FOREVER FANTASY ONLINE:

THE ONCE KING

BOOK 3 OF 3

RACHEL AARON / TRAVIS BACH

Series Information

Forever Fantasy Online

Last Bastion

The Once King

Copyright and Publishing Info

Aaron Bach, LLC
"Writing to Entertain and Inform."
Copyright © 2019 Rachel Aaron & Travis Bach

ISBN Paperback: 978-1-952367-03-8
ASIN eBook: B07Z57HC3P

Cover Illustration by Daniel Schmelling,
Cover Design by Rachel Aaron,
Editing provided by Red Adept Editing

Leylia's secret could unite them all or lead them to an eternity of undeath.

After the loss of Bastion, everyone who's not a zombie has holed up in FFO's sole remaining safe haven: the lowbie town of Windy Lake. But the undead armies never rest, and it's only a matter of time before the Once King's forces come to crush what's left of life in this world.

But Tina, James, and the rest of the players are facing a crisis of their own. After so long in this world, their human bodies are dying on the other side. If they don't find a way home soon, they may have nothing to go back to.

With time running out in two worlds, Tina and James face a horrible choice: do they spend their final days looking for a way to get back to their old bodies, or join the NPCs to fight for their new ones. But just when things look impossible, James learns a secret that might change everything. Only one catch: to pull it off, they're going to have to fight one raid boss no one, not even Tina, has ever beaten.

The Once King.

Content Warning
A note from Rachel Aaron

This a book about gamers. The characters talk like gamers, think like gamers, and act like gamers, which—as any gamer knows—is sometimes not very well. As such, this book will contain far more cursing, sexual situations, prejudice, and blood than my novels usually do.

That said, it's still us. Travis and I do not tolerate hate in our fiction any more than we do in real life. Just because a character says/does something awful does *not* mean that we agree with it, or that that person will not have to pay for their actions. This book deals with difficult issues many real people face, and we tried our best to give those issues the gravitas and realism they deserve. We might not have done everything perfectly, but Travis and I did our best to get it right.

The FFO series is our love letter to the online games we played obsessively for years. We wanted to show the amazing strength and resourcefulness of the gaming community without painting over its pitfalls. This book reflects that, and we hope that you love it as much as we do.

Thank you for reading and enjoy the story!

Chapter 1

Tina

Tina Anderson, aka Roxxy, aka guild leader of the Roughnecks Mercenary Company—or what was left of it—woke up in the shallow ditch of churned dirt she'd made for herself before passing out.

She came to with a wince, reaching up with stone fingers to brush the dust out of her lashes, which she just now noticed were made of copper wire just like her hair and sharp as little needles. Wincing again, Tina rolled onto her back to face the day, which was much darker than she'd expected. Several confused seconds later, her sleepy brain realized this was because she wasn't looking at the sky. She was staring at a wall of stretched hide. Someone had erected a tent over her while she slept. They'd also covered her in a blanket, which her fitful sleep had tied into a knot at her feet, though not before it had gotten covered in the greenish-gray mud made from her silvery blood mixing with the fine yellow soil.

Scowling at the mess, Tina grabbed the already ruined blanket and started scrubbing the remaining blood-mud off her armor and skin. There was a staggering amount of it, but thanks to the magical first aid the healers had poured into her, her body felt fine. Her stone limbs were supple and strong when she moved them, her core centered and still as a cave pillar.

Too bad the same couldn't be said for the rest of her.

Hands over her face to block the gray-white glare of the sun through the canvas, Tina flopped back into her dust wallow with enough force to shake the ground. The only reason she didn't dig herself even deeper in was because it wouldn't make a difference. No amount of dirt could block yesterday's failures. She'd failed to save Bastion City. She'd failed to find them a way home. She'd gotten them to safety, but too many people had died and been left behind. People who were never coming back. And to top it all off, she'd managed to have a giant public breakup with a guy she'd never actually been dating in the first place.

1

That last one had to be the shittiest world-first ever. Just remembering the look on SilentBlayde's face as she'd yelled at him made Tina want to burrow into the ground forever, but she didn't have the luxury of self-pity. She didn't know what time it was, but she could hear people moving around outside her tent. Clearly, her raid was awake, which meant she needed to be, too. So with that, Tina scrubbed the dust off her stonekin's chiseled face one more time, picked up her shield, and pushed back the tent flap to face the day.

The *blinding* day. Tina blinked in the glaring light, her emerald eyes turning the sunlight into a painfully bright rainbow that eventually condensed into a dusty field of tents and hundreds of players in dirty but still brightly glowing armor. There was so much to see, her dazzled brain didn't know what to make of it all for a moment. Then she remembered. Thanks to James, they'd evacuated everyone from Bastion to Windy Lake, the jubatus starter town in the Savanna zone. When she'd passed out yesterday afternoon, their camp had been a mob squatting in the sunbaked field that served as the town's festival grounds. Now the scrubby grassland had been transformed into a tent city big enough for all the Roughnecks, Trade Company, and Red Sands guilds. A short walk away at the lake's edge, masses of low-level players huddled beneath large open-sided pavilions like refugees.

No, not like. *Were.* They *were* refugees, all of them. Even the Roughnecks sitting around her were covered in ash and blood, their eyes vacant and haunted as they stared at their weapons or mechanically ate their rations. She was watching them just as bleakly when someone cleared their throat beside her.

Tina jumped, nearly knocking her tent over as she whirled to see Zen sitting cross-legged in the dusty grass right next to her tent flap. The elf looked exhausted, her normally luminous complexion dull and sunken with fatigue. Even her magically perfect leaf-green hair was limp, the curls

2

weighed down by dust and blood as she brushed them away from her face to look at Tina.

"Get enough sleep?"

"Yeah," Tina said after a moment, kneeling back down. "Thanks to you." The end of yesterday had been a mess of pain, heartbreak, and fear, but she still clearly remembered Zen offering to guard her sleep, a gift whose true value she was only now realizing. "Thank you for staying up to keep order. It must have been rough."

Zen shrugged. "I'm used to it. I worked a twelve-for-three night shift at the ER for ten years. Though I'm glad you're awake now for different reasons. Frank and I have been trying to keep a lid on things, but the whole damn world has been waiting for you with bated breath."

Tina looked around at the subdued camp. "Really?"

"They're too tired right now to make as big a stink as they want," Zen explained. "But people are upset. We took a hell of a beating yesterday, and it's brought a lot of issues to the surface. Specifically, people are arguing about what to do next."

"Seems reasonable." If she'd hadn't been too hung up on the past to think about the future, she'd have been worried about that too.

"Just because it's reasonable doesn't mean it's not a problem," the Ranger said quietly, her voice even more serious than usual. "We all chose to do the right thing yesterday and make peace because we weren't willing to kill everyone to get our way, but that was yesterday. Today's today, and people are starting to realize that we're stuck on the losing side of a fight the majority of the Roughnecks want nothing to do with. We made it to safety, but the Savanna's not *that* far from Bastion. It's only a matter of time before the Once King sends his army here to finish the job."

"And people don't want to fight that again," Tina finished, nodding. "I get it. I never want to see another skeleton again, either. But—"

"It's not just that they don't want to fight. This isn't our battle. We were supposed to be going home, not fighting a war."

3

"Finding a way home has always been the goal," Tina argued. "It still is, but we can't find a portal home when we're getting hammered by an undead army. Surely people understand that."

"They *do* understand," Zen said. "That's why no one's broken ranks yet. But while everyone was fine with fighting for Bastion, we're not in Bastion anymore. There's a lot of people pointing out—not incorrectly—that fighting here doesn't get us home. There's also a sizable group of people who *don't* want to go home at all. Frank, SB, Anders…I could go on, but you get the idea. They want to stay and stop the Once King before his army wipes what's left of Bastion off the map and this whole continent falls to the undead."

Tina closed her eyes. This was way too heavy to deal with first thing in the morning. *"Can* we stop him?"

"I have no idea," Zen admitted. "But Bastion is—*was*—the biggest, strongest kingdom in this world. We're looking at a very real tipping point in history here. It's not bragging to say that the Roughnecks are the strongest military force left. If we decide to leave, the king's remaining forces don't stand a chance."

"So the fate of the world depends on us?" Tina grumbled, scrubbing her hands over her stone face. "Damn, Zen. Lay it on a little harder."

"I'm just telling you the facts."

"I know, but it's not like we have a choice in this. If us leaving is going to get everyone killed, then we *have* to stay and fight. It's not like we know how to get home right now anyway. There's no harm in sticking around to save the world before we figure out how to leave it."

The issue seemed pretty cut and dried, but Zen was shaking her head.

"What?"

"Do you want to go back home, Tina?"

"Of course I want to go home!" What kind of question was that? Just because certain elves who should not be named wanted to stay didn't mean she was considering it. She was sick of being a rock. She wanted to be human

4

again, to eat pizza and hug her mom and swim in a lake without sinking to the bottom. But just because there was nothing for her here anymore didn't mean she was willing to let the Once King turn this whole world into the Deadlands. Yet when she said as much to Zen—minus the bit about heartbreak, of course—the Ranger only looked more dour.

"I think your heart is in the right place," the Ranger said. "But we might not have the luxury of getting everything we want. Did you live alone back in the real world?"

Tina shook her head. "I have roommates." Four of them, all just as broke as she was and crammed into a three-bedroom apartment to save on rent.

"That's good," Zen said, looking genuinely relieved. "They've probably already found your body and gotten you to a hospital, then. I live by myself." She tilted her head back to stare up at the bright sky. "We've already estimated there's roughly a ten-to-one time difference between this world and our own. That's a generous margin, but it still adds up. As of this morning, we've been trapped here for seven days. How long has my body been lying in my bed at home without food, water, or going to the bathroom? Sixteen hours? More?"

"Oh shit," Tina breathed, eyes going wide. "Are you dying?"

"Not yet," Zen said. "It takes more than one day for a healthy body to start having problems, but when I logged in to raid with you, I'd just started a three-day break. That means it'll be at least four days before someone notices I'm missing, and probably several more before they get worried enough to come looking for me. What state will I be in then?"

She'd asked the question, but her grim expression was all the answer Tina needed.

"It's not just me, either," Zen went on. "There are probably plenty of other people here who live alone or in bad circumstances or who are in weak health. Even for those in good positions, we have no way of knowing what's happening to our bodies on the other side. Some may already be dead. Point is: we're all on a timer. The longer a body stays in a coma, the less chance there is of coming out. If we want to go home, we have to get a move on. The longer we spend here, the more we risk not having bodies to go home to."

Tina cursed under her breath. She'd been so caught up in the emergencies in front of her, she hadn't even thought about what might be happening to the her she couldn't see. What if those days fighting to save lives in Bastion had been the few hours too many for their bodies back home?

"I wish we'd realized this sooner."

"Several of us have actually been worried about it for a while," Zen said honestly. "But you were already doing everything you could to get us home, so there was no point in harping on it. Now though…"

Now they had to choose. The Roughnecks were the best fighting force in the world. Tina had already known that, of course, but they'd proved it to everyone else yesterday when they'd taken on every undead boss in the game minus the Once King himself. If they said "screw this mess" and set out to search for a way home, they'd effectively be dooming everyone who stayed behind, including the players who didn't want to go back. Including SilentBlayde. If they *did* stay, though, there was still no guarantee they'd win. The Once King's army had kicked their asses in Bastion, and that was when they'd had a castle to fall back to. Out here they had nothing but grass and tents. If they fought again, people would die. Maybe everyone. If they went looking for a way back and couldn't find one, though, they'd be stuck wandering in a world filled with undead. Any way Tina imagined it, her people died. What the hell was she supposed to do?

"It's a pickle," Zen said at her panicked expression. "I'm sorry to dump this on you so soon after you and Silent—that is, I know you're dealing with your own problems right now, but we need you to make a decision. We've been through a lot together, and that's kept things civil so far, but if you don't give an order soon, the raid's going to split between those who want to fight and those who want to run, and none of us are going to survive if that happens."

Zen didn't have to tell Tina what would happen if their raid fell apart. It had been her greatest fear since this shitfest had started. Like hell was she letting it happen now, after everything they'd accomplished together. She just wished she knew which goal she was aiming them toward.

"Thanks for the heads-up, Zen," she said, rising to her feet.

"Just wanted to make sure you had the full situation before someone jumped on you," Zen replied, standing up as well. "Like I said, the whole world's been waiting for you to wake up. For what it's worth, though, the raid's held together this long. Debates have gotten heated, but I haven't had to shut down any real altercations. So long as you don't make any rash, unilateral decisions that stomp all over people's feelings, I think we stand a good chance at keeping things together."

"As if I'd ever—"

Zen's eyebrow arched so fast, Tina couldn't even finish that sentence. "I will steadfastly avoid doing anything of the sort," she said instead.

"That's all I can ask," the Ranger replied, pointed ears drooping as her mouth opened in a huge yawn. "And with that out of the way, I'm going to bed. I've been chasing people away from your tent all night. I've said my piece. Ball's in your court now, Roxxy. Don't drop it."

"I won't," Tina promised. "Thanks again, Zen. One more thing before you sack out, though."

"Yes?"

She opened her mouth then froze. She was about to tell Zen to forget about it when her brain blurted the words out anyway. "Is SB okay?"

She hated herself as she asked, but she didn't take the words back. Running the guild when she wasn't around was SilentBlayde's job, one he normally took very seriously. If Zen had been riding herd on people all night, that meant SB hadn't been around to do it, and while Tina was determined not to waste any more feelings on someone who clearly didn't give a shit about them, worrying over Haruto was a habit she couldn't just drop overnight.

"Not that I care where he spends his time," she clarified, twisting her armored hands together. "It's just not like him to abandon his responsibilities. If he's in trouble, I want to know, just as I would for anyone else in the raid."

Zen's expression showed that that excuse wasn't flying at all. "Of course he's not okay," she said with her usual bluntness. "But I saw James drag him off, so he's in good hands. Let his friends worry about him. You worry about us."

"Right," Tina said in a small voice. "Sorry."

Zen waved the apology away and crawled into the tent, curling her long, lithe body into the stonekin-shaped ditch Tina had left in the middle. She was asleep the moment she hit the ground. Tina paused just long enough to tuck the slightly muddy blanket around her narrow shoulders before slipping back outside, feeling like an idiot.

How pathetic could she be? Asking about her ex the day after she dumped him was just sad, especially considering how much else she had to worry about. Well, no more. She'd told him she was done, and it was time to start acting like it.

Unfortunately, Tina was *so* determined to focus on things other than SB, she forgot to watch where she was going as she stomped between the tents and ended up running face first into someone's chest in the process.

"OMG, I am *so* sorry," she cried, scrambling back to see who she'd just run over. "Run over" was the right term, too, because when a half-ton of armored stonekin bumped into someone, it usually resulted in serious injury. Fortunately—or maybe unfortunately—the person she'd run into this time was just about the only figure in the entire camp she could smack into and not damage. He was also the only person she could walk into and only come up to his chest. That was the advantage of being a five-skull raid boss, though. You were literally the biggest thing around.

"Your Majesty," Tina said, looking up at the towering figure of the Holy King of Bastion with a wince. Of course she'd crash into the *king*. Seriously, how much worse could today get? "Forgive me. I didn't mean—"

"No, no, it's all right," King Gregory said hastily, giving her an unsure smile that looked very out of place on his regal face. "I actually came here looking to bump into you, so this is quite fortuitous."

"You came here to see me?" Tina repeated, glancing down the empty path behind him. Not a lord or courtier or even a guard in sight. Not that a raid boss needed guards, but the lack of attendants struck her as very odd.

"I thought it would be best if we could talk casually, as players do," the king said, noting her note his lack of an entourage. "I came by earlier, but your Ranger told me that you were sleeping."

Tina blinked. Wow. When Zen had said everyone had been stalking her tent, she'd meant *everyone*.

"I wanted a chance to speak with you before the war meeting," Gregory went on, his speech speeding up, almost as if he were nervous. "It's critical that—"

"Wait," Tina interrupted. "War meeting? What war meeting?" No one had told her anything about a meeting.

"The leaders of the factions here are gathering at noon to discuss how we shall face the coming crisis," the king explained patiently. "All the player leaders were invited, though, of course, as leader of the Roughnecks, you are the one we most wish to speak with. It's no exaggeration to say that your group is invaluable in the coming battle against the Once King's armies. I've already asked your second in command, SilentBlayde, if you will be participating, but he claimed he could not speak for you."

Tina snorted. Good to know that SB still respected her enough not to put words in her mouth. Unfortunately, this meant she had to answer the king herself, and she didn't think he was going to like it. "I don't know what we're doing yet," she told him honestly. "I have to gather more information and talk about it with my people before we decide what's our best course."

That was a damn good dodge, Tina felt. But while Gregory wasn't the evil, Machiavellian king she'd assumed he was during the worst parts of the mess in Bastion, he still had far more political experience than she did, and he didn't miss a beat.

"Of course you must," the king said smoothly. "I know many of your number wish to return to your homes. I've already promised you access to my Portal Keepers in return for your great heroism in Bastion, but surely there is something else you desire. Lands, titles, money, wealth? I may be a displaced ruler, but until the Once King actually takes my head, all of the lands of Bastion are still at my disposal. You told me on the field of battle that yours was a mercenary company. What can I offer you to ensure your continued support?"

Tina sighed. That was as open-ended a bribe as she could ever have wished, but while money and power were great for those who wanted to stay, they didn't mean squat to the people who wanted to get home before their bodies died. She still didn't know what she was going to do about that, but playing the wrong hand now would split her guild, and that was a disaster no one could afford. So even though it went against every instinct she had, Tina forced herself to be patient.

"I can't tell you our price because I don't know what we want," she told the king. "We haven't even talked to the Portal Keepers yet, and I can't promise anything before I know how big a fight we're signing up for. Even after I get the details, I still have to discuss them with my people so we can vote, *and* I need to share what I learn with Assets and Cinco so that their guilds can decide."

Just listing it all out made Tina exhausted. When had leading a guild gotten so complicated? To her surprise, though, the king nodded like that had been exactly the nonanswer he'd expected her to give. "I understand it's a very complex issue," he said. "But if it makes your decision easier, I've already heard from Lord Assets that the majority of his Trade Company Guild wishes to stay here."

Tina blinked at the King. "*Lord* Assets?"

The giant man nodded. "My previous treasurer perished in the battle for Bastion, and Assets has already shown himself to be immensely qualified. He eagerly accepted the position of Lord of the Treasury, as well as the barony which comes with it."

"I bet he did," Tina said with a snort, leaving off that Assets—aka Bridget Walsh, former CFO of a Fortune 500 company and unrepentant exploitive capitalist—would likely be running the kingdom within a decade. She was about to warn Gregory not to give the greedy elf *too* much power when the king leaned in.

"But you could have even better," he said in a low voice, his face deadly serious. "Many of the noble titles in Bastion were given as rewards for victories in war. Help us defeat the Once King's army, and I could make you a duchess. Even a—"

"*Tina!*"

The sudden yell made them both jump as a tall Berserker—not as tall as Roxxy or the king but still freakishly huge for a human—stepped out of the forest of tents and elbowed his way into the conversation. "What we talking about?"

"Heya, Cinco," Tina said, too grateful for the distraction to be properly pissed at his rudeness. "The king came to get me for some sort of war meeting."

"Great, I was headed that way myself," the leader of the Red Sands guild said, putting out his arm. Tina stared at it for several seconds, uncomprehending, before she realized he was offering to walk her down the path like an old-fashioned gallant.

That image was so ridiculous she laughed, but while there was no way in hell she was going to loop her giant stone arm through his like some kind of armored debutante, she was happy to let the Berserker walk between her and the king, who kept asking for answers she couldn't give. Unfortunately, Cinco wasn't done yet.

11

"Hey, King," he said, grinning up at Gregory in a way that was not at all friendly, "I heard someone important asking for you on my way over. Seems like there's some problem or other that needs your attention. You should probably go deal with it."

That was the worst lie Tina had ever heard. From the pinched look on his face, Gregory felt the same way, but it was clear now that their "casual" chat was over, so he backed away with a sigh. "Thank you for your time, Miss Anderson," he said, bowing politely to Tina. "I'll see you at the meeting."

Unsure what else to say, Tina nodded back, watching guiltily as the gentle giant of a king straightened himself up and strode off, vanishing between the tents at a speed that would have been a sprint for a normal-sized person.

"Damn, Cinco," she said once Gregory was gone. "Did you just run off the king with a lie?"

"It wasn't a *lie*," CincoDeMurder replied casually. "I used to manage a call center back in college. There's *always* someone looking for the boss, so while I might not have heard anything specific, I'm sure it was true enough."

Tina rolled her eyes.

"This war meeting is serious business, though," Cinco went on. "Let's go that way, and I'll tell you what I know."

He offered her his arm again as he finished, only this time it didn't seem so foolish. Hearing Cinco talk about home had reminded her that inside Roxxy's hulking body, she was still Tina. SB had made it clear yesterday that he didn't care about that person, but Cinco was here offering his arm to her giant stone self, seemingly without caring how stupid it looked. And that was nice. Ridiculous, but it felt good to be reminded that *some* people thought she was worth the effort.

She still wasn't going to hold his hand, though.

"I'm fine like this," she said, folding her arms behind her. "So what you got?"

If her rebuff hurt his feelings, Cinco didn't show it. He just smiled and started leading the way out of the player camp into the main tent city of Windy Lake. "Have you heard about Lord Assets of Sell-Outia yet?"

Tina rolled her eyes. "*Oh* yeah. Gregory tried that shit on me, too. So what about you? Are you Count Cinco De Murdershire or something now? Because if so, you might want to treat your future boss with more respect."

"You mean the pushover king we almost dethroned yesterday?" Her fellow guild leader waved his hand like he was swatting a fly. "I'm never bowing to him. And for the record, I'm still pissed at you about that treaty you agreed to on our behalf."

Tina gave him a scathing look. "That's not the tune you were singing yesterday. You and Assets looked scared as shit when I came in. I saved all of our asses with that peace deal, and you know it. Don't you dare try to act like you didn't want me pulling your ass out of the fire now that you're safe."

Cinco put up his hands. "Whoa! Down, girl," he said. "I only brought it up because I wanted to make sure the same thing doesn't happen again today."

"What are you talking about?"

"Babe, we're going into a *war* meeting," he reminded her, exasperated. "In case King Pushover's personal visit wasn't a big enough clue, the NPCs are frothing at the mouth to get you on their side. Assets already ate up his bribe, but what else could you expect from a low-level bank alt whose only skill in life is screwing other people over? You and me, though, we're different. We're on top of this shit world. That's why everyone's willing to pay through the nose to get us on their side."

Tina sighed. "If you're asking me what I plan to do, I still don't—"

"I know," he said, giving her a superior look. "Your raiders aren't the only ones bickering over should we stay or should we go. I'm not asking you to choose one way or the other yet. I'm just saying don't make a choice for me again. Whatever the Roughnecks decide, Red Sands wants in, but you talk about that shit with me first before you sign any more NPC bullcrap, deal?"

"Fair enough," Tina said, holding out her hand. Cinco grabbed it with his usual crushing grip, but then his fingers grew gentle, lifting the back of her giant armored hand to his lips. When she gave him a *What the fuck?* look, he let her go with a wink, striding ahead down the dusty road toward the center of Windy Lake.

As expected of a town that had just had an active war teleported onto its doorstep, the jubatus city was a flurry of activity. The fierce cat-people of the Savanna ignored the blistering heat as they ran to and fro carrying medicines, weapons, and food to the various tents of wounded refugees and soldiers. The town's forges rang with frantic work, and everyone was shouting as different clans tried to coordinate with each other and with the groups of disgraced knights and players who were also trying to get their needs taken care of. The result was a noisy mass of hot, dusty chaos that even the ever-present winds couldn't tamp down. Thankfully, the war meeting was at the Naturalist's Lodge, the only wooden structure in all of Windy Lake, which also made it the quietest.

As usual, Cinco hopped up the stairs to enter first, though he did hold the curtain for her as Tina stepped into the mercifully shady but very crowded central chamber. There were so many furry, lashing tails, she had to slow to a crawl to avoid stepping on something she shouldn't and causing a diplomatic incident, but at least the break gave her a chance to survey the circular room.

In addition to the aforementioned important-looking cat-people attached to the tails, Tina spotted an extremely sour-looking Captain Hightower, commander of Bastion's City Guard. The Arch Sorcerer of Bastion—whose name she *still* didn't know—was there as well, as was High Priest Raffestain. The Bastion crowd was gathered around Gregory, who was seated at the head of a massive table beside an ancient battle-ax of a female jubatus Naturalist that Tina dimly remembered James referring to as

14

Gray Fang. Next to them, "Lord" Assets was lounging on a cushion, trying to look impressive. The well-dressed elf nodded imperiously at her and Cinco. Cinco responded by flicking him the bird, a gesture that, thankfully, no one else at the table seemed to realize the meaning of. For her part, Tina just focused on getting to the oversized pillow that was clearly meant for her without crushing anyone's limbs.

"Thank you all for coming," Gregory said when everyone was seated. "My deepest thanks to the Lords of the Savanna for aiding Bastion in our time of need. I am proud to stand once again with our friends of old."

This praise elicited a lot of preening from the line of old cats across the table. "It's in these hard times that a king learns who his true allies are," announced the tallest and most scarred of them, a great old terror of a jubatus named Rends Iron Hides, who also happened to be the cat James had decided was his new dad. Or whatever.

"Quite," Gregory agreed with a nervous smile. "Now that we've had a chance to settle the chaos, though, it is time to take stock of what we have and how we will go about defeating the undead menace ravaging our lands. Lord Assets will explain more."

It took everything Tina had not to roll her eyes as Assets stood up and pulled a folded piece of paper from the inside pocket of his replica-Armani suit.

"Thank you, Your Highness," the elf said in his clipped accent. "After a night of counting, it is my guild's best estimation that twenty-five thousand of Bastion's original citizens escaped the city's final collapse. I realize that's a terribly low number, but please keep in mind that the vast majority of the capital's population fled before the city was sealed by the Royal Knights. Of those who remained, twenty-five thousand is a higher-than-expected number that we should all be proud of."

He paused for applause, but none came. Tina didn't know about the jubatus, but everyone who'd been at Bastion knew that Assets was glossing over the fact that the number of dead and missing was likely ten times that of the surviving.

"Of the combined armies remaining from the attack on the capital, two thousand are former knights, three thousand are city guards, and we have an additional one thousand mixed units from the castle garrison, bringing our total combat-ready manpower to six thousand, give or take."

Tina blew out a breath. Those were lower numbers than she'd expected given the masses of men they'd seen marching down Bastion's Royal Mile. She felt a stab of guilt for her part in reducing the ranks of the king's armies, but she shoved it away just as quickly. She'd done what she'd had to do at the time, and her people were alive because of it. She refused to feel guilty over the deaths of those who'd willingly gone along with Malakai's shitty decisions, but she *was* feeling a lot worse about Bastion's prospects here in the Savanna—an emotion that was almost certainly on purpose since Assets was staring straight at her.

"Thanks to Windy Lake, we can count on another thousand jubatus warriors," the elf went on, blithely ignoring her pointed glare. "The king has also signed a deal with the gnolls—sorry, the *Grand Pack* of Red Canyon— who have agreed to lend us the use of their fortress at Red Canyon as well as pledging the assistance of an additional five thousand soldiers in exchange for a royal declaration of citizenship. This brings our total armed forces to twelve thousand. We have a high readiness level, and while supplies and replenishment are always an issue in any long campaign, the jubatus's high mobility and knowledge of the land should ensure we are always fighting on favorable ground."

He finished with a confident smile, reminding Tina of a salesman trying to reassure a nervous customer that this really was the deal of the century. She wasn't sure the NPCs were buying it, but they weren't the ones who spoke next.

"What about the other guys?" Cinco asked, his booming voice offensively loud in the crowded room. "Our numbers don't mean shit if we don't know what we're fighting against."

"I was getting to that," Assets said testily, turning his paper over. "Obviously, it's hard to get an accurate count of an army that has yet to arrive, but given what we observed in Bastion, we're expecting an attack force of at least a hundred thousand assorted undead."

"A hundred *thousand*," one of the cat lords repeated, his tail stiff as a board.

"Mindless zombies and reanimated animals," Assets assured him, as if that made it better. "Thanks to the Roughnecks' heroic efforts yesterday, the majority of the really dangerous foes—the former raid and dungeon bosses— are already defeated. We're expecting only a handful of serious intelligent enemies to assault the Savanna, of which only two should be five-skull rated."

He'd clearly meant that to be the good news, but no one at the table looked any happier, especially since Assets was still going. "But while we should be facing a much less powerful army than we did in Bastion, we still have two major problems before us. The first comes from the Great Bird Xthr, who has reported that the Once King's lich-lords have been hard at work reanimating large numbers of the dead we left behind in Bastion."

Gregory went pale. "What?"

"They're turning our fallen into zombies to use against us," Assets clarified, too caught up in his analytics to notice the horror on the king's face.

"Our people," Gregory whispered, voice trembling.

"May the Sun have mercy on their souls," the High Priest said, lowering his head.

Most of the heads at the table were lowered, actually. Those who'd fought in Bastion had seen this before, but the jubatus clan lords had no experience with the horror show that was fighting the Once King. Tina had thought they'd be more freaked out, but they took the grim news with surprising stoicism.

"This is not our first time facing the monsters who wear the faces of family and friends," Gray Fang said in a low, angry voice. "Windy Lake was regularly attacked by undead during the events of the Nightmare, with my own granddaughter, Lilac, as their leader." She shook her old gray head. "We know too well the Once King's cruelty, and we will not hesitate to strike."

"Good to hear," Assets said crisply, going back to his report. "These reanimations work for and against us. On the one hand, they add to the enemy's already swollen ranks, but raising so many zombies takes time, and time gives us the advantage."

Cinco snorted at that excessively rosy perspective. "You said there were two problems. What's the other one?"

"Ah," Assets said, looking down at his paper like he was hoping they'd forgotten that. "That would be the Blood General, Sanguilar. He's the only Dead Mountain raid boss the Roughnecks failed to kill at Bastion. He's also a top-tier five-skull who deals enormous damage and gains health every time something dies near him, making him virtually unkillable in army combat."

Assets said all of this as quickly as possible, but Tina could practically see the sunlight dim as a palpable sense of doom descended on the room. As the dread rose, every eye in the room started drifting toward her, making it clear what they all expected.

"What about the surrounding zones?" Gregory asked hopefully. "The Savanna is large, but this is all the Kingdom of Bastion. We are surrounded by allies on all sides. Could any of them be brought in to bolster our ranks?"

Rends Iron Hides, James's new sorta-dad, shook his head. "Shortly after launching our campaign to reclaim the Savanna, we sent scouts on our fastest runners to restore communications with our neighbors. The riders reached the borders well enough, but all of their reports have come back with ill tidings. As my brilliant son James already guessed, the zones around us were not as fortunate with their players as Windy Lake. Those who have not been decimated by player gangs have been inundated by out-of-control questlines left over from the Nightmare. We can expect no help from outside, and fleeing to another zone would mean running into additional unknown dangers."

The already crushing sense of doom grew even heavier with every word he spoke. Across the table, several of the important-looking cats were now openly burying their faces in their hands. Not that Tina could blame them. This really did look like the end of their world.

"What about the players?" asked a white-furred jubatus wearing a necklace of crackling stormcite.

Tina's head whipped back to Assets just in time to catch the end of a wink, filling her with fury as she realized that that question had almost certainly been prearranged. She shot Assets a searing look to see if she could trick any guilt to the surface, but the former corporate bigwig was apparently immune to shame, because he just kept rolling.

"What an excellent question from the head of the Water Born Clan," Assets said, flipping to the next page in his stack with a flourish. "The player army currently stands at three hundred high-level individuals. That may not sound like much to some of you"—the golden-haired elf glared pointedly at a young jubatus in the back who was rolling his slitted eyes—"but it's equivalent to roughly five thousand Royal Knights. Probably more."

"*Definitely* more," Cinco said.

"We also have an additional two thousand players below level fifty," Assets went on, ignoring the Berserker's rudeness. "They are classified as noncombatants under treaty and as such cannot legally be conscripted, but they can surely be convinced to volunteer to fight on their own given the right incentive."

Pleased as she was that Gregory was sticking to his word about her lowbies, Tina still expected this to spark an explosion from the NPCs. Every player higher than level ten was technically combat capable, and anyone over level thirty was a serious fighter compared to the jubatus and gnoll forces. They'd been small fry at Camp Comeback against level-eighty Knights, but they represented a considerable fighting force under the current circumstances. Even Assets at level twelve was technically more powerful than some of the civilian lords present, and from the grumbling going on around the table, the cats knew it.

"The players are indeed an invaluable force," Gregory said, his eyes on Tina. "One without whom I fear we cannot win."

"The East Bastion Trade Company has already pledged ourselves to the fight," Assets said. "But I cannot speak for the others."

He looked at Tina as he finished. Everyone did. There were technically two guild masters sitting in this tent, but every damn eye in the place was on her, and Tina was getting sick of it. She was about to say as much when CincoDeMurder suddenly stood up.

"I don't know where the Red Sands stand yet," he announced. "We've been made a generous offer by King Gregory, but unlike *some*"—he sneered at Assets—"we don't care about bullshit titles or land that will probably be overrun with undead soon. Me and my guys want to go back home to the real world."

"You would abandon everyone to save yourselves?!" cried the jubatus lord with the stormcite jewelry. "*Reprehensible!*"

"Call us whatever you want, kitty cat," Cinco snarled back. "You and your lot have been trying to kill us since day zero. We don't owe you shit on a brick."

"We killed you because you were plundering our city!" bellowed Captain Hightower.

"Oh, I'm sorry," Cinco said, cupping a hand to his ear. "I can't hear you over last week's genocide, or the fact that Windy Lake still has the *corpses of eight players* staked out in the sun by the water like scarecrows."

Tina jerked in surprise. She hadn't seen those, but then, she hadn't been paying much attention to her surroundings what with all the moping and war meetings and surprise visits from kings.

"Those are criminals," Gray Fang said sternly. "They tried to conquer Windy Lake shortly after the Nightmare broke and were punished accordingly."

"I'm sure it's *sooo* clear cut as that," Cinco sneered back.

This triggered more accusations and more shouting, filling the tent in a deafening cacophony until the king banged his fist on the table.

"*That's enough!*" Gregory yelled, shaking the ground with his enormous voice. When the room fell into terrified stillness, he cleared his throat and said, in a far gentler voice, "Roxxy of the Roughnecks has not yet spoken. I wish to hear what she has to say before we make any decisions."

With that, the whole room went back to staring at Tina, who sighed. Rude as it was, she'd been glad of Cinco's outburst. His "fuck you" attitude reminded her that the rich old lords at the table weren't innocents who needed her protection. That said...

"You didn't give the king a definitive answer yet, Cinco," Tina pointed out, turning to study the man sitting beside her. "You said you didn't owe them anything and that you want to go home, but you didn't say you *wouldn't* fight. Does that mean there's a circumstance in which you would?"

The red-armored Berserker crossed his muscular arms over his even more muscular chest. "Can't get nothing past you."

Tina shrugged her stone shoulders. "I just want to know what you're planning."

"Then we're stuck," he said angrily. "Because my plan depends on you."

"Come again?"

Cinco rolled his eyes like he couldn't believe she was making him say this. "Everyone knows the Roughnecks are the strongest group here," he spat. "At least when it comes to fighting monsters. You've got all the Dead

Mountain gear, and you're the only tank left in the world who can toe-to-toe it with a level-eighty raid boss." He glanced at Assets. "Twelve thousand soldiers? Who the fuck cares about that number? Half of them are so low level they're useless, and we all know you can't swarm-kill Sanguilar. Fucker gets health back every time someone dies in his vicinity. You could throw your whole army at him, and he'd only get more powerful."

The room fell deadly silent as Cinco turned back to Tina. "I'll put it bluntly: if you leave, this whole place is fucked. You and the Roughnecks, you're the power, and this whole king-and-pony show is just a ploy to guilt you into throwing your lot in with Bastion. But if you and I team up, there's nowhere in this shitty world we can't go. Player gangs? Zones overrun by questlines gone crazy? We can kill them all. There's nothing that can stand up to our two guilds combined, so my answer is 'I'm sticking with you.' Frankly, anything else is suicide."

If he hadn't put it so starkly, Tina would have been flattered by Cinco's faith in her abilities. But it was all too clear that the Berserker was just doing what he always did: looking out for number one. Not that she faulted him for it. Tina was doing the same, except her "number one" was an almost-full raid plus one stubborn brother, and they were the ones she answered for.

"I'm sorry," she said, shaking her head. "But I can't answer for the Roughnecks yet. Just like Red Sands, we have a lot of people who want to go home. Any other day, I'd say that if you want us to fight for you, all you have to do is pay up, but these aren't normal circumstances. I understand this is a do-or-die situation for you, but we've already been away too long. If we stay and fight, I'm worried some of my people might lose their shot at going home entirely, and I can't ask that of them. I won't order my raiders to give up their lives for yours."

"So that's a no?" the king said, his giant shoulders slumping.

"It's a wait-and-see," Tina replied, her stone lips quirking. "As I am regularly reminded, I'm not Queen Tina. I have to think of what everyone wants, not just me. We fought for access to the Portal Keepers, but I haven't even gotten to talk to them yet. For all I know, home might be just a spell away. I understand you're in a hurry, but I can't pledge my people to a fight without at least doing my homework first."

"The kingdom of Bastion is willing to offer *exceedingly* generous compensation for your help, Roxxy," Assets said. "Don't think of this as a question of home versus stay. Think of it as how rich and powerful you'd like to be while searching for the way back."

"More like 'how dead,'" CincoDeMurder growled, leaning closer to her. "This is a losing fight, Tina. We should bail *before* the trap closes this time."

"Are you even listening to me?" she cried, glaring at both of them. "For the last time, it's *not up to me!* You can throw all the bribes you want, but I can't answer yet!"

"This isn't a matter we can delay!" one of the jubatus lords shouted. "You're their leader, aren't you? Just tell your soldiers what they're doing and be done with it."

Tina threw back her head with a groan. She supposed this was an excellent opportunity to introduce these people to the concept of democracy, but she didn't feel like having that fight—or explaining the Roughnecks' internal politics—to a crowd of terrified feudal cats.

"Sorry," she said. "You'll just have to wait."

No one was happy with that answer. The king looked desperate, his officers looked furious, the cats were hissing, and Cinco and Assets were both clearly gearing up for another round. It was a lot of pressure, but one of the nice things about being an eight-hundred-pound stonekin was that no one could push her around. She'd said not yet, and she meant it, and damn if she was going to budge. She was already opening her mouth to ask the king where the Portal Keepers were so she could get on with the "how do we get home?" questions when James's dad-cat stood up.

"I think we have a solution to the problem."

Tina blinked. The old cat was grinning like a...well, like a cat, and she didn't like it at all. The annoying jubatus with the stormcite necklace was standing beside him, and the two of them were looking at her like she was a whole basket of canaries.

"Your Majesty," James's new dad said solemnly, "it is with great joy that I, Rends Iron Hides of the Claw Born tribe, along with my good friend, Reeds In Wind of the Water Born, announce the engagement of Morning Shimmer, first daughter of Water Born, to James, second son of Claw Born."

Tina was shaking when he finished, her vision tinting literal red. But maybe she actually was getting better at managing her anger, or maybe stonekin just took longer to work into a killing frenzy than humans, because her voice was only moderately deadly when she said, "What?"

"Your brother is marrying into a great and noble clan," Rend said, grinning at her like he'd just made the winning move. "You were not ready to commit your army when it was merely a battle of strangers, but this fight is now a *family* affair. You might be willing to leave us to die, but even a player won't abandon her brother. And it's a good match for James as well. Morning Shimmer is the most sought-after marriage in all the Four Clans. With this connection, your brother will have great standing in *two* noble families! Anyone would fight for such a glorious future, and if you value your brother's life, you will have no choice but to stay and fight with him."

All around the table, the jubatus lords murmured in admiration. It was clear all the cats thought Rend had just struck a finishing blow. King Gregory looked less sure, but Tina didn't give a shit about him. Her eyes were locked on Rend, her fists clenched so tightly she would have crushed her armored gauntlets if they hadn't been made of sun steel.

"You fucking *asshole!*"

"Roxxy," Assets said, his already pale face going the color of paper. "Calm down."

"*No!*" she roared, shooting to her feet so fast she almost flipped the table. Rage rose in her chest like magma from a volcano, because she knew

24

Rends was right. Not about James liking the power—she didn't think he cared if he was a noble cat or not—but since coming to this world, her lazy, class-flunking brother had become responsible to a fault, especially when it came to the NPCs. If his cat-dad said he had to stay and protect his new wife, he'd do it, never mind what his *actual* family thought. Hell, he was already buddies with the king. The only reason James wasn't pressuring her to stay and fight right now was because he wasn't here, but that didn't mean Tina was going to let these assholes use him against her.

"Fuck you for trying to corner me with my brother!" she yelled, booming voice shaking the ground. "I don't care if I have to burn this village to the ground myself, you are *not* marrying James off in absentia!"

"You dare threaten us?" Rends Iron Hides hissed, tail lashing.

"It's not a threat," Tina snarled back. "It's a *promise*. All I said was 'wait,' but you couldn't even last thirty seconds before using my brother to strong-arm me. Didn't James save this place? You're a special kind of under-handed asshole to repay him like this."

"I have jumped over my own tail for my *son,* James!" Rends roared at her. "He got a better marriage than my eldest! Morning Shimmer is first born of the clan head himself. Not only does her beauty have no rival, she is skilled in all the feminine arts required of a lord's daughter! She is the most desirable marriage within the Four Clans, yet she has selflessly agreed to marry a player for the sake of saving her family. We are all making sacrifices! How dare you accuse us of dishonor!"

"*Dishonor?*" Tina roared back. "You're the one saying that marrying my brother is a *sacrifice!*"

"Roxxy, be reasonable," Assets said sharply, grabbing her arm to whisper in her ear. "This is a legitimately medieval society. Lord Rends Iron Hides is being an exemplary clan head by their standards. You need to see it from their—"

25

"Shove it, Assets," Tina said, yanking out of his feeble grip to jab an armored finger in the golden elf's face. "This is as much your fault as his. You're letting them use my brother so you can keep your damn title!"

"The jubatus of Windy Lake are giving you a great honor!" yelled Captain Hightower, his face disgusted. "One they do not need to. I'll remind you that you and your Roughnecks are all citizens of Bastion now. Your low-level players are protected by treaty, but if His Majesty wished it, it would be entirely within his right to conscript the rest of you into military service." He bared his teeth. "If you cannot be reasoned, bribed, or shamed into doing the right thing, we can *make* you do it."

"Captain Hightower," the king said in a panic. "That's not—"

Tina didn't bother listening to the rest. She was killing mad, which meant she needed to get out of this situation before she did something she'd regret.

"Come on, Tina," Cinco said, rising to his feet. "These people aren't worth saving. You and me, we don't need this place. Let's bounce."

He pulled on her arm, but Tina didn't budge. She was dying to tell these assholes exactly where they could shove their damn threats. The only reason she didn't was because she'd promised Zen she wouldn't make rash decisions. She'd *promised*. Her people were trusting her to do the right thing, and she was trying her damnedest to figure out what that was when a frantic shout sounded outside the lodge's canvas door.

"Sir! You can't!"

The guard was still yelling when James burst into the lodge. He froze when the whole room turned to look at him, ears pressing flat against his head.

"James?" King Gregory said, breaking the silence. "What are you doing here? Is something wrong?"

The king's gentle question made her brother jump. "I..." he began, swallowing as his eyes scanned the scowling room before coming to a rest on

Tina. "I'm sorry to interrupt, Your Majesty, but I have something I must speak to my sister about immediately. I realize this is a bad time—"

"On the contrary," Tina said, shrugging out of Cinco's hold to put a massive hand on her brother's shoulder. "It's a *great* time. Let's go."

James cast a nervous look at the scowling nobles—especially his adoptive father, who looked angry enough to hork up a hairball—but there was nothing he could do. Tina was already marching them out of the lodge, firmly ignoring the glares digging like daggers into her back.

Twenty minutes earlier.

"**A**re you serious?"

James was in the Portal Keeper's yurt. In the far corner, the other portal mages were clumped together in a terrified, angry, purple-robed knot, but he wasn't even looking their direction. His eyes were locked on Leylia, holding her in place while the rest of his brain spun.

"Serious as a heart attack," Leylia said in her New York accent, sitting cross-legged on the wood-and-hide cot the jubatus had supplied. "Everything I just told you is legit, and I can prove it. I've got more, too, but I'm not giving out additional deets for free." She glanced at her fellow Portal Keepers, who were watching her with expressions of terrified hate. "As you can see, this information doesn't make me very popular with the locals. I'm happy to answer all your questions, but only if I get full player protection."

"I'm sure Tina would be fine offering you protection in exchange for this," James promised. "But she needs to hear it with her own ears first."

His sister was going to *flip*. This could change everything, but he had to do it right. Information like this could tear the world apart if handled incorrectly.

"Keep me from getting knifed, and I'll talk to whoever you want," Leylia promised.

James nodded and turned to his brother, but that idea died as soon as he saw Ar'Bati's face. Like the Portal Keepers, Fangs in Grass was radiating wrath like summer heat. It was clear he was fighting not to attack Leylia right then and there, which made him a very bad choice for guard duty. James had to get Tina himself, though. There was no way he was trusting something this sensitive to a messenger. The only way to get Tina here without letting the secret out was to fetch her himself, but he couldn't take Leylia with him. That left only one option.

"SilentBlayde?"

The elven Assassin didn't even look up. He was still sitting on the stool he'd flopped down on when they'd come in. His armor and body were filthy from the blood and ash of yesterday's battles, and there were dark circles under his eyes from a night of no sleep and general emotional trauma. He didn't look qualified to sit up straight, much less to protect what could be the most important source of information alive, but there was no one else.

"SB?" James said again.

The Assassin's blue eyes grudgingly flicked his direction.

"I'm going to get Tina so Leylia can tell her what she just told us," James explained. "I need you to protect her until I get back."

He wasn't sure his friend was parsing all of that, but SB gave him the slimmest of nods.

"If it will help Tina, I will keep this woman alive until you return," the elf said, shooting a look at the two male Portal Keepers that sent them scrambling even farther into the corner.

James didn't like the look on his friend's face one bit, but it got him what he needed right now, so he rolled with it. "Thanks, dude. I'm counting on you," he said, turning back to Leylia. "I'll bring my sister here, but I'll make it clear before she arrives that you'll only talk if one of the guilds guarantees your safety. That's the best I can do. Is it good enough?"

"It'll have to be," Leylia said, but her brown eyes were worried. "Are you *sure* your friend's okay?"

SB was nowhere near okay, but James trusted him to do this job at least. Maybe nothing else, but if there was one thing his friend was good at right now, it was looking scary.

"He'll be fine," he assured her. "*You'll* be fine. Just sit there. I'll be right back."

Grabbing the angrily vibrating Ar'Bati, James pulled them out the flap into the blazing heat of the noonday Savanna. The knight guarding the yurt was red faced and drenched in sweat, reminding James to be glad he was a jubatus and naturally adapted to this specific climate. He needed all the advantages he could get right now. But when he started down the street toward the player area, Ar'Bati dug his claws into the dirt.

"I can't be involved in this."

James sighed. "Fangs..."

"I want to skin her alive," his brother snarled. "I know I should be better, but eighty years of hatred don't just go away!"

"I know, but—"

"I can't be trusted around her," Fangs said angrily. "So I will take my mother's advice for once and remove myself from the situation. Come find me when you are no longer dealing with that woman."

With that, the tall cat-warrior turned on his heel and stalked away. James didn't bother chasing after him. As much as he wanted his adoptive brother's support, this was probably for the best. Honestly, he thought Fangs was handling it pretty well all things considered, but his reaction was a good reminder that Leylia's fears were not just paranoia. If the secret she'd told them got out to the general population of this world, James didn't think they'd all be as self-controlled as Ar'Bati. The quicker he got her under Tina's protection, the better their chances of going home, so he turned away from his brother's retreating back and started toward the center of town. A few feet later, he dropped to all fours, the Eclipsed Steel staff banging against his tail as he loped through the busy streets toward the player area.

Which turned out to be a total waste of time. Normally his sister's giant stonekin was easy to find, but he didn't see her at all in the chaos of the players' camp. He was frantically checking the tents when the Roughnecks' other tank—a man he'd known in game as DarkKnight but was apparently going by Frank these days—told him Roxxy had gone to a war meeting.

James didn't need more than that. There was only one place in Windy Lake where important meetings happened, so he turned right back around and ran at full speed toward the Naturalist Lodge. Sure enough, the front stairs were covered in guards and various anxious-looking assistants. One of them tried to stop him, but James blew right past, sprinting through the curtain into the tensest atmosphere of his life.

He froze the moment he got inside. He had no idea what was going on, but the whole room was staring at Tina as if she'd just threatened to burn down the village. She looked mad enough to do it, too, which was *never* good. For once, though, her mood seemed to improve when she spotted him.

"James," Gregory said in a voice that sounded both worried and relieved. "What are you doing here? Is something wrong?"

He was so off kilter from the sudden blasting attention that the gentle question made him flinch. Fortunately, Tina was still smiling at him, so James decided to ignore the kicked hornet's nest he'd apparently just stepped into and focus on the mission.

"I'm sorry to interrupt, Your Majesty," he said, addressing Gregory because that was what you did when there was a king in the room. "But I have something I must speak to my sister about immediately. I realize this is a bad time—"

"On the contrary," his sister said, grabbing his shoulder so hard James staggered. "It's a *great* time. Let's go."

He really should have said more. He'd come here for Tina, but just walking out while everyone was staring felt unspeakably rude, especially with Gregory looking so desperate. There was nothing James could do, though. His sister's hand was as heavy as the boulder it resembled. It would have been easier to fight a rockslide than to keep her from marching him out of the tent, and honestly, he didn't really want to. Their exit had been much more flagrant than he'd intended, but he couldn't fault Tina for wanting to get out of that antagonistic atmosphere.

"Killer timing, bro," she said in a relieved voice, confirming his suspicions. "What's the fire?"

"It's not a fire so much as a game changer," James told her excitedly, rising up on his toes and dropping his voice to a whisper. "I've been talking to the Portal Keepers all morning. Specifically, I've been talking to Leylia."

"Whoa," Tina said, her gemstone eyes going wide. "When you say 'Leylia,' do you mean *the* Leylia? As in 'Leylia's Disease'?"

He nodded rapidly. "This is big, T, but I don't want to say more here." He turned and looked pointedly at the crowd of guards and assistants hovering around the tent they'd just left. "If you'd just—"

"Way ahead of you," she said, keeping her own voice to a gravelly whisper. "But if we're talking about what I think we are, then the others will want to hear it, too. Let me get Cinco and Assets, and we'll go."

James stared, dumbstruck, as his sister—without argument, without demands, without further cajoling—stepped back into the lodge to fetch the other players. She reemerged a minute later with her fellow guild leaders, both of whom looked equal parts angry and curious.

"Okay," CincoDeMurder said when he spotted James. "You met the *actual* Leylia? As in the crazy lady who—"

"*Yes,*" James said frantically, cutting the Berserker off before he could blurt out "*the crazy lady who made FFO*" in the middle of the crowded steps packed full of guards and officials. "And you're going to want to hear what she has to say."

"Must we?" Assets sighed, giving Tina a put-out look. "I can't imagine it's more important than—"

"If James says it's important, it's important," Tina said, glaring at the elf like she was daring him to argue. Assets, being smart, did not, and Tina turned back to her brother. "Lead the way."

Her trust was enough to make James actually tear up a bit. He turned quickly to hide it, motioning for the other players to follow him back through the village toward the Portal Keepers' tent. "Before we talk to her, there's something I need to ask you," he said as they walked. "Leylia's information has the potential to make a lot of people very, very angry. She's afraid for her life, and from what she's told me already, I think she has good reason. She's willing to tell us everything, but only if we agree to protect her once it's out."

"I take it you mean protecting her from the NPCs," Cinco said, scratching the stubble on his square jaw. "Shouldn't be hard, but what's she got that's so bad?"

James looked around nervously. Fortunately, all of the jubatus on the road were giving the players a wide berth, so he decided to take a risk. "Leylia caused the Nightmare."

"Holy shit," Tina said.

"How?" Cinco asked at the same time.

"She said it was an accident," James whispered. "That's all I can tell you right now, but do you get why she's afraid? Every person in this village suffered horribly during the Nightmare. Imagine what they'd do to her if they knew she was the reason."

"I don't have to imagine," Tina said. "I've already seen what they were willing to do to us, and we didn't even know what the hell was going on." She looked down at James. "Do you think she can tell us how to get home?"

"She hinted at it," James said. "But she wouldn't say anything definitive without a promise of protection. I think she knows, though. At the very least, she can tell us how we got here. If we know that, maybe we can figure out how to get back."

"Good enough for me," Tina said.

"Me too," Cinco said, hooking his thumbs into the band of his ridiculously oversized metal belt. "Red Sands will do it. If any NPCs get within ten feet of her, we'll turn them into stains on the grass. Assuming her info is good, of course."

The casual violence of that statement was enough to make James's ears go flat. This was what he'd wanted, though, so he just nodded and resumed walking, leading the other players through the mess that was Bastion's refugee camp to the larger, guarded tent that had been erected for the Portal Keepers.

Sir Jamie opened the flap the moment they got close, and James darted into the tent's cool, dark interior. He sighed in relief when he spotted Leylia right where he'd left her, sitting on her cot under SB's watchful eye. Unfortunately, he didn't realize the rest of what he'd done until Tina pushed into the tent behind him and froze.

All at once, it was so silent he could hear his own blood in his ears. Next to him, SilentBlayde rose from his stool, his eyes locked on Tina like they were stuck there. For her part, Tina was as still as the stone that made her. She didn't even seem to be breathing.

"Tina..." SB began. "I—"

"Whatever," Tina said gruffly, turning away.

The look of hurt on SilentBlayde's face was so sharp even his mask couldn't hide it. He didn't say anything, though. Just quietly stepped back into the shadows as Tina focused all of her attention toward the brown-haired woman on the cot.

"Are you Leylia?"

"That's me," Leylia said, glancing nervously from James to Tina and back again. "Did James tell you my thing?"

"He did," Tina said, turning her body so that her back was to SB even though they were standing almost side by side in the yurt. "CincoDeMurder has volunteered his people to guard you. They'll keep you safe."

"We'll keep you better than safe," Cinco said, stepping up beside Tina and reaching way up to rest an arm on her shoulder. "What Tina here is forgetting to mention is that Red Sands was the best PvP guild in FFO. My guys are stone-cold killers. If some stupid NPC wants to polish their grudge, we'll polish the ground with his face."

"Gruesome, but good to know," Leylia said with a smile. "I feel better already."

"That said," Cinco went on. "You've gotta know you're still screwed in the long run. We've got you covered here, but Red Sands can't protect you for the rest of your life."

"That's fine," Leylia said. "I just need someone to watch my back until I can give the king the slip. I know this world better than anyone, and vanishing into the crowd is easy in a place with no internet or cameras. I've just gotta survive the next couple weeks, and I should be golden."

"Works for us," Tina said, crossing her arms. "We've satisfied our part of your bargain. Now talk."

"Okay, okay," Leylia said, and then she held out her hand. "Nice to meet you. I'm Leylia Reis, and yeah, I'm *the* Leylia."

Now that she was actually talking, James couldn't stop himself. "How'd you create the Nightmare?" he blurted.

Leylia winced. "I didn't set out to create it. I mean, what happened was totally my fault, but it wasn't intentional."

From the corner of the tent, one of the other two Portal Keepers made an angry sound, and James flinched. The last time she'd admitted her role, the two men had flown into a rage, forcing him to restrain them. They looked like they were about to try again, but they made it no more than a step before Tina's giant stone trunk of an arm stopped them.

"How did it happen?" Tina asked, completely ignoring the two NPC mages, who were already cowering back down. "Accident or not, knowing how this started could help us end it."

Leylia sighed. "I'm sure you all know all about Leylia's Disease, that whole can-never-wake-up lucid-dreaming problem?" When everyone nodded, she went on. "Well, the reason it's named after me is because I've had that problem my whole life. Like, before there was an FFO or even the VR Sensorium Engine. Everyone thought I was just crazy, and I thought so too at the time, but I know now it wasn't a mental disease. I was seeing all those things because I'm a natural-born Portal Keeper."

"What does that mean?" Assets asked, wiggling his way between the other, much-taller players.

"It means I have the ability to read the Infinite Unbounded Sky and connect magically to other worlds contained within it."

"That's stupid," Cinco said. "Our world doesn't have magic."

"*Au contraire,* Mr. Hunky Muscles," Leylia said, wagging her finger at him. "As its name suggests, the Infinite Sky is *infinite.* We're all part of it. Our home universe just happens to be in a very dark, very cold, very low-magic segment. That lowness makes natural Portal Keepers like me a one-in-a-lots-of-billions chance, but it does happen on occasion. Anyway, we didn't know any of this at the time, but my parents were loaded and determined that their only daughter wasn't going to spend her life in an asylum. That's why, when my therapist suggested embracing my visions as a way of learning to deal with them, they let me spend waaaayy too much money building a fully immersive VR version of the world I saw in my dreams. When I did, and the tab got too high, we decided to turn the world I'd built into a VR game to try to recoup some of the losses. And thus FFO was born!"

"Didn't that bother you?" James asked. "I mean, therapy is supposed to be private."

"Not at all," Leylia said, shaking her head. "Remember, I wasn't *actually* crazy. I built the digital version of this world based on the visions I saw of an *actual* place. It was always meant to have people, and FFO-the-game was a lot more fun than FFO-the-therapy-program. Also, I got to go down in history as the founder of the first full-immersion VR MMO RPG as opposed to a footnote in some psych journal, so there's that."

"I thought people with Leylia's were supposed to *avoid* playing FFO," Tina said. "Doesn't the game make your condition worse, not better?"

"Oh yeah, it was an *epic* failure as therapy," Leylia said. "And it gets worse. I didn't know it at the time, but as we were building the world that eventually became FFO, my Portal Keeper powers were slowly connecting the fake copy-world I was making with the real one. That would have been bad enough by itself, but the real kick came when we started letting other people in. All of a sudden, millions of players were walking around in the version of this world I'd painstakingly reproduced and treating it as real. Their participation reinforced my belief and made my waking dreams even more vivid. Eventually, the feedback loop got so strong, I couldn't tell which world was real anymore. The only time I felt normal was when I was playing FFO, and the more I played, the stronger my powers became until, a few weeks after the game's launch, we crossed the ten million–player threshold, and the Nightmare began."

"Wait," James said. "What's so special about ten million players?"

Leylia shrugged. "I have no idea. I don't even know if it was the number or if that day just happened to be the one when I crossed the line, but *something* happened." She tapped her slippered foot on the ground. "The game world of FFO was based on my connection to this real place. I know now that I was drawn to this world in particular because it lies at the center of the Unbounded Sky. Well, as much as anything can be the center of infinity. Anyway, what I'm trying to say is that this place is a very bright light, magically speaking. And since I was a Portal Keeper who had no idea what she was doing, I was drawn to it like a moth to a bug zapper, subconsciously reaching out to it first through my visions then through the game. The harder I reached, the closer I got, until one day *boom!* I smashed our two worlds together, and everyone who actually lived here got stuck in my version of their home."

"Incredible," James said when she finished. "It's like, by making FFO, you were casting a giant spell that connected our worlds."

Now that he'd said it, he could see just how it had happened. There were streams of magic in all people, lines of power that connected them to each other and the rest of the world. If Leylia had been born a Portal Keeper back on Earth, where there was no magic, it made sense that her lines would connect back to this place where power was rich and magic was plentiful. As

37

she'd built FFO off her visions, she'd strengthened that connection, and every new person she brought in would add their power to the spell. Even if the humans of Earth had only a tiny bit of mana due to their planet's low magical nature, enough grains of sand added up. Given how many millions of players FFO had had at its height, James had no problem believing all those tiny sparks could make something *big*, galvanizing Leylia's unconscious spell into an iron-clad trap strong enough to imprison the real residents of this world in her fake version. Including, apparently, Leylia herself.

"So how did *you* end up here?" James asked. "I mean, you clearly didn't get pulled in with the rest of us. Not only were you a Portal Keeper while this was still a game, you died in our world two years ago. It was all over the gaming news."

"Really? I'm dead?" Leylia took a moment to process that, and then she shrugged. "Honestly, I'm not too surprised. Bodies can't live long without their souls, and two years on Earth adds up to about twenty years in FFO time, which is about how long I've been here."

"Wait, that doesn't make sense," Tina said. "You said you started the Nightmare shortly after FFO launched, but that was eight years ago. If you only got stuck here *two* years ago, that means you got pulled in after the Nightmare but well before we arrived. How did that happen?"

James also wanted to know. This was the part of the story Leylia had refused to tell him without protection. She had it now, though, and her face broke into a grin.

"It was the Once King."

James couldn't have heard that right. "The *Once King*? As in the—"

"As in *the* Once King," Leylia said, nodding.

"How?" Tina demanded.

"It was pretty wild stuff," Leylia said. "I'd been playing FFO nearly twenty-four hours a day for a few years at that point. I was logged in as my GM character when it happened." She gestured down at her current body, which was definitely not a standard player-human model. "Super-cute, right?

I had the art department make her for me custom, and she's held up amazingly. Can you believe I'm over forty now? Anyway, I was working with the devs on that big city in the Verdancy we were building out to be the main hub for the Deadlands expansion pack. You know, making sure they had everything right, since FFO was still technically my therapy game. I was describing how the buildings should look to the art team when I heard this grim-broody voice go, 'The tree may not forgive it, but the ax offers its apologies. The trunk must be cut before the roots grow deeper.'"

Tina arched a copper eyebrow. "What does that mean?"

"I'm still not entirely sure," Leylia confessed. "But after it finished, I got hit with the wham-spin-wham and some serious sensory overload. When it was over, I woke up in this body in the middle of the *actual* Verdancy city I'd just been copying from my dreams to the game. But while I don't understand what he meant, there was no mistaking the voice. It was the Once King for sure."

"That's a pretty huge leap based off a voice you only heard once," Tina said, crossing her arms over her stonekin's heavily armored chest.

"It's not the sort of thing you forget," Leylia said. "You were in Bastion when he made his appearance there. You heard him speak. Could you *ever* mistake that voice for anything else?"

The moment she said it, James knew exactly what she meant. The Once King's voice wasn't just a sound. There was something in it that reached into your soul. Maybe something deep in his jubatus body still remembered that the last Celestial Elf was the world's first and primal king, or maybe you just didn't forget something that powerful. If the king's voice had had that same effect when he spoke through the Eclipsed Steel staff, James would never have mistaken it for a mere talking weapon. He absolutely believed Leylia when she said she knew the Once King's voice, and from the looks on their faces, so did Cinco and Assets. Tina, however, was still scowling.

"I don't get it," she said. "I didn't hear anything special. I mean, yeah, the Once King's got some serious projection, but so does Gregory. I thought it was just a raid boss thing."

"You wouldn't feel it," Leylia assured her. "Because you're not technically alive. Stonekin aren't born like normal people. The Bedrock kings forged you from magic deep in the ground. That's why stonekin can't be casters. It was never a balance issue, it's because you're not descended from Celestial Elves like the other races, which means you don't have the essence of the Unbounded Sky inside you. No sky, no mana, but also nothing that remembers the Once King's divine right to rule. Plus, stonekin are weapons who were made specifically to fight the Once King, so it makes total sense that you wouldn't be vulnerable to his commanding presence."

Tina didn't seem to know what to do with that information. James left her to ponder it and moved on. "His voice is solid proof enough for me," he said. "But what I want to know is *why* the Once King brought you here. What was he trying to accomplish?"

"How did he do it at all?" Assets asked sharply. "The Once King was introduced in the Deadlands expansion, which only launched a year ago. He wasn't even in the game yet when you claim to have been brought over two years ago, so how could he have done it?"

"Just because he wasn't in the game doesn't mean he wasn't *here*," Leylia said. "The Nightmare didn't take over the whole world at once. When I arrived, only a few places were frozen."

"Holy shit," Cinco said.

"What places?" James asked at the same time. As soon as the question was out, though, he realized he already knew the answer. "It was the places that were already in the game, wasn't it?"

"Bingo," Leylia said. "When I came in, the Nightmare had locked up the entire continent Bastion was on and every zone that was in the currently released seven expansions. It was *totally* spreading with the game, and man oh man, did the people who lived in the Verdancy know it. From their point of view, the rest of the world had been trapped in this repeating, dream-time-scape hell for decades. Garrond's Order fortress had been holding the line against the Once King's undead alone for almost thirty years by the time I got there. Even the lizard tribes of the Never Swamp had put aside their ancient grudge against humans to help keep the Order supplied so the fort wouldn't fall and flood their nests with undead. Shit was *dire*."

"Wow," Tina said. "I knew Garrond was hardcore, but that's ridiculous."

"If I'd known the Nightmare was taking over the world one expansion at a time, I would have stopped development," Leylia went on. "Too bad I didn't find out the truth until after I'd been brought over. I couldn't communicate with anyone back in our world, so I wasn't able to stop my company from rolling out the Deadlands expansion. The moment it went live, the Nightmare expanded again, and this time I was caught as well. One moment I was in the Order's fortress with Garrond, trying to figure out how to fix things; the next I was suddenly transported to Bastion and trapped there as a Portal Keeper NPC. Apparently someone on the dev team made me a memorial character there after I died, which was sweet I suppose, but damn, it was a trippy ten years." She shook her head. "They don't name it 'the Nightmare' for no reason. I'm *so* glad it's over."

"But we still don't know why the Once King brought you over," Tina pressed. "If he's really the reason we're here, that makes no sense at all. We're the only ones in this world who can kill him. Bringing us over seems like a really shitty strategy."

"Well, he's winning right now," Cinco reminded her. "And he never was beaten in the game."

"We're not done yet," Tina snapped back.

Leylia shrugged at them. "Heck if I know what goes on in the Once King's head. My best theory was that he thought bringing me here would stop the Nightmare from spreading. My magical reaching was the reason all of this happened, so it made sense that dragging me over would stop the damage. Unfortunately for everyone, it didn't work. Now that I know more about magic, my best guess is that all of the players' individual investments in the game world kept the connection alive despite my absence, which is why he brought all of you over as well. The spell had taken on a life of its own, so he had to do something equally huge to break it. That's my theory, anyway. But there's no way to know for sure."

Everyone fell silent as they thought about that. James especially was wracking his brain, leaning on his black staff as he struggled to come up with a magical theory that could explain everything they'd observed enough to reverse it. But while he didn't have any brilliant ideas, the cold bite of the cursed metal against his skin told him who might.

"I can ask him."

Every eye in the tent locked on James as he held up the Eclipsed Steel Staff. "The Once King can talk to me through this."

This revelation caused several gasps of alarm.

"Shit, for real?" Cinco asked.

"Can he hear us as well?" Assets demanded, stepping back. "Has the enemy been listening in this entire time?"

"I wouldn't be here if he could," James said. "It's pretty fuzzy, usually. I actually thought this was more of the typical cursed-talking-weapon type of setup until yesterday, when I heard him speak for real. I'm certain he's in here, though, if only as an echo. I'd talked to him plenty of times before I realized who I was actually speaking with."

"Well shit," Tina said. "Dial him up, then! If he really did bring us here, then he should be hella ready to send us back after what we did to his army."

"Are you sure talking to him is a good idea?" Cinco asked, the huge Berserker sounding uncharacteristically nervous. "I mean, isn't he like the enemy of all life and shit?"

"Can't hurt to ask," Tina said, grinning at her brother. "Get him on the line, James!"

"I'll try," James said, frowning at his staff. "I've never actually initiated contact, just replied when he spoke. Like you said, though, can't hurt to ask." He paused. "Um, if I start casting weird death magic, please shut me down."

"Will do," Tina promised, cracking her knuckles with a metallic *pang*. "Let's talk to a king."

James nodded and forced his eyes away from the cadre of giant people who might be tackling him in the next few minutes to focus on the staff in his hands. As always, the Eclipsed Steel felt cold and unpleasant against his skin. He ignored the wrongness and peered into the latticework of magics that ran through the too-black metal for a clue.

It was hard. The twisted flows of energy formed an unfathomably dense, multilayered matrix that spiraled horizontally, vertically, and maybe even in a third direction his brain couldn't grasp. Whatever was going on inside the staff, it was as far beyond his comprehension as quantum computing would have been. So since understanding how it worked clearly wasn't going to fly, James tried the stupid approach instead.

Hello, he thought at the staff, giving it a squeeze. *Mr. Once King?*

Nothing happened.

Hello? he thought again.

Still nothing.

"It's not working," James said. "Does anyone know the proper form of address for a king of the undead? I mean, 'Once King' is the name we gave him, but he has to have something else he calls himself."

"Hmm," Assets said, frowning. "Why don't you try..." He finished with a word in Old Elven that James had never heard in his life but whose very pronunciation carried a sense of awe and power straight to his bones.

"Wow," said James, Cinco, and Leylia at the same time. They all looked at each other and then at Assets.

"How'd you know that?" James asked, jealous that he hadn't gotten Old Elven as one of his languages from the transition.

For once, the Trade Co. guild leader didn't look smug about knowing something others didn't. "It's the only word of the Unbounded Language I know," he said, clearly shaken. "I don't know *how* I know it, but I know it means *King*. Unsurprisingly."

That was better than anything James could come up with. Staring hard at the Eclipsed Steel Staff again, he thought and said the word Assets had told him at the same time, doing his best to keep his voice reverent.

"*King.*"

For a long heartbeat, there was nothing but the cold tickle of cursed steel in his hands. Then James felt a stirring, like someone rousing from deep slumber.

Who dares speak my name without permission?

The sonorous voice came from the staff to sound directly in James's head, and he bounced excitedly. "I've got him!"

Tina nodded, looking ready to tackle him while everyone else took a nervous step back.

"Um, it is I, James the Player," James replied. "We conversed yesterday. Thank you once again for the honor of your reply."

He spoke seriously and slowly, trying for a respectful, courtly vibe, since James was pretty sure the Once King was a prideful ruler and, unlike Gregory, wouldn't forgive any faults of decorum now that they both knew who the other was. Sure enough, the answer that came from the staff sounded pleased.

You have learned my name and offer proper respect at last. Have you decided to join my cause and save your people from their suffering?

"I must humbly decline," James said nervously. "I wish only to ask why you brought us players to your world."

That is not the real question which I'm sure burns in your heart. The lovely voice of the ancient elf sounded deeply disappointed. *But I am proud of my actions, so I will answer you nonetheless. I brought you here to end the Nightmare that had consumed us all. I'd tried to stop the spread years ago in a more precise manner, but though I successfully felled the trunk, the roots clung on. Even my great plans had to be set aside for a time while I did the cutting necessary to free*

44

the world. Tragically, some souls were caught on this side of the Unbounded Sky as a result. My apologies. You players are now trapped here the same as all the rest. I am truly sorry to have doomed you, but know that you have helped me save something much greater than yourselves. This world should honor your sacrifice more than it does.

It wasn't so different from Leylia had guessed, but hearing the truth from the Once King himself gave their whole situation new gravitas. Hauling Leylia over hadn't stopped the Nightmare because the players were still participating in the game and perpetuating the collision of worlds. So the next time he reached, the Once King had just grabbed everyone, and this time it had worked. Without millions of players keeping it going, the connection between the fake and the real had snapped, and the Nightmare had finally broken. The rest of it—all the players' lives lost and ruined by the transition to FFO—were just the casualties of war. They were sacrifices the Once King had chosen to save his world from the disaster Leylia had forced onto it. James wasn't sure if he begrudged that or not, but there was no time to figure his feelings out. One did not keep ancient god-kings waiting.

"Thank you for telling me the truth," James said, struggling to keep his voice steady. "But if I may dare another question..."

What you dare is your business.

James nodded, taking a deep breath. Here went nothing. "I understand now that you brought us here to save your world. A great and noble act to be sure, but one that is no longer necessary. Now that the spell is broken and the Nightmare is over, is it within your great power to send us back home?"

There was a long pause before the answer came back.

I am sorry, James the Player, the Once King said, his flawless voice sad and sincere. *I do not have so much mana that I can expend it on such frivolities. Your world created the Nightmare, and you players have paid the price to fix it. As unfortunate as that is for you, you cannot deny it is fair. But I am not without mercy. If you surrender to me, I will allow you to pass painlessly into oblivion without having to serve in my armies. Such is the breadth of my magnanimity.*

45

He clearly thought he was being *very* generous with that offer, but James was too focused on the first part of what he'd said to pay much attention to the latter.

"So you *could* send us back if you had the mana?" he demanded, courtly speech forgotten. "How?"

I have not the breath to waste on outcomes that will never arrive, came the scornful reply. *This audience is over. If you desire to speak again, you may present yourself properly to me in person. I do not make a habit of paying calls to rude peasants.*

"Wait!" James cried, but the staff was already falling still in his hands as the Once King's presence faded. "*Damn!*"

"What'd he say?" Tina asked eagerly, dropping her ready-to-tackle stance.

James quickly recounted the conversation to the room at large. When he'd told them everything, CincoDeMurder slammed his fists together. "Hot damn!" the Berserker cried, turning to Tina. "This means I was right! If you and I get our raids together and head for the Dead Mountain, we can crush that smug fucker! We'll hold him down and beat him until he finds the mana to send us home!"

"Don't be stupid," Assets snapped. "Even during the game when we had rezzes, no friendly fire, and instant communication via voice chat, no one ever defeated the Once King. Also, since you clearly forgot, the Dead Mountain Fortress is on the opposite side of the *planet.* How are you even going to get there? Build a boat?"

Cinco glowered dangerously, but Assets had already dismissed him, turning to speak directly to Tina instead. "The smartest course of action is to band together and defeat his undead army here. After this kingdom's peace is restored, we can return to Bastion and use the Room of Arrivals to portal directly to the Deadlands. King Gregory would fall over himself to send you there with full logistical support. If you'd just be patient, you can have everything you want."

"You know a lot about patience, *Lord* Assets," Cinco snarled, forcing James to jump out of the way as the huge Berserker stepped forward. "You didn't make it a day before selling out to the locals, and for what? You were the one reading the damn numbers. You *know* this is an unwinnable fight. I thought you greedy Wall Street types were supposed to be smart!"

"It's not unwinnable if we all fight the enemy instead of each other," Assets snapped. "Our best chance of survival is to stay together. That means fighting with Bastion, and if I'm going to be the hero of a kingdom, I'm damn well going to get paid for it."

"What's the point of sticking together with an army of cannon fodder?" Cinco argued back. "Windy Lake's level what? Twenty? Maybe thirties? That's nothing. I could sneeze and kill a whole squad of those low-level bastards. We don't need a worthless kingdom providing worthless troops. Three high-end raids and the Once King at our feet, *that's* what we need!"

"And where am *I* supposed to live once he's sent you all home?" Assets said, fearlessly jabbing a finger into Cinco's burly chest. "What's left of this continent is about to be swarmed under! Windy Lake will be a *literal* ghost town before you can even make it to the coast. Why should I sacrifice my chance to live as a rich lord in this beautiful new body just so you can go back to your life as an internet tough guy living in his mother's basement?"

"*I don't live in my mom's basement!*" Cinco roared. "I have my own place, and it's fucking *sweet*. That said, my body is lying there alone right now! I'm dying of dehydration as we speak. We don't have time to fuck around!"

"You think I do?" Assets snapped. "I know exactly how high the wall we're up against here is, but I also know you don't throw out all your backup plans on a long shot. If you leave all of Bastion here to die while you go storm the Once King's castle, and you *can't* beat him, then you just sacrificed the whole world for *nothing*. And while I'm fine with you being stuck in a hell of your own making, I don't want to be a zombie forever because you're an elitist meathead who can't think past his own immediate needs!"

"*Guys!*" Tina said, too loudly for the tent, but at least it stopped the fight. "Shut up for a second. I just had a great idea."

Both Cinco and Assets glared murder at Tina. Just being in the same vicinity as that anger made James want to wilt by proxy, but his sister didn't seem to care at all. She actually looked excited, putting her armored hands proudly on her hips in a way that reminded James of when she'd first figured out how to beat him at cards when she was nine.

"I think Cinco is right," she announced. "We should attack the Once King as fast as we can."

Assets looked appalled. "You can't be serious—"

"I can and I am," she said. "You can spin shit into gold for the NPCs all you want, but we all know the undead army headed our way can't be beaten. We already fought it with our best and burned the city to a crisp with windfire powder, and we *still* lost. Now we're stuck out here in the plains with tons of refugees, no resupply, and no castle, while they have all of Bastion's dead. Face it, staying here in the current circumstances is suicide, but what if we could destroy that army before it even gets to us?"

"What do you mean?" James asked.

Tina's face split into an even bigger smile. "I mean, what if we took the problem out at the source? I'm not great at lore, but I know all the ghostfire in the world rises from the Great Pyre at the top of the Dead Mountain Fortress. That is an exact quote from the DMF loading screen, and if it is actually true..." She looked at Leylia, who nodded. "Then we don't have to beat the Once King at all. We just have to get past him long enough to smash the Great Pyre where all the ghostfire comes from. If we do that, all the undead in the world will suddenly become *dead*-dead. It's an instant and total win!"

She finished with a flourish, but Assets was already shaking his head. "It's a nice dream, Roxxy, but the Once King and his vaunted source of ghostfire are still in a castle on the other side of the world. Even if you could just walk in and stomp the flames out, we'd all be months dead before you got there."

"I still think Tina's on to something here," James said excitedly. "We're in trouble because the Once King sent his entire army to Bastion, and now that army's on its way to us. But if all the undead in the world are marching our direction, that means the Once King is *alone* in his fortress right now."

"Exactly," Tina said, flashing him a proud smile. "You saw what we fought in Bastion. Every damn raid boss, elite guard, and undead-whatever in the world got dragged through the Room of Arrivals to come fight us. But my Roughnecks killed almost all of those assholes yesterday, and there's no more respawning. If that's all true—and we *know* it is—then the Dead Mountain Fortress is *empty*. We won't have to battle our way through five terraces of two-skull patrols and giant intelligent raid bosses! We can just walk right in and go straight up to the Once King. He's never been more vulnerable!"

"But that plan still requires sacrificing Bastion," Assets said testily. "I wish you all would stop treating that part as inevitable and start thinking of ways to win here. The DMF will be just as empty *after* we save the biggest and most important kingdom in the world."

"But it *is* inevitable," Tina said, exasperated. "Seriously, dude, wake up. We can't win here, but we might be able to stall."

"Not for months," Assets said.

Tina shrugged. "Who said anything about months? The Deadlands are on the other side of the world, but I was there just three days ago. Fuck sailing—this is a world full of portals! There *has* to be a way to get to the Deadlands fast. If we can do that and you guys play good defense here, there's a chance we can destroy the Great Pyre and/or force the Once King into submission before his army even arrives!"

49

Assets clearly had not considered that angle. Cinco looked impressed as well, though not sold. "It's not a bad plan," he admitted. "But how does it get us home?"

Tina punched her hands together. "Easy. The Once King's stupid powerful, but he's still just one guy. All we have to do is get past him to the Great Pyre. We'll hold the ghostfire hostage until he agrees to send us all home. Once we're sure we've got our way out, we betray him and destroy the pyre anyway. Win-fucking-win."

"Sounds great to me," Leylia said, making the others jump. "Just one problem: this world isn't *actually* full of portals. One of the reasons the city of Bastion was so powerful in this world is that all teleports here rely on the network that runs through the Room of Arrivals, and that's kind of overrun with zombies."

"Minor detail," Tina said, reaching over to pull James to her side. "I'm sure my brother can figure it out."

James cringed in her hold. "I can?"

"You got us a portal out of Bastion," she reminded him. "And you know the back ways to get around this game better than anyone. If anyone can think up a way to get to the Deadlands without using the Room of Arrivals, it's you."

Desperate as he was to live up to his sister's unprecedented vote of confidence, James was drawing a blank. The anywhere scroll he'd used to evacuate them from Bastion had already been a super-out-of-the-box solution that someone else had thought up, *and* it had cost him his entire vault. He didn't exactly have another pile of treasures lying around. Even if he did, there wasn't a Schtumple Bank in the Savanna. The only branch he knew of outside of Bastion was in the ichthyian capital a mile under the Western Sea, not exactly convenient. There had to be *something*, though. He was wracking his brain for every tidbit of fast travel lore when Leylia swooped in and saved him.

"You guys need the Timeless Tunnels," the brunette said cheerily.

50

James gaped at her. "I've never heard of those."

"You wouldn't have," she said smugly. "Because they were never in the game. They're part of this world's actual history, but I've been dream-walking in this place since I can remember. I know way more about it than I was able to cram into FFO. The Timeless Tunnels are one of the bits that never made it in, mostly because the dev team thought a super-fast subterranean global transport system would unbalance game play. They absolutely exist, though, and bonus, the Bedrock Kings are extremely anti-undead. I'm sure they'd help if we asked."

"Cooooool…" Tina rumbled.

"Sounds awesome," James agreed. "How do we contact them?"

Leylia made a face. "That's the bit I'm not so sure about. Game-wise, I was planning to bring in the Bedrock Kings as key figures for expansion nine, the one after the Deadlands. We were gonna have a big opening event where some boss-ass ancient Naturalist used a stonekin general to summon them, but that's all developer stuff that bends the lore to match the game. Now that things are really real, hell if I know if it would actually work."

"Well, we have Naturalists and a stonekin," James said hopefully. "I'll get with my mentor Gray Fang and see if we can figure something out."

"I'm on board," Tina said, flashing them a marble-toothed grin. "If this works out, we can get people home in a timely fashion *and* save the world from an undead apocalypse! That ticks all the boxes I needed for my people."

"I like it as well," Assets said, making a show of cleaning his super-rare ruby shades. "I like any plan that saves Bastion, and I agree that beating one raid boss alone in his home is a much better proposition than taking on that ridiculous army a second time."

Tina nodded and turned to the other guild leader in the tent. "Cinco, how about you?"

The red-armored Berserker shrugged. "I already said I'd go along with whatever you did, and kicking the Once King's ass was my plan first, so count me in."

James breathed a sigh of relief. The trio of guild leaders had come here angry and combative, but now they were all wearing grins-of-future-ass-kickings, which seemed to be how they bonded. He was still wiping the nervous sweat off his brow when Tina suddenly leaned forward to loom menacingly over Assets.

"There's one more thing I want."

"Yes, Miss Anderson?" Assets said, slowly backing away.

Tina stopped that by grabbing the elf by the lapels of his faux-designer suit. "Just because we've got a good plan now doesn't mean I've forgotten what you did in that war meeting," she growled in Assets's face. "I know you and that Water Born cat were in cahoots, and while I can't speak for the Roughnecks, I *can* speak for myself. You're going to get James's wedding canceled, or I'm not tanking shit."

"My *what?*" James squeaked, looking at Tina in a panic.

"Your cat-dad is marrying you off to try to force me into staying and fighting here," his sister replied.

"It's a good marriage to a wonderful girl that James should at least consider," Assets choked out as Tina lifted him off his feet.

"But I can't get married!" James said frantically, wringing his tail in both hands. "I don't even know her! And I have to go home and pay off my debts. I can't leave a wife behind! But if I break the engagement, her family will be insulted, and the Claw Born will be horribly dishonored. This is a *disaster!*"

"Don't worry, bro," Tina said, baring her teeth at Assets, who was frantically trying to get away. "The new Lord of the Treasury is going to fix this for you. Aren't you, *Baron* Assets?"

"But—" Assets tried to say.

"Would you rather I fixed it?" she asked, giving the slender elf a shake. "'Cause I'm in a mood to solve the *fuck* out of this problem."

Assets began rapidly waving his arms. "No, no! Definitely not!" he cried. "I'll get this taken care of even if I have to marry her myself!"

"Glad we could come to an agreement," Tina said, letting her victim go.

Assets fell three feet to the ground. He landed with typical elven grace, but his hands were shaking as he frantically smoothed out his hair and suit. "Well," he huffed when he was decent. "I'd better get on that, then. Shall I inform the king of our plan?"

"*I'll* inform him, after I've talked to the Roughnecks," Tina said. "I think they'll like it, but it's not a done deal until we vote."

"Whatever you want," Assets said, hurrying out of the tent so fast he was practically running.

"Chump," Cinco snorted, flashing Tina a cocky grin. "I'm going to go tell my guild what's up and that we're on guard duty." He jerked his head at Leylia. "Mind keeping an eye on her until my boys arrive?"

"Sure," Tina said. "I need to talk to my brother anyway."

Cinco blew her a kiss and strolled out of the tent. When he was gone, James turned to his sister, tail still clutched in his hands. "Thank you," he muttered. "Thank you thank you *thank you*."

"Don't mention it," she said, reaching down to mush his ears with her huge hand. "Honestly, you were just a good excuse. I've been wanting to scream at Assets all morning. So how long until you can summon me some Earth Kings?"

"I can get moving on the research immediately," he said. "Leave it to me."

"Fantastic," she said, petting him again. "Thanks, J."

"No problem, T."

Cinco's guards arrived shortly after that. Once they knew their jobs—namely, murderize anyone who tried to touch Leylia—they settled in to watch, and Tina left to go inform her guild of the new situation. James watched her go with a hopefulness he hadn't felt in a long time. Scary as it had been, this whole incident had been the most positive interaction he'd had with his sister since he'd left for college. He was still basking in the warm glow of not being hated by his only sibling when he suddenly remembered something else he was supposed to be doing.

"Shit."

James whirled around, searching the small tent while Cinco's killers watched in amusement. No matter how hard he looked, though, there was no sign of movement in any of the shadows, which meant SilentBlayde was gone.

"Craaaap," James groaned, lurching out of the tent. Tina seemed surprisingly okay, but that was how Tina was. When shit got bad, she buried herself in work until she was too busy to think about anything she didn't want to. SB was the opposite. He brooded, badly, and right now—deeply depressed, sleep deprived, and barely out of his last breakdown—the last place he needed to be was alone.

Unfortunately, the whole point of the Assassin class was being hard to find. No matter where he looked, James found nothing, but he wasn't going to give up. Tina was trusting him to get on this Bedrock Kings problem, but he couldn't focus until he knew SilentBlayde was okay. Not that he really thought something bad was going to happen, but the last time James had blown off someone in SB's situation, he'd been left with a wrong that could never be undone. He'd sworn he'd never make that mistake again, so even though daylight was sliding through his fingers, James turned away from the Naturalists Lodge, where Gray Fang would be, and went off instead in search of his friend.

Chapter 3

Tina

Typically, gathering the Roughnecks together for a meeting was akin to herding cats. This time, however, there were no such problems. The moment Tina walked back into camp, raiders started popping out of the tents like prairie dogs. Even Zen was up and about despite the fact that she couldn't have gotten more than two hours of sleep. The only Roughneck Tina didn't see was SB, but that was probably for the best. Today had been hard enough already without adding her stupid emotions on top of the heap.

"Is everyone here?" she asked when the group gathered around her looked about the right size.

"Everyone who counts," Killbox called back. "What's the plan, boss?"

The trust in his voice made Tina both giddy and terrified. Looking out into the sea of expectant faces, Tina realized the crowd had divided itself into two groups. On her left were the people she knew wanted to stay—Frank, Anders, and several others. On her right were people who wanted to go home, starting with NekoBaby, who was right up front. Some, like Zen and Richard, were floating in the middle, but the crack in her guild was already clear. Even divided, though, they were all still looking at her. Looking for salvation. Tina just hoped she had it.

"All right," she said, keeping her normally booming stonekin voice down to make sure only her guild could hear this. "I know we're all anxious as shit, so I'm going to skip the pep talk and get straight to the point. I've got good news and bad news. Good news is, I think I've found us a way home."

A squeal of glee went up from NekoBaby's area of the audience. The others weren't so optimistic.

"What's the bad news?" Zen asked.

Tina blew out a breath. Here went nothing. "We gotta beat the Once King to do it."

The announcement fell like an anvil, crushing even Neko's excitement.

"But..." someone said in the silence. "Hasn't the Once King never been beaten? Like *ever*?"

"No one has ever killed him, no," Richard said in a dry voice. "Though not from lack of trying."

He would certainly know, Tina thought. His guild, *Richard's Inferno*, had been ranked number one in the world before repeated failures at the Once King fight had torn them apart. But she wasn't finished.

"That was before," she said boldly. "But as we keep learning over and over, this isn't a game now. We don't have to play by the rules anymore. If we want to bring four, five, or six raids to the fight, we can do that! We can beat him."

Frank raised his hand. "Uh...why do we have to kill him, again?" he asked when Tina pointed at him. "Sorry if it's a stupid question, but how does killing a guy on the other side of the world get people home?"

"Because he's the one who brought us here," Tina said.

Gasps flew up from the crowd, and she raised her hands. "I know you've got questions, but that's all I can say for now. Someone risked their life to tell me this info, and until I'm sure they won't die for it, I can't go into more detail. But what matters is that the Once King's the one who sucked us into this mess, which means he's the one who knows how to get us out."

"Shouldn't we be *not* killing him then?" ZeroDarkness asked.

"I didn't say 'kill,'" Tina pointed out. "I said 'beat.' Right now, the Once King has the power to send us home, he just doesn't want to, so my plan is to storm his house and kick his ass until he changes his mind. Once we've got him on the ropes, we'll negotiate how to get those of you who want to go home home. And for those of you who don't want to leave, we've got you covered, too. As soon as we've got our exit back to Earth secure, we're going to kill the Once King and stomp out the Great Pyre for good. No more ghostfire, no more undead, world saved." Her face split into a grin.

"You see? We don't have to choose! We can have our way home and eat it too! All we gotta do is beat the guy we were playing this game to beat in the first place, and we get everything we want. There might even be loot!"

A cheer went up from the crowd, and Tina let out the breath she hadn't realized she'd been holding. She was congratulating herself on a plan well sold when Zen raised her hand.

"What about the MDB?"

Tina winced. That was a good question. A *very* good question. One she didn't have an answer to yet.

"What's the MDB?" Frank asked, his voice exasperated. "Sorry to keep being the speed bump, but you folks use too many acronyms for me to keep up with, and that's saying something coming from an engineer."

"The MDB is the Million Damage Blast," Anders explained, his ichthyian fish-eyes even rounder than usual with worry. "It's the reason the original Roughneck raiding guild could never get the Once King past his second phase back in the game. Once he gets down to thirty percent health, he does a huge attack that hits everyone in the raid for one million damage, which is more than anyone can take. Roxxy's the only one tough enough to survive it, and only if she blows all her cooldowns."

"Not that it does any good," Zen added. "Knights don't have Raise Ally, and one tank can't DPS the Once King down the final thirty percent by herself. That's why no one's ever beaten him even though the Deadlands expansion has been out for a year. No matter how well you do before it goes off, the MDB is a guaranteed wipe."

"And now that he's no longer constrained by the game mechanics, there's no reason the Once King couldn't cast it at the very beginning of the fight rather than the end," Richard put in bleakly. "That would be the intelligent thing to do. Why fight at all when you can kill everyone facing you in one hit?"

This announcement made everyone look defeated, and Tina rushed to pull them back up before the whole raid collapsed. "The MDB is just a problem we don't know how to solve yet," she reminded them. "But we've done tons of impossible things over the last week! Remember Grel? How many impossible fights have we cheated our way through? We'll figure it out. It won't even be that hard. The Once King's sent his entire army to Bastion, remember? That means he's alone in the Dead Mountain Fortress. We can walk right in there and kill him."

"How are we even getting back to the Dead Mountain?" someone yelled from the back.

"My brother James is already working on that," Tina said. "We'll find a way to make it happen, but before we do anything, we need to vote. And not by class leaders, either. This decision affects everyone, so I want everyone to have a say."

NekoBaby snorted. "What's there to say? We barely escaped Bastion with our lives yesterday. If that army shows up again, we're D-E-D *dead*. We need to GTFO of the Savanna anyway. Might as well head back to where the good loot is." She cracked her knuckles. "Also, I don't know about the rest of you losers, but I owe the Once King for a few hundred thousand wipes. We Roughnecks spent four months dying to that bastard five nights a week! Saving the world's cool and all, but I want some payback."

"I'm in!" Killbox said excitedly. "I always wanted to be part of a world-first kill!"

"And with the removal of the game's mechanics, it might even be possible," Richard said, his stoic face as animated as Tina had ever seen it. "We could bring in two raids, or three! That way, even if the MDB kills the main group, the others can sweep in and finish the job while the spare healers resurrect everyone who died. The possibilities are endless now that we're no longer constrained by arbitrary limits like group size and instanced dungeons."

Everyone started talking excitedly after that. Tina let them. She needed the excitement and momentum if they were actually going to do the impossible. Personally, though, she agreed with Neko. There was no other choice. If they stayed here, they were almost certainly dead, and for what? Winning on the Grasslands was a temporary victory at best. Even if they smashed every last zombie, there were always more dead to raise. The Once King's army would simply rebuild and return, and they'd have to fight all over again. If they went to the Dead Mountain, though, they had a chance to solve the problem for good *and* get their way home. It was win/win all around, but Tina had finally had it beaten through her stone skull that she couldn't force her raid. If she tried to make them go a certain direction, even if it was obviously the best one, they'd fight her on principle. But if she gave them the information and waited for them to come to the same obvious conclusion she had, they'd all go along happily, thinking it was their idea.

At least, that's what she hoped.

"Okay," she said when the excited buzz had grown as loud as it seemed likely to go. "Time to vote. Who wants to stay here and die?"

No one raised their hands, and Tina's lips curled into a smirk. "Who wants to kick the Once King's ass, save the world, and win us a way home?"

There was lots of eye rolling at her choice of words, but every single hand in the crowd still shot up as high as it would go, and Tina's smirk turned into a victorious grin. "It's decided, then! Get your shit together and get ready to fight. Officers on me for specific instructions."

The crowd parted like a shot. While the majority of the raiders raced around preparing for battle, the class officers—minus, again, SilentBlayde, who was replaced by ZeroDarkness, the Roughnecks' only other Assassin—gathered in a clump around Tina.

"So what are we *really* going to do?" Neko asked the moment they were all together. "Not to be a buzz kill, but we couldn't get the Once King down to thirty percent reliably even back when we were a *real* raiding guild. How the hell are we going to do it now? We *still* don't have a full raid, and some of these people have no idea what they're doing." She looked pointedly at Killbox and Frank. "No offense."

"None taken," Frank assured her.

"We'll figure it out," Killbox said at the same time. "We figured Grel out."

"Yeah, 'cause he was big and stupid!" Neko snapped. "The Once King's smart, and he can *fly*. Now that the game's not making him stand there and let us hit him, what's to keep him from just flapping up and blasting us from the sky? How are we even going to make a plan? It's not like we can look up a tanking video on his new mechanics, and I doubt he'll be polite enough to give us multiple attempts."

"She's not wrong," Richard said, scowling under the glow of his eternally burning crown of flames. "We can't assume anything from the game anymore. If we're going to face him, we need a new strategy that uses our new strengths and makes up for our new weaknesses."

"There's a lot to work out," Tina agreed, grinning at them. "But that's what you guys are for! I want all of you to put your heads together and get me a plan to beat the Once King using the people and tools we've got. Cinco has already agreed to come with his Red Sands, so we'll have at least one extra raid. You work with that. Meanwhile, I'm going to go inform the NPCs of our decision before they decide to marry anyone else off."

Frank's eyebrows shot up. "Marry?"

"Long story," Tina grumbled.

"If only we had some way to practice before the fight," Richard said, completely ignoring everything Tina had just said. "As NekoBaby astutely pointed out, the Once King won't give us multiple shots. Whatever we do, we have to do it in one."

Tina's lips curled into a smile again. "I think I can help with that part," she said. "Let me go arrange some things. You guys just focus on coming up with a plan."

Neko saluted and squatted down next to Richard, who was already drawing diagrams in the dirt. Satisfied their survival was in the best hands possible, Tina turned around and started walking back toward the Naturalist Lodge to tell the king that the Roughnecks were all in.

***

"So let me be sure I have this correct," King Gregory said, looking nervously across the table at Tina and Cinco, who'd already been waiting at the lodge when she'd arrived. "You want to stop this invasion by defeating the Once King, enemy of all life?"

"Yep," Tina said. "No Once King, no ghostfire, no undead army. Problem freaking solved!"

"And what do we do in the meanwhile?" the king asked. "Even if James can find you a way to the Deadlands that won't take months, the undead army is marching toward us at this very moment."

"You'll just have to turtle up and deal," Cinco said with a shrug. "All you've gotta do is not die while we go out and solve the problem. Easy peasy."

"There is nothing easy about facing a siege while outnumbered by a superior enemy!" Captain Hightower yelled. Then his eyes narrowed. "How do we know you players aren't just running away?"

"Dude, do *you* want to fight the Once King?" Tina snapped. "'Cause that's the only way this is gonna end. Even if we stayed and stomped every zombie, they'd just make more. The only way to end this for real is to cut off the snake's head."

"What about going home?" one of the jubatus lords asked suspiciously. "I thought you players were all about that. Now you suddenly want to face the world's most powerful enemy for our sake? How do we know this isn't a trick?"

"For real?" Cinco growled, his eyes narrowing dangerously. "We offer to do the impossible, and *that's* your response? Do you furry fuckers want our help or not?"

"Let us worry about getting home," Tina said pointedly, stabbing a *shut up* elbow into Cinco's ribs. They'd already agreed not to say anything

61

about the Once King's role in bringing them here, because blabbing the truth would have put Leylia in even more danger and given the NPCs a new angle of attack. Just because they'd made peace didn't mean everyone was buddy-buddy, and it was an easy step from "brought over by the Once King" to "agent of the Once King." The last thing they needed was another reason for the people of this world to mistrust them, especially with what Tina was going to ask next.

"I'll handle my people," she told the nervous room. "But right now, our focus has to be on killing the Once King. With his army in Bastion, we'll never get a better shot to take him out and end this for good. Our raids are the only people in the world who have a chance of actually killing him. My officers are already working on a plan, and my brother James has a way to get us to the Deadlands before the army arrives, but we're still going to need help from you."

"What can we do?" King Gregory replied immediately, making Tina smile. Good to know *someone* saw the bigger picture.

"We're going to need supplies," she said. "There's nothing to eat in the Deadlands except dust and no water at all, so we'll need all of that plus tents and wagons to haul it. We can probably pick up some things from the Order fortress, but Commander Garrond was already stretched thin when we left him three days ago, and I don't imagine he's restocked yet."

"It's not as if we're stocked, either," Rends Iron Hides said grumpily. "But we'll see what we can do," he added after a look at the king.

"Fantastic," Tina said. "If you've got food and whatnot, that leaves just one thing we need before we're ready to face the final boss."

"What is that?" Gregory asked.

Tina grinned. "You."

The king jerked back. "Me? *Why?*"

"Human-scale raid bosses are the worst to fight," she explained. "Giants like Grel have their own issues, but at least they're easy to hit and damage without hurting our own people. When all that power gets crammed into a person-sized package, though, the whole fight dynamic changes. Malakai almost cleaned my clock twice, and let's be honest, the Blood General Sanguilar was too busy having fun and lording his supremacy over us yesterday to be serious. He didn't give us half the ass kicking he could have." Tina shuddered at the memory of those final minutes in Bastion when Sanguilar *had* been serious. He'd nearly killed her in one hit.

"The Once King is the strongest five-skull in existence," she went on. "If we're going to have a prayer of beating him, there's no room for mistakes. Whatever plan my people come up with, we're going to have to pull it off flawlessly on our first try. That kind of perfection requires a *lot* of practice, and since Your Highness *also* happens to be a five-skull raid boss, I'd like to train my troops with you."

The request was barely out of her mouth before Captain Hightower shot to his feet. "*Absolutely not!*" he roared, getting in her face. "You want His Majesty to fight a player raid? Preposterous! You were rebels just yesterday! We cannot put our king's life in your hands!"

Tina tried to push the four-skull captain out of her personal space unsuccessfully. "Who else are we supposed to train on? Desperate times, desperate measures, yo. Do you want us to win or not?"

"You can't possibly—"

"I'll do it," Gregory said.

"*Highness!*"

The king shook his head. "I've learned my lesson, Hightower. If I hadn't hidden in my castle after the Nightmare, the city might not have fallen to chaos. If I'd ridden out to face the players instead of letting others handle everything I found uncomfortable, I might have been able to save my knights from Malakai's hate. If I'd been a better king, we could have faced the Once King's invasion united and maybe triumphed. But I did none of those things, and now we are here. I will not make the same mistakes again. I will do whatever I can to ensure this grassland is not the end of Bastion."

"But Your Highness," Hightower begged. "Be reasonable! If any player in their number wished to kill you, you'd be handing them your head!"

"Come on, that's just dumb," Tina said. "If one player could down a five-skull raid boss, we wouldn't be in this situation. Also." She nodded at the ancient white-and-gold–robed elf sitting on the pillow to the king's left. "You've got High Sun Priest Whatshisname right there. You're a raid boss, but he's a raid boss *healer*. He can stand on the sidelines and toss heals at the king the whole time if it makes you feel better. Hell, half the Bastion army can be on standby if you want. I don't care who's watching so long as I get a real five-skull to train on."

That argument seemed to mollify Captain Hightower somewhat. At least he leaned back a bit and stopped shoving his hooked nose into her chin. But his griping was quickly replaced by the high priest's.

"I cannot," Raffestain said, shaking his head.

"Cannot what?"

"I cannot heal His Majesty," the golden-robed priest said somberly. "I am still too low on mana from the battle of Bastion."

Tina couldn't believe her ears. "*Whaaat?* How is that possible? Didn't the cats feed you?"

The wrinkly old elf harrumphed. "The hospitality of Windy Lake has been more than exemplary. I have eaten and slept all I care to. That is not the issue. What is is that I was four-skull rated in your game, which means I have over ten million mana. That might sound like an infinitely deep pool, but it goes quickly when you're healing an army, and my mana doesn't recover any faster than a player's no matter how much I eat and sleep." He sighed. "It will be days before I am full again. I need to save my strength for the battle here, and not just to heal our wounded. We brought the Bastion with us, but the crystal inside is still too weakened to be used again so soon. Without it, I am the only one present who can cast the Resplendent Aegis, which may well take all the mana I have left."

Up to this point, Tina heard just a bunch of excuses about recovery rates, but that last bit caught her attention. "Wait, the big golden anti-undead shield the Bastion put over the city was just a *spell*? As in something you can cast?"

The high priest nodded.

"Holy shit," Tina said, earning herself a cutting look, which she ignored. "Can you teach my Clerics to do that? 'Cause having my own portable version of the Bastion would be *really freaking useful* for when we go fight the lord of all undead."

The old elf shook his head again, which seemed to be a common theme with him. "Even if I was willing to teach it, I cannot. Unlike normal spells, the Resplendent Aegis isn't something I control. It is a prayer that beseeches the Sun's direct intervention. Only true priests—those who have devoted themselves entirely to the service of the Holy Sun—can request such a great blessing." He turned up his nose. "I *highly* doubt anyone in your band of robed hoodlums can even hear the voice of our great god."

As much as Tina wanted to call that out as racist bullshit, she was worried the old bastard had a point. She clearly remembered her conversation with Anders two days ago about this exact issue. He'd been worried that he was a fake priest stealing the power of a very real god. That said, Anders *had* been talking to the Sun at that time. Specifically, he'd been complaining about how the god was hard to understand and how its relationship with players was complicated, but those were all minor details Tina was sure they'd sort out. Point was, she had at least one priest she *knew* could talk to the Sun, and that would have to be good enough.

"I might have a guy who can prove you wrong," she said, leaning over the table at the high priest. "If I can get you a player the Sun will listen to, will you give him a chance?"

Raffestain thought about that for a moment, then he nodded. "Regardless of the current situation, the opportunity to turn a false cleric into a real one is a chance I can't ignore. I'll see if what you say is true."

"Works for me," Tina said with a clap of her hands. "Let's do this."

"What about His Majesty?" Captain Hightower snapped. "He needs a healer!"

"I will be fine, Hightower," the king said, smiling reassuringly at his captain before turning to Tina. "I am ready."

"Let's rock, then!" she said, turning to lead the way out of the lodge.

***

"Are you *sure* this is a good idea?" Zen asked her an hour later.

They were all standing in the middle of the rutted trade road just south of Windy Lake. In front of them, King Gregory stood in all his eight-foot-tall, sun metal–armored glory. The Dawn Blade, his family's ancient heirloom and one of the world's most powerful against the undead—and pretty much anything else—hung on his hip like a sheathed nuke. Behind him, Captain Hightower and two hundred of Bastion's former knights were waiting in the field on the edge of town. They were all sweating and looking miserable, but it was still a very imposing production, even if Gregory's nervous hand-wringing did ding the effect a bit.

"It'll be fine," Tina said, glad that her stonekin didn't seem to mind the heat any more than the cold. "Though we probably should have some water on hand in case anyone gets sunstroke. Full armor in this heat is beastly."

"I've already got water stations set up, but that's not what I'm talking about!" Zen snarled, rising onto her tiptoes to wave her lovely—and *very* magical—bow in Tina's face. "I meant should we really be having a mock battle with the king using our *real weapons*? It feels like this could get out of hand very, very fast."

"We don't have a choice," Tina argued, rapping her knuckles against her own golden sun–steel armor. "I'll go splat if I try to tank a five-skull in my underwear. Also, what else are we gonna fight with? Even steel swords

66

don't hold up at our level. It's magical weapons of legend or go home, so we might as well use what we've got."

Zen huffed in annoyance, and Tina smiled. "Relax! Gregory's a tanky type of boss. He's got five hundred million HP or something crazy like that."

"Not that crazy when you consider some of us deal over a hundred thousand damage per second," Zen pointed out. "It only took the Roughnecks two minutes to beat King Gregory during the Drunken King event last Oktoberfest. I know, I was there. I got the *Chug! Chug!* speed kill achievement at the same time you did."

"That was in-game DPS," Tina said dismissively. "Thanks to this friendly-fire bullshit, we can't get anywhere close to those numbers on a human-sized target. That's the whole reason we're doing this."

"But—"

"Zen, it'll be *fine*," Tina said, pointing at the sidelines, where a whole raid of low-level player healers had been pressed into king-management service. "If we can do enough damage to actually hurt Gregory through all those heals, then the Once King is gonna go down like a chump. This practice isn't even about doing damage, anyway. It's about us learning how to fight a raid boss who isn't the size of an apartment building."

"You're right there," said Killbox from behind them. "We suck balls at small targets. Gotta L2P if we wanna win."

"What does L2P mean again?" Frank asked from his position beside Tina. "Seriously, sometimes I swear y'all are speaking a different language."

"You're not half wrong," Tina said, laughing. "And L2P is 'learn to play,' which is exactly what we're going to do." She settled her shield on her arm and looked over her shoulder to check her troops, who were already arranged in the positioning Richard had deemed most optimal. "Ready?"

"No," ZeroDarkness said, stepping suddenly out of Frank's shadow. "Where's SB?"

"Tarnation!" Frank yelled, jumping a foot in the air. "Don't do that to a body!"

"Sorry," Zero told Frank, but the Assassin's slitted cat eyes never left Tina.

She wished they would. She knew why Zero was asking. SB wasn't just the Roughnecks' top damage dealer; he was her second in command. It was his job to know what was going on and give orders if she went down, but he didn't know anything about their current plan. He hadn't even shown up for the vote. But while that was fine with Tina, who didn't want to think about SilentBlayde right now in any capacity, it was a very bad look. It was also not a conversation she wanted to have out here in front of everyone. Or ever. But she had to say *something*.

"He was fine in the Malakai fight," she replied after a long pause. "He'll pick this one up, too. I'm not worried. Let's just do this."

Zero scowled and opened his mouth to say more, but Tina wasn't waiting around for any more awkwardness. She'd already started marching down the road toward the King of Bastion.

"Ready, Your Majesty?" she yelled.

Gregory nodded nervously. "I think so."

That was more warning than the Once King would give them, so Tina dug her boots into the ground and charged, hurtling her eight-hundred-pound stone body down the road straight at the king.

The giant man took an involuntary step back as the wall of Roughnecks charged after her, yelling their battle cries. Then Tina saw Gregory's pale face pull into a determined scowl as he raised his fist for the opening punch. Lifting her shield higher, Tina braced for impact, skidding to a stop and digging her boots into the dusty ground to stop herself from being thrown as the level-eighty five-skull king swung at her...

Bong.

Her shield made a gentle bell noise as Gregory's fist plunked against it, and Tina threw up her hands.

"*Stop!*" she yelled, grabbing Killbox by his collar as the Berserker charged past her with his ax raised high. "Stop, stop, *stop!* What was *that?*"

"A punch?" Gregory said sheepishly.

"More like a fist-bump."

Gregory dropped his eyes. "I didn't want to kill you."

"But that's the *point!*" Tina cried, getting so far into his face she was practically in his beard. "You're a raid boss! If I can't tank you, then I sure as hell can't tank the Once King. You're our only chance to learn how to do this right! If you wimp out on us, we're *all* going to die!"

"Sorry," Gregory said, eyes still on his feet, and Tina sighed. She felt like a heel yelling at the gentle king, but this was too important to be nice about.

"You have to *really* hit us," she scolded him. "Otherwise there's no point. And on that note, why are you even attacking me?"

The king looked confused. "Because you're the tank?"

"Exactly," Tina said. "I'm the one who's best suited to take your attacks, so why are you punching me when you could be punching *them?*" She pointed over her shoulder at the clump of healers and cloth-robed Sorcerers, many of whom were still holding spells ready for when she gave the order to resume. "They're the ones who are going to win this, not me. The Once King's not going to make the mistake of attacking the one person who's built to survive his blows. He's going to go after the squishies he can kill in one hit, so that's what you need to do, too."

Her words sent Gregory into a panic. "But I don't want to hurt them!"

"I don't want you to, either," Tina said, waving her shield at him. "That's why I'm going to learn how to *stop* you. But I can't do that if you just stand there and bap my shield like you're still a tank-and-spank fight from the game."

The king looked more dejected with every word, and Tina sighed. "Look," she said, lowering her voice. "This is training for you as well. There are a lot of players in this world who aren't as nice as we are. When else are

69

you going to get practice facing them? Now's your chance to learn how to use your status as a raid boss to protect your people. Don't waste it."

"That...that is a wise perspective," Gregory said with a nervous swallow. "I will keep it in mind."

"Good," Tina said, turning around to stomp back up the road. "Let's take it from the top. And remember: go for the healers first. If we lose them, we lose the fight, so they should always be your first priority."

"Right," Gregory said, clenching his fists.

"Roxxy," Killbox whispered nervously as they jogged back to their starting positions. "Should you really be telling him this?"

"Damn straight I should be," Tina growled. "You think the Once King's going to pull his punches?"

"But I don't want to die in a practice fight!" NekoBaby called from much farther away than Tina had thought she could hear. "Everyone who's died says it's ultra-horrible!"

"Then make sure you all stay on top of your heals," Tina yelled back, turning around to face her raid. "The Once King is the end boss of the Dead Mountain Fortress. He's going to be faster, stronger, and tougher than anything we've ever fought. He can cast and counterspell every type of magic in the game, has a giant health pool, hits like a goddamn truck, and if all that wasn't bad enough, he can *fly*." She shook her head. "If we can't handle 'Teddy Bear' Gregory, then we might as well pack it in right now. This is for real, people. But so we're not sitting around all day waiting on rezzes, we'll count a knockdown as a death. If Gregory gets to you and puts you in the dirt, you're officially 'dead' for the rest of that round. Sound good?"

It was obvious *no one* thought that sounded good, but they nodded anyway.

"Great," Tina said, getting her shield back into position. "Let's try this again."

She didn't give Gregory a warning this time. She just charged him with her shield like a linebacker. When he started backing up timidly again,

Tina switched up and came at him with her sword instead. Seeing the naked blade in her hands had the desired effect. All at once, Gregory's eyes went wide, and he lurched forward, grabbing her sword in his armored hand.

Tina's charge jerked to a stop. Malakai had grabbed her blade before, but being stuck in Gregory's grasp felt like her sword was stuck in a mountain. She couldn't rip it free, either, because the "wicked-sick" serrations that ran down her blade's back had locked into the sun steel chain of the monarch's gauntlet. She refused to let her weapon go, though, which turned out to be a very bad idea, as Gregory used her own sword like a handle to sling her sideways into Killbox.

She hit the Berserker like a boulder, taking them both down and leaving a giant gap in the front line. Getting the hang of things at last, Gregory charged through the break, steamrolling past her to plow into their shocked back line. Zen hit him in the leg with a rapid-fire attack, but the king had so much health and armor that her arrows just bounced off. Richard was casting a fire spell, but he was forced to drop it and teleport out of the way instead when the king turned his direction. Unable to grab the Sorcerer, the king grabbed Anders instead, his huge hands engulfing the ichthyian's entire fin-crested head as he lifted the kicking Cleric off his feet and prepared to throw him into the group of casters who were already fleeing.

"Stop!" Tina cried, pushing herself off Killbox. "That's a wipe!"

Gregory quickly set the struggling ichthyian down. "Are you all right, good sir?"

Anders's spines flexed erratically as he staggered away. "I'm okay," he gulped out, his fish eyes huge.

The king looked traumatized, but Tina clapped her metal-covered hands. "Now that's what I'm talking about!" she called, grinning at her players, most of whom looked every bit as horrified as the king. "This is the new reality, people. We've been fighting stupid undead bosses up to this point, but the Once King is *smart*. Smart raid bosses aren't going to sit there and let themselves be tanked while everyone else shoots them. They're going to move and charge and be all up in our business, and if we want to win, we've got to learn to handle that."

Everyone groaned and grumbled at that, but they all got back into position when Tina yelled, "Again!"

It was a bruising and humiliating rest of the afternoon. Gregory quickly learned that he could physically overpower almost any defense they tried to mount. She and Frank tried a few co-tanking strategies in attempt to make their front line harder to break, but it didn't really make much of a difference when Gregory could simply grab anyone who wasn't a tank and toss them out of the way. At one point, Tina, Frank, and Killbox were all hanging off His Royal Five-Skull-Ness like kids on a gorilla while he chased a fleeing NekoBaby.

Tina forced herself to stay relentlessly positive so the raid wouldn't crumble, but in reality she hated it more than anyone else. She prided herself on being the tank, the wall no enemy could cross, and Gregory was running circles around her. Worse, she didn't know how to make him *stop*. Gregory figured out a way around every strategy they tried. Having a raid boss who could feint and change targets at will was just impossible to deal with. Once, when they were trying out a strategy of using a ring of Berserkers to physically cage him in, Gregory grabbed Killbox by his ax and tossed him into a tree a hundred feet away.

It was a harsh reminder that no one was safe in this kind of fight, not that Tina needed to be reminded. Every time Gregory got around her, all she could think about was how easily Malakai had killed KatanaFatale. She never wanted that to happen again, but Gregory was simply impossible to control. She supposed it was a good lesson for the other Roughnecks to stop depending on her and learn to protect themselves, but that didn't mean much when a boss could kill you in one hit.

By the time the sun began to slide toward the horizon, tempers were running as hot as the day. Even Tina was struggling to stay upbeat when

Cinco and the Red Sands showed up to make everything a thousand times worse.

When the PvP guild arrived, Tina assumed it was to join the practice, but they just stood in the shade and laughed as Gregory plowed through spells, disarmed people with slaps, and used Roughnecks as human wrecking balls against each other. Finally, Tina had had enough. The king was soaked in sweat and red-faced anyway, so she called for a break. Everyone immediately went for the barrels Zen had set up along the roadside, dunking their heads in the warm water. This only made CincoDeMurder laugh harder as Tina stomped over.

"Damn, this is some funny shit to watch," he cackled, slapping her on her giant shoulder plate. "I thought I was gonna die when he caught Zero by his cloak and tied him up in it."

Tina gave him a killing look, and Cinco rolled his eyes. "Come on, don't be a stick. That shit's funny!" He nodded at her exhausted raid. "It's like watching a bunch of kids trying to wrestle an elephant."

This remark earned hoots of laugher from his PvPers, and Tina got an idea.

"Yeah, I guess us hug-box raiders just suck," she said, smiling down at him. "Why don't you PvP badasses show us how it's done?"

The red-armored Berserker grinned back at her. "Sure thing, sweetheart," he said, pushing off the tree he'd been leaning against. "Red Sands, fall in! Let's go show these Care Bears how *real* players fight!"

Tina motioned for him to go ahead, flopping down in the dirt to enjoy the show as Cinco arrogantly informed the King that his guild was next and they were "the real deal." Zen and several others came over to sit next to her in the shade, fanning themselves in the dusty late-afternoon heat as Red Sands started their attack.

Cinco was right about one thing: watching a raid fight Gregory *was* hilarious. Ten minutes after Cinco and his guild took the field, Tina could barely breathe from laughing so hard. She actually had to scramble out of the

73

way when Gregory launched a red blur into the branches over her head. Cinco crashed into the brush nearby a few moments later, cursing and coughing up lungfuls of yellow dust.

"Come on, dude," Tina said, reaching down to help him up. "I soloed a four-skull yesterday. Surely you can take down FFO's easiest boss with that overstocked raid of yours."

A chorus of "ooooooooohs" went up from the Roughnecks surrounding her, and NekoBaby even tossed in a "Sick burn!" They were still catcalling when Cinco slapped Tina's hand away.

"Fuck you," he huffed, hauling himself to his feet. "This isn't PvE or PvP, it's a circus of *bullshit*. Nothing works on that guy!" He glared murder at Gregory, who was currently using the Red Sands' top Assassin, Shankfest, like a cricket bat to knock over healers. "How the fuck did you beat Malakai, anyway?"

"I drowned him," Tina replied with what had to be the smuggest smile in the history of smug smiles.

"Yeah, well, fat lot of good that does us," Cinco snarled. "We're in a fucking desert right now."

"First, it's an arid grassland," Tina replied, wagging her finger at him. "And second, Windy Lake is just half a mile that way."

She pointed at the water glittering in the distance, and Cinco's face turned as red as his armor. "Fucking fuck you!" he yelled, leaving the Roughnecks to laugh at him as he stomped back to his raid, which was now lying in the road at Gregory's feet.

"Asshat," Neko said when he was gone. "You'd think Mr. World-Class-PvP would be better at losing."

"You'd think," Tina agreed, cupping her stone hands around her mouth to yell at Red Sands. "You guys can have one more round with Gregory. We're the primary raid for the Once King fight, so we need him back after that, but don't worry!" She pointed across the road at the eternally brooding Captain Hightower, who'd been watching them the entire afternoon. "You guys can go practice with Captain Training Wheels over there. He needs something to do."

CincoDeMurder answered her with a pair of middle fingers. Still laughing, Tina returned the gesture and then lowered her hand to receive NekoBaby's enthusiastic high-five.

At least the Red Sands' misery did wonders for the Roughnecks' morale. By the time Cinco's guild dragged themselves, humiliated, off the field, Tina's raiders were ready to go again. They were huddled up, discussing new strategies, while Gregory took a break when a wagon came bumping down the road they'd been using as a practice field.

Leaving the others to figure it out, Tina stepped over to the wagon just in time to see a white-robed acolyte scramble around to help the old elf who'd been sitting in the back. He'd removed his glittering robes for the trip, but Tina had no trouble recognizing High Priest Raffestain as he shuffled across the road to Tina, using his gold-tipped magical Sun Staff as a cane.

"Um, welcome," Tina said, unsure of how to address this man outside of formal affairs like war meetings. "Thanks for coming out."

"I came mostly out of concern for His Majesty," Raffestain said, glancing over at Gregory, who was gulping down water as fast as his guards could hand it to him and grinning like a kid on Christmas morning. "But I see my fears are misplaced."

"Oh yeah," Tina said, tilting her head at the groaning pile of Red Sands raiders. "His Majesty is doing fine. I'm more worried about us."

That earned her a smile from the old elf. "It seems I owe you my gratitude today, then."

Tina's copper eyebrows shot up. "Huh?"

Raffestain leaned on his gleaming staff. "I've known Gregory since he was a boy. He was always happy and carefree, as befits a third prince no one actually expected to inherit, but ever since his father and brothers died in the Forgiven Wars, he has been a prisoner of his own fear. Though peace was secured, he inherited a broken and troubled kingdom. That would be a challenge for any man, but then the Nightmare arrived and made everything worse. Receiving the power of a raid boss made Gregory a great asset for Bastion, but it was a curse for him. He could not stop thinking of his potential to hurt others, too afraid of what he could do if he was not always careful. That fear kept him paralyzed when we needed him most. I feared for a while that it had defeated him entirely. Now, though, seeing him like this." The priest looked at the laughing king with a sincere smile. "This is a Gregory I haven't seen in a long, long time. Even under such dire circumstances, it is a blessing."

"Glad we accomplished something," Tina said, trying not to sound too sour about it.

"Something indeed," the old elf said wistfully. Then he pulled himself straight. "Anyway, I have come as I promised. Present to me this player Cleric of yours so that we may judge him."

Tina didn't like the way the high priest said that, but this had been her idea, so she turned back to her raid. "*Anders!*"

The ichthyian must have been watching the High Priest since his arrival, because he was there before Tina finished bellowing his name. He stared at the old elf with fish eyes wide, spines flexing with anxiety. Raffestain appeared just as agitated, drumming his fingers on his golden staff as he squinted at Anders for several long, tense seconds.

"Have you truly talked to the Sun?" the high priest asked at last.

Anders nodded. "Sort of, yes. At least I think I did."

The old elf gave him a salty look. "And what did the Center of All Heavens have to say to you?"

Anders flinched, and Tina braced for disappointment. From what she remembered of their conversation back in Bastion, Anders had claimed that the Sun didn't use words. Maybe real priests could actually converse with it?

"I asked a lot of questions," Anders said, his voice warbling. "But the Sun never talked to me in words. Only meanings and feelings. It's impossible to describe."

Raffestain's scowl deepened. "It is as I feared," he said with a long sigh. "That is the correct answer."

"Feared?" Tina snapped, since Anders was too shocked to speak. "Why feared?"

The priest shot her a very normal look of pure annoyance, breaking his wiser-than-thou routine. "Because it means the Sun has accepted the feelings of a *player*." He spat the word out like a piece of rotten meat. "This is upsetting to say the least. From what I have seen, you are all unworthy of the Sun's light, much less its attention. But my god has spoken, and I have no choice but to accept the decision." He bowed his old head humbly. "The Sun is far wiser than I."

Tina had had it up to here with the nonstop player-hate, but she kept her mouth shut for Anders's sake. The Sun had already won this battle for them, anyway. The stuffy old priest would just have to eat it and like it.

"What do you know of the priesthood, young man?" Raffestain asked Anders.

"Only what I've read in the wiki," Anders replied in a nervous rush. "Priests serve for life, and there are three hundred rules they must live by, though I can only name the famous ones like avoiding exalted sleeping places, abstaining from dark magics, and not eating after high noon. There's also no lying, stealing, murder, sex, or alcohol."

The high priest looked impressed. "You are already more aware than some junior acolytes, then," he said, sounding amused despite himself. "But knowing that, are you willing to dedicate your life to the service of the Sun and the people it shines upon? Will you join the church after the Once King has been vanquished?"

That sounded like a pretty heavy question, but to Tina's surprise, Anders answered at once.

"Yes," he said, bowing his scaled fish head reverently. "I had already decided to stay, and I believe that a life of service to others is the only way forward for me. I would be honored if you would accept me into your order."

"That is a good answer," Raffestain said with a sigh of resignation. "Player or not, you sound no more wayward than the average young man who seeks the golden cloth." He looked around a moment, and then the elf pointed at a large rock sitting in the middle of the grassland to their west. "Sit there, face the Sun, and confirm your commitment. I will be with you shortly to teach you the spell that General Roxxy has requested."

"Yes sir," Anders said happily, bounding off through the grass toward the car-sized rock. But while he looked happy as a fish in water, Tina didn't like the way the old priest had sent him off.

"That's a stalling tactic if ever I've seen one," she said, crossing her arms over her chest. "Why aren't you teaching him the spell right now?"

Again, she got an annoyed glare. She gave him her best salty stare right back, and eventually the high priest sighed.

"I will tell you, because you are the one who will fight the Once King," he said, looking sadly at Anders, who was already scrambling onto the rock. "But you must swear by the Sun not to tell him, for his own sake."

"Why can't I tell him?"

The high priest kept his mouth firmly shut. When it was clear that was going to be that, Tina gave in. "Fine," she growled. "I swear by the Sun not to tell Anders whatever you're about to tell me."

She said it flippantly, but the moment the words were out of her mouth, Tina felt a strange presence behind her. When she turned to see what it was, the glare of the setting sun hit her like a blow. It wasn't just the light in her eyes, either. There was a weight to it, an enormous, distant power that made her feel singled out and incredibly small at the same time.

"Whoa," she said, taking a step back.

"I hope now you see how serious this is," Raffestain said, his old face pleased. "I said I would teach your Cleric the Resplendent Aegis spell if he could truly speak to the Sun, and I will keep my word, but I fear that this Anders will not be able to use it."

"Why not?" Tina demanded. "Because he's a player?"

The high priest shook his head. "For once, that has nothing to do with it. Wherever his soul came from, the Sun has found it worthy, which is all that matters. No. I'm afraid this problem is…personal in nature." He leaned closer, lowering his voice to a whisper. "He has a dark weight upon his soul. My guess is that he committed a sin of a great and serious nature. The Sun has already forgiven him, for its mercy is infinite, but he must be at peace with himself as well to invoke a power as pure as the Resplendent Aegis. He will have to atone and receive forgiveness from those he has wronged before his soul is light enough to do what you need him to do."

"Crap," Tina muttered, scrubbing her hands through her copper hair. She was pretty sure she knew what sin was weighing Anders's soul down, but obtaining absolution on that one was going to be hard. NekoBaby wasn't exactly the forgive-and-forget type. "Is there any other way to clean him up? An absolution spell or something?"

Raffestain shook his head. "This is not a matter that can be resolved with magic. As I said before, the Sun has already forgiven him. It loves us unconditionally no matter what we've done. Sins are the doings of men and must be resolved as such. The Sun knows this, and it is not above withholding its power in order to guide its children to the right path."

"Good for it," Tina grumbled, glancing down the road at NekoBaby, who was miming kicking Gregory in the balls. "But it's not like we've got the luxury of time, and I need that anti-undead ward." She sighed. "Is there any way to speed things up?"

The priest shook his head again, and Tina gritted her teeth. "Guess I'd better get Neko and Anders together for an emergency counseling sess—"

"*No*," Raffestain said, glaring at her. "You promised to say nothing, remember?"

"But it's for his own good!" Tina cried. "And all of our survival! Why can't I help?"

"He has to seek redemption for its own merits," Raffestain lectured. "Not because *you* need him to know a spell. If you interfere with this, you risk tainting his chance at salvation forever. That's why I made you swear."

"Oh, come *on*!" Tina cried, but the priest was already shuffling off. When he reached the edge of the grassy field that held Anders's rock, though, he turned back to her.

"Before I go, there is another matter I must warn you about."

It couldn't be worse than learning the only person capable of casting the spell they needed most couldn't actually cast it until he obtained forgiveness from the person who'd only grant it when hell froze over, so Tina motioned for him to go ahead.

"If you exchange words with the Once King, remember that he is the enemy of the Sun," the priest said in a low, angry voice. "He has rejected not only its great teachings but also its boundless love. He has turned his back on the light and sworn eternal hatred on his own creator. It is that hate, not the Great Pyre or the armies of undead, that makes the Once King the enemy of all life."

"Okaaaay," Tina said, arching an eyebrow. "I'll keep that in mind, but we're going there to beat him, not talk to him. Theological debate isn't happening."

Raffestain smiled at that. "For once, I am glad that you players are from another world," he said, his voice relieved. "Go forth with the Sun's blessings upon your inevitable victory."

"Back at'cha," Tina said, wanting this conversation to be over.

The High Priest made a sign of blessing and walked away, stepping high through the tall grass toward Anders. The ichthyian looked up excitedly when he approached. Penitently, too, which was good, because she needed him to learn that damn spell. The Resplendent Aegis imposed an eighty-percent damage debuff on any undead it touched. Even if Anders could only manage it for a few seconds, those might be the winning seconds against the Once King.

Unfortunately for everyone on the planet, there was nothing more she could do. Tina didn't know if the damage between Anders and NekoBaby *was* reconcilable, but if she was sworn not to interfere—and from the weight of the sun's light on her back, Tina suspected she was *hella* sworn—then the problem was officially out of her hands. It wasn't as if she didn't have enough problems of her own to deal with. All the Resplendent Aegises in the world wouldn't mean squat if she couldn't learn to tank a raid boss. Gregory was already back up and ready for another go, so she turned to tell her raid to get back in position...

And found Zen standing right behind her.

"*Whoa!*" she cried, jumping a foot in the air. "Don't do that!"

The green-haired Ranger shrugged at Tina's shock and stepped a little closer. "We need to talk."

Tina winced. People in Camp Comeback jokingly called Zen "Raid Mom" behind her back. Tina didn't know if Zen had kids in the real world or if it came from her IRL job as a nurse, but the elf had the stern parent routine down to a science, and as with any parent, nothing good ever followed "We need to talk."

"*Roxxy.*"

"I'm listening!" Tina said frantically. "What is it?"

She was *really* hoping that she'd read this wrong and that the Ranger had actually come over because she'd had a brilliant new idea for fighting King Gregory. No dice.

"SilentBlayde isn't here," Zen announced, glaring at her. "That's a problem."

Tina looked over the Ranger's head at the raid standing in a clump in the center of the road. "Is it, though? I mean, we've got tons of melee."

"That's not the point," the elf said angrily. "SilentBlayde is your second-in-command. He needs to be here learning this stuff more than any of us, but he's *not*, and you're letting it happen!"

Tina gritted her teeth. This was the last topic she wanted to deal with, but Zen didn't retreat an inch.

"I know exactly *why* SB's absent," the Ranger went on. "That's why I gave you both a pass at the start, but this is going to create a major liability if you let it continue. He hasn't been here for any of our learning fights, and we've learned a *lot*. If you get knocked out in battle, he won't know how to lead us."

"I know..." Tina said. "But—"

"But nothing," Zen snapped, crossing her arms over her chest. "When we signed the Roughnecks' new charter, you gave this guild a creed. We all pledged that we could fight each other as much as the enemy so long as we came together when it counted. Everyone here has stuck to that rule. Even Neko and Anders have worked as a team. I know you and SB are going through some shit, but this is get-in-line time. As a Roughneck, SB *needs* to be here. You can't let him be the exception."

"I *know*," Tina said again, rubbing her arms. "But I just can't, okay? It hasn't even been a full twenty-four hours since we...since I yelled at him. The wound is too fresh for me. Him being here is going to undermine everything."

"Him *not* being here is undermining things right now," Zen argued. "Do you not understand that his absence might get himself or someone else killed? You know how important this practice is—you're the one making us do it!"

Tina looked at the ground, and the Ranger sighed. "Look," she said, folding her willowy arms over her chest. "If you two can't do this, then maybe SB shouldn't stay in the Roughnecks."

Zen's words hit Tina like a truck. The idea of SB leaving hadn't even occurred to her. His was the second name on the charter after hers. She was the leader, but the Roughnecks had always been *their* guild, together. How could she kick him out?

But even as her heart balked, her brain recognized that Zen had a point. If she was serious about what she'd said yesterday, then it was over. *Really* over. Even though it wasn't technically a break-up since they'd never actually been together, being in a guild with your ex was *never* a good idea. Every time she looked at him, there would always be that hook, that pain. Tina didn't see that ever getting better, so maybe Zen was right. Maybe the healthy thing *would* be to kick him out so they could both move on.

Not right now, though. Even with bitterness set to maximum, Tina couldn't abandon SilentBlayde in this world with no group of players to fall back on. Maybe she could find him a new guild? Blayde had PvPed with Cinco's group several times; maybe she could get Red Sands to take him in. She owed them for poaching Richard anyway...

It was a logical solution that would solve a lot of problems, but as hurt as she was, Tina couldn't even think about actually going and doing it. If SB left the Roughnecks, that would be the end. Of course, it would have ended no matter what when she went home and he stayed here, but that was somewhere in the future. This was *now*, and right now...

"I can't," Tina said, her voice defeated. "I can't kick him out. Not yet. But I *do* need a new second." She looked hopefully at Zen. "What about you? You're practically doing the job already."

Zen's face pinched in anger, so much so that Tina took a step back. "I refuse."

Tina didn't understand. "Why not?"

"I will not be used as a prop so you can avoid dealing with your emotional baggage!" Zen yelled. "Find someone else!"

"But you're the best," Tina argued. "Please, Zen, we need you."

Those must have been the magic words, because the Ranger sighed. "Fine," she said through clenched teeth. "I'll do it for the good of the guild, but only if you go find SilentBlayde and tell him in person that he's being demoted. You have to deal with this before it bites us all in the butt, and don't think promoting me will let you avoid him! My first task as your second is going to be dragging SB to practice."

Tina couldn't think of a conversation she'd less like to have, but Zen was right. If she was going to demand the best from her people, then she needed to step up too. But while telling SB he was demoted was a lot better than telling him he was being kicked out of the guild, she still didn't want to do it right now.

"Can I do it tomorrow?" she asked in a small voice. "It's almost sunset, and James still hasn't gotten back to me about the portal to the Deadlands, so it's not like we're leaving tonight."

Zen rolled her eyes at the obvious dodge, but Tina must have looked really pathetic, because she had mercy. "Fine," the Ranger said. "But *first thing* tomorrow."

"First thing," Tina promised, walking back toward her raid, who was staring at Gregory in terror, and with good reason. The king was refreshed and up, swinging his sword merrily with way more energy than someone who'd been fighting raids all afternoon should have. It was clear they were in for yet another ass kicking, but Tina would rather fight the king for the rest of eternity than face what she had to do tomorrow. But tomorrow was tomorrow. Today was today, so Tina wiped the sad expression off her stone face and marched back to her officers to hear what plan they'd come up with this time to try to survive Gregory's onslaught.

Chapter 4

James

James *still* hadn't found SilentBlayde.

It had been hours since he'd left Leylia's tent. He'd looked everywhere, dodging jubatus as all of Windy Lake scrambled to prepare for Tina's plan to assault the Dead Mountain. An assault he was critical to and was supposed to be working on *right now*.

"Dammit, Haruto," James muttered, glaring up at the empty tree where he'd found his friend brooding early this morning. It wasn't that he didn't have sympathy for what SB was going through, but it was hard to be compassionate when the elf had brought this entirely on himself for reasons he *still* refused to talk about. James didn't have time for this foolishness, but he'd sworn he'd never leave a desperate friend alone again, so off he went to the last place he wanted to go but probably the first he should have checked: Tina's raid.

He found his sister standing in the middle of the south road with her entire guild. The king was there as well in full armor with his sword drawn. This frightened him at first—they'd been trying to kill each other a little over a day ago, after all—but his fears vanished when he saw Gregory's face. The king looked like he was having the time of his life. A moment later, James saw why as the Roughnecks charged in…and promptly got their clocks cleaned by Bastion's resident five-skull.

James was forced to leap out of the way as the king sent players flying. One actually landed right in front of him, sprawling in the grass at James's feet. Fortunately, in a long-overdue stroke of luck, the pained face that looked up at him was exactly the one James needed.

"Hey, ZeroDarkness," James said, grabbing a handful of green magics to start weaving a healing spell over the gasping Assassin. "How's practice going?"

"How does it look like it's going?" the jubatus groaned. "We're so fucking dead."

"I'm sure you'll figure it out," James said encouragingly as he rained healing down on Zero's head. The Assassin's look of pain vanished as the bliss of the magical healing hit him, and he rolled back to his feet with a whoop.

"Thanks for the pick-up," he said, brushing the dirt off his glowing leather armor. "But what are you doing here? Aren't you supposed to be making us a portal to the Deadlands or something?"

"I'm working on it," James lied. "But I've got a favor to ask you first. I'm looking for SB. Have you seen him?"

ZeroDarkness rolled his cat eyes in exasperation. "Oh yeah, I've seen him. Couldn't miss him. He's making the whole Lightless Realm even more gloomy than usual."

James let out a breath of relief. "Can you get him for me, please?"

"Sure thing," the Assassin said, vanishing into the small dark patch of shadow by James's feet. James barely had time to shudder at the feeling of something invisible sliding past his magic when Zero reappeared with a dirty elf slung over his shoulder.

Thinking SB had been knocked out, James leaped forward. Then he saw the elf's blue eyes were open. He wasn't unconscious; he was just limp, lying in a defeated heap over the feline Assassin's shoulder.

"Dude, that was just sad," ZeroDarkness said, dumping his payload unceremoniously on the ground. "All those times you beat me in duels, and you let me grab you just like that? Get your shit together, Blayde."

SilentBlayde said nothing. He just curled up into an even smaller ball on the dusty road. Shaking his head in disgust, Zero turned back to James. "You know him IRL, right? Tell him he needs to shape up, or his problems are only going to get worse, and I'm not talking about Roxxy."

That didn't sound good. "What *are* you talking about, then?"

"He knows," Zero said cryptically. "He's been eavesdropping from the shadows all afternoon. He knows *exactly* how much shit he's in."

Before James could ask for more, Zero vanished back into the Lightless Realm, leaving him alone with SilentBlayde, who still hadn't bothered to get up from where he'd been dumped.

"Blayde?" James asked tentatively, kneeling beside him. "Can you sit up?"

"What's the point?" SB muttered at the ground. "It's over. Just leave me alone."

James sighed in frustration and reached down to grab the elf's shoulder...only to let go again just as fast when he realized SilentBlayde's leather armor was still crusty with yesterday's ash and blood.

"I'm *not* going to leave you alone," he said stubbornly, scrubbing his hand on the grass. "You're being ridiculous, probably because you're filthy, you haven't slept yet, and I'm gonna guess starving too."

The elf's stomach rumbled loudly at that last one, and James smiled. "Come on," he said, grabbing his friend's arm. "If you won't take care of yourself, I guess it's up to me."

SB's head drooped lower, but he didn't resist as James hauled him to his feet and started dragging him toward the glittering expanse of Windy Lake. When they got to the edge, he made SB strip and go wash himself off in the warm, clean water. Meanwhile, James used a combination of wind and water magics to scrub the Assassin's filthy armor. It took two passes to get all the bloodstains out, but he didn't give the armor back once it was clean. Instead, when Blayde emerged from the water, James handed him a set of normal jubatus clothing from his backpack.

"Put it on," he ordered.

SilentBlayde did as he was told. The rough-woven shirt and trousers were baggy on the underfed elf, but they were comfortable, and the light color protected from the heat. When SB was decent, James grabbed his arm and started pulling him toward the Naturalist's Lodge.

The central room was just as busy as it had been when he'd burst in on the meeting earlier. All the clan heads and Gray Fang were still gathered around the table, while a flood of assistants transmitted a constant stream of orders and information. Catching his mentor's eye, James ducked into one of the wooden lodge's many side rooms. A few minutes later, Gray Fang joined him, her old yellow eyes watching SB warily.

"What's with him?" she asked, nodding at the deathly pale Assassin.

"Rough night," James said, settling himself on the rug-strewn floor. "But he's the best lore guy I know, and I need his help. Can we get him some food?"

"He's going to need more than food," the old Naturalist said, but she snagged an attendant, and soon a plate of meat and gravy-soaked bread was shoved under SilentBlayde's nose.

"So why are you here?" Gray Fang asked as SB began to eat mechanically. "I'm guessing it's not so I can feed your friend lunch."

James shook his head. "You've heard about Roxxy's plan to take on the Once King?"

"The lunacy has been explained to me, yes," the old cat said, lashing her gray tail. "I'm dreading to hear your part in it."

He smiled at her exasperated tone. "I promised I'd find a way to get the Roughnecks to the Deadlands through the Timeless Tunnels."

"I figured it was something like that," Gray Fang muttered, pulling out her long pipe and lighting it with an ember from the banked brazier in the corner. "You never make *small* promises, do you, James of Claw Born?"

James shrugged. "Radical ideas require radical effort, but I'm certain it's possible. The Bedrock Kings have been the Once King's enemies since their creation, *and* we've got a stonekin to talk to them with. That's two points in a line, we just have to make the connection."

"You say that like it's something we can do," the old cat snapped. "This is insanity. How did you even come up with this idea?"

He opened his mouth to tell her it was actually Leylia's idea but caught himself just in time. "It was the only thing everyone could agree on," he said instead.

"The only way out of your marriage, you mean," Gray Fang huffed. "Do you know how hard Rends worked on that deal? If you can't find a way home, you'll be sad you missed out." She paused to take a long draw off her pipe. "At least you were smart enough to get that new Lord Assets to do your dirty work for you. Once again, you've somehow managed to avoid all situations that would have shamed our family. You seem to have divine luck at avoiding damaging our honor, which I would love if you weren't constantly endangering it."

James smiled sheepishly. "Sorry, Grandma."

That earned him a smack between the ears but a good-natured one. "Well," Gray Fang said, settling back on her haunches. "Let's see if we can't dig our way out of the hole you've put us in."

He nodded eagerly. "The Bedrock Kings control the Timeless Tunnels, so our first step is to get their attention. Do you have any idea how to do that?"

"No," she said, reaching back to pat her hand against a stack of old rugs piled in the corner. "But these might."

James frowned at the dusty woven mats. "What are those?"

Rather than answer, Gray Fang grabbed a rug off the top and handed it to him. James took the thick mat of cloth gently with both hands. It was old and worn from many hands, but the image woven into it was still clear. Four elements—and not the Aristotelian ones—swirled together against a golden background. There was the Sun's red fire and the Moon's purple...whatever that was. Energy? There were also some white gusty lines that he assumed meant the Wind and blue waves which had to be the Water god.

"What are these?" James asked, looking harder at the rug pile, which he could now see was full of similarly woven images.

"The collected knowledge of our people," Gray Fang explained, leaning back on her pillow. "We pass most things down by word or song, but that method has its flaws. Us old cats don't always remember things right, so that which we cannot risk getting wrong gets woven into rugs to preserve it." She chuckled evilly. "It's usually the apprentice's job to reweave the damaged ones from scratch. I've remade that entire stack in my time. If you stick around long enough, you'll do it too. It'll serve you right for bringing so much trouble to my door."

Looking at what would have been the anthropological find of a century back home, James didn't think having to study these rugs would be a punishment. He was already wondering if there were any rugs with information about *Forever Fantasy Online*'s mysteriously absent Moon god, the one Xthr had named as his protector and the Grand Schtump referred to as "The Silent Moon."

"Anyway," Gray Fang went on. "If any jubatus on the grasslands has ever found a way to bring the Bedrock Kings to the surface, it'll be recorded in there. Your job is to dig through that pile until you find something we can use. And by 'dig' I mean carefully search while handling every weaving as if it were the Bastion itself."

"I will treat them with the utmost respect," James promised, holding the rug she'd handed him as carefully as he would a newborn child. "But where will you be?"

"Here," Gray Fang said, closing her eyes as she took another puff from her pipe, the smoke from which smelled suspiciously like a certain five-leafed plant back home. "You dropped all of Bastion on my head, and I've been dealing with life-or-death politics for a night and day now. I'm *tired*. You're the young apprentice brimming with energy and bright ideas. You can work. I'm going to sleep. Wake me up when you find something useful."

That was fine with James. He'd already pulled down a whole armful of rugs to start searching through. When he turned to ask SB's opinion on the larger-than-life elf figures stitched into the first one, though, the Assassin was already asleep, slumped over on the rug next to his empty plate.

"Some help you are," James whispered, but not unkindly. SilentBlayde's knowledge of FFO's lore had never been more than an excuse, anyway. Sleep was what his friend needed, so James tossed a blanket over him and let him be, shuffling over to the far side of the small room, where the afternoon sunlight had made a glowing square on the lodge's plank floor. Spreading the rugs out in the sunlight, James set to work, muttering his findings under his breath so he wouldn't wake anyone up.

***

Going through the rugs was more work than he'd anticipated. They looked simplistic at first glance, just a stack of rudimentary drawings depicting various magical concepts and important events from the Savanna's history. But the longer James studied them, the more he saw. Every stitch seemed to have something extra woven into it. Secret images were everywhere, expanding the simple tales with new information and nuance.

By the time the sun set, he was only a third of the way through the stack. When the constant meetings in the main room finally put out their lamps and adjourned for the night, James summoned glowing orbs of magical water to cast a shimmering aqua-colored light over the room so he could keep working. This gave him a horrible eyestrain headache that not even healing spells could fix, but he didn't dare stop.

It was a humbling night. James had always considered himself an expert on FFO's lore. It was one of the few areas in his life he'd ever felt confident about. But the longer he studied the rugs, the more he realized just how full of holes his knowledge was. There were so many important figures he didn't recognize, so many events he'd never heard of. Given that everything he knew about this world came from Leylia's waking dreams, the gaps weren't surprising, but James hadn't realized just how much he didn't

91

know until it was staring him in the face. He was still trying to get his brain around it when Gray Fang finally woke up.

"What time is it?" the old cat asked groggily.

James glanced out the window at the lightening sky. "About an hour before sunrise, I think."

Gray Fang made a face that turned into a yawn, stretching her long, bony body like the cat she resembled. "What progress have you made?"

"Well," James said, drawing the word out as he pointed at the smallest of the many piles he'd stacked the rugs into. "Those are the ones I understand, and the rest are the ones I don't."

His mentor chuckled. "Not as easy as you thought, eh?"

James shook his head. "I thought I knew everything there was to know about this world," he confessed. "But it turns out that I only know the big stuff, and not even all of that." His shoulders slumped. "I'm useless."

"Not useless," Gray Fang said, flashing him a smug, fanged smile. "You've learned the depth of your own ignorance, which is the first step toward actually knowing things."

That was one way to look at it, James supposed.

"Here," Gray Fang said, scooting closer. "Show me what you *did* understand, and we'll work from there."

Sighing in frustration, James turned to the small stack of rugs he had been able to decipher. He was showing them to Gray Fang when the pile of blankets in the corner stirred, and SilentBlayde sat up.

"Koko wa doko?" he muttered, rubbing his face.

"SB, dude, wake up," James replied in the Central tongue. "You're speaking Japanese."

The elf blinked and rubbed his face again. When he opened his blue eyes the next time, they were much more aware. "Sorry, James," he said, looking around at the wood-and-hide structure in confusion. "Why are we in the lodge?"

92

James didn't want to sour his friend's vastly improved mood with reminders of how he'd acted the night before, so he stuck to the most positive spin possible. "I had some work to do, and I was hoping you'd help me with it." He turned back to Gray Fang, who was staring at SB as if she were afraid he'd be sick on her floor at any moment. "Master, this is SilentBlayde. He knows more about FFO's history than any player I've met."

"Oh good," she said, her voice dripping with sarcasm. "Another child who thinks they know it all."

James winced, but if SB was insulted, his perfect face didn't show it. "Thank you for taking me in," he said, reaching over to retrieve his ninja mask from the corner, where James had stacked his armor. When the cover was back in place over his face, he turned to James and bowed so low his forehead hit the floor. "I am sorry I caused you so much trouble," he said, his words muffled by the rugs. "It won't happen again. Thank you for picking me up."

"Of course," James said, frantically pulling SB out of his kowtow before he died of embarrassment. "You're my friend. I'd never leave you to wallow. But if you're feeling up to it, I could really use your help."

Gray Fang gave him a scathing look. James responded with a pleading one. It was true SilentBlayde was looking much better after a night of sleep, but there was no way he was back to normal. Some nice, distracting, nothing-to-do-with-Tina busywork would do him good, and he really was the best lore guy James knew. Not that that seemed to mean much in the context of this world's actual history, but he needed this, and eventually Gray Fang sighed.

"I suppose another pair of hands can't hurt," the old cat harrumphed, pointing at the largest stack of rugs James hadn't been able to make heads or tails of. "Grab those and bring them here."

SB bowed again and did as he was told. He was setting the stack down carefully in front of Gray Fang when a young jubatus assistant poked her head through the curtain that separated the small side room from the lodge's main area.

"Elder Gray Fang?"

The old Naturalist looked up.

"General Roxxy is here to speak with an elf called SilentBlayde," she said, her voice transforming SB's name into a long series of whooshes and clicks as she translated the foreign words into the language of Wind and Grass. "She claims he is in your company."

James went stone still. Across from him, SB seemed to have frozen in place, his hands clutching the rugs so hard they shook. If Gray Fang noticed their discomfort, though, she gave no sign.

"He's here," she said, using tongs to grab an ember from the iron brazier to relight her pipe. "Send the stonekin in."

The girl bowed and vanished. A second later, the hide curtain was pushed aside to make room for the mass of stone and armor that was James's "little" sister. Tina had to turn sideways to get through the doorway without scraping the carved wooden frame. Once inside, she straightened up carefully, lifting her head until her copper dreadlocks brushed a beam in the ceiling.

James and SilentBlayde hastily stood up as well, not that it helped. James was tall by jubatus standards, and SB was an elf, a race that didn't seem to come in heights less than six feet, but they both still had to crane their necks back to meet Roxxy's emerald eyes, which seemed to be looking everywhere but them.

"Hey, sis," James said cheerfully, desperate to break the horribly uncomfortable silence. "What can we do for—"

"SilentBlayde."

James jumped. He'd never heard his sister say SB's name so sharply. From the look on the Assassin's face, neither had he.

"You've been missing practice," Roxxy continued, speaking the words so quickly and precisely James knew she must have practiced them beforehand. "This is unacceptable. Due to your excessive absences, it's the officers' opinion—and mine—that Zen should take your place as my second-in-command."

James gasped. Next to him, SB went pale as ash. Before either of them could say anything, though, Tina kept talking.

"But just because you've been demoted doesn't mean you're off the hook. This is serious get-in-line time. Everyone else in the Roughnecks is bringing their A game. If you can't do the same, it would be better for everyone if you left the guild entirely."

She said all of this in a rush, speaking so quickly and precisely James could almost hear her checking off bullet points—a fitting metaphor since SB looked like he was being shot.

"I've already talked to Cinco and Assets," she went on, her emerald eyes focusing on the support beam just above SilentBlayde's head. "They both have agreed to take you if you decide you'd rather not keep fighting with us. I'd suggest the Trade Company since nearly all of them are staying, which means you'll still have a functioning guild after the rest of us go home. Assets is in tight with the king, too, so he should be a strong ally. Anyway, the choice is yours. I've got to get ready for practice with Gregory now, so let Zen know what you decide."

With that, Tina turned on her heel and left. She was wiggling her huge stone frame back through the jubatus-sized doorway when SilentBlayde suddenly stepped forward.

"Wait."

Tina stopped mid-stoop. The sudden, perfect stillness of her stonekin was eerie and unsettling, and SB took a shaky breath.

"That's it?" he said in a small voice. "I'm cut out that fast?"

"You left me no choice," Tina replied, still not looking at him. "You're the one who decided to keep everything to yourself. If I knew why you were acting like this, I could tell everyone to STFU and give you space. But I don't, so I can't. All we know is that you're not stepping up when we need you to, and that's unacceptable. But the ball's in your court now. You can show up to practice as a Roughneck or go join another guild. Or stay here and talk lore all day with James, I don't care. Everything's on your terms now, just like you always wanted, so you do whatever. I'm getting back to work."

"Tina..." SB said, but she was already gone, ducking through the door so fast she took out a chunk of wood in the process.

"I'm sorry," James said when her thundering footsteps faded.

"Don't be," SilentBlayde whispered, his hands clenching so tight James was afraid he'd break something. "I knew this was coming."

James sat back down with a sigh. "It's not—"

"It is," his friend said hopelessly. "I overheard Zen talking about this yesterday, not that I blame her. She was absolutely right. My actions have been unacceptable. I'm *still*—"

He snapped his mouth shut, and James sighed again. He was happy that SB was taking responsibility, but the tone of his friend's voice was still worrisome. "What are you going to do?"

Rather than answer, SilentBlayde leaned down to replace the pile of rugs Gray Fang had asked him to bring her. When they were perfectly straight, he walked to the corner where James had stashed his things last night and started gathering his armor.

"Sorry I can't help you, James," he said in a dull, bitter voice. "But as you just heard, I have to get to practice."

James's face pulled into a furious frown. He wanted to be supportive of his friend, but while he was happy to see SB doing something other than mope, this was ridiculous. He'd thought they were done with the endless will-they-or-won't-they dance, but there Blayde was, picking up his swords to go back to the Roughnecks. Back into his sister's life when she'd obviously bent over backward to give him an honorable out. And he'd had enough.

"Haruto."

SilentBlayde went still, and James gritted his teeth. "I say this as your friend and as Tina's brother: piss or get off the pot."

"That saying doesn't translate well in Central," the elf said as he continued collecting his things. "I don't know what you mean."

"You know *exactly* what I mean," James growled. Not a normal growl, either, but the throaty lion sort that only jubatus could pull off. "I'm sick of watching you hurt my sister. She gave you every opportunity to tell her how you felt, and you threw it away. Now you want to run right back to her side like nothing's changed!"

"What else am I supposed to do?" SilentBlayde demanded, sliding his weapons into the sheaths at his hips. "I can't hide in the back with Assets while she fights the Once King alone!"

"She's not alone," James reminded him. "She has a whole guild to watch her back, but you're the only one who can fix what's wrong between the two of you."

"I'm trying," SB snapped.

"No, you're not," James snapped back. "If you aren't willing to let her into your life, then you don't get to demand to stay in hers. It's cruel, it's unfair, and frankly, it's hurting everyone. It's hurting *you.* You're the one dragging this out, so do us all a favor and *stop.*"

"How can you say that?" SilentBlayde demanded, his eyes betrayed above his mask. "I thought you were on my side!"

"I'm on both of your sides!" James yelled. "I want you *both* to be happy, or at least to stop stabbing each other in the heart. But frankly, at this point, I think you and Tina would both be better off if you never saw each other again. I hate to say that after everything you've been through together, but you've proved twice now that whatever secret you're hiding is more important to you than she is. You can't say you love her and then refuse to give her anything of yourself. It's grossly disingenuous. Don't you see that?"

Maybe Blayde *hadn't* seen it, because the elf stepped back in shock. Since it wasn't a big room, this put his back right up against the wall of the lodge. The moment he hit the wood, he collapsed in a heap, his long legs giving out to drop him into a pile on the floor. When James reached down to help him back up, though, the elf wouldn't even look at him.

"You're not wrong," he said at last, his long ears drooping as he slumped even lower onto the floor. "She would be better without me, but I can't leave her."

"Then tell her," James said, exasperated. "She loves you, you idiot. She's loved you for years now. All you have to do is let her in, and you'll both be—"

"I can't!" SB cried, his voice desperate. "If I tell her the truth, she'll despise me forever! I can't live with that!"

"You do realize that she's already dumped you, right?" James snarled, fed up at last. "And you're on the verge of being kicked out of her guild. You're already living in the worst-case scenario, so you might as well go for broke. Whatever happens if you tell her the truth, it can't be worse than this!"

"You're wrong," SilentBlayde said despairingly. "Things can *always* get worse." He looked down at his swords again, and then he started the long process of pushing himself up off the floor. "I need to get to practice."

James threw his hands into the air. "Did you hear *anything* I just said?"

"I did," Blayde said, glaring over his mask. "But you're wrong. I still have too much to lose. If staying in the Roughnecks is all I can have for now, I'll take it, but I won't give up. Even if she doesn't want me around, even if she leaves, I'll never let her face danger alone. I'll stay by her side no matter what. It's all I've got left to offer her."

James growled loudly enough to rattle the floorboards, but as he opened his mouth to tell his friend just how stupid and self-indulgent he was being, Gray Fang burst into a loud, excessively moist coughing fit. In the break the noise created, SB vanished into the shadows. James lurched after him, just in case, but the elf was already gone. Cursing under his breath, he turned to glare at Gray Fang.

"What was that about?"

"I had to cough," Gray Fang said innocently, puffing on her pipe. "And it was the fastest way to knock you out of a rut that was going nowhere."

"But—"

"You won't change that boy's mind with words," she said authoritatively. "Love-stupid people are immune to logic. He has to learn on his own, and *you* have a job to do. The fools can fight it out later. The best you can do for them now is figure out how to make sure there *is* a later."

Now it was James's turn to flop. He slumped onto the floor, hands catching his head with a noise of pure frustration. "I don't know if I can. I wasn't lying about SB. He really is a walking encyclopedia of FFO lore. I don't know two-thirds what he does. I can't even figure out a pile of rugs!"

"That's because you don't know our spoken history," Gray Fang said, holding up the closest rug with a grin. "These images are just anchoring points and visual aids. They're pretty useless if you don't know all the songs and tales that go with them."

James couldn't believe his pointed, fluffy ears. "Wait," he said, pushing back up. "You mean you let me stay up all night working on rugs you *knew* I couldn't decipher?!"

"Welcome to apprenticehood," Gray Fang replied, completely unrepentant. "You're not the first know-it-all student I've had. They all strut in with their tails high, but every one of them learns in the end. You will, too. Much faster now that you've seen just how much you don't know. So what do you say to me?"

Biting back the slew of smart remarks he'd like to say to that, James swallowed his pride and bowed low over his knees. "Wise master, would you help your poor apprentice with his research project?"

Gray Fang patted him on the head like he was a kitten. "I'd be glad to."

Chapter 5

Tina

"**I** am a stone Terminator," Tina told herself as she stood like a boulder in the middle of the road running south out of Windy Lake. "An emotionless undead-smashing machine crafted by the Bedrock Kings."

It sort of worked. She definitely felt like a lump of rock warming up under the Savanna's intense morning sun, but the chaos of feelings running beneath her stone skin was still far, *far* too human. Delivering SB's demotion and "show up or else" mandate had been every bit as painful as she'd feared, and that pissed her off. Seriously, how pathetic could she get? She was the one who'd put her foot down and dumped *him*, so why did seeing the hurt on his face still make her so upset? How did he still have the power to twist her insides into knots? Dammit, she should be better than this.

But just like her stone Terminator affirmations, saying the words didn't make them true. She was supposed to be the tank, the Roughnecks' fearless leader, but Tina just felt like a big fat fraud as her guild shuffled into the practice grounds. To top it off, the rising sun was blasting her right in the face. But while her instinct was to shield her eyes, Tina didn't, because the glare didn't actually bother her. Rocks didn't need to squint or blink. They didn't cry, either, which was why she was determined to become one with the fucking stone today. She was repeating this to herself over and over when she noticed a space opening up in the gathering crowd.

That caught her attention. Normally, her Roughnecks had zero respect for personal space. She didn't know if they did it for protection or if they were just impatient, but they usually piled on top of each other like kids. If they were keeping their distance, that meant the person was a threat or a pariah. Both were trouble, but when Tina looked over to see who was causing the disturbance, her eyes landed on an elven Assassin in top-tier black-and-red armor with two silver swords strapped at his sides.

Fuck.

Tina wasn't sure if she was relieved or pissed that he'd shown up. Part of her had wanted him to bail if only so she wouldn't have to face him again, but she should have known better. SilentBlayde would never let her get rid of him that easily, the jerk.

"What's shaking, Rocky Road?"

Tina jumped in surprise and looked down to see NekoBaby strutting over. The short jubatus started climbing her armor the moment she got close, scaling Tina's sun steel plate like a kitten going up a curtain to perch on her shoulder, a devious smile on her face. "Want to hear the gossip?"

Her eyes slid back to where SB was standing alone at the edge of the furiously whispering crowd of Roughnecks. "Not particularly."

"Don't be like that," Neko said, elbowing her in the cheek. "So get this: I had to save Killbox's life last night. He was hitting on this fly elven Sorceress chick. It started out okay, but then he started 'being himself,' so of course she got super offended and hit him with a fireball. I was laughing so hard I could barely cast the water spell to put him out. It was *hilarious!*"

"I'm sure it was," Tina muttered, not really paying attention. When her eyes started to slide back to SB, though, Neko whapped her in the face with her tail.

"Pay attention! I haven't even gotten to the good stuff yet! So waaaaaay more important than Killbox striking out, we figured out how the ichthyians get it on."

That got Tina's attention. "You did *what?*"

"Don't get all pearl-clutchy," the cat girl scolded her. "You know you want to hear about freaky fish sex here! Anyway, after a lot of trial and error, we learned that it takes three ichthyians to do the deed, and one of the guys has to change to a third temporary gender. Also, there's *sex ooze!* It's super gross! And..."

NekoBaby had a lot more to say on the subject of sex ooze. Tina wasn't actually interested in listening to Neko judge the shit out of ichthyians' sex lives, but she still appreciated the effort. NekoBaby might be the queen of drama, but all that gossip hounding had given her a sixth sense for awkward social situations, and it didn't take a genius to see that Tina was not taking SB's presence—or the whispers that came with it—well. Seeing her upset, Neko had done what Neko did best and brought Tina a distraction, like a cat bringing its owner a dead bird. And as awkward and inappropriate as that was, Tina appreciated it. It was nice to have a friend who cared enough to pull her away from the disaster her personal life had become, even if it did involve graphic descriptions of sex ooze. She was doing her best to look like she was listening without having to *actually* listen to Neko's oversharing when she spotted King Gregory coming down the road toward them with a tall female knight at his side.

"Anyway," NekoBaby went on, oblivious. "The lore says ichthyians can do it with elves, humans, and jubatus, but like, how does that *actually* work? We were trying to get two ichthyians and a nonichthyian together to test it out—you know, for science and shit—but no one would volunteer, the *prudes.*" She stopped, rapping her knuckles on Tina's metal hair. "Yo, Rockslide, are you listening? This is super-important the-birds-and-the-bees-and-the-fishes knowledge I'm conveying here!"

"Shhh," Tina said, turning around so Neko could see the approaching royal party. Now that they were closer, Tina realized she recognized the dour-faced woman walking at Gregory's side. Neko must have as well, because she gasped, claws digging into Tina's neck.

"Holy crappanoli! Isn't that the Knight trainer lady you took Camp Comeback from?"

It was none other. Neko scrambled off Tina's shoulder and back to the raid just in time as King Gregory stopped in front of them, raising his hand in greeting.

"Good morning, General Roxxy," he said warmly, gesturing to the knight beside him. "I trust you remember Dame Fiona Steelwall."

"How could I forget?" Tina asked, looking the tall—but still far shorter than her—woman up and down. "She threw a barrel of windfire powder at me."

"A fitting response, considering you were demanding that I surrender my base," Fiona replied without a hint of remorse.

"Dame Fiona is the new captain of Bastion's Royal Knights," Gregory said in a rush, clearly eager to escape. "She's heard about your plan to assault the Once King, and she believes she has some advice that may help. I'll just leave you two to discuss it."

With that, His Majesty scuttled off to join the crowd of Roughnecks, who welcomed him with laughs and slaps on the back and generally way more affection than one might expect given how the king had been tossing them into trees yesterday. The mood had been very different the night before when Tina had finally called a halt to practice, but then Gregory had swung by the Roughneck camp to apologize for getting carried away. More importantly, the king had brought booze as a way of making amends. Tina had no idea where he'd managed to find booze, but it had worked like a charm. The moment the Roughnecks saw the barrels of wine, Gregory had become her guild's new best friend. The king seemed to enjoy the revelry as well. He barely touched the wine himself, but that hadn't stopped him from partying just as hard as all the others while his guards cowered in alarm.

As a fellow giant person, Tina completely understood. It was hard to relax when you had to constantly worry about hurting the people around you. But—as they'd proven over and over again yesterday—the Roughnecks could take whatever Gregory dished out, and the effect on the usually timid king was profound. He was laughing just as loudly as the players now, taking Killbox's slaps on the back with infinite good nature and no lectures about proper decorum for a monarch. If she hadn't been in such a shit mood, Tina would have joined in. But she was in a shit mood, and she had shit to do, so she turned her back on the ridiculousness and returned her attention to the glaring knight.

"All right," she said, resting her giant stone hands on her hips. "What's this advice?"

Fiona Steelwall's hard face grew even harder. "Despite your unrepentant criminality, the king has informed me that you are now Bastion's last hope. Therefore, as a sworn defender of the crown, it is my duty to help you in whatever way I can."

Tina snorted. "No offense, *Dame*, but how can you help us? We're not bringing any royal troops to this shindig, and my Knights have already trained up all their skills. That said…" She trailed off, looking the three-skull Knight trainer's heavy armor up and down. "You want to come with us and try your hand at some real tanking? Because I could really use another geared meat shield who knows what she's doing."

Dame Fiona looked mortally offended. "I have no wish to engage with you or your *rabble*," she snapped, shooting a pointed glare at Gregory, who seemed to be testing just how many Roughnecks he could lift with one arm. "I could not leave even if I wished it. I am needed here to lead the Royal Knights in the battle *you* decided to leave at our feet. *But.*"

Tina arched an eyebrow. "But?"

Dame Fiona pulled herself even straighter. "While I still believe you to be a brigand and an honorless mercenary, His Majesty's forthright efforts toward peace have inspired me to give you the benefit of the doubt. With everyone giving everything they have toward our victory, it would be dishonorable of me to hold back, which is why I have come here in earnestness to tell you what I know of battle with the Once King."

That last part caught Tina's ear. "And what would that be?" she asked, without a trace of sarcasm this time.

Dame Fiona's voice grew somber as well. "I know a legendary Knight technique."

Those words sent Tina's brain screeching to a halt. "You know a *what?*"

"A legendary technique," she repeated, annoyed. "The Nightmare gave it to me ten years ago but didn't allow me to teach it to any players. I believe I am now the only one in the world who knows of it."

Tina nodded rapidly, fighting the urge to squeal with glee. Ten years ago this-world-time would have been one year ago Earth-time, which lined up with the release of the Deadlands expansion. "Is it for the Once King?!"

"The Nightmare called it 'One For All,'" Fiona said reverently. "I suspect it was intended to be revealed at the end of an epic Knight-class questline. I was already given some of the opening dialog, which is how I know that this ability was indeed intended to be used during the Once King encounter. How or in what capacity, though, I am uncertain. The Nightmare ended before the full quest could be implemented."

"That's fine," Tina said, grinning widely. "You've already said the magic words! So what does 'One For All' do?"

"It is a technique that allows you to focus a wide-area magical attack onto yourself alone," Fiona explained, removing the tower shield from her back and affixing it to her armored arm. "Bring me a Sorcerer, and I will demonstrate."

"You got it," Tina said, turning to bellow over her shoulder. "*Richard!*"

At the edge of the bawdy Roughneck circle, a tall Sorcerer with a crown of ever-burning flames on his head looked up from the book he'd been reading. "Yes?"

Whipping her arms excitedly through the air, Tina waved him over. She yelled for Anders as well, because having a healer on hand was always a good idea. It sounded like an even better idea after Fiona revealed what she wanted Richard to do.

"Let me make sure I've got this straight," Richard said, pointing his long finger at the dour knight captain. "You want me to cast a fire tornado *near* her but not on her. Correct?"

"Correct," Tina said, nodding at Dame Fiona, who was positioning herself several dozen feet down the road. "Fiona's a level-eighty three-skull. She can take it, and Anders will be ready with heals in case anything goes wrong." She glanced back at the ichthyian priest, who nodded and gripped his staff. Satisfied no one was going to die by accident, Tina turned back to her Sorcerer. "Light her up!"

With a final shrug, Richard obeyed, weaving his hands through the air in whip-like motions. Tina felt her stone skin heating as the magic built, and then a dust devil of orange flames twisted into being on the road ten feet behind Fiona's position. It rapidly grew in size, going from dust devil to full-scale tornado in a matter of seconds. When the cyclone of raging flames was as tall as a two-story building, Richard threw his hands over his head for the finish, unleashing a whirlwind of fire as wide as the road.

The nearby grass immediately caught fire. Naturalists from the raid stopped yakking with Gregory and ran over to douse the flames with frantic bursts of water magic. Since they seemed to have it in hand, Tina ignored the pending prairie fire and kept her eyes on Fiona, who was definitely living up to her name. Despite the wall of spinning flames roaring her direction, Fiona Steelwall didn't so much as flinch. Instead, she stomped down her feet in a wide stance, slammed her armored fists together with a loud clang, and yelled.

"One For All!"

Tina felt the pressure all the way to her core. The moment the old Knight spoke the words, something in the air inverted. Tina had no name, no words for that power, but it felt like the entire world had turned into a sinkhole with Fiona as its center. The size of it was staggering, leaving Tina gaping in awe as the roaring flame tornado shrank to a single frantically swirling pillar that charged down the road toward Fiona as if the blond knight were sucking it in.

When the spell reached her, her whole body was engulfed in roaring flames, but only for a moment. The fire looked no less powerful, but the storm was shrinking before Tina's eyes, condensing to a ball the size of a car, then a post box. As the tornado got smaller, the roaring flames that formed it increased their pitch, spinning faster and faster until, at last, the spell spun out of control. In the blink of an eye, all of Richard's expertly woven fire magic unraveled, collapsing into a pool of screaming flames.

Tina nodded appreciatively at what looked like a successful defense, and then she realized the screaming *wasn't* the flames. It was Fiona. Though it was no longer spinning, the raging inferno of Richard's Fire Tornado was still going, and it was stuck to Fiona like napalm. The Knight trainer fell to her knees as she watched, roaring in agony, and Tina screamed for a rescue.

"Put her out!" she ordered, voice booming. "Extinguish and heal *now!*"

The road lit up as Roughneck Naturalists conjured a torrent of bright-blue water at Fiona Steelwall. Anders moved at the same time, casting a pillar of golden light over the gasping Knight. When the flames were out, Tina rushed forward to help the woman up.

"Are you okay?"

"I'm fine," the blond Knight wheezed, knocking Tina's hand away to stand under her own power. "That was unnecessary."

"No offense, but it looked pretty damn necessary," Tina snapped. "You were a human bonfire."

"I can take one player's spell," Fiona said stiffly, tossing her sopping-wet braid over her shoulder. "But do you see now how difficult this skill is to use? One For All takes an attack meant for many and directs it solely at yourself. There is no reduction in power, no scaling down of damage. You must take *all* the pain meant for others as your own, hence the name 'One For All.' Activating it takes immense determination and discipline, as well as most of your strength. It is a tool meant to be used only in the most dire situations."

"It's definitely a skill that's only for the hardcore," Tina agreed, and then her face split into a giant grin. "I *love* it! Teach it to me!"

"Hold up! Are you crazy?" NekoBaby cried, shaking the water from her robes as she scampered over. "Did you see what that ho did to herself? That's a martyr skill!"

"She's right," Killbox agreed, coming over as well. "I didn't think anything could be too hardcore, but this is totally it. You should pass, boss."

"You guys don't get it," Tina said, turning to face the crowd of disturbed Roughnecks gathering around her. "This is the piece we've been missing! Think about it: One For All is an epic skill that was never launched, one specifically designed to let a single tank redirect a *wide-area magical attack* off a raid and onto herself. You know what that means, right?"

Everyone stared at her like she was mad.

"The Million Damage Blast!" Tina cried, throwing out her arms. "You know, the Once King's bullshit ultimate move that guaranteed wipes everyone when he reaches thirty percent? Of course we could never beat it. Because we didn't have *this*."

She threw her hand out toward Dame Fiona, who looked insulted, but not as insulted as Tina.

"I can't believe this bullshit," she snarled, clenching her stone fists. "I always thought the reason we hadn't beaten the Once King yet was because we hadn't figured out his trick, but there *was* no trick. Those stupid-ass developers put a legit unbeatable boss into the game! It was never our fault. We were up against an unwinnable fight! I bet we were mere weeks away from the patch that would have introduced the One For All questline, and then *everyone* would have the secret to getting the Once King from thirty percent to zero!"

At this proclamation, many in the crowd went "Ooooooh!" but not all. Among those who didn't was Zen.

"At the cost of the main tank's life," the Ranger said, stepping forward. "What good is an ability that gets you killed? Even if we do get the Once King to thirty percent, we can't finish him without you."

"You'll still have Frank," Tina argued, pointing at her off-tank, who looked terrified by the prospect. "He can handle things for the last third, and this is assuming the Once King *can* be tanked anymore. In case you didn't notice yesterday, I was doing a piss-poor job of keeping Gregory in line."

"That's a separate issue," Zen said, crossing her arms. "Forget the MDB. You're the only one with enough Stamina gear to not get one-shot killed by the Once King's normal attacks. You can't take those hits for us if you're dead."

"I bet I could survive if I paired One For All with Earthen Fortitude," Tina said. "That would reduce the damage."

"Not enough," Richard said in his dry, practical way. "Focusing an area-of-effect spell down to a single target seems to amplify its damage by an order of magnitude. I'm not sure what the exact multiplier is since we can no longer see the combat text, but concentrating the Million Damage Blast down to only yourself might result in a total hit of *ten* million damage. Even with Earthen Fortitude's ninety-percent reduction, you'd still be taking a one million damage hit, which is three hundred and fifty thousand more hit points than you possess. There's not enough buffs, barriers, or healing in the world to make up for such a large deficiency."

"Then fucking rez me," Tina snapped. "Cinco's raid will be there as backup, don't forget. If I die stopping the train, I expect all of you to haul my ass back into the fight. This is our *only* option, people. I don't mind taking a turn under the ax if that's what we have to do to save the world."

That response earned her lots of nervous looks from the dusty crowd. Given that their track record for in-battle resurrections was exactly zero, Tina couldn't fault their anxiety, but this wasn't up for debate. This skill was obviously how the Once King was meant to be defeated, and since she was the best geared and most experienced Knight in her raid—possibly in the *world*—that meant the task fell to her. Tina was fine with that. She trusted her people to save her even if they didn't. And if everything *did* go

110

tits up, well, there were worse ways to go out than being the hero who saved an entire world.

Honestly, Tina's biggest problem right now was the way the crowd was looking at her. More specifically, the way they were looking at her and SB. The raid group had actually shuffled out of the way to open a clear path between him and her, and Tina resented the hell out of it. SilentBlayde had nothing to do with this and zero right to comment.

But despite that, a small, weak part of Tina was still hoping he'd ask her not to do this, not to risk herself so recklessly, not to die. But Blayde said nothing. Instead, Fiona clanked up to Tina's side.

"Well spoken, Knight Roxxy," the old knight said, reaching up to clap Tina on the shoulder. "We may have been enemies, but I respect your courage. It will be my honor to teach you One For All so that you and your soldiers may scour the Once King from the face of this world."

"Thanks," Tina said, ripping her eyes off SB. She gave herself a shake and then clapped her hands together. "All right, everybody! Frank needs to practice being the main tank, so he's on point today while I'm off getting flambéed. One For All is the chance we've been looking for, but it doesn't mean anything if we can't figure out how to last more than ten minutes against Gregory over there, so no slacking!"

There was much grumbling at that, but no one actually tried to argue. They all just shuffled off down the wagon-rutted road toward Gregory, who was standing ready at the end. As they left, Tina caught several backward glances filled with what appeared to be genuine worry for her, which only made her even more determined. She would not let them down, not after she'd worked so hard to earn that caring.

Body stiffening with determination, Tina turned back to Fiona. "Let's get to this," she said, flashing the Knight trainer a cocky marble grin. "We're burning daylight when we should be burning me."

The stern captain nodded back. "Then let us begin."

To reduce the damage done to people and things, Tina and Richard both took off all their gear for the practice. This resulted in Tina making a spectacle of herself as she stomped around the trade road in her shorts, yelling and getting burned while Dame Fiona corrected her technique. Fiona Steelwall in teacher mode was a true hard-ass, too. Tina quickly learned that the Knight trainer was utterly demanding and had a brutal eye for imperfections. She took as much damage from Fiona's corrective swats as she did from Richard's fire.

Through it all, Tina had never been so glad she was a stonekin. There was no other way she could have put up with being engulfed in flames over and over, all day long. Richard tried to limit the damage as much as possible, but even without his robes and staff, he was still a level-eighty Sorcerer, and his fire *hurt*. Another person probably would have felt guilty over burning her alive again and again, but that was the great thing about Richard. The computer-like man was as solid as a stonekin in his own way. He understood this was how training had to be, so he just accepted it and did his job, paying Tina's screams of agony no more mind than he did her praise.

The healers were another story. As morning turned to afternoon, Tina had had to rotate through her entire roster of Naturalists and Clerics. Not because they were out of mana—she was a breeze to heal with no armor boosting her health—but because no one could take watching her get repeatedly burned alive for more than thirty minutes at a time. Even Dame Fiona started to hesitate as the rounds mounted up, but Tina refused to stop. Dogged persistence was what she had, and Tina needed every bit of it. Learning new techniques now wasn't as simple as hitting "accept" on a quest box. She had to actually practice, which started by learning how her other Knightly skills actually worked.

Before today, Tina had never thought to question how a nonmagical class like a Knight did obviously magical things like Ground Stomp or Iron Wall. Since all of her class skills had become instinct when FFO stopped being a game, she had very little understanding of the mechanics involved in using them—a fact Fiona Stonewall seemed to take as a personal offense.

"*No!*" the Knight cried when Tina failed yet again to suck in the fire properly. "I keep telling you, it's not in the feet. You have to *feel* the magic of the ground pulling toward you!"

"And I keep…telling you…I don't feel magic!" Tina panted, resting on her singed knees as the latest Naturalist in the healing rotation poured soothing magic over her burns. "How can I get my feet lined up with something I can't feel? Stonekin don't even *have* mana! That's why we can't be casters."

"Just because you don't have mana doesn't mean you can't move the world," Fiona said sternly. "Sorcerers, Clerics, and Naturalists grab magic and give it shape, but Knights work only with their will. You have to grab the enemy's spell with your determination and force it to you!"

"I *am* forcing," Tina snapped. "I'm stomping the crap out of that fire!"

"Anyone can stomp and clap. That's not what's important. You have to stop focusing so much on the physical motions. They're only there as guides. Will is what actually makes the technique work. You have to reach out of yourself and challenge that Fire Tornado until it charges you like the mad bull it is!" She stepped back with a clap of her hands. "Do it again!"

Those words made Tina want to cry. No matter how many times the Knight explained what she needed to do, it never got any clearer. But even when the thought of being burned yet again made her want to curl into a ball and whimper, she gritted her teeth and kept at it. She would not let this beat her, dammit.

And maybe that was the secret. Tina didn't think she was getting any better, but as she refused to admit defeat again and again and *again*, the Fire Tornadoes stopped rolling over her like avalanches and started getting smaller. She couldn't say what had changed, if anything, but pure stubbornness was also a form of will. Fortunately, it was one Tina had in spades, and the longer she kept at it, the better she got.

By the time the sun had fallen to the horizon, she was manhandling Richard's tornadoes like they were unruly farm animals. She hadn't even realized how much time had passed until she looked up and saw the Roughnecks and Gregory standing in a ring around her.

"Holy shit," Neko said, her cat eyes wide as she took in the blackened trade road. Everything within a hundred-foot radius of Tina's position had been burned to cinders. But while the ashy remains of her earlier failed attempts were everywhere, the ground surrounding Tina was cool and still without a trace of smoke.

Neko whistled appreciatively. "So did you figure it out?"

Tina gave her a shaky thumbs-up. "I got it," she said in a smoke-roughened voice. "Though I think I might have picked up a new fire phobia on the way." She laughed at her own joke, but no one in the Roughnecks laughed with her.

"You shouldn't push yourself this hard."

SilentBlayde's voice cut through the nervous murmurs like a knife. She hadn't even realized he was here, but when Tina raised her head again, there he was, standing in the back of the rapidly parting crowd, his face white with fury above his ever-present mask.

"This is too much, Tina," he said, the words shaking with anger.

"You don't get to tell me what's too much," Tina snarled back in a voice so bitter and sharp that even she didn't recognize it as hers. "You didn't get a say before, and you sure as shit don't get one now."

SB stiffened, and Tina braced for a fight. It never materialized, though, because the elf just turned on his heel and stalked away, his body pulled up tight with rage.

"Wow," NekoBaby said as he left. "He's been Mopey McMoper-Pants all day, and now he busts out?" She shook her head. "He must really hate seeing you get all burned and hurt and stuff."

"I don't care what he thinks," Tina said, but there was no more bite in her voice. After a day of burns and screaming at tornadoes and now this, she was drained dry. All she wanted to do now was bury herself in the dirt and cry. Or maybe scream; she hadn't decided yet. She was still thinking it over when Neko hopped onto her shoulders.

"Hey there, Rocky Road-On-Fire," the cat girl said in a suspiciously cheerful voice. "You get a chance yet to look at what James has been doing? 'Cause it sure as shit looks like he's building a new version of Stonehenge over by the lake."

That was just weird enough to make Tina forget about SB for a moment. She blinked furiously, wiping the wetness—pain tears, not tears-tears, she told herself furiously—from her eyes before looking over at the water that ran along the town's edge. Sure enough, she could see the black silhouettes of huge monolithic rocks against the setting sun.

"Whoa," Tina said, rubbing her eyes again. "What the hell are those?"

"We don't know," King Gregory said, gently pushing his way to the front even though, at his height, he could have easily spoken over the crowd. "But we are all dying of curiosity. I intend to go and investigate this personally." There was a pause, and then the king added proudly, "With my homies."

Killbox and Neko burst into fits of muffled laughter. Rolling her eyes at what was clearly *way* too much nonsense for her to deal with right now, Tina turned to thank Fiona and bid her farewell. When the Knight captain was gone, Tina put her armor back on slowly, wincing every time the metal bumped her skin, which was still sensitive despite gobs of healing. Apparently even magical stone got weak when you rapidly heated and cooled it over and over. She didn't see any cracks, though, so Tina ignored the pain. When she was back in her equipment, Tina fell in behind the king as he led the Roughnecks through the town toward James's rocks.

"So how'd it go today?" she asked Zen when the Ranger fell into step beside her.

"Pretty crazy without you there," Zen admitted. "I had to put some people in time out, which works a lot better on adults than you would think.

Everyone pulled it together in the end, though, and we discovered some, umm...*unique* tactics."

"What do you mean 'unique'?" Tina asked, slightly terrified. "Did you defeat him with the power of song or something?"

Zen's mouth quirked in a smile that was gone in a flash. "Not *that* unique, but I might have spent all our remaining money buying several hundred feet of enchanted chains."

"Chains?" Tina wrinkled her nose. "How does that work?"

"I'll have to show you later," Zen said. "It's pretty complicated and more than a little stupid, but what matters is that we've gotten our time up to fifteen minutes against Gregory before things start to fall apart."

"That's great!" Tina said excitedly. "Huge improvement, but why the hell are they making you *pay* for chains? We're saving the world here."

Zen shrugged. "Artisans still have to make a living just in case the world doesn't end. And it was a *lot* of metal, which isn't exactly in ready supply right now. He gave us a good price, though."

That was something, Tina supposed. "Well, if it got us from zero minutes to fifteen, then it was money well spent," she said. "Thanks for managing everything, Zen. One more question, though..."

Zen's long ears bobbed as the elven Ranger glanced at her. "Yes?"

Tina nodded up at the king, who was walking at the front of the raid with Killbox and NekoBaby crowded around him, thick as thieves. "What the hell have you been letting them teach Gregory?"

"So you're telling me you *don't* have a harem?" Killbox said at that exact moment, *loudly*.

"What about a posse?" NekoBaby cried. "*Please* tell me you've got a posse!"

When Gregory shook his head, both players groaned in dismay.

"No posse? Who gets you the hook-up on your weed, then?"

"And chicks!" Killbox added frantically. "Elf chicks, cat chicks, human chicks. This world is full of fly hunnies! Who's lining them up for you if you don't have a posse?"

"I-I have no need of such things," the king said, his ears turning redder by the second. "Concubines and harems would be extremely disrespectful to any future wife I might take. There's also the problem of bastard children. I would *never*—"

"Killbox," NekoBaby said, *super* seriously. "We've gotta teach the OG here how to king right. Dude is missing out hardcore. He is a *literal* boss. He should be ballin'!"

The Berserker nodded gravely. "True dat. We gotta fix this." His face brightened up. "I call chick-wrangling duty! You do plant magic 'n shit, so you're in charge of the chronic. He's tall, so we're gonna need a lot. We need a DJ, too. A player who can drop an actual beat so we're not stuck with some medieval bard shit."

"Would you two *knock it off?*" Zen hissed, darting away from Tina to shove herself between Neko and Killbox. "What have I told you two about not corrupting Gregory?" she scolded. "Do you have any idea how lucky we are to have a king who is a decent human being and not some overgrown man-child evil prince?!"

Tina bit her lip hard to keep from laughing. The last thing she wanted was to undermine Zen's new authority, but this shit was just so *funny*. She could almost imagine the Ranger with a spray bottle spritzing Killbox and Neko like they were a pair of misbehaving cats. The two Roughnecks certainly scattered like scolded pets, leaving Zen furiously glaring at their backs as they dove for the safety of the larger raid.

"Please don't listen to them, Your Majesty," Zen said, schooling her face and tucking her leaf-green hair back behind her long brown ears as she turned to face the king again. "They're idiots."

King Gregory blushed faintly as he smiled at her. "Do not fear, Ranger Kayla," he said in his rich baritone. "I'm committed to the dignity of the Holy Throne. That said, their teasing does not bother me. It is fun to talk of things of no consequence on occasion." Then the king stroked his red beard and added thoughtfully, "Though I do like the player idea that breweries should be open to the public with food and regular events. That's a change we should *definitely* implement."

"Breweries are a lot of fun," Zen admitted, slipping away from the king with a graceful bow before fleeing back to Tina with her inhuman speed.

"So," Tina said as the Ranger reappeared beside her. "Since when are you 'Ranger Kayla'?"

"Since I was born and baptized as Kayla Johnson," Zen replied irritably.

Tina blinked in surprise. "You mean that's your real name?"

"Yeah," the Ranger said, eyes narrowing. "Why?"

"Nothing!" Tina said quickly, waving her hands. "It's a great name! It's just…you've been going by Zen this whole time, so I figured you had some dark secret or something."

"Sorry I'm not as dramatic as the rest of you," Zen said with a huff. "I just like my character's name is all. Ranger Zen is beautiful, stylish, and deadly. Kayla Johnson is a forty-two-year-old nurse from Philly who lives alone in a fourth-floor walk-up with her three cats and plays too much FFO. Why wouldn't I choose to be the cool one?"

"Nothing wrong with that," Tina said with a grin. "I still can't decide between Roxxy and Tina. I'm much more curious as to why you're on a first-name basis with the king, though."

"So are you," Zen pointed out. "He calls you 'General Roxxy.'"

"That's because we've got the whole 'fellow commanders' thing going on," Tina said dismissively. "I'm also a rock. You're a hot elf. Totally different vibe."

Zen rolled her eyes.

"Sooooo," Tina said, wiggling her eyebrows. "Did you two have any 'moments' during training today?"

"I don't even know what that means."

"Oh, you know," Tina said, her voice dripping with innuendo.

"Tina, this is not a high school drama," Zen replied firmly. "We're just two sensible people forced to team up against the crazies."

"Awwww. So there was nothing? No moments at all?"

The Ranger shook her head. "Sorry to disappoint."

Tina leaned closer. "Would you have minded if there *was* a moment?"

"Would you stop?" Zen huffed, hunching her shoulders. "It's not like that! We're just..." She trailed off, her lithe body going still. Then she asked, "What happened to the lake?"

Tina was about to accuse her of dodging the questions when she realized all the Roughnecks around them had stopped as well. Straightening up from the stoop she'd been using to get into Zen's business, Tina looked over the heads of the crowd to see that Windy Lake was *much* lower than it had been that morning. The formerly glittering expanse was now a small pond ringed on all sides by a large collar of exposed mud. She was trying to figure out where the water could have gone when she heard yelling to their left.

"*Pull!*"

All the Roughnecks jumped as the tall yurt taking up the street beside them suddenly collapsed, and it wasn't the only one. Looking around, Tina saw that *all* the hide tents in Windy Lake were being disassembled. Up the road ahead of them, Lord Rends Iron Hides—AKA James's cat dad—was watching the controlled destruction from the steps of the Naturalist Lodge, his long arms folded tensely in front of him. At the sight, King Gregory detached himself from the latest group of Roughnecks that had glommed on to him and started hurrying forward. Stretching her long legs, Tina followed right behind him, jogging up to the king's side just as he reached the center of town, or what was left of it.

"Lord Rends," Gregory called, looking around at the rapidly vanishing jubatus village. "What is the situation?"

"Not good, Your Majesty," Rends replied, his old tail lashing. "Our scouts have reported that the quickest undead vanguard units have already been spotted in the northern grasslands, only a hundred miles from here. That's much faster than expected. We'd hoped the chaos of the runaway Spring Cleaning event would slow them down a little, but apparently even bandits know better than to get in the way of the undead."

"What is the plan now, then?" Gregory asked gravely.

"Same as before, just a bit faster," Rends replied, pointing down the road they'd just come from. "As planned, we're retreating to the Red Canyon fortress. It's got less water, but it's much more defensible. The gnolls left this morning to start preparations, and we've already drained most of the lake into the water wagons so we won't get caught dry if there's a siege. There's still much to do, but our skirmishers have ridden north to buy us what time they can while we move the rest of the town."

"Wait," Tina blurted. "You're moving the *whole* town?"

Rends gave her a disgusted look. "Of course. We're nomads. The only reason we've lived at Windy Lake for more than one season is because the Nightmare forced us to. We don't build a permanent settlement out of *tents.*"

"Oh," was all Tina could say to that.

"And what of our assault on the Once King?" Gregory asked.

Rends pointed a sharp claw in the direction of six stone pillars rising above the remaining yurts. "My brilliant son James has figured out a ritual, but Gray Fang says it won't be ready before sunrise tomorrow. Our goal is to have everyone packed and ready to leave by the time it is complete."

"And if it doesn't work?" Tina asked.

Rends gave her a fanged smile. "Then I hope you'll join us for our glorious last stand."

Tina ground her marble teeth. She didn't like how quickly their options were vanishing. They were only two days out of Bastion, and already they'd reached the "everything has to work perfectly or we're dead" stage. If anyone could pull off the miracle they needed, though, it was James. Her brother could drone on about FFO's magic for *hours*. If there was ever a time when that obsessive level of nerddom would pay off, this was it.

"I fear the time has come to end our training," the king said, his face grave as he turned to Tina. "We have learned much from one another these last two days. I pray that you are able to use those lessons to best the Once King and save us all." Gregory clenched his massive fists, whose strength all the Roughnecks had learned to respect. "For my part, I vow that I shall use what you have taught me to its fullest against the enemy. The Blood General Sanguilar will find no easy prey this time."

"Don't worry," Tina said, putting a hand on the huge king's shoulder. "You're going to be a rock star, and we're gonna teach the Once King just how terrifying we can be."

Behind her, the Roughnecks started to cheer and whistle, and Gregory smiled. "I believe you," he said, grinning at the raiders. "But it is not yet the time for goodbyes. See to your troops, General Roxxy. I must go to mine."

Tina winked. "Give 'em hell, Your Majesty."

Gregory smiled once more and left, striding away down the street that was now little more than a break in the chaos of collapsing tents. Staring after him, Tina lifted her hand and ordered everyone back to camp. She really wanted to go over and see what James was making, but it sounded like he didn't have time for distractions, and the sun was already setting. She still had to get everyone packed up and resupplied for a march through the Deadlands, not to mention get some sleep, since they might not have a chance to rest again before the fight.

But these practical concerns didn't stop her from worrying. After fidgeting around camp for several minutes, Tina gave in and ordered one of Zen's Rangers to run over to James's ritual site and ask if he needed her yet. When the answer came back "not until dawn," she was a little disappointed, but at least she knew the timeline.

"Okay, guys and gals," she boomed once everyone had eaten their dinner. "Get to your tents and enjoy your last night of being warm, 'cause we're hitting the Deadlands bright and early tomorrow."

There was much groaning when she mentioned the Once King's cold, ashy zone. If she hadn't been up front setting a good example, Tina would have joined them. She'd hoped never to set foot in that horrible gray landscape again, but here they were. "This won't be like last time," she promised. "We're the attackers now. We're going to march into the Dead Mountain Fortress like bosses, and then it's gonna be payback time!"

That got the raid cheering again. Tina let them rally for a good five minutes before ordering everyone to bed. When she was sure they were all moving to their tents at appropriate speed, she crammed one of the stupid magical rocks stonekin ate into her mouth and trundled off to her own bed-ditch in the ground, never noticing the elf-shaped shadow watching her silently from the shadow of the spindly trees.

Chapter 6

James

James stood in the middle of the dew-damp field, thankful once again for his superior jubatus night vision, which made it possible to read the rug's six-pointed diagrams in the predawn light. Behind him, every Naturalist in Windy Lake was sleeping on the mats Gray Fang had found for them, utterly exhausted. It turned out that raising six pillars of deep bedrock to the surface was one hell of a mana-intensive task, but they'd done it.

When the sun finally peeked over the horizon, its golden light fell upon a circle of six hexagonal stone pillars, each the size of a school bus. Outside the ring, the air was full of the noise of the grasslands: crying birds, whistling wind, the lap of the remaining lake water, the distant yells of the jubatus who were just now finishing up the packing of Windy Lake's yurts. But inside the circle of stones, all of that stopped, leaving only silence.

At first, James had thought the lack of sound meant something was wrong with the ritual he and Gray Fang had designed, but there was nothing wrong. It was the stone itself. Rock that had lived for so long in such a deep, primal place exuded quiet like fire radiated heat. Standing in their shadows, even the rattle of the carts leaving for Red Canyon was quashed beneath the heavy, oppressive quiet of the deep, dark bedrock. James was appreciating the rare stillness when he saw Ar'Bati marching toward him.

"Good morning, brother," James said, stepping out of the circle of silence so Ar'Bati could hear him. "Nice armor."

His adopted brother grinned widely. The tall jubatus warrior was dressed from head to toe in brand-new plate-and-chain Berserker armor. He still carried the two-handed sword he'd picked up in Red Canyon on his back, but its blade had been cleaned and freshly sharpened, amplifying its magical green glow to a blinding shine.

"Thank you," Ar'Bati said proudly, turning around so James could see the back. "It has excellent 'stats,' as you players would say. It was a gift to the Claw Born from the new Baron Assets of the Treasury."

James felt a twinge of apprehension. "You're *sure* it's a gift? Not like a loan or anything?" Because if there was anything he knew about Bastion's new accountant, it was that he could not be trusted.

"He said it was ours to keep, along with many other treasures," Fangs said proudly. "He has been very generous with gifts to our family. I think he wisely seeks to ally himself with the foremost clan of the Savanna."

Remembering Tina's ultimatum about breaking off his marriage, James wasn't so sure that was it. Before he could ask for more info, though, Ar'Bati tossed one of the two backpacks he was carrying at James's chest.

"That one's for you," Ar'Bati said with a fanged grin. "Sorry there's no tent for you to change in. Everything's already been packed, so the grasses will have to do."

Confused, James opened the pack to see a stack of newly stitched leather armor gleaming with magic runes. Breath quickening in excitement, he emptied the bag onto the grass at his feet. Inside were leather pants, a chest piece, and boots from the level-eighty Assassin set. It was all Agility gear, but someone had also included a shimmering cloth belt, cloak, and braces from the Heavenly Fire caster set. The magical golden silk was so incredibly soft and thick, James almost missed the +Intelligence amulet and rings that had been folded into the cloak.

All the new gear was player crafted and level eighty. James couldn't be certain without the item text, but he was pretty sure it was all rare quality, too. Nothing anywhere close to Tina's Dead Mountain raid gear, but every piece of this new equipment was still ten times better than the hodgepodge of level-forty equipment he'd scavenged from Red Canyon and was *still* wearing. He was running his hands over the glittering pile in delighted disbelief when he found a note tucked into the left boot.

Dear James,

124

Please inform your sister that I have done as she requested on the issue of your marriage. I have successfully intervened with both families, and you are no longer engaged. As such, General Roxxy's further involvement in this matter will **not** *be needed.*

> *Signed and Sealed,*
> *Baron Assets*
> *Lord of His Majesty's Treasury*
> *Head of the East Bastion Trade Company*

Given how Tina had "requested" his assistance—namely by lifting Assets off the ground and shaking him until he agreed—James wasn't surprised that Lord Assets had had a very open hand in smoothing things over. But while he was *very* relieved he would no longer have to marry…whatever her name was, he was too overwhelmed by the epic pile of loot that had been dropped into his hands to feel much of anything else. Just looking at the beautiful set of armor with its gleaming enchantments and perfectly straight stitching made his vision go blurry.

"I do not understand this crying-in-joy thing players do," Ar'Bati said as James wiped his wet eyes. "Is it not disgraceful?"

"It's a little disgraceful," James said, sniffing against the flood of unwelcome emotions. "Can I confess something to you?"

"Anything," Fangs said seriously. "I am your sworn brother. Our bond is stronger than blood."

James smiled in gratitude, clutching his new gear to his chest. "I gave up everything I owned to make the portals we evacuated through back in Bastion."

Ar'Bati's slit cat eyes went wide. "*Everything?*"

James nodded. "My entire bank vault. All my epic gear, millions of gold pieces, literal tons of irreplaceable items. Everything I'd spent the last eight years frantically collecting." He sniffed at the memory. "I know I don't need it since I'm eventually going home, but the loss still hurt. I've had to watch everyone walk around in their awesome gear and listen to them talk about how they're gonna spend all their gold if the bank ever reopens while I'm broke and stuck wearing crap I *stole from the dead.*"

James looked down at his mismatched armor, which still bore the bloodstains of the players he'd taken it from in that pit no matter how hard he scrubbed it, and his eyes closed in shame. "It feels stupid and petty when I say it out loud, but I've just been so...so *jealous* of all the other players. Especially the Roughnecks. I mean, that used to be me! I had all this amazing gear, and then..." He sighed, shoulders slumping. "I don't regret what I did. Giving up my vault saved everyone's lives in Bastion, but I still miss it. I know that's selfish and petty, but..."

He trailed off, and Fangs reached out to put a clawed hand on his shoulder. "There is no shame in missing things that are gone," the warrior said solemnly. "I didn't know you'd made such a sacrifice, but I am not surprised at all to hear it. Once again, you have done us all a great deed. I will make sure it does not go unrecognized."

"No, no," James said frantically. "That's not what I meant! I don't need recognition. I just wanted..."

To talk about it, James finished in his head. He'd needed to tell someone, to admit that he was mourning, even if it was for something as selfish as his lost loot. So many people had lost friends and relatives—actual living beings—and here he was crying over gear. Just thinking about that made him feel like a monster, but it was still a relief to get it out. He was opening his mouth to thank his brother for listening when Ar'Bati hauled back and socked him in the arm.

"*Ow!*" James cried, jumping back. "What was that for?!"

"For not speaking up sooner!" his brother said. "Your pain is my pain, but I cannot help you bear it if you don't tell me when things are wrong! Also, what is this nonsense about not needing recognition? You must learn that it is good for a warrior to brag sometimes. How are we to feast in your honor if you keep your great deeds secret?"

James had to laugh at that. "Sorry to deny you a party."

"Do not worry," Fangs said with a murderous grin. "We will have the greatest celebration the grasslands have ever seen when we return home with the Once King's head on a spear. For now, though, you should get dressed. The day's trouble is already headed this way."

The warrior's ears twitched back toward town, and James raised his head to see a large crowd of armed players walking their direction.

Gasping at how much time he'd lost, James dove into the cover of the closest pillar and began stripping off his old armor. As always, it was a relief to remove the bloodstained pieces. Every time he touched them, he swore he could see the ashen faces of the dead players he'd taken them from staring back at him accusingly. The haunting image was so strong James didn't even bother putting his old armor back in the sack. He simply abandoned the bloodstained leather in the grass, glad to be rid of it.

Finally free of his old sins, James started shoving his body into his new equipment. When he put a leg into the pants, it felt like they were going to be too tight. That wouldn't be surprising given that the armorer hadn't had his measurements, but it was still a huge disappointment. As he wiggled more, though, James realized he was being silly. The pants weren't too small for him. Form-fitting leather armor was just really, *really* hard to put on.

Once he realized that, things went much faster. It was true the armorer couldn't have known his exact size, but like every other player who'd gotten stuck, James was living in a stock body model. His measurements were the same as every other male jubatus player's, and once he actually managed to get it over his limbs, the skin-tight leather fit him like a glove.

The cloth caster pieces went on much more easily, but when he reached for the glowing tendrils to bind the new gear's magic to his own in order to activate the enchantments woven into the silk, James was forced to stop and catch his breath. After so long in his scavenged equipment, donning proper level-eighty gear was a rush. With each piece he connected, binding the new gear to his soul so that it became his alone, James felt lighter on his feet. His mind and fingers became more nimble, and his head swam as his mana pool expanded exponentially. He wasn't sure what it had been before, but he was certain his old maximum was less than half of what he had access to now. James grinned as he imagined what life was going to be like with more than twice his old mana pool and probably double his previous health. Definitely awesome, he decided.

Feeling proud and powerful as only a giant upgrade could make someone, James emerged from the stone's shadow just in time to witness the arrival of the player army.

As always, Tina was out in front, towering head and shoulders over everyone else and almost painful to look at with the dawn light reflecting off her mirror-bright sun steel armor. Beside her was CincoDeMurder, the overmuscled Berserker with the blood-red skull-themed outfit. The two of them made an imposing spearhead for the column of more than a hundred armed and travel-ready players who marched behind them in orderly rows. When they reached the circle of the pillars, Tina held up her hand, and the whole procession stopped on a dime.

"Morning, James," she said, flashing him a marble grin. "You ready for this?"

"Ready as I'll ever be," he replied nervously, eying the army she'd brought. "But T, you *do* know we're just talking to them, right?" He pointed at the giant stone circle. "Gray Fang and I figured out how to ring the doorbell, so to speak, but I still don't know how the Timeless Tunnels work or if the Bedrock Kings will even answer. There are a lot of ways this might not work."

"It'll be what it'll be," his sister said with a shrug of her giant shoulders. "Whatever happens, we're out of time. Whether we go to the Deadlands or not, we can't stay here. The Once King's army is only a day away, and hell if we're fighting that mess on an open plain."

Ears drooping at the grim news, James turned and pointed at the low, flat boulder placed at the center of the stone circle he and the rest of Windy Lake's Naturalists had spent all night raising from the ground. "Go stand there, then, and let's give it a shot. Uh, just you," he added when Cinco tried to follow her.

"Why only Roxxy?" the Berserker demanded.

"Only a stonekin can call upon the Bedrock Kings," James explained. "Everyone else has to stay outside, or the magic won't work."

The red Berserker looked nonplussed as Tina strode forward to take her place at the center of the circle. "Wow, it's quiet in here," she said as she hopped up onto the pedestal. "So what do I do now?"

"Get their attention," James replied, reaching out to touch the cold pillar pulled up from the deepest depths. "This circle is basically a giant magical telephone. I'm pretty sure the Bedrock Kings will be able to hear anything you say, though whether they'll talk back is another matter. You'll probably want to lead with something impressive. You know, a great and noble speech fancy enough to get the attention of multiple ancient kings."

"Great, I love speeches," Tina said excitedly. "I've already got something in mind. Dial them up!"

Trying not to look as nervous as he felt, James picked up his Eclipsed Steel staff from where he'd left it in the grass and touched it to the closest pillar of bedrock. The contact connected his mana to the large flows of amber energy in the ground, lines he and Gray Fang had spent all of last night anchoring into a spiraling pattern that tied the six pillars together. From there, though, it was up to him.

James began to sweat. Back in Bastion, he'd learned that true casting—actually weaving magic, not just triggering the spells given to him by the game—was simple in theory but infinitely complex in execution. Casters used their internal mana to grab magic from the surrounding world, and then they wove or spun or mashed that power into the shape needed to achieve the desired effect. From there, the final component of any spell was the caster's will. Will was the force that pushed the gathered energies out of their dormant state and into an active one. The caster also imparted intent, guiding the energies' transformation in the desired direction.

At least, that was how it went in theory. In practice, James had learned that form was tricky, and matching his will to it was even trickier. His huge mana pool made him great at grunt work like hauling up pillars or blasting things, but this was different. The spiral of magic he and Gray Fang had built was bigger and more complicated than anything else he'd ever attempted. Just getting the massive web lined up correctly so that it wouldn't explode or cause a giant sinkhole when he activated it had taken most of the night. Now, he could only hope they hadn't missed anything as he stepped into the circle with her, using his staff to sweep his mana toward the center.

Tina gasped. The web surrounding her rock had multiple streams of energy that he and Gray Fang had purposefully left loose. Now James's mana snagged them up. Once he had them all, he swung his staff through the air, using the weapon like a hook as he moved in circles around Tina, looping the glowing lines around his giant sister. As the magic settled into her, he realized he could see the flows of green and amber that made up her stonekin existence rising to meet them. That was totally expected, since stonekin were completely artificial magical creations, but what he hadn't expected was just how many *different* types of magic flowed inside her. He'd never even thought to consider magic as more than its broadest categories—fire, water, air, and so forth—but there had to be a thousand different colors of amber, gold, and green coiled up inside her stone body.

Any other time, James would have stopped the spell right there so he could study them, but magical investigations would have to wait. Tina was fully wrapped in glowing earth magics now, tied up like a fly at the center of a giant web of power that stretched between the six pillars. When James was certain she was as magically connected as she was ever going to get, he stopped circling and pressed the tip of his staff to the center of her chest, pushing on the giant spell as hard as he could with his own mana as he galvanized his will into a single word.

"*Speak.*"

Tina jumped like he'd dumped a bucket of ice water over her head. She looked at James in confusion next, but he'd already fallen to his knees, his chest heaving from the sudden expenditure of so much mana. This was it, though, so he forced himself to gasp out, "You're on!"

"Hello," Tina said, her unsure voice echoing inside the stones like a drop of water in a silent cave. "Testing, testing?"

"Remember, dramatic!" James hissed at her. "These are former Celestial Elves! They expect pomp."

Tina looked embarrassed for a moment. Then she straightened up and got herself together, projecting her booming voice through the unnatural silence of the bedrock circle.

"Hear me, great kings of the deep strata! I am Roxxy the stonekin! Though I was not made by your hands, we share the same enemy. Lend me your aid so that we may turn history upon its head and defeat the lord of the ghostfire this day!"

As his sister's words echoed from pillar to pillar, she shot him a *"Good enough?"* sort of look. James gave her an enthusiastic thumbs-up in return, but he lost it a second later when the ground started to move, making him flail for balance.

James had never been in an earthquake, but he was pretty sure this was what it felt like. All through the grasslands, the ground was bucking and undulating, causing the remaining villagers of Windy Lake to cry out and clutch their overloaded wagons. Players dove out of the way as the field they were standing on split open to form a giant ravine that ran straight through the middle of the stone circle. The crack actually ran directly under James's feet, forcing him to leap onto Tina's boulder before he was dropped into the void. As the chasm grew deeper, James was sure he'd just gotten them all killed, but the bedrock pillars were actually the only things that *weren't* shaking. The ground around them was gone, but he and Tina were safe and secure on top of the flat boulder, the only steady point in a sea of quaking ground.

Then, slowly, the six stone pillars of the circle began to move as well, their huge forms twisting and shaping into something new. The deep, hard bedrock moved like potter's clay being shaped by a giant invisible hand working in extreme slow motion. James couldn't even say how long it took, but eventually the towering stone pillars transformed themselves into three stone men and three stone women, each standing at least twenty feet tall.

"Our stonekin has called," they spoke, their six rumbling voices harmonizing to become one booming sound. "And so we have answered. Behold the Bedrock Kings!"

"Holy shit!" squeaked Tina, crouching next to her brother on the boulder, which was now a lone pillar of stone in the middle of a vast black ravine. "I didn't think they'd show up in person!"

"We should bow or something," James whispered back, cowering behind her. "Show respect!"

He followed his own advice by dropping into a low bow. A second later, Tina did the same, bowing at the waist until her body formed a ninety-degree angle, which seemed to please the kings immensely.

"You are a player-made stonekin," the six boomed. "Despite this, you are our child. We watch over you the same as we care for all creations of the deep stone."

"Uh, thank you," Tina said, straightening back up. "I appreciate the—"

"You, Roxxy, have done many things," they boomed over her. "You have done...*well!*"

"Huh?" Tina said, confused. James didn't get it, either. The Bedrock Kings' stone faces were as expressionless as statues, but their voices were full of joy.

"We sculpted our stonekin as weapons to fight the Once King," the giant stones said. "They were created to be as unstoppable and tireless as the

132

undead they destroyed. You were not made by our hands, and yet you have exceeded even our greatest expectations. You have bested the king's generals, broken his weapons, and saved his enemies from undeath! Of all our stonekin, you, Roxxy, have accomplished the most." Six expressionless stone faces split into smiles. "We are so proud of you!"

Tina began to shake. Alarmed, James looked up to see his sister was…well, not actually crying, but it was a very near thing. For a moment, he couldn't understand what was wrong. They were praising her; why would she be upset? Then, feeling like an ass, James realized that *was* the reason. He couldn't remember their parents ever telling Tina "good job" or "we're proud of you." They'd always been too busy with their work or James's problems to notice his little sister's accomplishments. She'd told him as much herself, but he'd never actually stopped to consider how much that must have hurt her until he saw her reduced almost to tears by the praise of giant stone authority figures she'd never even met.

"Thank you," Tina said, wiping her face. "I did my best. But if you've been watching me all this time, why haven't you come to help before? We've nearly lost so many times."

"But you did not lose," the kings replied as one. "You stood firm as the mountains, the rock upon which the undead break. Now you seek to challenge the Once King himself, and so we are here."

"Thank you," Tina said again. Then she grinned up at the giant stone figures. "So are you going to help us fight him? Because you guys look like total bosses!"

The giant royal figures exchanged unreadable stone glances. "We cannot," they intoned at last, reaching up in unison to lay their giant stone hands upon their smooth carved backs. "We are but shadows, ruins of what we once were, and the Once King was ever the best of us. Also, the prison he has shut himself away within is protected from the Sun and all its children. Even if we wished it, we cannot enter."

James's ears fell.

"So does that mean you can't take us into the Deadlands?" Tina asked, voicing his fears.

"This is correct."

"Damn," Tina said. Then her eyes lit up again. "I don't suppose you have an army of totally awesome stonekin we could borrow instead?"

"We do not," the six replied without a trace of humor. "There are only ever one hundred natural stonekin at any given time. Currently, they are scattered far and wide as generals and commanders, holding the line against the undead in other corners of the world."

Fat lot of good that did them here. James was wracking his brain for something else they could ask for that the Bedrock Kings *could* do when the stone monarchs suddenly added, "We cannot transport you to the doorstep of the Dead Mountain, but the Verdancy is within our reach. If we take you to the edge of our enemy's realm, will you crash upon him?"

"Like a fucking rockslide," Tina promised, pounding her fists together.

James winced at her rude choice of words, but as with everything else Tina did, the Bedrock Kings ate it up.

"Well spoken, little creation!" they cried, their entwined voices humming with satisfaction. "Ready your fleshlings for the fight. We shall open the way!"

The words were barely out of the stone giants' mouths when the chasm James and Tina's rock was sticking out of like a toothpick suddenly rumbled again. Grabbing his sister so he wouldn't fall off, James watched in amazement as new stone rose from the seemingly endless black depths, forming a flat path leading down.

"The Timeless Tunnels are yours," the kings said as the crowd of players crept forward to gawk at the new road, which was as wide as a highway, going down into the ground in front of them. "We have but one last request."

"Go for it," Tina said.

Though still expressionless, James would have sworn that the Bedrock Kings' stone faces grew sad. "We know that you must save the world from He Who Was Once King, but as his followers and former friends, we also beseech you to save him from himself."

"Save the Once King?" Tina repeated, arching a copper eyebrow. "You know the plan is to beat him, blackmail him into doing what we want, and then most likely kill him, right?"

"We know," the towering statues replied, their voices blending into a melancholy chord. "He has earned your ire and your vengeance, but he was our king once. For all that he became our enemy, he never once betrayed us. It was he who said we shouldn't descend from the Unbounded Sky, he who gave up his own freedom to help us once we became trapped here. When we raised our prayers to the heavens for salvation, it was our king who warned us of the Sun's treachery. When it was done, it was he who tended our wounds and tried his best to give us new purpose. Even when we moved on to new lives and new forms, he remained king, endlessly alive and alone. Such is his devotion to his duty."

James stared at them in shock. He'd never heard the Once King described that way, but the stone giants' plea reminded him of what Lilac had said after he and Ar'Bati saved her from the lich's orb. She'd claimed she'd heard the Once King's voice speaking in her head and that he'd apologized. That description had never lined up with anything else James knew of FFO's ultimate end boss, but now the Bedrock Kings—beings who'd literally created stone super-soldiers to fight the undead—also seemed to be asking for leniency, and it just didn't make sense. He had so many questions: Why had the Celestial Elves descended from the Unbounded Sky? Why had the Once King been against it? And where exactly had they descended *to*?

That line of thought brought up yet more mysteries. Long ago, a famous FFO streamer had pointed out that the game world appeared to have no name. This observation had kicked off a frenzy of exploration, data mining, and conspiracy theories as people tried to figure out why a fantasy

135

game lacked such an obvious fantasy element as a world name, but no one had ever found a solid answer. Even the development company had been tight-lipped. James had been too busy frantically leveling to care about the controversy back in the day, but now that he lived here, he realized he'd never heard any of FFO's actual residents refer to their world by name. "Earth" was an English word that had no parallel in Central or any other language he knew. As a Naturalist, James called the magic he cast on dirt and rocks "earth magic," but that was only his brain's translation of the concept. Gray Fang and Thunder Paw always called it "Sculpting the Foundation" or "the Deep Sea of Amber." They'd never used an actual word for the ground they were standing on other than "ground" or "dirt."

The questions were still buzzing in his head when Tina stepped forward.

"What are you talking about?" she demanded, glaring at each of the Bedrock Kings in turn. "Devoted to duty? He *made* the undead! He's working to destroy the world as we speak. That's not something a good king does. He doesn't deserve mercy!"

"He would not take it if you offered," the six replied. "Such is his pride. But it is not entirely his fault. He is as he was made to be: the once and only king."

Tina gritted her teeth in frustration, and the stone giants smiled. "We do not ask you to understand," they said gently. "Only that you promise not to rob him of his dignity or deny him respect in defeat."

"Fine, fine," she grumbled. "I solemnly swear that we'll kick his ass in the politest way possible. So—with that same great politeness—can we go now? If you're dropping us in the Verdancy, that's two extra days of walking we didn't know we'd have to do. If we don't get a move on, there's not going to be any world left to save."

"You speak bluntly and true," said the six, raising their arms in unison. "Go with our blessings, little stonekin. Go and grant him the peace of death."

With that, the six stone giants turned back into six giant rocks. It happened so suddenly this time that James caught himself staring at the crags that had been faces like he still expected it to talk. The unnatural silence of the stones was still there, though, muting the players' nervous chatter as they edged toward the lip of the road the kings had left for them, an immense stone highway leading straight down into the dark. Standing above it on the pillar, James swore he could feel air blowing in and out of the dark like breaths, ruffling his fur with every puff.

"Right," Tina said, her voice only shaking a little as she stared into the void. Then, as always, she pulled it together.

"Okay, everyone!" she yelled, hopping off her pillar onto the new road. "Don't act like it's your first time walking into a giant magical cave that looks like it's going to eat you. *March!*

No one laughed at her joke, but they did obey, shuffling after Roxxy into the dark. Summoning a ball of glowing water so he wouldn't trip and break his nose, James crept after her as well, though he was very relieved when Ar'Bati emerged from the crowd to join him.

"Well done, James," his brother said, grinning into the dark. "The rocks have given us a sally! Onward to the death of our enemy!"

James shook his head in awe. "Do you *ever* feel fear, Fangs?"

"Of course," his brother said. "But fear is useless. Bloodlust makes a far better marching partner." He nodded hungrily at the wall of impenetrable darkness ahead of Roxxy's looming shape. "Think of it. At the end of this tunnel, our oldest enemy waits, vulnerable and alone. How can I be afraid when I know I will soon sink my blade into the Once King's neck?"

"Never thought of it that way," James replied, unsure if that advice did anything for him. It was, however, *very* Fangs-like, which amused him enough to keep the worst of the panic at bay as the sun vanished overhead.

"Don't dawdle!" Tina yelled over her shoulder at the crowd. "The faster we walk, the sooner we get out of here and on to punching the Once King in the face. Game clock's running. Chop chop!"

With much grumbling and trepidation, the players crept on. As they went forward, the wide tunnel they were following constricted and curved downward sharply, just like a throat. That was an observation James *really* could have done without, so he decided to focus on the little ball of glowing water he'd formed above his staff, pointedly ignoring how the circle of light it shed at his feet was *way* smaller than it should have been.

They walked for what felt like a very long time. How long exactly was hard to say. He'd often heard of caves referred to as "timeless," but this was insane. The moment the daylight from the mouth of the tunnel behind them vanished, James was suddenly unable to say if he'd been down here for an hour or a day or a century. Clearly, the Timeless Tunnels had been well named.

Fortunately, there was no chance of getting lost. The tunnel was dark as pitch, but it had no turns or forks. It simply went endlessly down, the stone walls eating the noise of the raid instead of bouncing it back as they should. Some players tried to chat, and Cinco even tried to strike up a bawdy marching song, but the silence of the place won in the end. With no way to talk and nothing to see, James was left alone with what was inside his own head, and soon he was lost in thoughts of home.

He could already see himself waking up in a hospital and trying to explain to his parents what had happened. He was certain they wouldn't believe him, but they'd have no choice once all the other players who returned started telling corroborating stories. The knowledge that he'd lose his magic when he went back was already making him depressed, but James hoped he'd get to keep his knowledge of FFO's languages. How cool would it be to be fluent in two tongues that were completely alien to Earth? Not that he could do anything with that knowledge except document the languages for linguists, but it would still be cool to help preserve and study them.

Not that he'd be needed for that, of course. There'd be plenty of other, much more educated former players to study languages and tell the story of what had happened here. Once the novelty faded, James would go back to being just another face in the crowd. A deeply in debt face with no degree and no prospects.

His shoulders slumped in the dark. Who was he kidding? Coming back from getting stuck into a game wasn't special when you were one of thousands. It didn't matter if he could still speak of Wind and Grass or not; he'd still be a loser working three minimum-wage jobs seventy hours a week just to make his rent and debt payments. *That* was what he was fighting so hard to return to: thirty more years of being a slave to his past self's stupidity. If it hadn't meant sticking his parents with his debts, James would have stayed in this world in a heartbeat. He had family here, and friends. The nameless world of FFO was the only place in the universe he'd actually managed to do things right. But even he wasn't *that* irresponsible. He'd made his mess, and he'd go home and fix it. It was the least he could do after screwing up his family's—and Tina's—lives so spectacularly.

But even knowing that he was doing the right thing did little to lessen the crushing weight on James's shoulders as he marched endlessly through the dark. Oddly, he didn't appear to be the only one. Everyone looked glum and introspective as they shuffled on and on and on until, without warning, the sound returned.

It felt like taking off a pair of noise-canceling headphones. All at once, the oppressive dark and quiet vanished, replaced with the bright glow of player armor and the loud echo of voices bouncing off walls as they normally did. The moment they realized it was over, the army of players burst into relieved chatter, filling the cave with whoops and crude jokes about holes. Tina yelled at everyone to quiet down and pointed ahead, which was when James noticed the eternally downward-sloping road was now going *up*.

He surged forward. Sure enough, there was a light in front of them. A cold, gloomy gray one that reminded him of winter clouds, but it was still daylight. The air smelled different as well, a cold ashy scent very different from the wet, mineral-y cave-scent of the Timeless Tunnels. He was breathing through his nose to get a better sense of it when the road they'd been following abruptly ended, dumping them out at the base of the tallest mountains James had ever seen.

"Hey!" someone yelled excitedly. "We're in the pass to the Deadlands!"

James was almost trampled as the rest of the raid rushed toward the gray daylight. He jumped to the side, shielding his eyes against the light that—though dim for morning—was still blinding after the dark. Even after his eyes adjusted, though, his brain had a hard time making sense of what they were seeing. He'd been to the Deadlands countless times back in the game, but seeing them in person, for real, was another experience entirely.

The raid was standing at the mouth of a lifeless mountain pass. Behind them, far, far down the crumbling gray slope, James could just barely make out the bright-green treetops of the Verdancy. That was the only color, though. Everything else around them was gray—gray rocks, gray trunks of long-dead trees, gray dust swirling up to low gray clouds. There was so much monotonous gray blending together that he almost missed the giant stone fortress blocking their path forward.

He had no idea *how*. The building was enormous, a manmade cliff of once-white, now gray-stained stone that blocked the entire pass between the mountains. On top of the walls, between the swirls of gray ash, James spotted banners of the Holy Sun fluttering from the battlements. There were soldiers up there as well, tiny figures wearing dusty but still faintly gleaming golden armor.

They must have spotted the players at the same time James saw them, because all the little armored figures on the walls started to scramble as he watched. Horns sounded next, sending sharp alarm calls echoing off the mountains as bowmen flooded onto the walls. Behind him, the player army drew their weapons in reply, but Tina waved them down.

"Relax," she said, striding purposefully down the pass toward the walls. "I got this."

"What does she have against a fortress?" Fangs snarled in his ear. James had no idea, but he had a feeling they were about to find out.

*I*t's like déjà vu all over again.

Tina stomped up the mountain pass toward the fortress of the Order of the Golden Sun. Up on the battlements, soldiers wearing the Order's golden tabard were freaking out and pointing their bows at her *again*. Not that Tina could blame them. She'd just led two full raids of players out of the side of a mountain on their flank. Of *course* they were in a panic. She just hoped no one got spooked enough to do something stupid before she could explain.

"*Players!*" someone shouted in a panicked voice from the wall.

Tina's jaw ticked in annoyance. Seriously? This again? She'd thought they'd at least be able to recognize the world's only female stonekin who wore full Dead Mountain tanking gear, especially after how hard she'd saved their asses not a week ago. She was about to yell at them to stop being insulting when CincoDeMurder jogged up to join her, his face grim.

"Those fucking rocks," he swore, his eyes locked on the wall bristling with bowmen. "They dropped us right on the Order's doorstep. We gotta find cover. I remember the Order's NPCs hit like girls, but with that many arrows, it won't matter. We're going to get pincushioned."

"Don't worry," Tina said, hopping up on a nearby rock. "It's all under control."

"How is *that* under control?" Cinco snarled, stabbing an armored finger at the battlements, which were getting more packed by the second.

Rather than waste more time explaining, Tina took a deep breath, drawing on the full capacity of her stonekin's booming voice as she cupped her hands around her mouth. "Hey up there!" she bellowed. "It's cool, we're friendlies! Go tell Garrond that the Roughnecks are back!"

Her shout echoed off the towering mountains, the words bouncing down the pass loudly enough to be heard all the way to the Verdancy. Up on the battlements, not a single weapon was lowered. A guard did run off, though, which Tina decided was good enough.

"You know these guys?" Cinco asked as she lowered her hands.

"'Course I know them," she said proudly. "Remember that epic fight against Grel'Darm we keep telling you about? This is where it happened." She nodded at the imposing fortress. "They know us just fine. I'm just hoping Garrond has gotten over being pissy at me for demolishing the front of his fort enough to let us back in."

"Hopefully? Demolished?" Cinco repeated, his brown eyes roving nervously over the crowded battlements. "You sure like to leave big footprints, don't you?"

"Size twenty-two, man," Tina replied, leaning down to rap her armored knuckles against her metal boot. "I don't do anything small."

Cinco arched a bushy black eyebrow at that. Before he could say anything else, though, the crowd on top of the wall parted, and a massive man in gleaming white-and-gold armor stepped onto the battlements.

"Why have you returned to my fortress?" Commander Garrond boomed from the walls. "Have you decided to accept my offer and join the Order of the Golden Sun?"

"Sorry, but we're not becoming paladins today," Tina shouted back, waving her arm at the army of top-geared players behind her. "But we *are* here to kill the Once King. Mind opening the doors and letting us into the Deadlands? Our ride dropped us off on the wrong side of your fort."

It was a really bum deal that they were so far away. Tina would have given an arm to see Garrond's face after that one. But while she couldn't see if she'd made the eternally grumpy commander crack a smile, his voice sounded more excited than she'd ever heard him before when he shouted back.

"If that's the case, then you are very welcome!" He turned back to his men. "Open the gates! The Roughnecks have returned!"

Tina let out a quiet breath of relief as the fort's huge wood-and-iron back doors began to open. The rest of her raid wasn't nearly so tactful. They whooped in surprise and delight, talking loudly about ungrateful, trigger-happy NPCs who'd *better* open those doors. Thankfully, they didn't have giant stonekin voices, and their impolitic comments were quickly drowned out by the crunch of hundreds of armored boots as the army made its way down the pass toward the now-open gates.

Despite Garrond's warm welcome, Tina was still half expecting to find the entire Order arrayed to trap them again. When they entered the fortress this time, though, the tall commander met her on foot with only a dozen of his soldiers. Everyone else was busy.

Only the side of the Order Fortress that faced the Deadlands had a double gate. The back door to the Verdancy opened directly into the fort's inner courtyard, which was even crazier and more busy than the last time Tina had been here. She couldn't see the front of the base, so she had no idea what Garrond had done with the collapsed gate-keep or the rubble pile they'd left Grel'Darm's body buried under, but the commander had definitely been busy. In addition to the soldiers coming down from the battlements, the yard was packed with the scores of covered wagons and ready troops waiting to muster out.

"What's with the wagon train?" Tina asked as Garrond walked up to her. "You guys going on safari?"

"It is good to see you as well," Garrond said dryly, nodding to the wagons. "And those are for our campaign. Three days ago, my scouts reported that all signs of movement within the Dead Mountain Fortress had ceased. We dread to think where they went, but so far as we can tell, the Once King's stronghold now sits empty. The legends say that the Enemy of All Life cannot leave his fortress or the ghostfire for long, if at all. If he is truly alone in there, then we would be fools to waste this chance."

Tina chuckled. "Great minds think alike. We're also here to take advantage of the fact that the Once King's home alone."

Garrond's eyes narrowed skeptically. "I usually regret asking you for explanations, but how is that possible? I sent your raid to Bastion. How did you get back here so quickly? And how did you know of the enemy's situation?"

"Well," Tina said, looking back at her army. "About that..."

***

It took an hour of explaining and several corroborating witnesses, but eventually, Tina got Garrond to believe that she really had been sent here by King Gregory in a Hail Mary play to save the world. Once the commander got that straight in his giant raid-boss head, though, he'd launched into action with impressive efficiency. That was how, not three hours later, Tina found herself at the head of an honest-to-god army.

"This is so fucking sweet," she said, breathing in the Deadlands' dusty air as she led the raiders—and two *thousand* of Garrond's Order soldiers—through the ruins that had once been the Order Fortress's front gate. "Does anyone else feel the pure fucking awesome that is this moment?"

"I gotta say, I did not see this coming," CincoDeMurder confessed, looking over his shoulder at the glittering holy army behind them. "It's boss as hell, though."

It was more than boss. They had two full raids of top-geared players, *all* the soldiers of the Order—who were the best undead-killing NPCs in the game—and an entire wagon train of the supplies, tents, and skilled artisans needed to keep it all rolling. They also had their very own level-eighty-two, four-skull paladin *badass*, which was the cherry on top. The commander's stats were almost as good as Gregory's, but unlike the Teddy Bear King, Garrond had the guts to actually use them. The salty old man looked ready to take on the Once King with nothing but his teeth. Truly, it did not get better than this.

"I can't believe it's really happening!" Tina said giddily, hopping over the rubble pile that was all that remained of their epic fight with Grel'Darm. "Something is *actually* going right for once!" She cracked her huge stone knuckles. "I'm soooooo ready to get some revenge on this place! We're gonna pulverize everything and anything undead that stands between us and that mountain."

"Save some for us, killer," Cinco said, bumping her shoulder playfully.

Tina pushed him away. "No way. I call dibs on everything. It's payback time! Roughnecks to the front!"

Grinning evilly, Tina ignored Cinco's eye-roll and jogged ahead, leading her guild to the front of the pack as they crossed the cratered battlefield where they'd beaten the first army the Once King had sent after them. Seeing all those smashed siege engines filled her with joy and a renewed sense that the momentum was *finally* on their side. Even the cold dust that was already working its way into the joints of her armor couldn't bring down her good mood as Tina led the glittering column down the broken road and into the long, narrow, claustrophobic valley that led to the Dead Mountain.

To her great dismay, they saw no undead in the first hour of marching. They were close to the Order's patrol area, though, so she didn't think too much of it, and she didn't let down her guard. She aggressively sent out five-person hunter-killer teams ahead of the main army with orders to smash anything that moved without a pulse. But despite everyone's eagerness to kill something evil, all the teams came back empty-handed.

As morning turned to afternoon, Tina stopped dispatching squads and went back to the far more efficient—but much more boring—tactic of using Rangers and Assassins as scouts instead. She kept a team of grade-A ass kickers assembled and waiting, though, all of them holding their weapons and walking right behind her for the ambush she *knew* had to be waiting around one of the jagged, rocky bends.

But it never came. The army marched in nervous silence made all the more ominous by the sheer desolation of this place. For her part, Tina couldn't decide if the state of things was good or bad. The empty zone reeked of a trap, but while she looked at every cliff and cave as if it might disgorge the entire contents of the Deadlands' patrols on top of her head, she never spotted so much as a single skeleton.

It was enough to make anyone paranoid. The first day of marching ended without a single sword swing, but Tina felt like she'd been in a fight since dawn. Too agitated to sleep and stuck in a body that didn't really require such niceties anyway, Tina volunteered to take the role of night watch commander so the softer, fleshier leaders could rest. She paced and checked sentries all through the dark, freezing night, but when the weak dawn finally broke over the mountains, all was still eerily quiet. Even the vultures were gone.

As the second day's march got moving, they passed the wooded hill where Grel'Darm had ambushed the Roughnecks what felt like forever ago. Everyone avoided looking as they passed, but Tina couldn't help looking through the clump of dead trees for the crater the raid boss's giant club had left in the ground—the crater that probably still held David's crushed remains.

We got your revenge, David, she thought wistfully, looking up at the eternally cloudy sky no sunlight had ever penetrated. *I hope you saw it.*

There was no reply, of course. Just the wind and the scrape of armored boots as the army wound its way down the cracked road.

At least they made good time. Tina was amazed at how the miles flew by when everyone had food and water, didn't have to fight random undead, and were all following orders. Garrond's troops couldn't move as fast as the ultra-geared players, but even with the Order slowing things down, the second day's traveling ended just a few miles shy of the Dead Mountain Fortress's front gate. They made camp in the black mountain's towering shadow, trying not to look too hard at the barren, sky-high slopes

147

crisscrossed with endless battlements and twinkling cauldrons of ghostfire. Even trying to avoid it, though, there was no denying that their suspicions appeared to be correct.

Every other time Tina had stood on this plain, the giant mountain dominating her view had been covered in undead. Flying undead, climbing undead, huge patrols of undead soldiers marching on the battlements. This time, though, there was nothing. The mountain was as still and empty as every other bit of the Deadlands they'd walked through, and while that was the entire reason they were here, seeing it with her own eyes made Tina more nervous than ever.

She didn't sleep the second night, either. Instead, she stayed up and studied the fortress, going so far as to borrow Garrond's spyglass just to make sure she wasn't missing anything. After months of raiding, she knew that stupid mountain inside and out. There were plenty of rooms she couldn't see, but from the outside, at least, it really did look empty. A couple times, she thought she saw something in the shadows behind the giant pillars of blue-white fire that lined the upper battlements, but she was never able to tell for sure. She was certain, however, that the same couldn't be said for them. They were an army camping in his front yard. The Once King *had* to know they were here. He was undoubtedly watching them at this very moment from his terrace on the mountain's peak, but no matter how many times she looked, Tina never saw him.

Finally, dawn came. As the gray sky began to lighten, Tina, Cinco, and Garrond gathered in the large command tent the Order had set up at the center of camp to plan their attack. Since moving everything would take too much time, they made the decision to leave all the supply wagons and tents here. The army would march the last few miles to the fortress with only basic backpacks containing the food and water they'd need for today. Once they took the bottom of the fortress, they'd move their camp inside the walls to continue the siege from there. Assuming this siege took more than one day, of course.

148

After that, there wasn't much left to discuss. Everyone had been up and ready since first light, so Tina took the lead again, marching their army down the last few miles of crumbling road to the mountain. When they reached the broken stretch where the Roughnecks had first woken up after the transition, Tina saw that the enormous black doors to the raid dungeon were closed tight. That was a new development. Every time she'd been here in the game, the gates had been open to allow the armies of skeleton patrols to walk through. She didn't think doors were going to be a problem for their group, but the unexpected change made her wary as they crept closer through the heavy silence.

When they were less than a hundred feet from the heavy doors with their carved skulls and ghostfire sconces, Tina lifted her fist to bring the army to a halt. The Roughnecks lined up in an orderly rectangle to her left, while Red Sands stopped in perfect rows to her right. Behind them, rank upon rank of golden Order soldiers waited. Over the rustling jingle of heavy armor, the *tick-tick* of catapult cranks could be heard as the Order's siege weapons were loaded and aimed at the mountain's empty battlements.

"Okay," Tina told her troops, her booming voice feeling both too loud and too small for the huge, silent fortress behind her. "This is it. Time to knock on hell's door and—"

A chorus of gasps interrupted her. Hands shot up from the orderly ranks of players to point at something over her head. Stomach clenching, Tina pulled her sword and whirled around, scanning the courtyard and the battlements. But the enemy wasn't on the battlements or at the door.

He was in the sky.

A lone figure was gliding through the dusty gray air above the mountain. He flew as silently as an owl but graceful as only an elf could be. Clad in glittering black armor that looked unsettlingly similar to her own sun steel tanking set, the figure should have been far too heavy for flight, but the weight didn't seem to bother him at all. He swooped down as lightly as a falling feather, his huge ash-gray wings spreading to check his speed as he alighted on the broken steps right in front of the fortress's closed doors, less than a hundred feet away.

Tina took an involuntary step back. The winged elf was enormous. Not as big as Grel, but definitely taller than King Gregory. Bigger than her for sure, and just as heavily armored. An elegantly curved sword of Eclipsed Steel hung from his hip, but the last Celestial Elf did not draw it. He simply stood at the gate, his flawlessly beautiful face lit by the ghoulish, bluish light of the ghostfire braziers as he gazed down on them, his thin lips curled in a slight, sad smile.

"Welcome," he said, his voice somehow soft and booming at the same time, filling the valley that his mountain dead-ended. "To the end of this miserable world."

Tina gripped her blade hard, her breathing coming so fast she would have hyperventilated if she'd still been human. Shit. *Shit.* Behind her, she could feel the fear spreading through her raid as they all came to the same realization, but no one panicked. That detail didn't escape the Once King.

"I commend you all for facing your fate so bravely," he said, his slight smile widening. "Surrender now, and I promise your deaths will be painless."

"Not likely," Tina growled, pulling hard on all the bravado she could muster as she stepped forward and pointed her sword at the winged elf's chest. "I am Roxxy of the Roughnecks, and we didn't come here to surrender."

The Once King looked down at her, a novel experience for a stonekin. "I remember you," he said, his voice amused. "Of all the children who made a game of the Nightmare, you faced me the most tenaciously." His lips quirked. "Foolish girl. How many times have you lain dead at my feet? You should know better than any that you cannot defeat me. Why do you waste your people's lives? You know it is hopeless." He waved his black-gauntleted hand at her army. "Abandon this act of desperation, and I will send the ghostfire to consume your souls and set you free from this shackled eternity."

Tina's answer to that was a bloodthirsty grin. The Once King remembered her! Sure, he remembered *beating* her, but that was only because the bullshit game mechanics had been on his side. Tina had the missing piece now, though. She had One For All, she had an army, and she was going to use both of them to shove those haughty words right back down his graceful throat.

"Big talk from a king who's home alone in an empty castle," she yelled back, lifting her own voice until it boomed off the barren slopes just as loudly as his. "You gonna flap back up to your roost, or are you going to step out here and save us the trouble of digging you out of your nest?"

She knew he'd say no. What boss would agree to fight his challengers on an open field where they could fully use their advantage of numbers? But she needed to show her people—and herself—that she wasn't afraid. She didn't know why the Once King had decided to come out and talk to them, but Tina fully expected him to throw a few more threats in their direction and fly back to safety. That would have been the smart thing to do, so she was shocked when the Once King drew his sword instead.

The black Eclipsed Steel blade burst into brilliant blue-white ghostfire the moment it left its sheath. The flare of it was so bright after the dimness of the Deadlands that Tina was forced to shield her eyes. When she could see again, the Once King had taken a step forward.

"I do not need my army to face such a small threat," he said, pointing his flaming blade at her. "I showed you great respect just now, Roxxy of the Roughnecks. I gave you the chance to save your people. But it is ever the burden of a king to do what others can't. If you are not wise enough to free your followers from the shackles of life, then I will do it for you."

With that, the towering elf fanned his ash-gray wings wide and lifted back into the air.

Holy shit! Tina thought as he rose. That was just supposed to be pregame smack talk. The boss wasn't supposed to come at them *now*. But he was plunging straight at her, which meant they were really about to do this. Right now.

"Plan A, everyone!" she bellowed, yanking her shield up. *"Go! Go! Go!"*

Her yells snapped the players out of their shock, and the ranks behind her broke into chaos. The Roughnecks leaped forward to get into position around her while Cinco's Red Sands bolted for the crumbling old walls on the roadside for cover. Tina couldn't tell if Garrond's troops were following the plan and fanning out to surround the area, but she didn't dare take her eyes off the enemy to check. Her vision was filled with the Once King as he surged forward. He dove at her from the gray sky like a falcon, his ghostfire-wreathed sword leaving a glowing trail in the air behind him as he aimed it straight for her head.

"Frank!" she screamed, hunkering down.

Her fellow tank was at her side in an instant. Just like in their training, Tina slammed her shield into the ground and wedged her shoulder against Frank's to lock their guards. *"Steady Ground!"* they called out in unison as the ashy soil beneath their boots turned to bedrock, anchoring the two tanks in place. A split second later, the unstoppable force that was FFO's most powerful five-skull slammed into their shield wall.

Their armor screamed under the impact, and an explosion of ghostfire blew sky high, turning the bottoms of the low clouds from gray to ghostly white. For a horrible moment, Tina was sure her shield was about to disintegrate from the pressure, but the divine sun steel held together, splitting the attack into a Y of shockwaves that roared out behind them, pulverizing the road and knocking scores of Order soldiers over like bowling pins.

It rattled Tina as well. Even with her shield directing the force around her, the impact of the Once King's hit was still enough to rattle her around inside her armor like a nut in a shell. A few days ago, that would have left her staggering, but she'd learned over and over during the practice fights with Gregory that the five-skulls didn't daze like she did. If she

152

staggered or flinched, showed any weakness at all, it was over, so she sucked up the hit and stood firm, waiting behind her defense until, at last, an elegant hand wrapped in glittering black armor slid into her view to grab the lip of her shield.

Tina whipped her shield out of the way and lurched backward. The Once King's burning blade shot through the opening she'd left only to land on Frank's shield as he stepped into the gap with practiced precision, freeing Tina to whirl around and bash her giant bulwark into the Once King's now undefended right side. Killbox moved at the same time, attacking with his giant ax from the king's swordless left. Meanwhile, ZeroDarkness and SilentBlayde emerged halfway from the shadows at the king's feet, their long blades going for his hamstrings.

It all went beautifully. The five of them came together even faster than they had during practice, but quick as they'd been, their attack hit only air. With a blast of his giant wings, the Once King launched up and backward, escaping their trap to land safely fifty feet away.

As his black boots touched down gracefully in the dust, despair hit Tina like a punch in the gut. That had been one of their best combos against Gregory, and they hadn't even scratched him. She was starting to wonder if his bravado earlier hadn't been just talk—if they really *were* totally outmatched—when the king lifted his face, and she saw his eyes were wide with surprise. It was just a flash, a momentary crack before the mask of haughtiness slammed back into place, but it was enough.

"*HA!*" she cried, pointing her sword at him. "Almost got ya, didn't we? How's it feel now that you don't have bullshit game mechanics to hide behind?"

"You are rash," the Once King replied, sheathing his sword in the blink of an eye. "As you have been freed of the Nightmare's arbitrary limitations, so too have I."

He raised his hands as he spoke. Behind him, all the ghostfire in the fortress followed the motion, the blue-white flames shooting high from their

153

sconces, leaping up to meet their king. As the undead fire flared, the Once King's hands began to glow bright purple, and Tina's heart stopped. She knew that casting animation. It had been beaten into her subconscious over countless nights of wipes and defeats. This time, though, she knew what to do.

"*It's the Million Damage Blast!*" she yelled, shoving Frank out of the way as she charged ahead. "I've got it! Get ready to rez me!"

The Once King didn't move as she ran at him, sliding to a halt practically on top of his feet. The king was even taller up close, his head a solid two feet above Roxxy's already impressive eight. But though she was now close enough to stab him without even stretching, the Once King didn't even flinch.

"Foolish child," he said, his deep voice strained from the effort of controlling the enormous magic flaring in his hands. "Raise Ally will not undo this damage. Even Garrond cannot save you."

The Once King's calm words poured ice into her veins, but Tina refused to step back. This was it. It had come much faster than she'd expected, but this was the moment they'd trained for. All those times she'd been burned learning Fiona's technique, all her promises to Gregory and the Roughnecks and herself. This was it. If she couldn't take this hit, it was over, so Tina swallowed her fear and slammed her shield down practically on top of the Once King's toes, roaring her defiance in his face.

"Earthen Fortitude!" she bellowed. And then, "*One For All!*"

The gloating look vanished from the Once King's face. "How do you know that technique?"

Tina's answer was a cocky grin, because the flaring magic in his hands had already reached its unstoppable crescendo. She was lifting her finger to flick him off one last time when she heard a familiar voice screaming over the roar.

"Tina, *no!*" SilentBlayde cried, his terrified voice somewhere to her right. "*It's the wrong color!*"

154

With those words, Tina's confidence collapsed, because he was right. The casting motion was the same as what she remembered, but the Million Damage Blast was made from ghostfire, which meant it glowed *blue*-white. This spell was purple, which was a color she'd never seen the Once King use before.

Shit.

The king smiled cruelly as the realization dawned on Tina's face. It was the wrong spell. She'd used One For All on the *wrong spell*. She didn't even know what this one did, but it was far too late to escape. Violet energies were already erupting from the Once King's hands. The pulse was bright enough to light up the entire valley, huge enough to hit every person in her army before One For All grabbed it by the horns and turned it back around, forcing the enormous magic into a single spear aimed right at her.

As it turned, all Tina could think about was how much bigger this was than Richard's Fire Tornado. Grabbing that spell had felt like catching an out-of-control fire hose. This was like trying to wrestle the sea. But while Tina was more sure than ever that she'd fucked up, she didn't dare let the spell go. It might not be the MDB, but whatever the purple magic did, she was certain it meant the Roughnecks no good, which meant it was her job to stop it. She just hoped someone was waiting with a rez, because this was going to *hurt*.

That was Tina's last thought before the iron grip of One For All crashed the valley-sized spell down on top of her. As the purple energy flooded into her body, her insides went *wham*, then *spin*, then *wham* again, turning the world to blurry slush as Tina slid into the dark.

***

This couldn't be happening.

SilentBlayde blinked furiously to clear the purple flash from his eyes as he scrambled over the broken ground toward Tina. With every step, he reminded himself that this was the plan. Even if she'd grabbed the wrong spell, she'd told the raid to expect this. The healers knew. They were probably casting a resurrection right this moment. That knowledge was little comfort when he was running over stones that had been turned to sand by the Once King's blast, but he clung to it anyway, because it was all he had. His mission now was to get Tina's body away from the Once King so the healers could do their job, but when his eyes finally cleared enough to see what was actually in front of him, the sight that waited knocked all those plans clean out of his head.

When he'd last seen Tina, before the blast went off, she'd been standing in front of the Once King as strong and defiant as a mountain. Now, though, he saw nothing. The Once King was still there—doubled over from the impact of the spell but still clearly up and kicking—but the road in front of him was empty. All that was left of the place where Tina had made her stand was a blackened crater with a glittering heap of sun steel armor at the bottom.

Empty armor.

The world slowed to a crawl. In the crater, the golden armor that had once held Roxxy clattered on the dusty ground. Her shield fell on top of it as he watched, the huge length of the tower toppling over like a felled tree. It was still crashing onto the pile when he dashed forward, moving faster than he'd ever moved before.

But still not fast enough. He reached the armor before the shield hit the ground, but it didn't matter, because Tina wasn't there. Just empty pieces of metal clattering on the ground like a shed husk. Above him, the Once King groaned and sagged, staring at the empty armor as if he didn't know what to make of it either. Then, suddenly, he laughed.

"So that's who you really are," he whispered in a quiet, amused voice. "Not what I expected of the Roughnecks' great leader."

There was more, but SilentBlayde couldn't hear it over his pounding heart. He'd never known such terror or despair as he did at that moment, digging through the heavy golden armor for any sign of Tina. She *had* to be there. Even if she was crushed, there had to be something they could resurrect. Something he could save. She couldn't be gone. He refused to accept it.

She couldn't really be gone.

That thought sent his panic to nearly debilitating levels. Almost from the moment he'd met Tina when they were both level one, he'd been enamored. The infatuation that had sparked that first day in Bastion had quickly flared into an impossible love. For seven years, his entire life had revolved around being with Tina as much as possible, because he knew their time was limited. She wasn't trapped like him. He'd always known she'd eventually move on from FFO, get busy with a career and out-of-game responsibilities, maybe even start a family. He'd lived in constant dread of the day she'd get on and tell him she'd gotten a boyfriend, or didn't get on at all. Dreaded the day he would lose her.

The transition had saved him from all of that. SilentBlayde had supported Tina's efforts to go home because supporting her was what he did, but he'd always known their efforts to find a way back had been little more than grasping at straws. That was why he'd come back to the Roughnecks even when everyone had told him to leave. He knew if he could just stay in her life long enough, he'd find a way to salvage things eventually. They were finally both together in the same place, and he loved her so much. There *had* to be a way to fix the damage he'd done in Bastion. He'd just needed more time to figure it out.

But now, in one purple flash, all that time was gone. Above him, the Once King was retreating, staggering back from Tina's crater to his fortress. It was the weakest the elf had ever looked, but the thought of chasing him for a finishing blow never even entered Blayde's mind. He was too busy clawing through Tina's armor, shoving the hundred-pound, stonekin-sized pieces aside for a sign—*any* sign—that what his eyes were telling him was wrong.

Dimly, in the distance, he saw Frank and Killbox running in to join him, but while he could definitely have used the extra muscle, SB was too frantic to wait. With a shove that took all his strength, he heaved her giant breastplate out of the dust and forced himself to look inside, determined to save what was left of her, even if it was only ashes. But as he stared into the huge cavern of armor that had protected Roxxy's stone chest, he saw something that made his frantic shaking go utterly still.

Inside the curve of the sun steel, curled into a tiny ball of pink and white, was a girl. She was very small, thin as a rail, and barely five feet tall with fine curly hair that surrounded her head like a chestnut storm cloud. Her face was turned away from him, but that didn't matter. SB would know her anywhere. It was Tina. Not Roxxy but **Tina**: The real, beautiful, flesh-and-blood person.

By this point, several more Roughnecks had run up to join him. Ignoring the chaos of their shouted questions, Blayde reached into the armor with shaking hands, his eyes wide with a hope so desperate and terrifying it hurt. When he slid his trembling fingers under her, her bare skin was soft and so warm he could feel it even through his gloves. Her chest moved as he watched, her narrow ribcage rising and falling with her breath. The movement made his own chest ache, because she was alive. Tina was *alive*.

And very, very naked.

Too relieved to be embarrassed, SB tore the cloak from his shoulders and wrapped it around her body. She was so short the red silk half cape covered her all the way to her knees. Lifting her gently, he pulled her into his arms next, cradling her body against his as he scrambled out of the crater. He had to get Tina away from here. He didn't know if the fight was over or if the Once King had just temporarily stepped back, but he had to get her away from him. She was so small. So delicate and mortal and *not* made of stone. He could already feel the warmth leaving her body as the cold of the Deadlands crept in, making her shiver violently. Clutching her shape protectively to his, SB was about to turn and bolt when someone caught his arm.

158

He whirled around to see Frank's pale face. He was about to order the tank to let go of him when a long shadow fell over them both. Curling his body around Tina's, SB raised his head to see that the Once King had jumped back up to the mountain's lowest ring battlements. That was still way too close, but the king no longer looked in the mood for a fight. He actually looked like he was having trouble staying upright, gripping the stone for support with one armored hand as he sneered down at them.

"It seems that fate favors no one this day," he said, his booming voice clearly straining not to wobble. "Very well, then. We shall have our battle in the way of the game after all. If you can make it through my fortress in one piece, I will deign to fight you all again. Until then, think on my offer. Your deaths are inevitable, but I am always glad to free a soul from suffering. You do not have to endure this world. When we meet again, I will grant you peace."

With that, the Once King turned with a dramatic swish of his feathery wings and walked away. There was no magic, no dramatic launch. He just strode back into the battlements, his motions stiff as if he were trying to hide a limp as he vanished into the fortifications of the Dead Mountain.

When he was gone, SilentBlayde gave the order he'd been dying to give all morning. "Roughnecks, retreat!"

The words rang clear and loud through the shocked silence, but nobody moved. Instead, the raid looked at Zen, whom SB hadn't even noticed was standing less than a foot away.

The Ranger looked like death. Gray ash coated her dark skin, and there was blood dripping through her green hair from a wound on her temple, which surprised him. He hadn't seen Zen get hit, but then, he hadn't been paying attention to anything except Tina. Maybe it *was* a good thing he'd been demoted, because even now, he didn't care about her wounds or the rest of the raid. All he cared about was getting Tina to safety. He was about to carry her away when Zen grabbed his arm.

"Fuck," she whispered, her green eyes wide as she stared at the small, naked girl fiercely guarded by SB's arms and cloak. "Is that—"

He nodded, and the Ranger swore again. "We're retreating!" she cried, looking over her shoulder at the stunned raid. "Everyone fall back to camp!"

No one argued, not even Garrond. As quickly as they'd rolled up, the army retreated from the front of the Dead Mountain. As the crowd started to move, Zen put her hand on Frank's shoulder. "Get her gear," she said quietly, tilting her head at the glittering pile of Tina's legendary armor on the ground.

Frank nodded and hunched over, gathering Tina's things into his arms. It was so huge that Killbox had to help as well. When the two of them had picked it all up, Zen motioned for everyone to follow her back to the protective circle of the Roughnecks.

SB's poor, overworked heart clenched in appreciation. While Red Sands and Garrond's troops had beat a hasty retreat, the Roughnecks had moved in closer to form a wall. When Zen gave the order to move out, Blayde found himself surrounded by a ring of his fellow officers, which he would have found comforting if they hadn't slowed him down. It wasn't that they were dragging their feet—everyone was so eager to get away from the Once King that they were practically running—but no one could move as fast as he could, and Tina's body was getting colder by the second. His cloak wasn't anywhere near thick enough for the biting cold of the Deadlands, and she was so *small*. So tiny and fragile and vulnerable, her breaths coming in little puffs through the gap in the cloth that covered her face. He was picking up the pace when she shifted slightly in his arms, pressing her nose against his chest as she burrowed for warmth.

It got harder to think after that. He was dimly aware of Garrond and Cinco shouting orders as they reentered the camp they'd set up at the entrance to the Dead Mountain's valley the previous night, but he didn't really pay attention to the rest of the army. His focus was on Tina's breathing, the irrefutable proof that she was alive.

She was *alive*.

He began to shake again as the relief and wonder he'd felt when he'd first picked her out of the crater crashed over him once more. It still didn't seem possible, but the proof was right there in his arms. Tina wasn't dead. He hadn't lost her forever. She was *here*, not as stone but as her real self. It was a miracle, a true miracle, one of many he'd experienced since this began.

This time, though, Haruto was determined not to waste it.

Chapter 8

James

James scrambled to keep up as the army poured back into camp. He couldn't see SB or Tina through the protective ring of Roughnecks up ahead, but he decided that was a good thing. The rest of the army was on edge enough as it was. The last thing they needed was more chaos before they even knew what had happened.

Thankfully, Tina's head Ranger Zen was on the ball. Not two minutes after they entered camp, she'd commandeered Garrond's command tent and set up a ring of Roughnecks to guard it. SB had already taken Tina inside, so James asked Ar'Bati to help keep watch and went in after him.

Despite being the biggest they'd brought with them, the command tent was still no larger than a standard six-man camping tent from back home. There was enough room to stand up if you weren't a stonekin and stayed toward the center, but it was still cramped, and the canvas sides did little to block the Deadlands' biting wind. By the time James entered, SB had already kicked the wooden folding table covered in maps to the side and laid Tina down on the commander's own wooden cot, the only bed in the entire camp that wasn't a woolen bedroll on the ground. He was covering her in blankets as he knelt at her side, his eyes filled with love and wonder above his mask.

James winced. A week ago, he would have found that touching. Now it just looked like trouble. Sure enough, when he took a step closer, SilentBlayde whirled around, hand falling to his sword. He stopped when he saw who it was, but James put his hands up anyway.

"Easy," he said. "It's just me."

The elf nodded and looked embarrassed, but he didn't move to let James in. He actually scooted even closer to Tina's bedside, and James sighed. *Definitely* trouble.

162

"Okay, I'm here," Zen said, her brusque voice all business as she ducked through the tent flap. "How's she look?"

"Like she's asleep," SB reported, reaching up to brush the curling brown hair out of Tina's face.

"That's better than dead," Zen said, taking off her leather gloves. When her hands were bare, she walked over to the bucket in the corner and started washing them. It looked like hard, cold work with no towel and only a scrap of oil soap, but she kept at it until every nail was scrubbed. When her fingers were finally clean enough to meet her standards, Zen turned around to glare at SB.

"Out."

SilentBlayde didn't move.

"That was not a suggestion," Zen said sharply. "I'm a nurse, remember? I have to examine her."

"I'll keep out of your way," he promised. "But I'm not leaving her."

"That's not your choice," the Ranger snapped. "I know you two are in an 'it's complicated' stage, but right now you're not her boyfriend or her SO or anything else that qualifies you to have a say in her treatment."

"You're not telling James to get out," SB argued.

"James is her brother and a healer!"

"Zen," James said quietly. "Just let him stay."

The Ranger turned her death stare on him. "He has no right to stay with the patient."

"I know," James said quickly. "But this isn't a hospital, and he's not doing any harm. Besides." He dropped his voice to a whisper. "I don't think we're getting him out of here without a fight. Blayde was the top-ranked Assassin back when this was just a game. He wouldn't hurt us, but neither of us is good enough to move him if he doesn't want to be moved. A loyal guard for Tina might be useful right now, anyway, so let's just let him be."

Zen's expression told James exactly how *not cool* she was with that decision, but James was Tina's family, and SB clearly wasn't budging.

"He can stay for guard duty," the nurse said grudgingly, glaring at SB. "But you don't get a say in care, and you have to respect her privacy. Got it?"

SilentBlayde nodded and spun around, putting his back to Tina. When Zen was sure he wasn't peeking, she reached out and folded the covers down to reveal Tina's body.

James winced when he saw her. Not because she looked bad—she actually looked surprisingly good considering what she'd just been through—but he'd gotten so used to seeing her as the giant stone Roxxy. Compared to that, the scrawny girl in the bed looked as fragile as a porcelain doll. He noticed with a pang of guilt that she was even thinner than when he'd seen her at Christmas, a detail Zen didn't miss, either.

"She looks malnourished," the nurse said disapprovingly, placing her finger in the deep hollow of Tina's collarbone. "Is that new?"

"Not really," James admitted. "Tina lives on Pop-Tarts, coffee, and cup ramen, so I don't think this is a result of the Once King if that's what you're asking."

Zen rolled her eyes. "It's a miracle she doesn't have scurvy with a diet like that," she said scornfully, reaching up to check Tina's pulse. "Other than being all bones, though, she seems healthy enough. Heart rate's good, breathing is normal."

"Magically, she looks fine as well," James said, pointing at the lines of glowing blue and green life magic he could see weaving through her. "No trace of ghostfire whatsoever."

They all let out a relieved breath.

"So what is she, then?" Zen asked, her voice uncertain. "I mean, she looks like a normal human to me, but how did she get here?"

That was the million-dollar question. James leaned forward, running his hand—his large, suddenly incredibly alien-looking cat hand—down Tina's cheek to feel the magic inside her. But while everything seemed normal and healthy—none of the dips or disruptions he typically felt in wounded people—she was also remarkably empty.

"She has no mana," he reported. "Or at least if she does, it's so small that I can't see it."

"What does that mean?" SB asked suddenly.

"I don't know," James confessed. "But Roxxy didn't have mana either. No stonekin does, which is why they can't be casters. Humans have it, at least the humans from this world, but Tina's not from this world."

"You think this is her *actual* body, then?" SilentBlayde said excitedly, looking over his shoulder with a clearly determined effort to keep his eyes *only* on James, not the girl on the cot beside him. "As in brought over from Earth?"

"It has to be her real body," Zen said, picking up Tina's arm and turning it over to show James the small bruise on the inside of her elbow. "That's an IV mark. Plus, she smells like a hospital."

"You're sure?" James asked.

"I've worked in hospitals for twenty years," Zen replied scornfully. "I'd know that smell anywhere. Also, there's no isopropyl alcohol in this world, so it's not like she could have picked it up anywhere else." She looked down at Tina with a worried expression. "However she arrived here, she was getting treatment in a modern medical facility no more than an hour ago. That means someone found her body, which is good. The real question, though, is what is she *now*?"

James looked hard at his sister, staring at the lines of power he could see flowing inside her. Even without mana, there was clearly magic inside her, but from what Leylia had said about all worlds being part of the Infinite Sky, that could have been there from Earth. That wasn't what Zen was asking, though. She wanted to know what *everyone* would want to know, which was, was Tina still level eighty?

He was still figuring out how to answer that when a loud shout sounded from outside, and Cinco burst into the tent.

He hadn't made it one step before SB was in front of him, swords in hand. "Get out."

"Holy shit," the huge Berserker said, ignoring the silver sword pressing into his stomach as he leaned over to get a better look at Tina before Zen frantically covered her back up. "It's true."

"Get. *Out.*" Blayde said again, his voice deadly.

"Stuff it, pretty boy," the Berserker snarled, reaching for his own weapon. "This is my army, too. I have a right to know if the mission is fucked or not, and it's looking pretty fucked."

"It's not *fucked*," SilentBlayde said, sneering at the profanity. "Roxxy's still alive!"

Now it was Cinco's turn to sneer. "That's not Roxxy," he said, stabbing his finger at Tina. "*That* is a little girl. Does she even have a level?"

"We don't know," James said, moving to stand between the raging Berserker and his sister. "I haven't figured out how to tell levels yet by looking. We'll just have to wait until she wakes up."

"What's the point?" Cinco snarled. "We're totally screwed! The Once King took the only tank in the world who actually knew how to handle him and turned her into a fucking middle-schooler!"

"She's twenty-one," SB snapped.

"Cinco, stop throwing a fit and think about what you just said," James said at the same time, pointing at his sister. "This isn't just some random female human body. This is Tina. The *real* Tina, as in from *Earth*. Do you get what that means?"

Cinco nodded. "It means we're fucked."

"It means we're *right*," James said, his voice caught between anger and excitement. "This proves that the Once King really is the connection between our worlds! If he could bring Tina's real body over here, then surely he can send us all back home!"

The Berserker looked unconvinced. "*If* we can beat him, which was always a pretty big *if*. Without Roxxy, I'd say it's damn near impossible. She was the most geared tank left on the planet and the only one who had experience fighting the Once King. How the fuck are we supposed to do this without her?"

"You're not," SB said angrily. "She's going to wake up!"

"And then what, huh?" Cinco demanded, sneering at Tina. "She can't tank shit like that. I knew she was small from her video channel, but she barely looks like she's hit puberty. She's not even tall enough to use as cover!"

"There are plenty of female human tanks," SB argued. "And she's taller than a schtumple Knight, and they can tank just fine."

"But does she still have her Knight class abilities?" Zen asked nervously. "Is she even a player anymore, or is she just...human?"

The tent fell silent as everyone looked at James.

"I don't know," he said, rubbing the back of his head. "We *can't* know anything until she wakes up."

"So wake her up," Cinco said, reaching out to grab Tina's shoulder. He barely made it an inch before SB's sword flashed, and the Berserker snatched his hand back with a yelp.

"The hell is your problem?!" Cinco roared, gripping his bleeding hand.

"I said 'don't touch her,'" SB replied with a scathing glare. "She'll wake up when she wakes up. You'll just have to wait."

"Fuck that," the Berserker snapped. "I don't have time for this Sleeping Beauty shit. You saw how the Once King left the fight. Dude is wrecked! We need to be out there kicking him while he's down, not sitting around here."

"Kicking him with what?" Zen demanded. "Roxxy's the only player in the world who's learned the One For All ability. Without her, all it'll take is one MDB and you're dead."

"Secret abilities don't mean shit if the girl using them is too small to fit into her armor," Cinco growled, grabbing a cloth from Garrond's personal effects to wrap around his bleeding hand. "Also, the Million Damage Blast takes a shit-ton of mana, and it doesn't look like the Once King's got any of that left. We need to move before that changes."

He paused, clearly expecting them to agree. When they didn't, his face turned red. "Fine! You idiots can sit here playing mama hen all you want. I'm going to go see if I can scrape a win out of the dirt before we lose our chance."

With a final rude gesture at SB, the leader of the Red Sands turned and stomped out of the tent.

"I'll go keep an eye on him," Zen grumbled, tucking the blanket firmly around Tina. "Nothing more I can do for her without modern equipment, anyway. Let me know when she wakes up, okay?"

"I will," James said, but the Ranger wasn't looking at him. She was watching SB, who was staring at the tent flap with murder in his eyes.

"I'll protect her," he promised, hands on his swords. "I've beaten Shankfest in duels before. If he tries anything, I'll slit his throat."

"Glad to see we're on the same wavelength," Zen said, giving the Assassin one final pointed look before slipping out after Cinco.

James slumped when she was gone. What a disaster this was turning out to be, and he had a bad feeling things were only going to get worse. He wasn't worried about Tina herself—SB looked ready to take on a raid singlehandedly right now—but there was a lot more to being main tank than just the skills. When she got back on her feet, and he was certain she would, there was a lot she still needed to win, and James was going to make certain she had it.

"I'm going out as well," he announced, standing up. "Take care of her, Blayde."

"I'll watch her better than I watch myself."

Considering how badly his friend had been taking care of himself recently, that statement didn't have the weight SB had no doubt intended, but James let it slide. SilentBlayde might be coming off a low period, but if there was anything he could trust the elf with, it was this.

With that, James waved farewell and slipped out of the tent. He'd barely made it past the circle of guarding Roughnecks when Fangs grabbed him.

"Well?" his adopted brother asked.

"She's alive and healthy," James reported. "Beyond that, though…" He shrugged. "We don't know, and we can't know until she wakes up."

Fangs nodded sharply. "And how long will that be?"

James shrugged again. "I've never seen someone dragged between worlds. It took the rest of us about an hour to wake up from the sensory overload when we first got here, so maybe this will be the same, but there's no way to know for sure. But Tina's okay for now. I've left her in SilentBlayde's care. He'll watch out for her."

The head warrior looked skeptical. "Are you sure you can trust that elf? He doesn't seem…reliable."

"Oh yes," James said, remembering the loving, almost worshipful way SB had stared at his sister. "When it comes to protecting Tina, I trust him with my life."

Ar'Bati gaped at him. "James, he *stabbed* you. He stabbed *me*."

"Bad choice of words," James said quickly. "But at the time, he was stabbing us for Tina, so my point still stands."

"If you say so," his brother grumbled. "So what will *we* be doing, then?"

James leaned closer and lowered his voice. "We're going to find her gear. I trust my sister to tank no matter what body she's in, but a lot of her power and toughness comes from the stats provided by her end-game raiding armor. I know the Roughnecks collected it, but I don't trust Cinco as far as I can throw him, so I'm going to go make sure it's safe."

It was the least he could do. Despite all his assurances, James was more afraid for Tina than he'd ever been in his life. The car ride to the hospital after he'd broken her arm when they were kids was nothing compared to this terror. Tina was here, in this world, as *herself*. For all he knew, she was back to being a completely unmagical library sciences undergrad, which meant she could be killed by damage most players would consider a paper cut. That would have been terrifying enough back in Bastion or Windy Lake, but *here*—camped out on the Once King's doorstep, the most dangerous place on the *planet*—it was enough to turn his body to jelly.

"Your sister will be safe," Ar'Bati assured him when he saw his brother trembling. "But may I ask you a question?"

"Sure," James said, striding off. "If you can do it while we walk."

That was a tall request. The camp they'd made last night was just off the main road at the mouth of the valley that dead-ended at the Dead Mountain Fortress. The extra-steep cliffs turned the normally narrow pass into an echo chamber, and the player army had never been more agitated. James didn't think word of Tina's condition was out yet, but everyone had seen her go down in front of the Once King, which meant it was all anyone could talk about. *Loudly.* Most of it was legitimate worry for their leader, but James cringed every time he heard Roxxy's name. Even if Tina did recover fully, would all those players and soldiers follow a general who wasn't an eight-foot-tall stone killing machine? Would they listen at all?

"James?"

"Sorry," he said, looking back at his brother. "You were saying?"

Ar'Bati lashed his tail in annoyance. "I *said* that I saw your sister's true form when the Assassin passed me. She was definitely not what I was expecting. How old is she?"

"Not you too, Fangs," James groaned. "Tina's not a child! She's just short and baby faced. It's a family thing. My real face looks young, too. I'm twenty-eight, and I *still* get carded every time I go out."

Fangs scowled. "Carded?"

"Never mind," James said. "The point is, Tina's a lot more than she appears. People always dismiss her because of how she looks, but she created one of the world's top raiding guilds *and* one of the most popular FFO gamer video channels while she was still in high school. She's not to be underestimated."

"I did not mean to question her honor," Ar'Bati said defensively. "I only asked because you seemed so worried. She is your sister, but you are *my* brother. If your Tina has been robbed of her abilities as a warrior, then we must look after her the same as we would any of our family who was wounded in battle."

James stopped walking, stunned. "Really?"

"Of course!" Fangs said, offended. "The Claw Born look after our own! Tina is your family as you are ours. Of *course* we will care for her. I only asked her age because I needed to know if it would be more appropriate for Father to adopt her as well or to find her a husband."

James had been touched by Fangs's fore-thoughtfulness right up until the H-word. The idea of Rends trying to marry Tina off as a means of "saving" her sent his hackles straight up. He'd had more than enough of his foster father using marriage as a solution to everything. But that was a problem for him to take up with Rends. Fangs was just trying to be helpful, and backward as that help might be, he so did not deserve to have it thrown back in his face.

"Thank you, brother," James said, clapping a hand on Fangs's shoulder. "It's a kind offer, but I'm sure Tina will recover. Even if she doesn't, she wanted to go home anyway, so I don't think she'll need the Claw Born's help. But thank you for being there for us. It means a lot."

"Speak nothing of it," Fangs said gruffly, his fur puffy with embarrassment. "It is the least we can do after all you have sacrificed for our clan and kingdom. We are just eager to pay out our gratitude, that's all."

Leaving his brother to his embarrassment, James straightened up and began scanning the anxiously whispering player crowd for Frank. He didn't find the off tank on the first glance, but that was a good thing. If Frank had Tina's armor, then he was smart to lie low. Fortunately, James had a very good idea of who would know where he was, and she was impossible to miss.

James turned on his heel and started walking back toward the tent where Tina was, though not all the way. His target was the big knot of Roughnecks standing in front of it. Specifically, he needed the short Naturalist in the middle.

"Neko!" he called when he spotted her. "Can I ask you a question?"

The healer lit up the moment she heard her name and started bounding over, much to his brother's discomfort.

"Must we ask *her*?" Ar'Bati asked with a cringe.

"If something's happening in the Roughnecks, Neko knows," James replied. Then he smiled. "You don't have to say anything."

Fangs heaved a sigh of deep relief as NekoBaby bounded up. "James! Angry Cat!" she cried in false delight. "What's shaking? Here to eat some tacos?"

Before James could even respond to that lunacy, the Naturalist dropped her voice. "Seriously, WTF is going on? Everyone's saying Roxxy is down hardcore, but SB won't let me into the tent, the *bastard*. But you have to know what's up. You'd tell me if Tina was dying, right?"

"She's not dying," James assured her. "She's...well, you'll see. But I need to find Frank. Do you know where he is?"

Neko flashed him a grin. "Oh yeah, we've got Old F on lockdown because we're total pros and shit. Follow me."

Neko dropped to all fours and bounded off. Being jubatus as well, James and Ar'Bati followed suit, racing through the camp like three mad cats until they reached a lonely tent at the edge with a suspicious number of Roughnecks milling around it. The raiders all looked relieved when they saw James, but no one looked as happy as Frank did when Neko pulled open the tent flap.

"James!" Frank said, looking up from the pile of giant plate he was sitting on like a big armored hen. "You're a sight for sore eyes!"

172

"If the handoff's been made, I'm going to get back to the boss lady," Neko said as James and Ar'Bati crawled inside. "You guys can keep Frank the Tank company."

"I could use it," Frank said as the Naturalist scampered off. "I've been worried sick out here, and no one will tell me nothing! Is Roxxy okay?"

"She's alive and safe," James assured him. "SB and Zen are taking care of her, but she's going to want her armor when she wakes up."

"I bet she will," Frank said, but the Knight's face was still pale beneath his face guard. "About that, though…"

"What about it?" James asked frantically.

"I don't rightly know how to explain it," Frank said, standing up. "Probably easier if I just show you."

Frank lifted the cloak he'd been using to shield Tina's gear, and James uttered a loud curse. Tina's sun steel armor was all there, along with her sword and shield. They'd even remembered to grab her magical rings and amulet, but something was off. The normally gleaming gold-white plate was dull and listless, looking more like a heap of scrap than a suit of legend. Even her sword had gone dark, the blood-red runes barely visible on the black blade. But more troubling than the lack of glow was the emptiness. James hadn't realized something that wasn't alive could feel so lifeless, but every piece of Tina's armor radiated a wrongness, like it was lacking something vital. Probably because it was.

"I don't know what happened to it," Frank said, picking up a dull gauntlet. "It never looked like this when she was wearing it. I'm worried that big winged One King fella did something."

"Once King," James corrected quietly, kneeling to inspect Tina's shield. "And he didn't do anything. There's nothing wrong with her armor. It's just become unbound."

"Oh," Frank said, face breaking into a smile. "Is that good?"

It was James's worst-case scenario. No, scratch that. The *worst* case would have been if her armor had been destroyed. This was better, though not by much, and he still didn't know what he was going to do about it.

All magical armor—whether worn by players or NPCs—had to be magically bound to the bearer's soul before it could be used to its full potential. Once bound, the connection could only be severed by the wearer's death, which was why James had been able to scavenge his old magical gear off player corpses back at Red Canyon. Normally, bound gear meant stealing someone's armor was impossible unless you killed them, but Roxxy's body had *vanished*, and apparently that had been enough to snap the connection.

They could always *re*bind it, of course, but that would require Tina to be awake, magically capable, and level eighty, all uncertainties right now. Meanwhile, her armor was sitting around like a treasure chest with its lock bashed off. Without the soul binding tying it to her, all of Tina's gear—the best-in-the-world tanking set she'd built over a year of raiding the Dead Mountain—was essentially up for grabs to anyone who came by and put it on.

Which, James was sure, was exactly Cinco's plan.

"We have to get this back to Tina as soon as possible," he whispered, motioning for Frank to put his cloak back over the pile.

"Why?" Frank asked.

James kept his mouth shut. He trusted Frank implicitly, but the tent was small and made of canvas. He didn't know who else might be listening, and free top-tier raid gear was a temptation any player would have a hard time resisting. The less said the better, but as he motioned for Frank to start gathering Tina's things, the atmosphere in the tiny tent shifted, almost as if it had become lighter. More empty.

"Did you guys feel that?"

"Feel what?" Frank asked innocently, but Ar'Bati's hand rose to the handle of his sword.

"I felt it," the jubatus warrior growled. "Something followed us."

174

Cursing himself for an idiot, James looked around at the streams of magic flowing through the tent. He didn't see any disturbances, but he did notice the shadows—the huge, deep shadows behind each of them stretching out in the tent's muffled light.

"Shit," he whispered. "I think we were being spied on from the Lightless Realm." He looked at Tina's armor. "We have to move this."

"I thought we'd already agreed to move it," Frank grumbled.

"I mean *right now*," James said frantically, struggling to pick up Roxxy's enormous breastplate. "We have to get it out of here before—"

The loud stomp of boots outside cut him off, and then James's cat ears caught the loud, cocky voice of the Red Sands's guild leader just outside.

"Good job, Shankfest," CincoDeMurder said as a red-armored hand grabbed the flap to their tent. James barely had time to put his body between the entrance and Tina's armor before the Berserker stuck his head in.

"Hello, boys," Cinco said, flashing them a predatory grin. "Looks like you've got what I need."

James and Ar'Bati both growled while Frank sat himself back down on the pile of Tina's armor like a rock. Outside, the Roughnecks on guard were shouting angrily, but they fell silent shortly after. When Cinco reached out and snatched the entire tent off from on top of them, James saw why. The whole Red Sands guild was here and armed to the teeth, their weapons pointed at the Roughnecks guards, who were now badly outnumbered.

"Thanks for leading me to the jackpot," Cinco said, nodding to James, who bared his teeth. The Berserker winked back and turned his attention to Frank. "Heya, Frankie," he said jovially. "There's been a change in plans. We're on a timeline and Roxxy's indisposed, so I'm going to be taking her breastplate, bracers, and boots so my boy Brody can complete his set." He pointed at a tall Knight in the back, who was staring at the pile of Tina's armor and drooling. "I'm also going to need that shield for Garrond. He's not technically a tank, but he's still a four-skull badass, which means he'll do a better job than you. No offense."

"None taken," Frank said, sitting even tighter. "But I'm not giving you Roxxy's stuff."

Cinco's eyes narrowed. "'No' is not a word you get to say, *old man*," he growled. "We're not playing around. This is mission-critical shit, so fork it over."

"No," Frank said again.

"No," James said at the same time.

The leader of Red Sands turned his salty gaze on him, but James didn't budge. Wouldn't budge. He didn't care how nobly Cinco dressed his intentions, this was stealing. His sister had spent a year's worth of nights and weekends prying that armor from the hellishly hard Dead Mountain Fortress. Even if she couldn't tank anymore—which was not a forgone conclusion—it was still *hers*.

"You're out of line, Cinco," James said, tail lashing. "That armor belongs to Roxxy and you know it, so back off."

"You're the one out of line, little cat," Cinco growled back. "You've got less ground to stand on than anyone, because you know the truth: Roxxy's a gimp now. She's not going to be wearing that armor anymore. Hell, the breastplate is bigger than she is!"

That drew a laugh from the other Red Sands, and Cinco's smile grew meaner. "Face it, bro," he said in a sneering voice. "Queen Tina's reign is over, and her backup Frank's a sniveling coward."

"Frank is *not* a coward!" one of the Roughnecks yelled. "He's been in every fight Roxxy has, and he's never backed down!"

"Of course he's a coward!" Cinco yelled back. "What else can you call someone who shakes in his boots every time he's forced to play his damn class? Dude's got no backbone. A real pity since he's the second-best-geared Knight now." He arched an eyebrow at Frank. "Maybe we should relieve him of his shit, too? You know, do our civic duty to keep such fine gear from going to waste."

"That ain't a nice thing to say," Frank replied, his voice shaking slightly but his body still firmly set on top of Tina's armor. "But no means no. Now get."

The calm dismissal was enough to make Cinco jerk in surprise. Then his face turned an ugly purple. "You don't get it, do you?" he roared. "We don't have time for this bullshit! The Once King is weak! We should be tearing his fort down around his ears, not sitting here wasting time waiting on *one person*! This whole army is chewing its fingernails waiting to see if Tina's going to make it. Meanwhile, our enemy's getting the chance to recover all his mana so he can blast us again. Well, fuck that!" He stabbed his finger at Tina's stuff. "Armor for Brody. Shield for Garrond. *Move!*"

"*No!*" James yelled, shoving his body between Cinco and Frank. "That armor is Tina's! Even if she can never use it again, we're not giving it to *you!*"

Cinco put his hand on the butt of his spear and stepped forward, his giant boots landing perilously close to James's feet. "I'm not asking nicely again," the Berserker said in a quiet, deadly voice. "You've got one second to hand over that gear before Shankfest and I take it."

"We're not afraid of you," growled Ar'Bati, drawing his sword.

We should be, James thought. Bravado aside, he knew CincoDeMurder's reputation. The guy was a multiple-season PvP world champion, and Shankfest was the Assassin who'd done it all with him. Gameplay skills aside, he'd also heard that Cinco was a HEMA tournament winner who'd done at least some MMA, which meant James couldn't use the same tricks he'd pulled to beat SB. SilentBlayde had the advantage of gear, but Cinco was an experienced fighter in game and out. He was also a proven killer who outweighed James and Ar'Bati combined.

It was not a good match-up, especially with Shankfest in the mix. The Assassin had already pulled out his lightning maces and was twirling them in his hands, giving James a "you know what's coming" grin. James responded by getting out his Eclipsed Steel staff, but he'd barely gotten his hand to the weapon's grip when he heard the heavy clink of armor behind him.

"Boy," Frank said, rising to his feet. "You'd better back off."

Cinco scoffed. "What's this? Trying to prove you aren't an over-geared sissy? Way too late for that, baby doll."

Frank shrugged off the insults. "I know I'm scared a lot, but I ain't ashamed of it. Have you *seen* what us Roughnecks have fought? We've gone up against some scary business. 'Course I got the shakes. But even if I was shamefaced about it, I ain't got nothing to prove to an overgrown schoolyard bully like you."

"Get to the point, Grandpa," Cinco growled.

Frank's mustache rose in a smug grin. "My point, son, is that you done screwed up. You got all your boys together for this here robbery, but you forgot that you're in the middle of the Roughnecks' camp."

Before Cinco could respond to that, Frank drew his sword and held it up like a rallying banner. Beyond the circle of the Red Sands, a shout rose up in answer, and James looked to see that Cinco's group was surrounded on all sides by Roughnecks, as well as an astonishing number of soldiers from the Order. Zen was there too, bow drawn, as were Anders and Richard and everyone else. James wasn't certain exactly when it had happened, but suddenly Tina's whole guild was here, forming a ring of stone-faced, furious raiders around Cinco's band of PvPers, who now looked much less sure. Even Cinco looked cowed, lowering his spear as he stepped back.

"That's right," Frank said as Cinco backed away. "We ain't letting you take anything that belongs to the Roughnecks' Roxxy, so you'd best skedaddle. Be a real shame if something happened to our backup raid."

Cursing under his breath, Cinco sheathed his spear, but he didn't back down. He was still glaring at Frank like he might just attack anyway when an angry, familiar voice rose from behind the crowd.

"What the fuck is going on here?"

Chapter 9

Tina

Tina woke to the strangest mixture of feelings. She felt weak and small and tired but also comfortable, snuggled into bed under a warm mountain of blankets. She didn't remember going to bed, though. Maybe she was getting sick? She'd definitely been playing too much FFO, because the dream she'd just had had been the *worst*. She'd been stuck in Roxxy's body, leading a pick-up group into the Dead Mountain to fight the Once King. Talk about a lost cause. She was just glad it was over and she was finally back at home. She must have left her VR helmet turned on when she collapsed, though, because she could still hear FFO's iconic loading music softly from somewhere to the left of her head.

Oh well, she thought, turning to snuggle deeper into the blankets. She'd deal with that later. Right now, all she wanted was to sleep for another few...

Tina's hazy thoughts trailed off as her nose rubbed against the scratchy wool of the blanket. She didn't own a scratchy wool blanket. Whatever was on top of her, it wasn't her comforter. This also wasn't her bed. Her bed wasn't hard and lumpy and reeking of wood smoke and horses. What the hell?

Her eyes popped open, darting around in confusion. She was in a tent. Not a modern tent, either. It was a canvas tent tied up with ropes, and she wasn't alone. There was someone sitting on the ground beside her, humming FFO's loading theme in a beautiful low voice. The music stopped when she moved, and then a man's face appeared above hers—a masked elven face so breathtakingly handsome it was physically intimidating.

"Tina?" the gorgeous man said in SilentBlayde's voice. "Are you awake?"

Tina had no idea. She could barely think with those blue eyes—the purest, most beautiful sky blue she'd ever seen—looking into hers.

179

Everything was overwhelming, actually. The cold was too intense, the smell of dust and metal too sharp. Even the weight of the blankets felt like it was going to crush her. Where was she? What the hell was going on?

"Is she up?" asked a cutesy, high-pitched voice excitedly. Then the relative warmth of the tent was broken by a blast of freezing wind right before a giant cat face shoved its way into her field of vision.

"Rocky Road!" the cat girl squealed, making Tina's ears ring. "You're alive!"

"You said you'd be quiet!" the handsome elf hissed angrily.

"I *am* being quiet," the cat argued. "This is quiet for me! Anyway, she's not sleeping anymore, so what does it matter if—"

"Ugh," Tina groaned, reaching up to rub her face. "Neko, what the—"

She froze, fingers going still against her skin. Her soft, *fleshy* skin. There was hair, too. Her own unruly, curly brown hair hung in a tangle around her face like it did every morning at home, but this *wasn't* home. It was Garrond's command tent, except everything looked enormous, like the whole world had suddenly doubled in...

Tina froze, heart revving up like a race car in her chest. Her narrow, *human* chest. Of their own accord, her hands leaped to her neck and shoulders, then down under the blankets to check her stomach, but every part she touched was fleshy and bony and very much *not* hewn from stone.

Oh no, she thought as her lungs began sucking in air at a frantic rate. *No no **no**.*

"Tina," said the smooth elven voice as gloved hands grabbed hers, the masculine fingers completely engulfing her tiny fists. "Tina, calm down. You're safe. It's just us. Don't freak—"

Tina shoved him away. She was breathing so fast now that her vision was getting dark. Her body felt small and weak and wrong, and her brain was overflowing with so many physical sensations and emotions she didn't know which to feel first.

"She's gonna blow!" NekoBaby cried, scrambling off the bed.

180

But Tina didn't blow. She screamed instead, a high-pitched, panicked shriek as the raging chaos inside finally bubbled over.

She wasn't sure what happened after that. She must have passed out at least a little, because when Tina became aware again, there were a lot more voices in the tent. She cringed into the lumpy rope mattress, trying to get away, but someone with hands like cold iron grabbed her head and jerked her back into place, prying her eyes open to shine a bright light inside.

"Well," said Zen's no-nonsense voice. "She's definitely awake."

The light vanished, leaving Tina blinking away spots. When she could see again, her vision was filled with shockingly beautiful, giant people staring down at her.

She recognized Zen first. The dark-skinned elven Ranger's neon-green hair was a dead giveaway, but Tina didn't remember her being so *tall*. She towered over NekoBaby, who was squeezed in right beside her, ears up and curious. Even the diminutive cat girl looked gigantic to Tina, who was starting to feel a bit like Alice after a lot of ill-advised drinking in a really rough Wonderland. But scary as the changes were, it was the third figure who made her want to run and hide.

Hovering next to NekoBaby, his face so close to hers she could have leaned up and kissed it, was SilentBlayde. He'd been here the whole time, she realized, but now that she actually knew what she was looking at—or rather *who* she was looking at—Tina's body was having a serious malfunction. He'd taken off his mask at some point, giving her a clear view of his sharply angled jaw and flawless elven features. His pale blond hair glowed like sunlight in the dim tent, and when he leaned closer, her bare shoulder came into contact with the leather-wrapped iron of his perfectly sculpted chest, causing her face to heat to surface-of-the-sun levels.

"You're really flushed," Zen noted, her own supernaturally beautiful face pulled into a worried frown. "How do you feel?"

Like a fucking idiot. Forcing her eyes away from SB, Tina scooted back to the far corner of the bed with the blankets pulled up to her chin to hide her body. Her frail, bony, totally *naked* human body.

That thought almost started her hyperventilating again, and Zen's hands flew up. "Easy," the nurse said. "Just breathe normally and you'll be fine."

"I don't feel fine," Tina said, then stopped. Was that *her* voice? It sounded like hers, but it was so small. Small and pathetic and *terrified.* "I think I'm freaking out."

"That's to be expected," Zen said. "You've been through a lot."

"Do you want a heal?" Neko asked, raising a green-glowing paw-hand. "'Cause I've got the good drugs if you need 'em."

Tina shook her head. The last thing she wanted was to feel anything else, even the euphoria of magical healing. She already felt like her head was swimming in a sea of sensations she couldn't handle, especially with SilentBlayde so close and unfairly handsome. God, he even *smelled* delicious. All she wanted to do was kick everyone else out and crawl all over him.

Face burning hotter than ever, Tina pinned her eyes firmly to the blanket and motioned Zen closer. "Can you make him leave?" she whispered in the elf's long ear when the Ranger leaned down. "I'm going to do something stupid if he stays."

Zen nodded and straightened back up. "Everyone out."

"Aww," Neko groaned, but she went. SB, however, did not.

"You too, Blayde," Zen said, crossing her arms over her chest.

Tina couldn't even raise her eyes to see if he obeyed. She tried listening instead, but the Assassin never made noise, so she had no idea if he'd left until Zen said, "He's gone."

"Thanks," Tina breathed, covering her burning face with her hands. "Sorry to be weird, but I can't handle him right now."

"It's not weird at all," Zen said gently. "We've had nearly two weeks to get used to being this way. It must all be really shocking to you now that you're not a stonekin anymore."

That was putting it mildly. Tina hadn't realized just how much Roxxy's stony indifference to fleshy concerns had insulated her until it was stripped away. "It's pretty intense," she admitted. "How have you all coped?"

"We haven't," the Ranger said with a silvery laugh. "Remember Camp Comeback's 'Inappropriate Sex Hill'?"

Tina blushed even redder. "Oh yeah."

Her embarrassment wasn't helped by Zen's proximity. The elven Ranger's beauty was incredibly intimidating. Zen had a supermodel's face and a willowy dancer's body with mathematically perfect curves. Her salon-smooth emerald-green hair fell in picturesque curls around her elegant shoulders, and her long, dark lashes looked like they were coated in fresh, flawless mascara despite no such thing existing in this place. It was kinda scary being next to someone that perfect, and it made Tina all too aware of just how *im*perfect she'd become.

Zen had already pulled back the blanket to examine her, so Tina took the plunge and looked down to see…well, herself. She wasn't sure what she'd been expecting, but it was incredibly bizarre to see her normal body—short, scrawny, pale, flat-chested, bony—in this world. Being Roxxy had left a lot to be desired, but she'd still been a huge, gorgeous, totally cut stone lady. Now she was just Tina. Frizzy-haired, awkward, *normal* Tina, surrounded by people who looked like gods.

"I feel fine, really," Tina said when she couldn't stand Zen's examination any longer. "What I'd really like are some clothes."

"That I can do," Zen said, handing Tina a large square of folded cloth from the table beside them. "Garrond brought tons of extra uniforms for the Order. It's a man's undershirt, but it should work as a dress for you."

Because she was so short.

"Thanks," Tina muttered glumly, pulling the scratchy wool shirt over her head. At least it was warm.

"Okay," she said when she was no longer naked. "Tell me what happened."

"I was hoping *you* could tell us," Zen said, sitting down on the end of Tina's cot. "After you used One For All to soak up whatever the Once King did, your armor fell apart. SilentBlayde found you like this inside Roxxy's chestplate."

The thought of SB seeing her naked made Tina blush all over again. If she hadn't already wasted too much of their precious time on stupid boy-drama, she would have sunk straight down into the floor. "How did you escape the Once King?" she asked when she could speak again.

"We didn't," Zen said. "He retreated. Richard thinks whatever spell he cast to bring your real body over here used up all his mana, which makes sense to me. You were the only casualty."

"I'm already being counted out?" Tina said angrily, then she stopped, looking down at her fragile, human hands. Why was she even asking that? Of *course* they'd counted her out. They'd followed Roxxy here, not some little girl. SB had found her *inside* her stonekin's chest piece like a mouse hiding in a log. As always, no one followed Tiny Tina, and why should they? As she looked right now, she wouldn't follow her, either.

"Stop that," Zen said sharply.

Tina looked up in surprise, the tears she hadn't realized she'd shed slipping down her cheeks. "Why?" she asked, scrubbing her face. "Look at me. It's over."

"It's *not* over," the Ranger snapped, glaring at her. "*Some* people are jumping to conclusions, but the Roughnecks never doubted you. We retreated because you were hurt, not because we'd given up. Everyone's been waiting for you to wake up to see if you're still level eighty and can stand with us, not because of how you look." She smiled. "Stonekin or human, you're our Roxxy. We don't want another leader."

No words could have hit Tina harder. She tried not to cry, but the return of volatile human emotions after so long as a stonekin was too much. It only took a few seconds before she doubled over with a sob, clutching the blanket to her face. Zen, being wise, said nothing. She just sat there, rubbing Tina's back until her muffled gasps finally subsided.

"I'm sorry," Tina said when it was done. "I don't mean to be a basket case. It's just…I've been working my whole life to hear someone say that, you know?"

"It's the truth," Zen said, smiling at her. "But if you're stable, we've still got some big questions to answer. You being human isn't a problem—we've got plenty of those—but we need to know if you're still level eighty or not."

Tina nodded, pulling herself straight. "That's fair. But how do we tell? There's no interface anymore."

"I don't know," Zen said with a shrug. "But all your gear is from the DMF raid, and that requires level-eighty minimum. If you can put it back on, that should be proof enough."

"What are we waiting for, then?" Tina asked excitedly, getting out of the bed. "Let's go get my stuff!"

Zen put a hand on her shoulder. "About that," she said. "All of your armor became unbound when your body disappeared. Frank's guarding it, but we need to be cautious. I don't have to tell you how much damage a pile of unclaimed raiding gear could do in a camp full of players."

Damn straight she didn't. Tina had seen guilds ripped apart by fights over loot. She could only imagine how many people would kill for Roxxy's stuff, especially since gear no longer seemed to drop, a fact NekoBaby had loudly bemoaned during their boss extermination run in the fight for Bastion.

"I'll just have to get it back on fast, then," Tina said, planting her bare feet on the dusty ground. "Let's go."

Zen nodded and pulled back the flap. Adjusting her shirt-dress, Tina marched out of the tent...and nearly ran face first into a perfectly sculpted, leather-armored chest.

The only reason it was "nearly" rather than "face planted" was because the chest's owner jumped out of the way with impossible grace. "Tina," SB said when he landed, his blue eyes watching her above his mask with a desperate expression. "Are you—"

Tina shoved past him. It was cruel, but she couldn't afford to be distracted right now, and SilentBlayde was more distracting than he'd ever been. Good god, even exhausted and dusty from the Deadlands, he looked like a model fresh off a photo shoot. Just seeing him made her brain go soft, so she kept her eyes ruthlessly turned away, following Zen straight across the camp.

It was a terrifying journey. Being in a tent with Zen was one thing, but actually walking through the army of players was like stepping onto Mount Olympus. With the exception of the schtumples and a few of the female jubatus like NekoBaby, who was bounding along beside her, *everyone* was more than six feet tall. Some of the Berserkers were closer to seven, and GneissGuy, their only remaining stonekin, looked like a legit monster towering head and shoulders above the already towering crowd. Walking among them, Tina had never felt smaller or uglier, but she knew better than to let it show. She might not be Roxxy anymore, but she knew how to keep her face stony.

It helped enormously that she had her friends surrounding her. The other players might not notice Tina, but they got out of Zen's way fast, and Neko's hissing kept anyone who did stare from getting too close. She hadn't dared looked back yet, but she could feel SilentBlayde behind her, watching her back. That made her feel a lot better than it should have, but now was not the time to be picky. It was clear she was going to need all the help she could get as the crowd parted, and the situation came into view.

The first thing she saw was James. Her brother was looking fiercer than she'd ever seen him, standing in front of Cinco's giant red-armored form with his fangs bared and his tail lashing. His Taco-Cat brother and Frank were backing him up, but the head of Red Sands didn't seem worried about them. His eyes were sliding warily over the circle of Roughnecks surrounding him and his guild. It looked like a standoff, which confused her for a moment. This sort of hostility shouldn't have been happening between allies. Then she saw the pile of glittering gear beneath Frank's protective crouch, and everything became clear.

"What the fuck is going on here?"

Her real voice was nowhere near as commanding as Roxxy's, but she was pissed enough that it worked anyway. The moment she spoke, all the raiders looked her way, including Cinco, who looked her up and down with a sneer of disgust.

Tina gave him one back. "Stealing someone's gear, Cinco?" she said, crossing her arms over her chest in an effort to hide how ridiculous she looked in the oversized shirt. "That's a new low."

Cinco didn't even try to deny it. "Just doing what had to be done," he said casually, giving her a charming smile that didn't touch his eyes. "I've got tanks, and we've still got a boss to pwn, so I thought I'd put your stuff to use, seeing how you can't wear it anymore. Waste not, want not."

"We'll waste *you!*" NekoBaby hissed, fur standing on end. "That's Roxxy's gear, you thieving hack!"

The gathered Roughnecks made dangerous noises of agreement, and Tina narrowed her eyes. "How do you know I can't wear it?"

Cinco snorted and waved at her tiny body. "Because I have eyes. You're what, three feet tall? You couldn't even wear schtumple armor."

"News flash, genius," Tina snapped. "Those armor drops fit any class. By your logic, your tank wouldn't be able to wear my stuff either since he's not a stonekin. Maybe you never saw this since all your gear came from the PvP vendor, but *real* raid armor—the kind you get from killing bosses—

187

resizes itself magically to fit whoever binds it." She stabbed a finger at the pile of gear. "That's *my* stuff. All I have to do is rebind it, and it'll fit me just fine."

"Assuming you can," Cinco snapped. "You don't look level eighty to me, kiddo."

A muscle in Tina's face twitched, but she forced herself not to rise to the bait. "Only one way to find out."

She marched forward, ignoring the sharp rocks digging into her bare feet as she crossed the gray, dusty ground. Like everyone else, Cinco was a *lot* bigger up close, but she forced herself to ignore him, walking straight ahead until she was standing over the dusty pile of her armor, which was nearly as tall as she was. This position also put her right next to James, which was a huge relief. Even in this body, she could feel the magic radiating off him like electricity. It made her feel safe, as did the familiar weight of SB's presence in her shadow. She didn't know if the two of them would be enough to stop Cinco from trying anything, but damn if they wouldn't make it hurt.

"T," James said quietly as she reached down to grab her tanking necklace, the only piece of her gear small enough that she could actually pick it up. "Go slow. We still don't know if you're actually level eighty, and your stuff is *really* magical. If you try to bind it and you're not strong enough, it might fry your brain."

"If I'm not level eighty, I'm dead anyway," Tina whispered back, glancing over her shoulder at Cinco. "Because over my dead body is the only way that asshole's getting any of my stuff. Now how do I do this?"

In the game, binding gear had been as simple as putting it on and clicking the "accept" button. Tina didn't think it was going to be that easy now, though. The amulet in her hands was absolutely massive. The links of sun steel chain were as thick as Tina's wrist, and the fire ruby pendant was the size of a soup bowl. The necklace had been tackily huge even when she'd been a stonekin. As a human, she couldn't even use it as a belt.

"Let me help," James said, putting his furry hands over hers where she was gripping the amulet. "Now that there's no interface, you have to be able to see mana to bind things, and you couldn't do that even as a stonekin. I'm going to tie the magic in the item to yours, and then we'll see what happens." He gave her a nervous look. "Ready?"

Tina blew out a shaky breath. "Ready."

James bit his lip. "Are you sure? Because this could really—"

"Do it, James."

The look on his face was not reassuring, but Tina refused to chicken out. Her whole guild was watching. Zen, Neko, Frank, SB—they were all here standing up for her. She'd fought her whole life to earn that kind of trust and respect. She'd wear the stupid necklace even if it set her on fire.

Hands shaking on hers, her brother nodded and stared down at the necklace, his eyes getting that faraway look they always took on when he was seeing things she couldn't. He let go of her a moment later, reaching down toward his stomach in the motion all casters used to start their spells. Taking hold of his mana, Tina supposed, not that she had experience with any of that. She just hoped it worked, because so far, James's magic looked like just a bunch of hand-waving. She was starting to worry nothing was happening when, in one swift motion, her brother stabbed his hand into her stomach.

That was what it felt like, anyway. Tina gasped and looked down to see James hadn't actually plunged his fingers into her guts. He was just pressing them against her ribcage, his fingertips moving like he was sorting through a web of very small, very complicated threads. The tiny motions sent waves of nausea rolling through her. She was fighting not to be sick all over him when, suddenly, it was over.

Power surged through her body as James removed his hand, sweeping away the nausea and every other feeling of weakness. The crushing weight in her hands vanished next, leaving the amulet feeling more like a feather than a bowling ball as the magical necklace's hundred-plus Stamina and Strength kicked in.

"Mwahahaha...*Yes!*" Tina laughed, drunk on the power.

"Are you all right?" James asked nervously. "Did it work?"

"*Oh* yeah!" Tina whooped, clapping James on the shoulder so hard he staggered. "I feel fucking fantastic!"

James and Zen exchanged a worried look, and Tina realized she needed to get her act together.

"I'm fine, really," she said, much more sanely this time. "It's just intense. You try doubling your base stats and see how you feel. It's heady stuff."

Zen frowned. "If it worked, why does it still look like that?"

Blinking in surprise, Tina looked down at her necklace...which was still stonekin-sized. "Shit," she said, grabbing the giant ruby in both hands. "Why isn't it getting smaller?! It always got smaller in the game!"

"This isn't a game anymore," James reminded her.

"Well, that's a problem," Tina whispered frantically, glancing at Cinco, who was watching all of this with a murderous scowl. "Stats are no good if the gear doesn't fit!"

"You need a crafter."

Tina jumped and looked over to see SB, who was suddenly standing right beside her. "We had this problem making armor at Camp Comeback, remember?" the elf whispered, his voice smooth and professional and tightly controlled.

Tina scowled, trying to recall. Her smithing at Camp Comeback had been a blur of cranking out armor and weapons as fast as physically possible. As the only max-skill blacksmith, her time had been super valuable, so she'd left the actual fitting and binding of gear to the lower-level smiths. When she didn't answer immediately, Blayde helped her out.

"You need to use the Prayer to the Silent Moon to resize it."

"Oh yeah," she said, feeling dumb. In her defense, she usually only made gear for herself, which meant it didn't need resizing. Also, this was a necklace, not plate armor, which meant her intuitive blacksmithing knowledge wasn't kicking in. She didn't even know if she *could* use her skill on things that weren't armor.

"Can you do it?" she asked SB. "You're a jewel crafter."

The words were out of her mouth before Tina realized what she'd said. If it wouldn't have made her look like an idiot, she would have eaten those words right back and just tied the oversized necklace around her shoulders, but everyone was staring. Both the Roughnecks and Red Sands were clustered around her, watching with bated breath to see how this played out. Backing out because she couldn't handle her feelings around her ex would prove she was every bit as weak as Cinco thought, so Tina set her jaw and stared SilentBlayde right in his breathtaking eyes.

"Please," she said through gritted teeth.

Hands shaking, SilentBlayde reached out to take the giant amulet. Removing his gloves, he ran his fingers over the fire ruby's beveled surface, muttering under his breath as he went.

"What's this Prayer to the Silent Moon?" James whispered to Tina while the elf worked.

She gaped at him. "Don't you know? I thought you were Mr. Lore."

"Yeah, but I'm not a crafter," her brother said defensively. "My skills are herbalism and alchemy."

Tina grinned. It wasn't every day she got one up on her walking wiki of a brother, and she took great pride in explaining it to him. "The Prayer to the Silent Moon is a side skill that any crafter can learn. You don't even have to get it if you don't care, but it's super useful if you want to sell your stuff on the auction house. You know how everything you make is automatically sized for your character, right? Well, the Prayer to the Silent Moon fixes that. It makes your stuff flexible so it can change to fit whoever buys it and you're not stuck selling to only other female stonekin or whatever."

"I get that part," James said. "But why is it a prayer to the *Moon*? I thought the Moon god was gone."

191

"Hell if I know," Tina said with a shrug. "It's just the name of the skill. Makes sense, though. I mean, the moon is always changing, so if you want your stuff to change as well, that's who you'd want to pray to."

James looked at her as if she'd just said something deeply profound. Before Tina could ask him what was up, though, the amulet in SB's hands flashed bright purple. When the light faded, the giant necklace was less than half the size it had been originally. It was still comically huge—the ruby was the size of her fist, and the chain was long enough to hang to her belly button—but it slid easily over her head when SB gave it back, resting on her shoulders like it had been made to be there.

"Hell yeah," she said, grinning down at the giant gem. Then she raised her eyes to Cinco, who looked like he'd just taken a big bite out of a rotten fish. "That good enough for you?"

"No," the Berserker growled, giving her the ugliest sneer Tina had ever seen. "This doesn't change shit."

"What are you talking about?" Tina demanded. "You said you were taking my gear because you didn't know if I could wear it, but guess what, jackass." She thumped the amulet around her neck. "I can wear it just fine."

"And that doesn't change shit," Cinco snarled back. "Look at you! You look like a kid playing dress-up. You think you can tank the Once King?"

Tina scowled. "I know I can. Once I've got my gear—"

"Fuck your gear!" he roared. "You're the one who's always going on about how this isn't a game anymore, but a game is the only place where it makes sense that a *little girl*"—he gave her a shove that made her step back —"can take hits from a dude who's literally ten feet tall. Roxxy made sense. Roxxy was a mountain! You're ninety pounds of bones and hair."

"I won't be once I have my stuff!" Tina yelled.

"No, then you'll be ninety pounds of bones in a tin can," the Berserker spat. "All that magical bullcrap is doing is juicing you up so you won't die in one hit, but it can't change physics. You're still too small, too

192

light, too weak, and too short. It doesn't matter what kind of monkey suit you wear. The Once King's sword can still go right over your head to chop off ours." His lip curled in disgust. "Face it, sweetheart, you're done. Being level eighty doesn't change who you are, and you're literally too short for this ride. If you were really serious about winning, you'd give that armor to a guy who's big enough to actually make good use of it instead of milking the stats to shore up your short-girl complex."

Tina clenched her fists so tight her nails cut into her palm. How dare he. How *dare* he. "You think gear is what makes me a tank?!"

"If the shoe fits, baby," Cinco snarled back, looking around at his guild, who were all nodding in agreement. "We didn't come all the way out here so you could play dress-up. We're here to save the goddamn world, and we've never had a better chance. We all saw the Once King stagger away. Bitch is weak, which means we've got to hit him hard and hit him now, before he manas up." He shoved his giant hand into Tina's face. "Give me that armor and I'll put it on a man who can actually do the job. We'll give your shield to Garrond, and then we'll take our fucking army and tear that stupid elf's wings off! All you have to do is sit your pretty ass down in your elf boyfriend's tent and wait for us to come back."

Tina bared her teeth at him. "And if I don't?"

Cinco leaned down, flashing her a savage grin. "Then I'll fucking take it. We're the PvP guild. You're a pick-up raid of filthy casuals whose only actually good player just turned into a little *fucking* girl. You don't stand a chance."

Tina stared up at his looming face, wishing like hell he wasn't so much bigger. He never would have said this shit to Roxxy, but that was the whole problem, wasn't it? He'd respected Roxxy precisely because he couldn't push her around, but Tina was weak. Tina was nothing, and so he'd stomped all over her just like he did the NPCs. She couldn't even claim she hadn't known. Cinco showed his true colors every chance he got, but he'd been so good at flattering her ego that she'd ignored the warning signs. Now he'd turned on her, and Tina felt like an idiot for not seeing it coming.

But if he thought she was just going to roll over because he was huge and scary, he had another think coming. She'd seen the Red Sands fight King Gregory. They couldn't even handle the gentle king for five minutes before they fell apart. Tina knew the Once King's battle-math by heart. It took nine minutes minimum to get him down to thirty percent health, and that was with a full Dead Mountain–geared raid going whole hog on him. There was no chance that sort of damage was going to happen with their current makeup, which meant his plan was doomed from the start. The Red Sands players were just too aggressive and dickish, too eager to take risks to deal their damage. Those traits made them great against fellow players, but they didn't have the patience or teamwork needed for a long fight against a real five-skull, and that was why they failed. Her armor wouldn't change that any more than putting a shield on Garrond would make him a tank.

That was the bit that *really* ticked her off. The Order's commander was a four-skull with millions of health. All that HP meant he could take hits all day, but he was a paladin, not a Knight. He specialized in smiting shit and cleaving it in half with his giant sword, not tanking. He had none of the abilities that let him *avoid* getting damaged, which was what made player Knights so powerful. If Cinco put Garrond in the fight, keeping his giant health pool full would run the healers dry in no time. It was a stupid idea that was going to get a lot of people killed, and the fact that Cinco didn't realize that proved that he had no idea what he was talking about.

But as much as Tina was dying to rub all of that in Cinco's smug face, the situation was rapidly deteriorating. All around her, players were taking sides, the Roughnecks and Red Sands facing off like they were ready to throw down here and now. But while Tina would bet on her people in a heartbeat, any fight here was one they couldn't afford. Their strategy to beat the Once King relied on Cinco's raid being there to act as backup. If they killed each other now, they wouldn't have the manpower to do what they'd actually come to the Deadlands to do.

Any fool could have seen that, but it didn't look like Cinco was going to take no—or any sort of logic—for an answer. There was only one type of reply macho assholes like him would listen to. Fortunately, it was one Tina was all too happy to give.

"You're a fucking idiot," she told him. "But fine. If you want my armor so badly, I'll make you an offer."

"You're acting like you've still got options here," CincoDeMurder said haughtily. "But I'll play. What you got, Care Bear?"

Tina bared her teeth at the old insult. "Duel me," she growled. "To the perma-death."

A murmur went through the crowd as Cinco's eyes widened in shock. "Are you crazy?" he spat.

"No, I'm serious," Tina replied, sneering up at him since she couldn't sneer down. "My gear is mine. The only way you're getting it from me is if you're personally willing and able to kill me and unbind it that way." She lifted her chin. "You think I can't tank just cause I'm in this body now? Fight me yourself and prove it. Winner gets my armor. Loser doesn't get a rez."

By the time she finished, all the raiders were silent in shock, but Cinco just set his jaw and reached out slowly with the hand that wasn't holding his spear to poke his finger into the hollow of Tina's chest. "You think I won't hit you because you're a girl?" he said quietly. "Cause I will. I'll fucking kill you and strip the armor off your cold, dead body. Just see if I don't."

He pushed as he spoke, forcing Tina to stiffen her body to avoid being pushed over. Cinco increased the pressure with ease, causing her bare feet to slide backward through the dirt as he extended his arm. She ended up traveling a full foot before he ran out of reach, but at least she didn't fall.

"Talk doesn't mean shit," Tina said, drawing herself up to her full four-foot-eleven-and-a-half inches. "Man up and say you'll accept, or get the fuck out of my face."

"It's your death wish, baby," Cinco said, spreading his hands. "I'll give you one hour to get your gear back on, 'cause I'm a gentleman." He turned and pointed toward the edge of camp, where a deep, rocky gorge cut the dusty ground like a scar. "We'll do it over there by the cliff. It'll give me a nice place to pitch your corpse after I strip your armor."

"Deal," Tina said, looking over her shoulder at Frank, who was still crouched protectively over her gear. "Help me carry my stuff back to the command tent. I've got an idiot to spank."

Nodding nervously, Frank gathered her armor into his arms. Tina tried to help, but with only the amulet, the only things she could carry were her bracers, rings, and belt. Frank and Zen picked up the rest while the Roughnecks stood guard, and then the whole raid marched together back to the command tent.

The walk back across camp felt like miles. Part of that was her new short legs, but mostly it was Tina. It had been easy to be brave while Cinco was in her face pissing her off, but now that it was over, the reality of what she'd just done grew starker with every step. By the time she got to the tent, she was shaking violently. The only reason she didn't break down was because everyone was still watching.

"Thank you for having my back," she told her raid.

"Least we could do," Frank said, setting her giant chest piece on the dirt floor of the tent. "That man's a right bastard, pardon my French."

"He's a dirty thieving ninja is what he is," Neko said fiercely, tail lashing. "Ooooooooh, I wish the Report command still worked! I'd get the GMs to ban hammer him so *hard*."

Scared as she was, that image made Tina laugh. "I'd love to see that," she said. "But there are no GMs anymore. We gotta settle this ourselves."

"We could get Garrond," Zen suggested. "He could put Cinco in his place."

Tina was sure he could, but there was no way she was running to the paladin for help. Not after those words.

"No," she said firmly, clenching her hands in an effort to get her shaking under control. "If we appeal to Garrond, Cinco will just do it again the moment he sees an opening. The only way we'll have peace again is if he understands on a visceral level that he can't push me—or any of us—around."

The Ranger arched a perfect green eyebrow. "You sure? Because it's not too late."

"Trust me, it's waaaay too late," Tina said with a wry smile. "I made this bed. I'll lie in it. Now everyone get out except James. I've only got an hour, and Roxxy had a *lot* of gear."

With a lot of nervous looks, her officers left the tent, but the presence in her shadow didn't. Annoyed, Tina reached up and opened the vent at the top of the tent to let in the sunlight. It was weak, gray, Deadlands light, but at just after noon, it was still enough to banish the shadows, and the elf hiding inside them. When she was sure they were alone, Tina took a deep breath and turned to her brother.

"All right," she said, hating how her voice shook. "How screwed am I?"

Instead of answering, her brother reached out and pulled her into a hug. Tina hugged him back, squeezing her eyes tight so she wouldn't cry. It was stupid, since this whole thing had been her idea, but now that it was done, all she could think about was how bad a gamble she'd made. Cinco was a PvP champion, and she'd challenged him on his turf. She'd tanked much bigger baddies than him, but those had been NPCs and monsters, and she'd had a raid to back her up. One on one with another human was a different beast entirely. A dangerous, deadly one.

"Super screwed," she muttered into his chest.

"You're not screwed," James said. "I mean, I wouldn't say challenging a known killer to a duel to the death is the *best* idea you've ever had, but I understand why you did it, and I think you can win."

"How?" Tina asked hopefully. "Do you have a trick up your sleeve? Some crazy-awesome new move you can teach me that he won't expect?"

James shook his head. "I've been trying to think of one, but Cinco's the real deal. He's an actual martial artist, not someone who's been relying on his stats and moves from the game."

"You mean like me," Tina said flatly.

"That's not what I said," James protested, putting up his hands. "I'm just saying Cinco is a tough match, and as much as I'd like to, I can't teach you to be a judo master in an hour. But I still think you can do it."

"But how?" Tina asked again, looking down at her scrawny, frail body. "If I was still Roxxy, I could crush him with my weight or something, but I'm not a stonekin anymore. I'm just a...just a *Tina!*"

"What's that matter?" James asked with a smile. "Roxxy wasn't bigger than Grel'Darm or Sanguilar, and she wasn't stronger than Malakai, but you still won those fights. You don't need to be a stonekin to beat him, T. If I didn't believe that, I'd be out there sabotaging Cinco right now."

"Really?" she said, surprised. "Wow. I mean, that's so unlike you."

"What's unlike me?" James demanded, flattening his ears and thumping his tail and generally looking so much like an offended cat that Tina almost laughed. "That I knew you were the awesomeness all along and not just your stonekin? I have more faith in you than you think."

"No, no," Tina said. "I meant that you'd stoop to sabotaging Cinco. That seems really underhanded for you. I'm shook." *And touched*, she added to herself.

"Of course I'd sabotage him," James said viciously. "Cinco's reasons are bullshit, and I'm not letting some asshole kill my sister. I'd poison him myself if I didn't think you could win, and I'd have plenty of help doing so."

He glanced at the small shadow under the bed as he finished, the only one left in the room, and Tina sighed. She could guess which Roughneck Assassin was lurking down there, but she didn't try to force him out again. Cinco had sneaky Assassins, too, and her side might not be the only one considering some prefight foul play.

"We'll figure it out," she said, reaching down to grab her gauntlet. "For now, though, let's get this binding thing rolling. We don't exactly have the luxury of time, but at least we have armor I can work with myself. You tie the magic to me, I'll resize."

James nodded and got to work, spreading his fingers over the enchanted sun steel to collect the threads of power only he could see.

It took almost the full hour to get her fully re-equipped. While nothing had had as dramatic an effect as the amulet, Tina's head still swam with each new piece she donned. Once she had all her armor on again, she was strong enough to pick up her sword and shield. The massive bulwark was still a tower shield by her new standard, but Tina was painfully aware of how the slab of metal was no longer something that could flatten a car just by falling on it.

Everything was like that. Her armor was still beautiful and legendary and powerful, just....smaller. And in this new world, that mattered a lot. Still, Tina felt much more confident with her full set equipped.

"I have so many questions about density and the conservation of mass right now," James said as he healed up all the extra health her new stats had added. "I don't think the universe works the way we think it does."

"Says the guy casting magic," Tina replied, laughing. "Thanks for the help, by the way."

James nodded, but his eyes were more worried than ever. They were getting her now slightly too-long cape arranged over her shoulders when the tent flap opened, and a huge figure entered the tent. Tina froze, hand falling to her sword before she recognized the golden armor and dour expression of her favorite fortress boss.

"Hello, Garrond," she said, hiding her nerves with bravado. "Come to get your tent back?"

"No," Commander Garrond said, giving her a fed-up look. "I've come to inform you that the Order will not be taking a side in this disagreement."

"Didn't think you would be," Tina said, sliding her sword into its sheath, which had thankfully resized itself at the same time her weapon had. "But at least this means I don't have to worry about you helping Cinco."

"I would never," the paladin said distastefully. "This is a matter of honor. You have been a frustrating ally, Roxxy of the Roughnecks, but I hold great respect for you as a fellow warrior. Foolish as I feel you are being, it is your right to demand satisfaction from one who has wronged you as CincoDeMurder has. I wish you good fortune, and may the Sun's blessings shine on your righteousness this day."

"Thanks," Tina said, but Garrond didn't wait for her response. He was already walking away, leaving her staring at his giant back as he strode across the camp toward the circle of players that was already forming at the gorge's edge.

"Right," she said, fixing her shield on her arm. "Let's do this."

Wincing at the cold wind that bit her exposed ears as she strode out of the tent, Tina wished she'd thought to make herself a helmet back at Camp Comeback. It hadn't seemed like a big deal back when she'd had metal hair and a stone skull, but now that she was oh-so-breakable flesh and bone, the lack of protection seemed like a serious oversight. But while her head felt dangerously exposed, Tina could feel the power in her grip when she clenched her fist. It was impossible to know for sure without an interface, but she was pretty sure all of her base stats were back to normal, minus a few bonuses from going from stonekin to human. She *really* hoped that lost racial two-percent armor bonus didn't come back to haunt her, not that there was a choice. For better or worse, she was doing this, so she pushed her braided hair over her shoulder and held her bare head high, striding as fast as her short legs would take her toward the steep ravine at the camp's edge.

The clearing near the edge of the gorge was packed with players from both guilds. When Tina reached the Roughneck group, they parted to make a path for her. Seeing her in armor, shield and all, NekoBaby started clapping. Others joined in, and the applause rapidly grew to cheers. By the time she reached the battlefield, her raid was going wild. If she hadn't had her game face on, it would have made her cry.

"Thanks for being here, everyone," she said when the applause subsided. "I can't say how much it means to me. Now keep your eyes peeled, 'cause I'm gonna show this fool what happens when you step on the Roughnecks."

"That's my line, darlin'," called a voice behind her.

Wincing, Tina turned around to see CincoDeMurder standing with his spear drawn at the edge of the ravine, right where he'd said he'd be.

"Took your sweet time," he said, pointing his spear at the dull afternoon sky, the brightest it got in the Deadlands. "Not too late to beg for mercy."

Walking into the empty space between the two guilds, Tina stamped her feet on the dusty ground. "I could say the same to you," she growled, drawing her sword. "Remember the rules! This is a one-on-one duel to the perma-death. Loser doesn't get a rez."

"And winner gets your gear," Cinco said, looking her up and down. "All of it."

"That was the agreement," she admitted. "But getting to keep my own armor is a pretty shitty prize for me, so how about this. If I win, I'll let you live, but I'm the boss from here on out. I say jump, you say how high, no back talk."

"Deal," Cinco said with a hungry smile. "Not that it matters, since you'll be dead."

201

"We'll see about that," Tina growled, jerking her head toward Commander Garrond, who was watching from a safe distance with his soldiers. "Since Garrond's neutral, he can start us off. Would you give the signal, Commander?"

The paladin nodded and lifted his sword. "Remember that the Sun bears witness to all our actions," he proclaimed in his booming raid boss voice. "Fighters, prepare yourselves!"

CincoDeMurder twirled his spear, its long crimson blade gleaming wickedly in the dim light of the Deadlands. When he was done showing off, he stepped into a fighting stance, putting both hands on the weapon as he leveled it at Tina.

"Ready!" he called.

Tina raised her shield and drew her own blade. The point of the heavy, black-and-red–runed short sword quivered as she hefted it into guard position. Cursing silently, she stamped her feet in an attempt to banish the shaking that had never really stopped. For the first time ever, she wished they'd had some booze in camp. A shot to steady her nerves would have been really nice right now. Terrible idea, but nice.

"Ready," she said.

Garrond nodded and slashed his sword down, the golden blade falling like the day's last sunlight through the dust. "*Fight!*"

The word had barely reached Tina's ear before CincoDeMurder launched himself at her. The massive man charged in like a freight train, his spear tip moving so fast she couldn't have seen it if it hadn't been going straight for her eyes. Tina stepped back instinctively, throwing up her shield. She wasn't sure if it was luck or raw experience, but the top of the tower shield came up on time to deflect the blow over her head.

But not quite far enough.

Tina gasped in pain. Cinco's thrust had missed her eyes, but the edge of his razor-sharp spear still grazed the top of her scalp, slicing a gash across her unprotected head. Immediately, hot, wet blood began to pour down the side of her face. The wound wasn't actually deep, and the pain was minimal once the initial shock was over, but it still stopped Tina in her tracks.

What followed was a fear that was hard to put into words. She'd been hurt plenty of times before, and far worse than this, but Roxxy's blood had been silver and cold. Now, hot, coppery, *red* blood was running into her eyes and down her cheek, bringing with it an inescapable feeling of mortal danger that she'd never experienced as a stonekin. That was *her* blood coating the spear tip Cinco was pulling back for another strike. *Her* soft, not-granite skin he'd just sliced open. Not Roxxy's, not her character's. *Hers.*

All at once, Tina couldn't breathe. She staggered away from Cinco, raising her shield in pure human terror. When the dreaded red spear came flying at her again, she moved her shield frantically to guard her face. In her panic, though, she left her legs exposed, and Cinco's blade flashed down to stab her in the thigh.

Pain blossomed again, much worse than the scalp wound. As she frantically tried to adjust her position, Tina saw Cinco's eyes flash red, the tell-tale sign of the Berserker's Frenzied Strikes ability. Panicked, terrified, Tina reflexively activated Iron Wall.

It was a stupid, wasteful move. As Killbox had explained to her after their duel, Frenzied Strikes rooted the Berserker in place, meaning she could have just stepped out of the way. But she was not thinking, and Iron Wall was the most comforting of all her defenses. The ability took over her body, overriding her fear-induced fumbling and forcing her limbs back into the correct positions as a powerful series of attacks came in. Enchanted metals screamed as Cinco's spear slammed into her shield with all the highly geared Berserker's weight and strength behind it. Iron Wall forced her to duck a split second later, saving her unguarded eyes from the spray of sparks, but the supernatural skill couldn't last forever.

Like all of her defensive abilities, Iron Wall's duration was measured in seconds, and not many of them. Tina took the chance to slash wildly at Cinco while the ability kept her shield-work flawless. The massive Berserker parried her short attacks with ease, laughing at her as he did. He didn't even seem to care that her shield blocked every one of his blows. He just kept thrusting, hammering her with all his strength as her boots slid back in the dust.

He'd beaten her back almost five feet before Tina realized she *had* to get a grip. This desperate flailing was going to get her killed, and in a really pathetic way, but it was just so *hard*. Roxxy had been more than just extra height and weight. She'd been Tina's foundation, her rock in every sense of the word. Without her, Tina felt exposed and vulnerable, weaker than even Cinco had accused her of being. If she didn't find a way to pull herself together fast, though, her life was going to end at the bottom of a ravine.

That macabre realization was still passing through her mind when Iron Wall ran out. All at once, her supernaturally perfect shield work stopped. A heartbeat later, a stab slipped through to puncture the armor over her left arm. More pain, more panic, more red blood on the ground. Gasping, Tina hunkered down behind her shield for better cover.

Cinco must have been waiting for that. The moment her shield went up, he grabbed the top, armored fingers digging into the metal. The sight made her panic even harder. She didn't know how much Strength his gear had, but it was a lot more than hers. If Cinco ripped her shield away, she—

"*Tina!*" someone shouted in an elven voice. "He's not Malakai!"

That was obvious, but the statement still hit her like a punch, knocking her out of her panic. Good grief, what was she *doing*? The pain and blood were scary, yes, but she'd only taken three small wounds. She wasn't fighting Malakai or Sanguilar or even King Gregory—bosses whose every hit could be fatal. This was just another player, one whom she outgeared. Yeah, he'd gotten some hits in, but Tina wouldn't even have called for healing on something this small in a normal fight, so why was she acting like she was dying now?

Why was she acting like she'd already lost?

Furious with herself, Tina planted her feet, using her superior leverage to rip her shield out of the Berserker's grasp. The sudden loss of his grip left Cinco overextended, and Tina seized her chance, slashing up with her sword. He must have been getting comfortable whaling on her, because Cinco's face went slack with surprise as her sword shot past his completely open guard to slice a deep gouge through the chain mail covering his leg.

For a shining moment, Tina felt victory flowing into her as blood dripped out of Cinco. But even though his spear strike was still overextended, the Berserker didn't miss a beat. He didn't even seem to feel the wound as he turned and slammed his bloody knee into her armored stomach.

Tina grunted. She had plates guarding her torso, so the blow didn't actually hurt, but it did drive her back with a whoosh. Still, the fact that he couldn't mangle her armor with an unarmed attack helped her further realize the truth that had been shouted at her earlier. This *wasn't* the Malakai fight. Cinco was stronger than her by seven, maybe eight hundred Strength. That was a lot, but it was still small potatoes compared to a raid boss. She shouldn't be this afraid of him. It was unbecoming of the world's best tank.

That small spark of shame quickly burst into a bonfire. She'd shrugged off way worse beatings than this. Aside from the new color of her blood, there was nothing scary at all about what had happened so far. Good thing, too, because if Tina wanted to win, she was gonna have to step up. Cinco had the advantage of strength and reach, but she had HP and experience. It was time to be a damn tank.

Fired up, Tina charged Cinco head on, slashing at him with each step. He danced back easily, calmly keeping up with the storm of jabs. He even found time to counterattack, his spear moving lightning fast. Two jabs bounced off her shield, and she parried a third, but one got her in the arm again. The cut wasn't deep and didn't hurt much, but it still made her blood boil. She was attacking this guy all out, and he was *still* getting hits in.

Fuming, Tina forced herself to stop charging like a mad bear and pay attention. She'd avoided PvP at all costs back in the game. She hadn't needed the gear, and arena fights were pointless and frustrating. Also, she was a *very* bad loser. But she couldn't play as much FFO as she had without learning to recognize a true pro when she saw one, and Cinco was most definitely that. Unlike her, he didn't make any big risky moves. His attacks were compact and endless, flowing together in a way that turned his offense into his defense. Every time she messed up, he was quick to exploit it, and while he'd been full of insults earlier, he didn't waste his breath talking smack now. Instead, the Berserker's eyes were locked on her hands and feet, his face a mask of intense concentration as he circled to her left. Taking note, Tina pivoted with him, keeping her shield up to catch his countless strikes as she scrambled to think of a way to trick him into using his stun.

That was the Berserker's big move. If he stunned her, she'd be left defenseless while he had open season on her weak points. Even by not using it, Cinco had the advantage, because she couldn't use any of her big moves without worrying the stun was coming. If she gave him an opening, he'd slam her senseless, bring her health down with Frenzied Strikes, and then use Execution for a finishing critical hit.

That combo wouldn't be enough to kill her normally, but it would be if she let him keep whittling her down, which was probably why Cinco was sticking to small attacks. She needed to do something definitive while she still had the higher health pool, so Tina decided to take a chance and give him what he wanted.

Steeling her courage, she charged in, swinging her shield at him like a car door. Thanks to her new short arms, Cinco hopped out of the way easily, leaving her entire front open. It was irresistible bait, if such madness could be called bait, and she knew he'd taken it when she finally saw him crack a smile.

Sure enough, the butt of his spear flew up, shooting right toward her head for the Berserker's infamously long stun. But Tina had already learned the hard way that abilities were predictable, and he was using Head Slam in a textbook manner. All it took was a single step back and a lift of her arm, and Cinco's spear crashed into the back of Tina's sword rather than her head. Another turn of her wrist, and the spear's shaft was caught between the ridiculous serrations on the back of her crimson-runed tanking blade. Twisting her hilt back, Tina trapped his weapon and then pulled hard.

But not hard enough. Cursing, Cinco pulled back, using his superior strength to drag her forward instead. As her feet slid across the dirt, Tina activated Steady Ground, and her whole body rooted itself in place. This resulted in a very satisfying look of surprise on Cinco's face as his momentum stopped cold. The Berserker's superior strength was useless against her immobility, and the sudden change threw him off balance, giving Tina the edge she needed to haul CincoDeMurder completely off his feet and straight into her oncoming shield.

His nose made an immensely satisfying *crunch* as her Bash ability collided with his face. Shield Bash was the Knight class's stun. It only lasted two seconds, not nearly as long as the Berserker's Head Slam, but two seconds was all she needed. As Cinco stumbled back incoherently, Tina grabbed the shaft of his spear with her shield hand and yanked. When the weapon didn't come free, she chopped down on his arm with her sword.

That got his hand open. He dropped the spear with a gasp, and Tina tossed it over her shoulder into the gorge behind them. Cinco's eyes went from calculating to furious as his weapon clattered down the rocky slope, and then he bared his teeth like an animal.

"You fucking *bitch!*" he roared. "I'll make you die slow for that!"

"Big talk from a guy who leaks that bad from two scratches," Tina shot back, smirking at Cinco's bloody arm and leg. "Are you wearing any Stamina at all?"

Cinco's answer was to rush her, his empty hands going for her shield again. Snatching her bulwark back, Tina stepped in and slashed with her sword instead, happy to let Cinco choose which hand he wanted to lose. He blocked on his right bracer, but the red steel was too thin. Tina felt the hit all the way up her arm as her sword connected and sprayed Cinco's blood across the ashy ground. It wasn't quite enough to actually chop off his hand, but the wound was deep.

That didn't stop him, though. Roaring like he was an actual berserker, CincoDeMurder grabbed Tina's wrist with his bloody hand. He seized the base of her sword arm with his other, and then, using her arms like a lever, he hauled her off her feet.

Tina had never felt the loss of her stonekin more as her legs flew kicking into the air. Roaring with fury, Cinco lifted her high over his shoulders, and then the world went spinning as he threw her down into the bloody dirt.

The impact knocked the wind out of her and made her drop her sword. A normal person would have lain there trying to get air back into her lungs, but Tina had fought too many raid bosses to make that mistake. Stopping was fatal, and her body knew it. She was already throwing herself sideways, chest seizing for breath as her arms scrambled across the dirt to push herself up. She'd just managed to get back onto her hands and knees when Cinco's crushing weight landed on top of her.

A thick-muscled arm snaked around her neck, squeezing into the space between her armor's protective collar and her chin to clamp down on her throat. At the same time, his other arm came up under her armpit, locking his forearm across her chest and grabbing his other wrist to cinch the choke. Scrambling, Tina beat at his arms with her fists, but he was stronger and bigger and had all the leverage. She could have held out, but she *still* hadn't gotten back the breath he'd knocked out of her when he'd thrown her down. Add in the choke, and her vision was already starting to dim, her movements growing smaller and weaker with every hit.

"This is it, girl," Cinco huffed in her ear, "Say good night, 'cause you ain't *ever* waking up."

Too short on breath to curse him back, Tina ignored him and focused on getting free. Unfortunately, her options were very limited in this position. Her shield was useless with Cinco behind and on top of her, and her sword was lying in the dust several feet away. Even if she could have reached it, Cinco's hold under her armpit locked her sword arm at a useless angle. She could only bend it at the elbow, and not with any strength. Her shield arm was free, though, and she raised it frantically, swinging it behind her in an attempt to bash his head with the metal edge. But Cinco's giant shoulder plates—the ones covered in skulls—actually did their job as armor and blocked the hits, leaving her exhausted and *still* unable to breathe.

Unwilling to give up, Tina gritted her teeth and pushed with her legs. Cinco had her arms on lockdown, but he'd left her her feet, and while she wasn't as strong as he was, her epic armor's stats still made her superhuman. Keeping hunched over to balance him on her back, Tina stood up in a rush, lifting the Berserker off the ground. The huge man kicked and scrambled with his feet, but though he was only able to touch the ground with a tiptoe, he still didn't let go.

This was bad. Her lungs were screaming for air now, and the strength in her knees was fading fast. Tina stumbled to the right as the Berserker grew heavier, then she stumbled again as the ground under her feet crumbled, sending a slide of rocks clattering down into the gorge below.

Great, she thought, staggering away from the cliff. Not only was she about to lose consciousness, she was on the edge of the ravine. Even if she jumped, Cinco could simply let go of her to save himself. The sides weren't *that* steep. All he'd have to do was catch hold of rock and climb back up while she fell to her death.

Tina's vision was going in and out now, causing her panic to rise again. Cursing, Tina shoved it back down and forced herself to *think*. Cinco was choking her out, but that was air, not HP. She still had almost all of her health pool, and she was way more armored than he was. Shuffling her feet on the loose soil, Tina looked down into the ravine. She couldn't see the bottom through the deep shadow of the mountains above them, but she knew it was a long fall. Way too long for someone who put all his stats into strength rather than health.

A smile spread over Tina's darkening face. Couldn't tank, huh? A frail little girl, was she? She'd fucking show him how weak she was.

With all her remaining strength, Tina lifted her right foot and brought it down hard to activate her Ground Stomp ability. The wide-area taunt smashed the edge of the gorge to powder, sending golden lines of energy spidering across the dirt for twenty feet in all directions. Massive cracks followed, exploding through the rock, and then Tina felt the blessed rush of air in her lungs as Cinco's grasp vanished.

"You crazy ho!" he cried, wheeling his arms for balance as he tried to jump away, but it was too late. Tina's Ground Stomp had completely destabilized the already-crumbling cliff, causing the whole edge to tip sideways. Then, with a final thunderous *crack*, a good forty feet of old, weathered stone broke free and began to slide, taking them both over the edge in an avalanche of rocks and dust.

Tina pulled her shield over her face as the ground vanished from below her feet. Somewhere to her left, she heard Cinco screaming as the landslide swallowed him. She wanted to scream too, but she was too busy gasping in all the air she could. Light vanished as the river of rocks and dirt engulfed her, carrying her down into the darkness of the ravine like a leaf over a waterfall. Her armor groaned and shook as boulders the size of car engines slammed into her, but terrifying as it was, Tina still had her ace. *Earthen Fortitude, baby!* she thought with a grin, activating the big damage-stopping ability that was going to save her from being crushed to death.

Nothing happened.

Panicking, Tina tried again, her mind shoving at the reflexive ability that usually felt as natural as moving her fingers, but it didn't come. There was no embrace of the Bedrock Kings, no comforting mountain rising up from the deep earth to save her. Her body remained stubbornly soft and fleshy as the rockslide knocked her around like a pinball. It wasn't until the weight of stone crashed down on top of her, though, that Tina realized *why*.

The Bedrock Kings couldn't save her because she was no longer theirs to save. Earthen Fortitude was a stonekin-only ability. Human Knights had their own big damage cooldown, but she hadn't thought to learn it from Frank during the hour of prep time Cinco had given her—a seemingly fatal miscalculation as she slid farther and farther into the dark.

Curling into a ball behind the wall of her shield, Tina gave herself up for buried. The only luck she had was that she landed on her back. Above her, the landslide was still going, entombing her body beneath who knew how much dirt and stone. Years of tanking reflex had kept her shield in position in front of her, creating a pocket of air between her body and the rocks above, but the weight pushing down on her was so intense, the only part of her body she could actually move was her head.

As the thunder of the landslide finally began to quiet, Tina took a moment to assess her position. Her god-forged armor and shield had kept her from being crushed, but she was trapped, buried alive under tons of rock no amount of strength could have moved. She must have hit her head on the way down, because she could feel warm wetness running down her scalp into her armor. A *lot* of wetness, which would have been more frightening if she hadn't been convinced the lack of air would kill her first. Thanks to the faint glow of her armor, Tina could see the pocket her shield had created between the rocks and her body, but that was it. There were no cracks she could see, no daylight coming down through the wall of rocks and dirt above her. Once the oxygen she'd trapped in with herself was gone, that was it. She was dead.

Breathing as shallowly as she could, Tina closed her eyes and tried to come to terms with that. It was easier than she'd anticipated. She'd nearly bitten the dust so many times now, facing the real thing felt strangely anticlimactic. Her greatest regret was that she was leaving her guild to face the Once King without a tank. At least she'd run him out of mana before she'd gone down. As she'd learned from Raffestain, NPCs with giant mana pools couldn't recover any more quickly than players. No mana meant no Million Damage Blast, which meant the Roughnecks still had a chance even without One For All.

Even without her.

Tina's lip began to quiver. *No,* she ordered, squeezing her eyes tighter. She was *not* going to cry. She would die with dignity, dammit. It was the least she could do after getting carried away and killing both herself and Cinco. Dammit, she was supposed to win and get that idiot under control so they could stick to the plan! Now everything was ruined, and it was all her fault, as usual. She couldn't even give someone else her armor since it was buried with her under a million tons of rock.

Her regrets felt even heavier than the landslide. So many mistakes, so many things she should have done differently. Done better. As she heaved for more useless air, Tina almost thought she smelled the scent of the sky. That had to be a hallucination, but at least it reminded her of SilentBlayde. Alone in the crushing dark that was soon to be her tomb, Tina could admit she regretted not getting a kiss before she went. Sure, she was still mad at him, but there'd been a brief hour there when she'd been her and he'd been him, the only hour in seven years of longing where they'd overlapped. Not that a kiss would have changed the whole "dying pointlessly in a rockslide" thing, but it would have been nice to have one less regret.

At least I get to die with my pride.

It didn't feel worth it. She knew she'd been right, but Tina still felt bad about how she'd ended things with SB back in Bastion. More specifically, she regretted the extreme way she'd blown up. The reckoning had been a long time coming, but she wanted to believe that if things had come to a head under less extreme circumstances, she would have been kinder, used better words instead of throwing everything in his face. Maybe, if life had been more peaceful, they could have sorted it out, and then she'd have had a final wonderful memory to keep her warm in this grave of her own making.

212

Thoroughly depressed, Tina breathed in deep, because really, what was the point of saving air when there was no hope of rescue? She was only delaying the inevitable and apparently buying more time to make herself miserable. When she breathed in deep again, though, the smell of the sky was still there, sweet and bright and full of life, like a puff of summer wind against her ear.

Tina froze. That wasn't a hallucination. There really was air moving against the skin of her left ear. It happened again a second later, a slight flutter, almost like someone was blowing on her earlobe. Jerking in surprise, Tina tried to roll over, but the weight pushing down on her was too heavy. The best she could manage was to turn her head, tilting her chin up as she breathed in through her nose.

There was no mistaking it this time. That was *definitely* the smell of the high clouds. When the next puff of it hit her in the face, Tina saw them. Lips. In the darkness just above her, a pair of masculine, elven lips emerged from the shadows to blow a long breath of sky-scented air into her tiny pocket. They vanished back into the Lightless Realm a second later, and Tina closed her eyes with a sob.

Fuck, Blayde.

How was she supposed to stay mad at him when he did things like this!? Here she was, lost beneath tons of rubble, practically dead, and he *still* hadn't given up. She had no idea how he'd found her or what he'd put himself through to do it, but his lips appeared again a few moments later, blowing another life-giving breath into her stone tomb.

Tears running down her face, Tina turned herself sideways with the last of her strength. A trail of dirt landed in her eyes for her trouble, stinging bitterly, but she ignored it, tilting her neck back until it felt like it was going to crack. It was a painful position, but Tina didn't care. She had to be ready, because she might not get another chance, so she braced her body and waited. Then, when his lips appeared again from the tiny shadow in the dirt above her head, Tina pushed up to meet them with her own.

He froze when she made contact, his lips hard as the stone that was crushing her. Then they softened, melting into hers as SilentBlayde kissed her back. They held the kiss for as long as they could, then SB breathed his air into her lungs and vanished, leaving her gasping and flushed. He reappeared a minute later, but even she couldn't manage a repeat of that position. Instead, Tina satisfied herself by inhaling as he exhaled.

Minutes crept by as they kept up that pattern. Exhale and inhale, his breath to hers. Tina counted the seconds between his visits so she'd know when he'd be back, which was how she noticed that the gaps were getting longer. He always reappeared, but his breaths got more ragged each time, chilling her to the bone. Was there air in the Lightless Realm underground? Probably not. Also, how was he reaching her? The Lightless Realm let you move from shadow to shadow, not through solid ground. She was at the bottom of a ravine with what had to be tons of rock on top of her. How was he getting through?

Horror sank in as Tina realized the truth. He was using his speed. Even in a rockslide there were gaps, and down in the dark ravine, there were plenty of shadows. He must have been dashing between them, moving so quickly his body was never in one place long enough to be crushed. Tina shook her head in wonder at how he'd figured that out *and* had also found a safe position in which to pause to exhale. It was damn clever and hard as hell, the sort of feat only someone who'd mastered the Lightless Realm could pull off. It was also going to get him killed. They'd already seen what happened when he pushed his speed too far. If he kept this up, he'd die from hypoxia again. Would he kill himself trying to save her?

Tina was shocked by how well she knew the answer. SilentBlayde would *absolutely* die for her. There was no doubt in her mind, and the next gap confirmed it. It was thirty seconds, his longest yet. The air was getting dangerously thin by the time she felt his presence again, and Tina steeled herself to make it his last.

"Stop," she said.

"No," SB replied.

Tina shook her head. "I'm not letting you go down with me."

"That's my choice."

"No more, Blayde," she ordered, voice shaking. "Please don't make me beg."

The pause that followed was so long that Tina thought he'd obeyed. Then his soft voice whispered in the dark.

"You can call me Haruto if you want."

Tina sniffed as his presence vanished. Damn it. She'd ordered him to go, but she hadn't wanted it to end like this. The proof of how much he still cared was worse than dying thinking she'd ruined everything. At least before she'd had closure. Now she was sitting in the dark counting seconds, torn between hoping he'd come back and praying he'd stay away. Not that she had control, of course. She'd already made her grave, but that didn't stop her from counting as the seconds crept by.

Forty-five.

Fifty.

One minute.

Tina imagined SB dead in the Lightless Realm, trapped under rocks with her because he was too stubborn to let her go.

A minute thirty.

Maybe someone had stopped him? She hoped so. He needed to live. *She* needed him to live. Not even death could save her from the guilt if she got him killed.

One minute forty-five.

Tina had just about given up when she felt another puff of air. Delighted and furious at the same time, she rolled over to yell at him only to pause halfway. This air didn't smell like the sky. It smelled like cat breath. Wrinkling her nose, Tina breathed it in anyway, holding the fishy, meaty air in her lungs as long as she could, but she didn't actually need to. Once they started, the cat-breath puffs came at regular intervals, keeping her from the brink of death. Then, five minutes of fish-air later, she heard the sound of rocks moving above her, followed by a deafening *crack*. Golden light streamed around the edges of her shield, and then sweet, fresh, dusty air flooded into her tomb. Tina was gulping when an excited shout sounded over her head.

"We've found her!"

Tina blinked in wonder. That was James's voice, and he wasn't alone.

"Get that rock, muscle boy!" NekoBaby ordered. "We're almost OOM!"

Metal boots crunched next to her head, and then the crushing weight pinning her down vanished as Killbox and Frank heaved a massive rock off her shield. Hands appeared next, grabbing her arms and shoulders as her friends hauled her up and out of the Tina-shaped hole she'd made in the ground. Nearby, Anders stood with his staff held high, bathing the bottom of the rocky gorge in golden, healing light. A moment later, ZeroDarkness stepped out of the shadows and gave her a feline smirk.

"Where's SilentBlayde?" were the first words out of Tina's mouth when she could speak. Considering the guildwide effort to save her, it really should have been "Thank you," but Tina had to know if SB was collapsed somewhere in the Lightless Realm so they could save him. She was about to ask again when Neko grinned and pointed up the gorge.

"Over there."

Wiping the gritty tears out of her eyes, Tina whirled and saw SB. He was alive, panting on the ground next to a furious Zen. But while the nurse was definitely angry, even her scowl looked relieved. They all did, and Tina lowered her head in shame.

"Thanks, guys," she said, leaning on her shield. "I really screwed the pooch this time. Sorry you had to excavate me."

"'S cool," NekoBaby said with a cocky fanged smile. "We invented some wicked sick earth-bending magic to find—*Whoa!*"

The cat girl was nearly knocked over as James burst through, throwing his arms around his sister so hard it was practically a tackle. "*I'm so glad you're alive!*" her brother cried, his damp whiskers tickling her cheeks.

"I'm fine, thanks to you all," she said, patting him on the back.

James sobbed against her, and then he jerked back and grabbed her shoulders, glaring at her in fury. "*Never* do that again!"

"Not planning on it," Tina promised, then she gave him a smile. "But weren't you the one who said you were confident I'd figure out a way to beat Cinco?"

"I didn't think you'd do it with a landslide!" James shouted. "Seriously, what were you thinking?"

She'd been thinking about how to win, a determination that now felt a little silly and selfish as she looked around at the stricken faces of her friends.

"Thank you," she said again, her chest tight. "Thank you all for saving me."

"Don't you worry about it," Frank said, tugging at his mustache. "We knew you'd win."

James released her as more Roughnecks crowded in. As they took turns slapping her on the back, Tina noticed there were no Red Sands at the bottom of the ravine.

"Wait," she said, looking around. "What happened to Cinco? Is he dead?"

NekoBaby rolled her slitted cat eyes. "Nah. Garrond saved him, the big softy."

"*What?!*" Tina cried. Not that she'd actually wanted to kill Cinco. Her plan had always been to beat him and then use that victory as a leash to keep him in line. Things had just gotten out of hand, as duels to the death were wont to do. She was mostly pissed that the paladin had decided to save the idiot Berserker and not *her*.

"He was actually trying to save you both," Anders explained when she mentioned it. "Garrond has an area-of-effect version of Raise Ally. It operates on a fixed distance, so it skips the typical line-of-sight restrictions. More importantly, it causes a massive pillar of holy light to fly up at each target. He cast it so we could find your bodies under the landslide, but it only worked on Cinco because he was the only one who was dead. When we didn't see your flash, we knew you were still alive, which was good and bad, since it meant we had to find you the hard way and fast."

"Hold up," Tina said, eyes going wide. "If Cinco died, that means I *won*!" She pumped a fist in the air. "*Oh* yeah!"

The jubilant move sent a shock of pain down her side, and Tina winced, slumping back onto her shield for support. Anders's heal had restored her HP and patched up the bloody gash on her head, but Tina was still wrecked from the trauma of the duel and being buried alive. To add insult to injury, her stomach chose that moment to growl loudly, reminding her that her last meal had been an IV back on Earth.

"If we're done here, can we go back to camp?" Tina asked. "Not to be a wuss, but I feel like I haven't eaten in two days."

"Absolutely," James said, his face suddenly dour. "We need to finish taking care of you. Magical healing can only do so much, and your body's still fresh out of the hospital. This hasn't exactly been the easiest first day."

That was the understatement of the century. Fortunately for Tina's pride, everyone seemed desperate to get back to camp. Her raid looked as exhausted as she felt, their glowing armor dusty and bedraggled from frantically digging in the Deadlands' ashy dirt. The thin gray daylight of the zone was fading anyway, a sure sign that the pitch-black darkness of the undead valley's night would be upon them shortly, along with the subzero temperatures. Getting back to the warmth and pseudo-safety of their tents was the right move to make, so Tina gave the order to retreat. It'd give the Once King more time to recover his mana, but she didn't think they could beat him right now even if the king had both hands tied behind his back.

The assault on the Dead Mountain Fortress could wait until tomorrow. Tonight, they were done.

Her command was met with tired cheers as everyone began the terrifying process of climbing up the crooked stairway some Naturalist had hastily carved into the side of the gorge. Tina let them go ahead. She wasn't confident enough in her balance to attempt those stairs yet, and there was something very important she still had to do.

Zen had finished her lecture and moved on to the examination part of things by the time Tina came over. She was checking SilentBlayde's eyes for broken blood vessels when Tina cleared her throat, but she didn't roll her eyes or make a comment or do anything Tina expected. Instead, the tall Ranger gave her a knowing smile and moved away, squeezing Tina's shoulder briefly as she flowed gracefully past.

When she was gone, Tina turned to SilentBlayde, who was still panting on the ground with his face wrap dangling open, his lips faintly blue as his body fought to recover its oxygen. Now that she knew what they felt like, seeing those lips made her blush scarlet, and Tina snapped her eyes to the ground before she made an idiot of herself.

"Thanks, Haruto," she said, keeping her voice steady through sheer force of will. "I owe you one."

There was a crunch as the elf sat up, and Tina held her breath. Waiting for what, she had no idea, but it never happened. Before she or Blayde could say another word, James showed up to pull her away, babbling about all sorts of practical, responsible things like getting her food and washing the blood out of her hair. Unable to fight anymore, Tina let her brother drag her over to the line of players going up the stairs, painfully aware of SB's eyes on her back as she began the long, slow climb out of the gorge.

Chapter 10

James

James's first hour back at camp was entirely consumed with fretting over his little sister. He got her soup and other soft, nutritious foods suitable for a stomach that hadn't eaten in a couple of days. Garrond had already given up on his command tent, so she had a bed and blankets, and Zen showed up later with a bucket of hot water to help get the blood out of her hair and armor. There was quite a lot of blood, actually, which was much harder to deal with than James had anticipated. Seeing blood on Tina was a lot more traumatic than seeing it on Roxxy had been. But thanks to excessive magical healing, there was no lasting damage, and James was soon left with nothing to do.

Worried and anxious, James paced the perimeter of the Roughnecks' camp. Ostensibly, he was keeping an eye on the Red Sands in case they decided to get revenge, but even he had to admit it hardly seemed necessary. The PvP guild's camp was dark and depressed. Everyone stuck to their tents, especially Cinco, who was sulking so hard James was surprised he hadn't created a sinkhole. Climbing one of the dead trees to gain an observation point in case something happened, James was settling in for a long night when he heard someone calling his name.

James looked down to see Fangs in Grass glaring at him from the ground. "Stop looking for problems and get down here!" his brother yelled. "I got us dinner, but I'm not carrying it up a tree."

James didn't particularly want dinner, but he was certain his brother would uproot the tree if he made him wait, so he hopped back down, landing on all fours as always. When he stood up again, though, he saw that someone else was standing with the head warrior. It was one of the Roughnecks' Sorcerers, a tall man wearing the limited-edition movie event headpiece that looked like a crown of flames. He must have been pressed into service by James's brother, because he was currently attempting to juggle three steaming bowls of jerky stew. James took one quickly before it ended up on the ground, blowing on the steaming liquid as the poor Sorcerer shook his overheated hands.

"Thanks," James said, taking a seat by one of the fires that were scattered all over the camp. "So, umm…" He frowned at the Sorcerer, who'd taken a seat across the fire from him. "I'm sorry, I feel like I should know you, but I don't. I'm James."

The lean Sorcerer nodded. "I know," he said in a flat, almost monotone voice. "I'm Richard."

James nearly dropped his stew. "Wait, Richard? As in *the* Richard, god of the Sorcerer forums?" When the tall man nodded, James's face broke into a grin. "Oh, dude, I gotta thank you so much for the ichthyian legendary rep grind guide you wrote for casters! I would have never gotten the *Any Fin Is Possible* achievement without you."

"You're welcome," Richard said perfunctorily, then his thin brows pulled together. "To be honest, though, that guide had an unacceptable number of inaccuracies after the last patch. I was working on an updated version, but then this happened."

He waved idly at the dark mountains rising all around them, and James scooted closer. "So is that the *Prometheus's Fire* promo crown?" he asked, gazing enviously at the ring of fire floating above the human Sorcerer's dark hair. "I heard they only gave them out to a thousand people! I'm so jealous."

"Don't be," Richard replied with a hint of annoyance, the only emotion he'd shown so far. "I cannot remove it and thus live in constant fear of its mild ambient heat causing an unexpected ignition."

"Oh," James said. He hadn't considered the practical difficulties of having a crown of flames dancing around on your head *all* the time. Kind of made him glad he hadn't gotten a piece of rare collectors' loot for once. "So what brings you here?" he asked, switching to something less awkward. "Did you need something from Tina?"

That was the only reason James could think of for a Roughneck to seek him out, but Richard shook his head. "Actually, I was looking for you," he said, setting his untouched bowl of stew aside. "Your name on the forums was Heal-a-Hoop, was it not?"

When James nodded, the Sorcerer's dour face broke into something almost like a smile. "Excellent. I've been a fan of your discovery posts about rare locations in the game since FFO's beta. You are also a caster who, I have been informed, possesses a greater-than-average understanding of postgame magic. These combined areas of knowledge make you the perfect candidate for the conversation I wish to have about today's extraordinary events."

As Richard spoke, James forgot all about the dangerous drama that had gone down between guilds. He'd gotten so caught up in his sister's crisis that he'd almost forgotten about the event that had thrown them into disarray in the first place.

"Tina's real body is here," he said, setting his own bowl down as well. "That's what you want to talk about, isn't it?"

"What else is there?" Richard asked, looking genuinely baffled. "The Once King cast a spell that transferred a *real physical body* from our world to this one! Why is everyone not talking about this?!"

"Maybe because it's not that big a surprise?" Ar'Bati said around a mouthful of stew. "We already know the Once King's the one who brought you players here. That's the whole reason for this campaign."

"But those were just our *souls*," Richard argued. "At least, that's the going hypothesis. This is different. The Once King's magic transported a physical body from our world to this one, *without* killing it! That's a huge jump up from what we previously believed he could do!"

"I don't know," Fangs grumbled, licking his whiskers. "I think he was a fool. I've heard both ears full about this Million Damage Blast of his. Why didn't he cast that instead? He did not know Roxxy possessed the One For All at the time. So far as he was aware, he could have killed us all right there and won, so why didn't he?"

James had wondered that as well. "I bet it was because of Garrond," he said, scratching his whiskers thoughtfully. "As a top-tier four-skull, Garrond has over a hundred million HP. That means the Million Damage Blast wouldn't have been enough to kill him, *and*—as we just saw in the gorge this afternoon—he has a mass area rez. The MDB is super powerful, but it takes a ton of mana. There's no point in wasting all that energy if you're unable to kill the one guy who can rez everyone else."

"But why cast this spell instead?" Ar'Bati pressed. "It took so much mana he couldn't even fly after casting it, but what was the point of sending Roxxy back to her true body if he did not also eliminate her level and class skills? She's just as dangerous to him now as she was before, so why bother?"

"Actually, that purple spell is very dangerous to us," Richard stated flatly. "You do not know our original forms, Ar'Bati of the Four Clans. Only the best players have made it to this time and place, but that means we are all people whose real lives enabled us to play *far* too much FFO." He pointed at his youthful face. "People who spend the majority of their waking lives under VR helmets are not known for taking care of their physical bodies. We look hale and healthy in this place because that was how we designed our characters, but how many of us are physically disabled or impaired back in our world? How many suffer from chronic illness or even the simple impairments of advanced age? I bet there are many in this camp who would quickly die without their daily medications."

Given that his own life had been a constant struggle of figuring out how to play as much FFO as possible without losing so much sleep he went batty, James could only wince at how accurate Richard's assessment was. He also had to wonder just who Richard was in real life. Given the sheer volume of knowledge and theorycraft the world-famous Sorcerer had contributed to the community, James got the feeling he played a *lot*. Like SB-levels of a lot, which didn't leave much time for a job or a family or really anything else.

"I see," Ar'Bati said, nodding gravely. "If that's the case, then Roxxy's actions did indeed save the day. We are lucky she was not among the elderly or infirm."

"For real," James said. "But you're missing the important bit. It's not just good luck that he wasted his spell changing Roxxy into Tina. We now have physical evidence that the Once King can send us home! We already knew he could touch Earth magically, but we didn't have proof that it worked outside of the context of the Nightmare. But the Nightmare's been over for almost two weeks now, and he was *still* able to bring Tina's body over! That means the connection is still there."

"But that is to his advantage as well," Richard said cautiously. "Now that we know for certain the Once King—and *only* the Once King—can send us home, the next logical move would be for him to use that knowledge against us."

James went quiet, thinking that over. "I see your point," he whispered, scooting around the fire so that he was sitting right next to the Sorcerer. "Don't spread this around, but I actually already asked the Once King if he would be willing to send us home."

Richard's eyes went wide. "You've *spoken* to the Once King? *How?*"

"It's complicated," James hedged, keeping his eyes carefully away from the black staff he'd left on the ground by his old seat. "And it wasn't for very long, but I did get a chance to talk to him about this exact subject, and he claimed to have no interest. That was back when he thought he was winning, though. Now that we're at his gates, he might see things differently, and that raises a difficult question: What do we do if the Once King offers to send us back, but only if we abandon the fight?"

Ar'Bati bared his fangs. "There is no question! Half the players here have already made it clear they'd happily feed this world to the ghostfire if it meant they could go home."

"And I would be among those who would fight them to the death to save it," Richard said, his face lighting up with a rare flash of emotion. "I've

224

spent the better part of my life in this world. It is a land of beauty and magic that is far more my home than anywhere my physical body lies. I will not allow it to become a cold hell of undeath!"

"I feel the same way," James said, flashing the suddenly emotional Sorcerer a grin. "But my brother's right. There are a lot of people here who *don't* care and who will absolutely sell this world out for a way back to their own. I'm not saying the people who want to go home are wrong to feel that way, but if the Once King makes us an offer, we're going to be caught in a lose-lose situation. Half of us will want to go, half of us will want to stay, and all the Once King will have to do to defeat us is stand back and let us fight it out among ourselves. We have to figure out how to avoid that scenario at all costs *before* tomorrow's assault begins. Otherwise, we'll be finding out where people stand in the worst way possible."

"The solution is obvious," Richard said, calm once again. "We need a third option. If we could figure out how the purple spell works, we might be able to copy its effects or even reverse them! If we can master how to cross the barrier between this world and Earth on our own, the Once King will have no power over us, and this problem will be solved."

"Whoa," James said, putting up his hands. "I've learned a little about magic, but what you're talking about is way over my head, and probably yours. Not to cast doubt on your abilities, but the Once King is the oldest Celestial Elf and the first creation of the Sun. He has a mastery and understanding of the magic of the Unbounded Sky we couldn't hope to match even if we had a thousand years to study, never mind one night."

Richard's face fell into a stubborn scowl. But while he was clearly trying to think up an argument to counter James, he must not have found it, because he said nothing. James was silent, too, staring into the fire as he struggled to think of a way out, some end scenario in which they weren't all at the Once King's mercy, but he couldn't find one. As always, every path he explored came right back to the Once King, and the more he thought about that, the more he realized that his very first plan might have actually been the right one after all.

"I think we need to talk to the Once King again," he said. "Before the battle."

"Are you mad?" Fangs snapped. "Why would you even consider talking to the enemy of all life? Especially considering he already turned you down!"

"There's a lot of reasons," James argued. "Starting with the fact that the Once King is a rational being. He's not some cackling evil overlord who wants to destroy everything just because. Whenever I've talked to him, he's always seemed more resigned than angry."

"You say that," Ar'Bati growled. "But I have felt the ghostfire. I *know* the hatred for all life which burns within it. So do you!"

"I do know," James agreed. "And that's why this makes no sense! The more I learn about the Once King, the more I realize he's not like the ghostfire or his undead. They devour everything with irrational hatred, but every time I've talked to the king, he's been calm and rational. I wouldn't say he's nice, but he's definitely not some raging lunatic. Whatever he's doing with the ghostfire, he's doing it for a reason. If we could find a way to help him achieve that purpose *without* killing everyone else on the planet, imagine the possibilities. Imagine if he wasn't our enemy!"

"James," Ar'Bati growled. "You cannot talk down a man who has been the enemy of all life for a thousand years! Words cannot sway such determination."

"But we still don't know *why* he made the ghostfire or started this conflict in the first place," James said. "It wasn't in the game lore, and Gray Fang didn't know either. I'm starting to think that *no one* knows why the Once King does what he does, but that doesn't mean he does it for no reason. You call him the enemy of all life, but the ghostfire doesn't make undead plants, and the only animals that turn are the ones that are useful as weapons, big boars and wolves and whatnot. Otherwise, the ghostfire passes right over them. I mean, have you ever seen an undead rabbit?"

"No," Ar'Bati admitted grudgingly. "But that doesn't help us. We're not animals."

"We're not," James admitted. "But it's a start. Do you remember what the Lich of Red Canyon told us? He said that all Celestial Elves used to have wings, but they got burned off. Have either of you ever heard of that event? Because I've never read anything about it."

"It was definitely not in the wiki or any accessible in-game lore," Richard agreed. "I've read it all, and this is the first I've heard of burned wings."

"Exactly," James said. "I've already seen how there's a *lot* going on in this world that we don't know. Remember what the Bedrock Kings said about the Sun's betrayal? They claim the Once King tried to warn them because he was a good king, but everything I've ever heard or read about the Sun says it is a being of boundless mercy and goodness. The priests certainly seem to think so. And while the Sun wouldn't be the first god to have a complicated mythology, all the peoples of this world who worship the Sun see it as a wholesome and benevolent being. I find it very odd that such a seemingly universally beloved divinity would be capable of betrayal."

"There are many contradictions," Richard agreed.

"They're everywhere," James said, baring his teeth in frustration. "*It's* everywhere!"

"It what?" Ar'Bati asked.

"Bad history," James said, rising to his feet. "We're on the edge of something big. I can feel it. The Once King's constantly talking about saving people through death, but other than general nihilistic comments on the pointlessness of existence, he's never actually said what specifically he wants to save us from. There's no way the Once King would be going through all this trouble and putting himself in so much danger to make a philosophical point. There's something missing, some big piece of the puzzle that we don't

227

know yet. We can't fix this problem without knowing what started it, but if it's not in the game lore or the actual history, then the only person we can ask is the Once King himself. He's the crux of all of this."

Fangs in the Grass set his bowl down and stood to clap James on the shoulder. "It is clear you are convinced," he said. "I am not yet, but I have learned to trust in your wisdom. If you say this is the only way, I believe you."

James blinked at him in shock. "Really?"

Ar'Bati nodded, and James had to blink again hard to hold back the sudden tears. He'd been a screw-up for so long that he didn't know if he was ever going to be used to people just...trusting him. *Believing* in him. He still didn't know if he deserved it, but he was absolutely determined not to let his brother's faith down.

"Thank you," he said, reaching up to squeeze Fangs's hand.

"Are you going tonight, then?" Richard asked in his flat, casual way.

"Yes," James said, reaching down to grab his Eclipsed Steel Staff. "The assault is tomorrow morning, and there's no stopping it. If we're going to talk to the Once King, it has to be tonight."

"I wish you luck, then," Richard said, standing up as well. "I'd love to go with you—the Once King knows more about magic than any being in this world that's not actually a god—but I'm the Roughnecks' Sorcerer Officer, and I'm pretty sure I'd be missed. I'll stay here and delay things to buy you as much time as possible. And if the Once King does agree to stop fighting, please tell him I'm eager to talk with him."

"I will," James promised. "Thank you."

The Sorcerer nodded and left, drumming his fingers thoughtfully on his staff as he walked away through the circles of the fires. When he was gone, James turned to Ar'Bati. "Can you pack up our stuff and meet me on the Dead Mountain side of camp? I've got one more thing I need to take care of before we go."

"Certainly," Fangs said. "But surely it would be better to make haste? You said yourself this is the most important mission, perhaps in the entire world. What is it you need to do that's worth delaying that?"

James took a shaky breath. "I gotta tell Tina where I'm going."

***

James *really* didn't want to do this.

He was standing a few yards from the command tent Tina had ended up taking over, going back and forth with himself about what was best. If he snuck out under cover of night, he'd save himself a lot of time and avoid a potentially disastrous confrontation. He hadn't forgotten what had happened the last time he'd told Tina his plans. He and Fangs had ended up under NekoBaby's paw, and he didn't have time to deal with that again. On the other hand, sneaking out and kicking up huge amounts of trouble Tina might have to save him from later wasn't being a good brother. The two of them had made huge progress since Bastion, and James didn't want to jeopardize that by running off without telling her. He also didn't want to go back to being the sort of person who asked for forgiveness rather than permission. That was just another name for being irresponsible, and James was done running from his problems.

Not that that made them easier to deal with.

He was still going back and forth when he realized how much time he was wasting. All around him, the camp was filled with the nervous murmurs of people who knew this might be their last night alive. This whole army could be marching off to die tomorrow. He might be able to stop that, and here he was wasting precious time being afraid of his baby sister.

Thoroughly ashamed, James steeled his spine and marched up to her tent. The guards didn't even issue a challenge. They just waved him through, letting James walk right up to the lowered tent flap.

229

"Tina?" James called through the thick canvas. "It's me. I need to talk to you."

For a moment, there was only silence, then a muffled groan rose from inside. "Do you know what time it is? I actually need sleep now that I'm fleshy, you know."

"I know," James said, voice shaking. "But this is important."

"It's always important," she grumbled, but the rustling blankets told him she was getting up. "Come on in."

James pushed into the tent to find his sister sitting on her cot in full armor, which was a surprise. The last time he'd seen her, she'd been in a tub, scrubbing dried blood off her skin while Zen asked her math questions to make sure she didn't have a concussion. But while her frizzy brown hair was still damp and her eyes were bleary, she looked ready for combat at a moment's notice, which was a pretty wise way to be considering everything that had happened to her that day.

"All right, I'm awake," she said as James moved her shield aside to make himself a place to sit. "Now tell me what's so important."

"There's no easy way to say this, so I'm just going to lay it out," James said as he sank down to the ground beside her. "I'm going to the Dead Mountain to talk to the Once King. Tonight."

His sister's eyes widened, and then she closed them, reaching up to rub her temples. "Okay," she said slowly. "Why would you want to do that?"

James immediately launched into the explanation he'd rehearsed on the way over. Before he'd gotten through two sentences, though, Tina held up her hand.

"Don't take this the wrong way, J, but I just realized I don't actually want to hear it. I'm sure you've got a whole list of great reasons for doing this, but if you tell me, we're going to argue, because at the end of the day, we both know that if you go into the DMF alone there's a good chance you're gonna die and be made undead and then I'm gonna have to kill you and *I don't want to do that.*"

230

"I know," James said, trying not to sound as upset as he felt. "I knew from the beginning that this might be a one-way trip, but I think it's worth the risk. If it makes you feel better, though, I promise I'll return to you alive or not at all."

"That's even worse!" Tina cried, her angry glare changing into desperation, which was much, much worse. "Damn it, James, I just got you back! Why do you have to run off and get killed? I know the world is at stake, but we've already got a plan. We go in, we kick the Once King's butt, make him send home whoever wants to go home, and the ones who stay stomp out the ghostfire. Easy peasy, done and done. We've *got* this, so can you please just back off and let me handle things for once?"

"No," James said. "Because I *don't* think it's going to be that easy. There's so much that we don't know, things that might change the entire situation! I can't sit back and let everyone march into a situation that might be much, *much* worse than we think when there's a chance to *not* do that. Going to the Once King myself is the only way I can get the answers I'm looking for. The moment we show up with an army, the fight is on. But if I go to him alone, I won't be a threat, which means he might actually talk to me. That's the best thing I can do for us. The best I can do for *you*."

"I don't need you to do anything for me!" Tina said angrily. "I'm the tank! I protect you, not the other way around. All you have to do is worry about yourself instead of everyone else. How is that so hard to understand?"

"Because I already did that, and I've regretted it every day since!" James yelled. "I won't make that mistake again!"

"Whoa," Tina said, jerking back in surprise at his explosion. Then her eyes narrowed suspiciously. "We're not talking about the Once King anymore, are we?"

James took a deep breath. He hadn't meant for things to go this direction. Now that they had, though, he found it very fitting. He'd always meant to tell her this someday, and what better time was there than his possibly last night alive?

"Do you remember the summer I ran home from college?"

"How could I not?" Tina said, her voice so resentful it hurt. "It was the worst summer of my life."

"Mine, too," he admitted, making her do a double take.

"Oh," she said quietly, her expression confused, as if she'd never thought of it that way before. "All right," she said, scooting forward. "Go ahead. I'm listening."

He knew she was, and that was what made this so hard. "Something happened," he said, forcing the words out. "At school."

"I figured."

She didn't say it in a mean way, but the words still made him flinch. "I knew I'd been slacking," he said defensively. "Playing too much FFO, letting my grades slide. I was working extra hard on my finals to try to save the semester. You know, get my act together. But then..."

He trailed off, unable to continue. He didn't know why. The words were right there on his tongue, but he'd kept this secret for so long now, pulling it out felt like removing a rib. But if anyone deserved to know what had happened, it was Tina. Of everyone he'd hurt—those who were still alive to feel it, anyway—his sister had suffered the most for his actions. He couldn't risk dying without telling her why.

"It happened during the last week of finals," he said, his voice so thin she had to lean in to hear it. "I was up late studying when I got a call from my friend Grayson. He was upset and wanted to talk. I told him I couldn't, that I was studying. He...he started crying, begging me to come over. I knew something was off, I could hear it in his voice, but I'd put off studying for so long and had so much cramming left to do, so I..."

He fell silent again. Tina didn't say anything either. She just sat perfectly still, waiting for him to finish.

"I brushed him off and hung up," James choked out at last. "They found him in the river the next morning. He'd thrown himself off the bridge." He looked down, shoulders hunching in a sob. "I didn't even pass my test."

There was a soft clink as Tina removed her armored glove. Then her small, pale hand appeared on his, squeezing him tight.

"The cops told me later that I was the last person he'd called," James whispered, reaching up to rub the wet fur around his eyes. "All he'd wanted was to talk. I could have done that. I could have saved him, but I was too busy thinking of myself."

He couldn't say more. His throat simply wouldn't work. Even now, years later in another world, he remembered that morning with perfect clarity: the police knocking on his door, how annoyed he'd been that they were making him late, and then the pictures. The reality of what he'd done going off like a bomb. Later, the school counselors had told him over and over that Grayson's death wasn't his fault, but they hadn't been there. They hadn't seen how annoyed he was when he'd hung up, the way he'd rolled his eyes at Grayson's "drama." They didn't know how selfish he was, but James did.

"It was my fault," he whispered, turning his hand over to grab Tina's tight.

"It wasn't."

"It *was*," he said fiercely, head snapping up to look at her at last. "I *knew* something was wrong, I just didn't care. I might not have physically pushed him off that bridge, but I couldn't be bothered to extend my hand when Grayson begged for it. I don't see how that's any different."

"James," Tina sighed, but he held up his hand.

"I've hated everything about myself since that morning," he went on, desperate to have it all out. "I couldn't handle college after that. I tried anyway, but I flopped and screwed you over in the process. Everything I did, I failed. The only reason I didn't kill myself too was because I'd already seen how much that would hurt everyone around me, so I ran instead. Ran from you, ran from college, ran from all my other friends. I ran and hid in FFO

233

because that was the only place where I could be someone who wasn't me." He dropped his head with a sigh. "I'm sorry your brother is such a piece of shit."

The tent was silent when he finished. Then Tina's armor clinked again as she rose up on her knees to wrap her arms around him. "I love you, James," she whispered, hugging him so gently he didn't know how she managed it in all that plate. "Thanks for telling me."

The soft words hit him like a wave. It didn't seem real that she was acting like this. He'd been so sure she'd be disgusted, that she'd look down on him even more, but Tina did none of that. She just held him tight, petting his head with her hands. It felt so nice—both the petting and the relief of finally having it all out in the open—that he slumped into her, his whole body relaxing in a way he hadn't in years. A minute later, he became aware of a faint vibration running through his bones. It got louder as he listened, and then, to his shock, Tina began to snicker.

"Oh my god, *dude*," she said, choking on her laughter. "Jubatus *purr!*"

"I guess we do," he said, mortified. "Sorry."

"No, no, I'm sorry," she said, desperately trying to get a hold of herself. "I don't mean to laugh, it's just *super* funny. I wonder if Neko knows."

"We can sorta meow, growl, and roar too," James admitted, allowing himself to grin at the ridiculousness of it all. "I bet if someone put a box down, I'd have an irresistible urge to sit in it."

They both lost it after that. Tina laughed so hard she fell over. James went down beside her, clutching his sides as years of tension and fear flowed out of his body. When it was finally over, Tina pushed up on an elbow to grin down at him.

"Feel better?"

"I do, yeah," James said, drying his face with his cloak.

"Good," she said, and then she punched him in the arm. *Hard.*

"Ow!" James cried, jerking away from the unexpected violence. "What was that for?"

234

"For being mean to James," she said, not appreciating the irony or the contradiction. "You're *not* a piece of shit. I couldn't go five minutes in Windy Lake without someone telling me about how my brother saved the town. Seriously, Rends would *not* shut up about your selfless heroics, and Gregory told me three times about all the stuff you did to save us in Bastion. Sure, you messed up in the past. So did I. But in the here and now, you're a hero seventeen times over, so you are *not* allowed to be mean to yourself. I'd clobber someone if I heard them saying the shit about you that you said to yourself. Don't think I won't do the same to you."

"You sound like Ar'Bati," James grumbled, rubbing his arm sourly.

"Yeah, well, sometimes Angry Cat gets it right," Tina said, reaching down to yank him up off the floor. "So we cool now?"

James nodded meekly, wondering how she'd managed to turn this around on him. "We're cool. Thanks, T."

Tina nodded and sat back down on her bedroll, satisfied. "Okay, so you're going into the DMF tonight to talk to the Once King," she said, reminding James that he hadn't actually come here for a giant confessional. "What do you need from me?"

"Uh, permission?" James said nervously.

"Granted," Tina replied. "Thanks for asking. Anything else?"

"That's about it," he said. "Fangs and I are going to seek an audience to—"

"Nope, nope," Tina said, putting up her hands. "Don't want to hear, remember? If you tell me, I'm going to freak out, so let's just leave it at you've got an idea, and I'm going to trust you to carry it out *without* turning into a zombie. Deal?"

"Deal," James said.

"Great," she said, looking relieved. "And if you get stuck, just hide somewhere and wait for us. I'll find you even if I have to turn over every stone on that damn mountain."

"Will do," James said, and then he smiled. "Thank you."

"You can thank me by not dying," she snapped. "No undeath allowed, either. I'm not above trapping you in some kind of zombie-comedy-movie situation, I'm warning you."

James laughed at the idea, but it rang a bit hollow since undeath was a real threat here. There wasn't much else to say after that, and he was sure Ar'Bati was waiting impatiently for him, so James leaned down to hug her again. "Good-bye, Tina," he said. "I'll see you in the fortress."

"Bye, James," she replied, hugging him back. "See you soon."

James winked at her and ducked out of the tent. The camp was dark and quiet when he emerged, the fires banked for the night, though he still didn't think anyone was sleeping. Thankfully, his jubatus eyes worked as well in the Deadlands as they had in the Grasslands. He made it through the whole camp without tripping over a single rope. He spotted Ar'Bati waiting exactly where he'd told him to, standing under a copse of dead trees with two packs slung over his shoulders and his sword on his back, its soft green light illuminating his face like a ghost.

"How did it go?" he whispered when James got close.

"Surprisingly well," James whispered back, reaching up to catch the pack Fangs tossed at him. "We're not fleeing in the night, if that's what you're wondering."

"Good to know," the warrior said, standing a bit straighter. "Not that I fear her, but your sister is not someone I want on my heels ever again."

"Me neither," James agreed, looking up at where the Dead Mountain cast an even darker blotch against the moonless sky. "Ready to do this?"

His brother turned without a word, marching down the broken road away from camp toward the ever-looming spire of the Once King's fortress.

Chapter 11
Tina

Tina couldn't sleep.

She'd tried after James left, but all she'd managed was to find new ways to get her armor caught in the blankets. She was grateful her brother had told her he was going, but now she had to worry about him, and it was driving her insane. At least he'd finally let her in on what had happened all those years ago. She'd known it was bad, but for once, the truth had been worse than her imagination. Poor James. He hadn't deserved any of that, and he definitely hadn't deserved all her yelling. She'd felt so righteous at the time, but looking back, all Tina could see was a selfish teenager too caught up in her own woes to realize that her brother was suffering too.

They really were two peas in a pod, weren't they?

Well, she was going to do better. James was the savior of multiple cities at this point. If anyone could make the Once King listen, it was him. And if he didn't, Tina would be there to save his tail. Or zombie tail, as the case might be.

But she was not going to think about that. She was going to keep her damn word and trust her brother and get some sleep because she was a responsible leader, and these things mattered. It helped that she already knew exactly how much trouble she'd make if she tried to stop him. Neko was *still* complaining about—

"Halt."

The sudden command made her jump. Then she flopped back down, remembering the guards Zen had insisted on posting. It made sense, she supposed, but knowing there were people standing right outside her tent made sleeping even harder. She was totally going to dismiss them as soon as whoever this was went away.

"Roxxy's asleep," the guard said, his voice offensively loud through the canvas. "Take it to Zen or Richard."

Well, maybe there were a *few* perks to having—

"This is personal," a smooth elven voice replied, derailing her thoughts completely. "I just want a word."

Tina shrank down in her armor. *Craaaaaap.* And here she'd thought the night couldn't get any longer. She was tempted to stay quiet and let the guard—who'd totally just proved his worth—deal with it, but that would be cowardly. It would also be wrong. Sitting in the dark tent, it was all too easy to remember how she'd felt trapped under the landslide. All those regrets had made an absolute mess of her heart. Scratch that; her heart had been a mess since Bastion, and it wasn't going to straighten itself out until she dealt with this. She wasn't sure how it would go—probably horrifically—but James wasn't the only one who could die tomorrow. Tina was determined that the next time she faced that void, she would do so with a clear conscience, so she stood up and opened the flap, sticking her hand out to tap the back of the huge Berserker blocking her door.

"It's okay," she said when he turned around. "You can let him in, and you guys can have the rest of the night off. I'm good to guard myself now."

She rapped her knuckles against her armored chest, and the Berserker smiled in relief. "Right-o, boss," he said, happily trotting off to his bed. The other guard, a jubatus Cleric, went more slowly, making Tina feel even better about her decision. However this went, it was bound to be painfully personal. Personal and *way* too interesting to trust a guard to keep his ears shut. Even if she'd had faith he wouldn't talk, the last thing Tina wanted right now was an audience, so she stood in the door, glaring until the Cleric was gone. Only when he'd climbed fully into his tent did she finally turn and look at the man she'd been steadfastly avoiding this whole time.

"Come in if you're gonna."

SilentBlayde ducked into the tent so fast he seemed to teleport, clearly wanting to get inside before she changed her mind. Tina wasn't sure she hadn't, but she was in this up to her neck now. When she turned around, he was taking off his helmet, revealing blond hair that was messy for once.

She had no idea how that had happened. So far as she knew, elves *always* had perfect hair. She was about to ask if he'd made an effort to get it that tangled when he reached up and unhooked his mask.

Tina went still. SB treated his helmet like any other piece of clothing, but his ninja mask was special. It was just a vanity item, it didn't even have stats, but he acted like it was vital for breathing or something, and she'd never known why. Because he'd never told her, not even when she'd begged.

Which was the entire problem.

With that thought, the old anger flared bright and hot. She was a fool for letting him in—for putting herself through this *again*. How many times did she have to get burned before she learned? She was opening her mouth to tell him she'd changed her mind when SB said, "I'm sorry."

"You've said that before," Tina reminded him, crossing her arms over her chest.

"Not like this," he said, looking at her with those damn sad eyes that never failed to make her act like an idiot. "I'm sorry for how I've treated you. I shut you out and used secrets to control you unfairly. That wasn't my intention, but it was still wrong. *I* was wrong, and I'm sorry."

Tina looked down at her metal boots, clenching her fists against the stupid wave of hope that kept surging back up no matter how many times she stomped it down. Dammit, she'd sworn she wasn't going to do this to herself again. She was *not*.

"Why are you telling me this now?" she demanded, clutching her anger like a shield. "Is it because I'm human? I'm not an asexual hunk of stone anymore, so suddenly you feel bad? That's fucking convenient."

"That's not why!" SB cried, though Tina wasn't above feeling gratified at how red his face turned.

"Is it because you think I'm weak now?" she demanded. "I don't need a protector."

239

Those handsome lips twitched. "Tina, I watched you pick up a fully armored Berserker just a few hours ago. No one who sees you do anything could ever think you're weak."

Well, that was gratifying, but she was not going to be flattered into forgiveness. She was already breaking a thousand promises to herself just by letting him in here. If not for what had happened under the rockslide, she wouldn't even be looking at him.

"Then why?" she asked, hating how desperate her voice sounded. "Why are we still doing this?"

"Because I lost you twice today," SilentBlayde said, his voice cracking. "Once when I thought the Once King had disintegrated you and again in the landslide. Both times were worse than anything I could have imagined, but once was enough to teach me that a future without you was worse than any damage I could do by telling you the truth."

Tina's heart began to pound so hard she felt lightheaded. She hid it by sitting down, her armor clattering musically as she propped her knees in front of her and rested her arms on them. "Then prove it," she challenged him, her face as stony as she could make it. "Tell me why I couldn't visit you in Japan."

There was a pause, and Tina sighed. He wasn't going to do it. She'd been an idiot to think he could ever—

"My full name is Haruto Watanabe," he said, speaking in a clipped, tight voice like he was forcing the words out through sheer will. "I'm sorry I never told you before. I couldn't risk you using it to figure out where I lived."

"Why didn't you want me to know where you lived?" Tina asked, shocked. Not that he didn't want her to know but that he was actually telling her something personal. "Were you on the run or something?"

SilentBlayde shook his head. "It's not like that," he said, sinking down to sit on his knees Japanese style in front of her. "I didn't want you to know anything about my life outside the game because I was afraid you'd hate me."

240

"Wait," Tina said angrily. "You were afraid I'd hate you, so you refused to tell me anything to the point where I got so fed up and insulted that I dumped you in front of everyone?"

Technically, she hadn't dumped him since they'd never been together in the first place, but Tina wasn't in the mood for splitting hairs, and SB didn't contradict her.

"Yes," he said, shamefaced. "I'd rather you be mad at me for lying than risk you knowing the truth. I can live with you being angry or even kicking me out of the guild, but I couldn't live if you hated me."

"I don't hate you," Tina said, hurt he'd even think that. "I could *never* hate you. I think I've proved that. I mean, if what happened in Bastion didn't do it, what could?"

He stared at the ground. "You don't know the real me."

"Stop."

SB looked up, confused, and Tina glowered. "You're doing it again," she told him. "I'm not tolerating this 'you don't know and I'm not telling you' game anymore. If you want to be in my life, tell me the truth and let me decide my own feelings. Trying to manipulate me like this is *not* cool, and I'm not putting up with it any longer. If you're here to say something, say it. Otherwise, get out."

"Sorry," he whispered, his body shaking. "I don't mean to, it's just...." He took a deep breath. "I've borne this shame my whole life. It's hard to say out loud."

Seeing the pain on his face made it impossible for Tina to stay mad. The urge to hug him and tell him it was okay was overwhelming, but she couldn't, because it *wasn't* okay. If she gave in and let him off easy, they'd just go right back to the same limbo they'd been in for the last seven years. She couldn't do that again. It was put-up-or-shut-up time, no more outs, but that didn't mean he had to do this alone.

"I'm here," she said quietly, reaching out to put her hand, which was still bare from James's visit, on his knee. "Whatever you have to say, I'll listen, and if it's something I can help with, I will. Just let me in. Please."

"There's no helping this," he whispered, staring at the ground without really seeing it. "It's unfixable. But I'll tell you anyway, because you deserve to know why I am the way I am."

Tina didn't like the way he said that, but she nodded and sat back, holding her breath until, after what felt like eternity, he looked at her.

"My sister is also my mother," he said in a small voice. "I am my family's dirty secret, our great shame. I've been shut in by them for my whole life. That's why I could play FFO ninety hours a week. VR was my only escape."

Tina stared at him, shocked. "They locked you up?"

SB nodded, a tiny jerk of his head. "Since I was eight. That was when..."

He stopped, fisting his hands on his knees. Tina kept her mouth shut, giving him all the time he needed.

"When I was little, I thought my mother was my father's wife," he explained, as if that were abnormal. "But I didn't understand why she hated me. I didn't know why she never took me shopping or to the park like the other mothers I could see from my window. I thought it had something to do with the way our neighbors whispered, but when I told her I didn't care what they said, she screamed that I never should have been born."

Tina clenched her jaw, shaking with rage. She wanted to hurt the woman who'd done this to him, but she couldn't. The wrong was locked away in the past where she couldn't reach it, and Haruto wasn't finished.

"I knew something was wrong with me after that," he went on, not looking at her. "But I was too afraid to ask. My father was an angry man. He would beat us if we said anything to upset him. The woman I thought was my mother wore makeup to cover the bruises, but I couldn't. It was safer to stay in my room. The only person who was never cruel to me was my sister.

She just pretended I didn't exist. I started doing that too, eventually: pretending I wasn't there or that I was invisible. It was so much easier that way."

Tina nodded, unsure what to say, but SB wasn't looking at her anymore.

"It worked for a while. My father was a big believer in keeping up appearances. He had an important job at a big company, and while he never looked at me unless he had to, he insisted we all get dressed up and go out for important events like festivals. You know, pretend to be a normal family. It was during one of these that it happened. It was the spring right after I turned eight. We were on our blanket at our local sakura festival, viewing the flowers. The whole neighborhood was there, whispering as usual. We were ignoring them, but then the lady who lived in the house next to ours came over. She was drunk. *Very* drunk. Enough to walk right up to me and comment on how much I looked like my sister."

His perfect jaw clenched. "My father flew into a rage. He said we were leaving at once, but I didn't want to. I was having a good time being outside with other people for once, and I didn't understand why everyone was so angry. Why shouldn't siblings look alike? I didn't know yet what the rest of the neighborhood had known since before I was born, but my father was pulling my arm. When I tried to pull back, he..."

"He hit you?" Tina guessed, her heart breaking.

"It was worse," Haruto said in a tiny voice. "He picked me up and shoved me in the car. When we got home, he beat me so bad I had to go to the hospital. I was there for a month, but the doctors...they couldn't fix the damage. I remember being in the room when they told my parents my jaw would never be the same. My father just laughed and said that was fine, because at least now no one could say I looked like them."

He took a shuddering breath. "That was my first clue. I didn't learn the rest until later: how he'd raped my sister when she was thirteen, how he'd forced her to have the baby. Forced her to have me. She lived with us until she was twenty-three, when she left to get married. The whole time, she never looked at me. Never said a word. My father's wife was the one who finally told me the truth. She said I should know what I'd done. How I'd broken their family."

"But you didn't do anything!" Tina said fiercely. "None of this was your fault! Your father was the criminal. He should have been arrested!"

"The police wouldn't help," he said bitterly. "It was a family matter, and my father was a big local businessman. Even when I was in the hospital, no one said a word. That was when I knew for certain that no matter how much evil he did, no one was ever going to save me. All I could do was run and hide in games, the only place where he couldn't get me."

His body pulled tighter as he looked up at her at last. "So there you have it. My father is evil, and I'm a mangled monster born of an unclean union. I thought the transition had set me free, but my actions in Bastion proved that I've inherited much from my beast of a father. He's still in me, even now." He dropped his eyes. "I understand if you choose to revile me."

By the time he finished, Tina was so mad she was shaking—not at SB, but at the fact that his father was safe back on Earth and she couldn't pound him into a bloody paste. She wanted to rip apart everyone who'd made him feel this way, but she couldn't, and her anger was scaring SB. He'd just bared his soul and was clearly expecting rejection, and she was sitting here plotting murder. He needed better from her, so Tina shoved her anger away and focused on what was important.

"Thank you so much for telling me something so painful," she said. "I can see now why you didn't want to tell me before, but it's okay. All of that is in the past. It doesn't affect who you are right now."

"But it *does*," SB said, his voice thick. "Don't you see? I can't escape! Even here, in another world, I can't get away from what I am!"

"You're right," Tina said. "You *can't* get away from who you are, and that's a great thing, because who you are is a good person. Always was, always will be."

"You're wrong," he argued desperately. "I murdered innocents in Bastion. I stabbed James! I thought I had a new start, a chance to be washed clean, but all I've done is prove over and over that I am that monster's son. If anything, I'm worse. At least he never killed anyone in his anger." He hid his face. "I'm worse."

Tina grabbed Blayde's hands and pulled them away. "You are *nothing* like your father," she said angrily, staring hard into his blue eyes. "That man is a vile, reprehensible fucker who raped one child and beat the other. You are a sweet, kind, generous person whose only crime is trying so hard to be good that you screw things up by keeping all these burdens to yourself."

"But I'm not!" SilentBlayde cried, ripping his hands out of her grip. "You should hate me! I deserve it. I'm disgusting!"

He stood up then, darting around her toward the door like he was leaving. Panicked, Tina leaped up and grabbed him again, stopping him with her superior strength.

"Haruto!"

He went still in her grasp, and she let go at once, refusing to hold him with violence. He'd had far too much of that in his life already, and she was determined he would never feel it again. But she couldn't let him leave. Not like this.

"Please don't go," she said instead, her voice shaking. "I need you to listen to me. I don't think you're disgusting or a monster or any of those things, and I hate when you say them about yourself. I know you. I know who you are and what you've done, and I don't hate you at all. I will *never* hate you. I..."

Her voice faltered, but there'd never been a more important moment, so Tina gave her pride the shove and told him the truth. "I love you. I loved you back on Earth, and I *still* love you every bit as much now that I know everything. So please stay with me. Please don't go."

245

It was the closest to begging she'd ever come, but Tina didn't care. She'd plead on her knees if it would just make him listen. She was about to go ahead and get down there when SB finally turned around.

"Really?" he whispered in a tremulous voice.

"Really," Tina said, face heating. "How can you even ask that? You know I've had a crush on you for—"

"*I love you too!*" SilentBlayde cried, jumping back to grab her hand in his. "I've loved you since level one, back when we first grouped up seven years ago!"

Tina blushed harder. "You mean when I was Roxxy?" She looked down anxiously at her human body. "Um…it's not going to be a problem now that I'm not her anymore, right? I can't turn back into a stonekin."

Blayde vigorously shook his head. "I love *you*," he said emphatically. "It doesn't matter what body you're in or what character you play. You're the one I want. From the first time we partied together, you were the coolest person I'd ever met. You were brave and funny and fearless and always charging ahead toward amazing things. I've had a massive crush on you since that very first night, and it's only gotten stronger the more we've played together. What could I call this feeling but love?"

By this point, Tina's face was so red she thought she'd spontaneously combust. She knew she must look terrible, but SilentBlayde was staring at her like she was the only thing he could see.

"Do you know how hard it was not to tell you?" he whispered, reaching out to brush his elegant elven hand through her floofy hair. "When I saw you in real life on the web cam after we started making videos together, I knew I was doomed. The real you was just too beautiful. I wanted you so badly I could die, but I was the monster locked in my family's attic. I knew I could never actually be with you, but I couldn't bring myself to let you go. For seven years, I've lived in terror of the day when you quit FFO and I'd never see you again. It made me desperate, and I did so many stupid things because of that fear. I'm sorry."

His hand was still in her hair, his long fingers threading through the wild curls with a wonder Tina couldn't understand. Then again, maybe she could. She certainly had the same feeling when she reached out her own shaking hand to place it on his chest, grinning when she felt the shiver run through him.

"It's funny you should say that," she said, moving closer. "Because I thought you were super cool when I first met you, too. You were so smart and together, and you always had my back. I loved getting us into trouble just for the fun of seeing how you'd get us out."

"You were attracted to me because I was competent?" SB asked, raising an eyebrow.

"And funny and kinda underhanded," she added, taking another step. "Also a handsome elf. That's an important factor, not gonna lie. Plus you were good at your class, which is always hot." She grinned. "There's more. I could stand here listing reasons why I love you all day. Maybe I will, just to watch you squirm."

That was a bluff. Now that she was two steps in, Tina was *very* aware of how close he was. She understood now why he'd always been self-conscious about his face, but that handsome, perfect, elven face was the only one she'd ever known for SilentBlayde. Part of her felt guilty for that. She wanted to see his real face at least once, if only to prove that she'd love him no matter what he looked like. But if this was how they were stuck, she was fine with that, especially when he was looking at her as he was now, his sky-blue eyes filled with adoration. When he looked at her like that, the chill of the Deadlands vanished. She was much too warm, actually, and wearing way too much metal.

That, at least, she could fix. Keeping her eyes on his, Tina pulled her hand off his chest and reached up to brush her fingers over the runes that held her magical armor together. A few moves was all it took to send the protective metal falling off her like a shed carapace, leaving her dressed in only the oversized shirt Zen had given her. Eyes wide, SB took a nervous half step back, but Tina didn't give him a chance. She was already closing the distance again, wrapping her bare arms around his neck.

He went stone still as she settled against him, his body so tight she didn't see how he was still breathing. "Um…Tina…" he managed at last, his perfect face adorably red. "Are you…that is…"

"You're not the only one who's been wanting all these years," she told him quietly, rising until their faces were mere inches apart. "The only reason I pushed you away was because you wouldn't tell me the truth. It was *never* because I didn't want you." She smiled, tilting her head. "Seriously, did you miss how hard I chased after you all these years? I thought I was pretty obvious."

SB didn't seem to know what to say to that, so Tina made the decision for him, rising on her tiptoes to close the distance between their heights with the kiss she'd been waiting for for what felt like her whole life.

***

SilentBlayde's mind was in chaos. He'd told her everything, thought it was over. But now, somehow, here he was with her soft body pressed up against his chest, and she was kissing him.

Tina was *kissing* him.

That thought drove all the others away. His legs were threatening to give out, so he sank to the ground. The moment he sat down, Tina settled herself in his lap, her slight weight resting fully on top of him, her arms around his neck, her soft chest against his, her lips on his mouth, the scent and warmth of her hair filling his senses. It was overwhelming. It was *heaven*.

Shaking, he reached up to wrap his arms around her as well. He'd imagined this moment for so many years now. All that time, it'd only ever been something that could happen in a dream, but he wasn't dreaming now.

They were here on the ground in Garrond's command tent. Both of them, wrapped together.

And Tina was *still* kissing him!

Shivering with unhealthy levels of excitement, SB peeled his gloves off and tossed them on the ground. No longer bound by leather, he was free to reach up and cup the side of her face with his bare hand. Her skin was even softer than it had looked on camera, but the real thrill came when Tina leaned into his touch, her body melting into his as she broke the kiss at last to start pressing tiny, feather-light kisses all over his face.

He was going to die, he decided. Just keel right over from joy. The only reason he didn't was because that would mean he'd have to stop touching Tina. He'd already run his other hand down her back, feeling the delicate curve of her spine through the rough fabric of the shirt she wore like a dress.

A dress with nothing under it.

He almost did die then. One didn't exactly meet a lot of girls locked in an attic, but SB had only had eyes for Tina since he was fifteen. She'd been his obsession, his joy, his best friend, his greatest tragedy, and his reason for living, the person he wanted most and the one thing he could never have. But all those contradictions were in the past, lost in another world. In *this* world, right now, the love of his life was kissing him like there was nothing else she'd rather do, and so SB held on for her sake, throwing himself into the moment. The greatest miracle of his life.

He kissed her with everything he had, determined to make up in enthusiasm what he lacked in experience. He got his face to the side and slowly worked his way from her collar up her neck, paying careful attention to her reactions. When she made a good sound, he did that again, determined to make this as world-changing for her as it was for him. He was *so* focused on her reactions, actually, that he was caught completely off guard when Tina reached up to run a mischievous finger over the long arch of his left ear.

He broke away with a gasp, making Tina jump. "Sorry," she said, a beautiful flush spreading over her cheeks. "Did I hurt you?"

"No," he breathed, his whole body twitching. "God, no. It just surprised me. I didn't know my ears were ticklish."

A devilish light gleamed in her eyes. "Reaaaaaaaaally," she said, grinning like a cat with a mouse as she reached up to do it again.

He could have dodged, but SB didn't want to. It was far more enjoyable to be caught, even if it did end up with him writhing with laughter on the ground as she tickled him mercilessly. "Stop, stop!" he cried when he couldn't take it any longer.

Laughing so hard she could scarcely breathe, Tina did as he asked, collapsing on his chest to catch her breath. Then they both stopped breathing entirely as they realized their new position. SB was lying on the ground with Tina on top of him, their bodies separated only by her shirt and his armor. He was about to apologize—for what, he didn't even know, it just felt like the right thing to do—when Tina got that look in her eye again.

"You have too much clothing on," she informed him, tapping her fingers against the black-and-red leather.

Blayde went still all over again, but this time it was in fear. He hated being naked. Hated being seen by anyone, actually, which was why he wore a mask. But that was all damage left over from the old world. This was here, where he was a different person with a different face, and the love of his life was waiting for him. He'd almost lost her because of his past once. Was he really going to let it happen again?

Breathing hard, SB sat up and ran his fingers down the runes hidden along the side of his chest piece. When the armor loosened, he wiggled out of it, peeling off the leather and the undershirt that protected his body in the same motion. As it came free, he glanced nervously down at his chest. His father had hit him there too, leaving ugly dents and scars. He was so used to seeing them, he was surprised when he looked down and found SilentBlayde's flawless skin, the lean muscles straight and unmarred.

250

He was reaching down in wonder when Tina beat him to it, her small, pale fingers touching his character's Photoshop-perfect abs greedily. "Now the rest," she whispered, her brown eyes warm and giddy.

Who could say no to that? He did as she asked, stripping off all his remaining armor. With every new bit of him that came into view, the feeling of freedom deepened. It was like when he'd caught sight of his face in the mirror back in Bastion, but more. Bigger. He hadn't realized how much he'd worn this body like a mask until he was sitting naked on Tina's cot. But as she stared at him in open appreciation, it finally occurred to SilentBlayde that he was truly reborn. He didn't know what he'd done to deserve such a miracle, but he was not going to keep them waiting any longer.

With that, he reached out for her with both arms. Tina came eagerly, but when he started to lift her shirt so she could be as naked as he was, she grabbed his hands.

"Sorry," he said, letting go at once. "Am I going too fast?"

"No, no, it's not that," she said, her brows furrowed in frustration. "It's just…You're this glorious magical creature with perfect golden everything, and I'm, you know, *me*." She sighed. "Gotta be a hell of a disappointment."

"You could never be a disappointment," he told her, reaching up to cup her face. "You're everything I've ever wanted."

She gave him an incredulous look. "You wanted a frizzy-haired short girl with stumpy legs and no boobs?"

"I wanted *you*," he reminded her. "And I've *always* thought you were beautiful. Why do you think I didn't say anything the first time you video called me?"

"You said your mic was broken!"

"My mic was fine," he said, leaning in with a smile. "*I* was broken. Seeing you for the first time left me unable to speak Japanese, much less English."

251

Tina threw back her head as her cheeks went scarlet. "Oh, that's it," she said. "You've done it now."

"Done what?"

"Been too sweet," she murmured, leaning in to kiss him again.

He kissed her back desperately, determined to show her just how lovely he thought she was. He'd always hated when Tina disparaged herself, but he'd never been able to fight back without giving his feelings away. Now all that was done, though, he was determined to make sure she knew she was beautiful every single day. Not that that would be hard. She was even more lovely in person than she'd been on the screen. Cameras couldn't capture the warmth of her skin or the light in her eyes as she leaned back and peeled off the shirt, leaving her naked in front of him.

Now he couldn't speak. Fortunately, words were unnecessary, because Tina was already kissing him again, dragging him down with her to the cot.

SB didn't do much thinking after that. His brain was completely consumed by the physical experience of Tina and the desperate need to remember every single second. He didn't know what he was doing, but he was certain they were headed somewhere *very* good when Tina suddenly stopped again.

"What's wrong?" he asked.

She gave him a funny look, and SB realized he'd just said that in the wrong language. Shaking his head to get his brain back online, he asked again in English and was treated by the rare sight of Tina looking flustered.

"I'm, um, a virgin," she said, twisting her fingers anxiously through his hair. "I mean, I know what's supposed to happen, but we're already way further than I've ever gone, so...yeah. Just nervous and stuff."

"Nothing wrong with that," he told her. "I've never done it either."

She didn't look surprised by that. Not that she should be what with his confession that he'd been a prisoner in his own house, but something was still off. Her body was rigid, and her fists were balled up in the blankets, almost as if she were trying to hold on.

"I want to," she told him quickly when she saw where he was looking. "It's just, you're a lot bigger than me now, like physically taller, and it's kind of...I mean, I don't know what I'm—" She gritted her teeth in frustration. "You know what, never mind. I'm ready. Let's do this."

She reached for him then, but SB caught her hands. "Tina," he said gently. "You're not tanking me."

She looked insulted by that, and he sighed. "Let's not go so fast," he whispered, leaning in. "I don't know what I'm doing, either."

That made her laugh at least. "Some pair we are."

"Noobs the both of us," he agreed, sliding up to nibble her ear. "But we learn fast."

Tina didn't have a comeback for that one. She just gasped underneath him, almost making him forget that going slow was his idea. But he knew he'd only get one chance to make their first time right, so Blayde forced himself to calm down and move slowly. Slooowly. Holding back, until...

Tina grabbed his shoulders. "Now," she whispered.

That was all he could take. With that word, the dam of SilentBlayde's self-control shattered. Fortunately, Tina was right there with him. It was awkward and silly and undignified in places, but even with both of them fumbling their way through, being with her was better than he'd known to imagine. Even trying his best to commit every moment to memory, there were long stretches when all he could do was hold on and be happy. So ridiculously, stupidly happy that he almost broke out laughing right in the middle. Tina would *not* take that well, though, so he held it in, kissing her through his smile until there was nothing left in him but her.

When it was over, they both collapsed, panting, onto the cot. SB didn't think the poor wooden frame was made for such abuse, but despite being obnoxiously loud, it had performed like a champ. Not that he would have noticed if it had dumped them on the ground, but he was happy they didn't have to lie in the dirt as Tina wrapped herself around him with a deeply contented sigh.

"I think we aced that."

"I don't know," he said with mock thoughtfulness. "I think we might have to try again. Maybe several more times."

She laughed. "Not unless you want to get a healer in here."

He froze, suddenly terrified. "Did I hurt you?" Because Tina would absolutely tank her way through if she thought she had to. He was already cursing himself for a thoughtless fool when she shook her head.

"Nah," she said, smiling so contentedly his fear couldn't hold up. "I'm just not used to that particular movement yet. But I'm a fast learner. Give me a bit and you'll be the one begging for mercy."

Now it was his turn to laugh. "Not everything's a competition, you know."

"Says you," she replied, reaching up to play with a lock of his hair. "At least I finally understand why people make such idiots of themselves over sex. It's pretty awesome."

"It is," SB agreed contentedly. Then his face broke into a grin. "I'm glad our first time was *fucking in tents*."

Tina buried her face in his chest with a groan, then she looked up. "Would you say we're *on a roll* now?" she asked, patting the bedroll beneath them.

"Our virginity is definitely *past tents*."

He was pretty damn proud of that one, but then Tina scooted up to whisper in his year. "Just lemme know when your tent pole is up again."

He choked, turning so bright red he had to surrender the pun battle. Smirking in victory, Tina settled into his chest like a smug cat, pulling the blanket tight over herself against the Deadlands' chill.

They lay like that for a long time. That was perfectly fine with SB. He was still in awe over the fact that Tina was really here, with him. He was hoping she'd fall asleep on his chest—because that would be *adorable*—when she whispered, "I'm sorry."

"For what?"

Tina pushed up on her elbow to give him a serious look. "I'm sorry I didn't do more to help you. I knew there had to be a reason you were hiding so much, and I had a feeling it was bad, but I was too afraid of driving you away to press the issue. Now, after hearing how bad it was, I feel like I should have."

"It's all right," he said quickly. "You didn't know because I didn't tell you. Even if you had, what could you have done? We were two broke kids with an ocean between us."

"We could have done *something*," she argued, stubborn as ever. "Our video channel was making bank those last couple of months. I could have saved up enough to send you a plane ticket to Seattle. Once you were in the States, I could have married you to get you your green card, and then you'd never have had to go back. Your dad couldn't have done shit about it from all the way…"

She was still talking, but SilentBlayde's brain had hung on one sentence and could not let it go. The words were stuck on repeat in his head, but no matter how many times they circled, he still couldn't believe they were real.

"Sorry," he interrupted. "Could you say that part again?"

Tina blinked. "Which part? The one where I punch your dad and cause an international incident?"

"No," he said, heart hammering. "The part where you said you'd marry me."

Tina went quiet as she realized what she'd just said. "Oh," she whispered, blushing furiously. "Well, I mean, it's practical. Marriage would have been the easiest way to make you a US citizen and get you out of Japan. I wasn't really—"

"Would you *still* marry me even if I don't need citizenship anymore?"

Tina's cheeks turned an even more charming shade of red as a wondrous smile spread over her face. "Let me get this straight," she said, looking him in the eyes. "Are you asking me to marry you?"

SilentBlayde nodded frantically. "If you'll have me. I don't have access to my bank right now, so I don't have the ring, but I can make you one in the morning, and..." He trailed off, furious at himself for making a mess of this. How many romantic American movies had he watched preparing for the tiny, *tiny* chance he ever found himself in this scenario? Dammit, he could do better.

"Christina Anderson," he said, getting into a position that was as close to one knee as he could manage without actually getting up and risking knocking her off the bed. "Will you marry me?"

Tina put a finger to her lips, giving his proposal careful consideration. Then her composure broke, and she started kissing him all over.

"Hell yes!"

***

Tina had seen SilentBlayde in a lot of intense situations, good ones and bad. But she'd never seen him look as desperately happy as he did right now, which was saying something considering how they'd spent the last hour.

"We'll get Garrond to do it," he said in a rush once he'd finally stopped kissing her. "He's a paladin of the Sun. The wiki categorized those as warrior-priests, so he should be able to officiate a marriage. I'll make us rings as soon as it's light, and he can marry us before the battle. Then, after we win and there's peace again, I'll negotiate with the bank to get the wedding dress and tux sets out of my vault so we can have a real wedding in Bastion."

"Wait, wait," Tina said, laughing. "The tux I understand, but why do you also have the wedding *dress?*"

SB turned red. "You know...Just in case, someday maybe..."

"I'm just teasing you," she said, reaching up to tickle his ear, her new favorite target. "I know you've got every collectible in the game. I bet you have the Valentine's Day Sexy Apron, too."

His neck-to-hair blush told her everything, and Tina laughed again. "Hope it's not stonekin sized."

"It's adjustable," he said, still red-faced. "But I think the Spring Fling Dress would suit you better."

Tina frowned, trying to remember which of FFO's many ridiculous holiday-themed vanity costumes he was talking about. "Is that the big floofy one with all the ruffles?"

SB nodded eagerly. "I have all six colors."

"But those things cost a thousand tickets each at the seasonal vendor!" Tina arched an eyebrow. "Just how many dresses have you been hoarding?!"

"I think it'd be nice for you to have something not-armor to wear on our honeymoon," he replied, deftly changing the subject. "There's that schtumple resort town with all the hot springs up in the Ever Winter Mountains. It was built as a gag quest zone for the Christmas events, but you could reach it all year. I wonder if it still exists."

Tina lay back down on his chest with a yawn. "If it doesn't, we'll find something else. Let's just ask the king where nobles go on vacation. Rich people get the best shit in every world. I bet we can find a tropical island somewhere with pristine private beaches the locals would be happy to rent out to the Great General Tina Anderson and SilentBlayde, adviser to the king."

She snickered at her own ridiculousness. When SB didn't join her, Tina looked up to see him frowning. "It sounds silly when you say our names together like that," he said quietly. "I don't have to be SilentBlayde-with-a-y anymore. You know who I really am, so you can call me Haruto if you like it better."

"Nah, I know that name makes you flinch," she said. "Now that the secrecy issue is resolved, I'd much rather call you by the name *you* prefer. And anyway, you've always been SilentBlayde to me."

She'd hoped that would relax him, but he looked more upset than ever. "What about going home?"

Tina thought a moment, then she shrugged. "It's cool. I'll stay here with you."

His blue eyes went wide. "*Really?!*"

Tina nodded. "I mostly wanted to go home because I was trapped as a stonekin. Being a rock *sucked*. Now that I'm human again, though, it's not as big a deal. Don't get me wrong, I'm gonna miss my smartphone and air conditioning hella bad, but I can't make you leave all this"—she gestured at the Assassin's literally magical elven body—"and go back to your old crap life."

"But what about your degree?" he pressed. "You worked so hard to get to college! I can't ask you to give that up for me."

"Dude," Tina said, grinning wide. "We're rich and powerful and famous here. Also, this world has no public library or public education! Forget being *a* librarian. I could be *the* librarian who kicks off this world's version of the Enlightenment! It wouldn't even be that hard. The literacy rate in Bastion is *actually* medieval, and they don't even have the Gutenberg press yet. It's all wood-block printing or hand copying. There's nowhere to go but up! Just imagine the possibilities!"

"So, to be clear, you're *not* giving up the life you wanted just for me?" SB asked, still nervous.

"Not at all," Tina assured him. "It'll take a few years to return this place to not-smoking-crater status, but once we fix the damage, we'll be legendary heroes living in a *legit* magical kingdom! I can't go back to the normal world after that."

SB's chest dipped below her as he let out a long breath. "Thank you," he said, whispering the words in the most sincere and heartfelt way Tina had ever heard. "But, just so you know, I would have gone back for you."

"I know," she said, stretching up to kiss him. "I love you."

They *really* should have gone to sleep after that. Tina's now-fleshy body certainly wanted to, but her brain was too abuzz and happy with all the things she wanted to do with SB in the future. They lay cuddled in the tent for hours, joking about how Dungeons & Dragons would be a contemporary RPG here and how, if the bank refused to give them their gold, they should invent collectible card games to sell to traders and nobility in order to finance Tina's dream public library system. Tina also felt that romance novels would be the way to mad money once she had a movable-type system up and running. SB wanted manga but wasn't sure how they'd do that without insane levels of lithography.

In the end, they agreed to try it all. Tina was still thinking about using griffin riders to facilitate a worldwide interlibrary loan system when she fell asleep on SilentBlayde's chest. Wrapped in warm blankets and the sweet smell of the sky, she dreamed that they were already married and living in Bastion in an anachronistically trendy modern apartment filled with books. There was a hot tub and "elven" Ikea furniture, too, which even her dream-self realized was ridiculous, but the image was so warm and nice that Tina couldn't bring herself to care.

It was such a good dream that she clung to it even when the first light of dawn hit her face through the tent walls. When she managed to open her eyes at last, she was alone in the bed.

Tina sat up in a panic, but the fear vanished as fast as it had come when she spotted SB's silver swords on the table they'd shoved into the corner. Knowing he'd never go far without those, Tina stretched and got up. She put on her shirt then her armor and opened the tent flap to greet the cold gray light that counted as morning in the Deadlands. Thankfully, the delicious smell of cooked oats was already in the air, making her stomach rumble.

Other players were already clustered around the cook fires. Lots of people waved excitedly when they saw her, and Frank gave her a particularly enthusiastic thumbs-up. It wasn't until Killbox gave her a too-knowing "yeah girl" nod complete with "victory" two-finger symbols that she started to get worried.

"*Tina!* Over here!"

Tina looked over to see NekoBaby jumping and waving by one of the fires. Next to her, Zen was crumbling dried plants into a small pot set over the embers. The Ranger didn't even glance up as Tina walked over. Neko, on the other hand, was practically puffy with anticipation, swishing her tail and patting the log beside her until Tina sat down.

"Good morning," Tina said carefully. She was getting a weird vibe here, and she wasn't sure yet if it was a good one or a bad one.

"Goooooooood morning to you, too!" Neko said in a singsong voice with a big wink tossed in. "Want some meaty oatmeal?"

She thrust her bowl at Tina, who looked down to see that it was, in fact, oatmeal cooked with what appeared to be chunks of dried meat. "Uh, thanks."

"You're welcome," the cat girl purred. "The chefs say it's great for stamina, and I bet you need a lot of that after last night, ehhhhhhh ehhhhh?"

The cat girl wiggled her eyebrows up and down in blatant suggestion, and Tina's face heated to roughly the temperature of the surface of the sun.

"You know?" she whispered.

"Baby, *everyone* knows," Neko said, no longer able to contain her excitement. "Not only did SB walk into your tent last night and not come out until morning, but you two are *loud!*" She fanned herself with her clawed fingers. "Such passionate! Much canvas walls! *Wow!*"

Tina hunched over, attempting to crawl into her bowl of meaty oatmeal.

"Aww, don't be shy!" Neko said, scooting closer. "You two made me *so* much money in the betting pool! I knew you couldn't stay away from that hot elf luvvin!"

Tina shrank further into her bowl.

"So how was it? Like, are we talking sweet make-up sex or hot angry sex? *Spill!*"

"*Neko,*" Zen said sharply.

The cat girl whirled on Zen with a *Really?!* look, which the Ranger ignored. "Here," she said instead, pouring the water she'd been feeding herbs into out of the pot and into a battered metal mug, which she then handed to Tina. "Drink this."

"What is it?" Tina asked, sniffing the cup, which smelled a lot like dirt. "Some kind of tea?"

"It's what you asked me to find back at Camp Comeback," Zen replied in her flattest, just-the-facts nursing voice. "I'll give you the herbs so you can make it yourself. Drink one cup with food every morning to prevent pregnancy. It'll make you nauseous and screw your hormones up big time, but it's the best solution I could find. You'll just have to make do until we can ask the local Naturalists about finding something better."

Tina couldn't even bring herself to nod. Zen's informational lecture was somehow even more embarrassing than Neko's comments, which didn't feel possible. Not that she was mad—Zen was just doing exactly what she'd asked—but she felt so *stupid*. She'd been on birth control since she was a teenager, so she hadn't even thought about protection, but there *was* no birth control pill here. How could she have been so reckless? If she got pregnant here, in medieval times, in the middle of a war... Tina shuddered at the thought.

"Thank you, Zen," she said, chugging the hot tea so fast she burned her mouth.

"Just doing my job," the nurse said with a shrug. Then she smiled. "Glad you two worked it out."

"Oh yeah!" Neko cheered, throwing up her paws. "High fives for get'n *biz-ay!*"

Tina left her hanging, choosing to finish her tea instead while pointedly ignoring the huge smiles everyone seemed to be flashing her as they walked by. "Is it possible to die of embarrassment?"

"Don't worry about it," Zen said with a chuckle. "Half the camp was doing the whole 'we might die tomorrow' thing last night. Now eat. Today's the day, and you need your strength."

Accepting her second bowl of boiling-hot meat-oatmeal with a side of utter mortification, Tina wolfed it down, doing her best to ignore NekoBaby's bragging about how smart she'd been to give Tina "The Talk" back at Windy Lake. By the time the cat girl moved on to how many people *totally* owed her now that she'd been so *super* right, Tina had finished breakfast and was really looking forward to the part of the day where all she had to deal with was beating a never-defeated boss for the fate of the world.

"Rats," Neko said suddenly, ears drooping. "Fun's over. Here comes Commander Stick-Up-His-Butt."

Sure enough, Commander Garrond was making his way through the busy camp in their direction, and in the giant man's wake was SilentBlayde. The paladin's bushy eyebrows were tightly furrowed, which told her nothing. Garrond could frown at victory. He would definitely take offense if she didn't greet him properly, though, so she rose to her feet, brushing the ash from the fire off her armor as Garrond came to a stop in front of her.

"Good morning, Commander," Tina said, trying hard not to blush, which was difficult since the whole camp had stopped eating to look at them, and SB was *right there*, standing at the commander's side with his hands suspiciously held behind his back.

"General Roxxy," Garrond said, nodding in greeting. "It is my understanding that I am to officiate a *marriage* this morning."

The commander said this in the same way Tina's dad used to say "do taxes," but she felt like her eyes were going to bug out of her head. She'd thought SB had just been getting carried away with the whole prebattle wedding talk, but he was nodding furiously when she glanced at him. When Tina nodded too, the commander sighed so deeply his armor clanked.

"I could lecture you about how this is neither the time nor the place," he said in a defeated voice. "But I've learned the futility of attempting to make players move at anything other than their own pace. If I agree to this foolishness, will it get the Roughnecks ready for the assault faster?"

"Quicker than if you fight it, yeah," Tina said, grinning at SB, who looked adorably stubborn. "It doesn't have to be a complicated wedding."

"It won't be," Garrond promised, pointing east. "Five minutes. Over by that tree."

He tromped off, leaving Tina to be nearly trampled as an excited NekoBaby blew past her like a shot to go tell everyone the news. She was still recovering her balance when SilentBlayde stepped in to offer her his arm—and one of the rings he'd been hiding behind his back.

"I'm sorry they're just gold," he said apologetically. "I wanted sunmetal, but there was none around."

Tina was about to say a plain band was fine when she actually looked at the ring he'd just placed in her hand. "*Just* gold?" she said incredulously, holding up the incredibly intricate woven circle of delicate gold filigree he'd given her. "Dude, if this was back on Earth, we'd have been getting rings from the dollar store. How did you manage something this fancy out here?"

"I *am* a max-level jewelcrafter," SB said proudly. "The hardest part was finding the metal, actually. I ended up trading Garrond the location of the Order's missing Hammer of Last Light for the coins in his pouch."

"Nice work," Tina said, impressed. Then she frowned. "How long until Garrond realizes there's no way he's going to get it since the Hammer of Last Light is locked in a temple at the bottom of the ocean?"

263

SilentBlayde shrugged. "He's a resourceful guy. I'm sure he'll figure it out."

Tina shook her head and slid her arm through his, strolling together toward the tree, where Garrond was already waiting impatiently.

"Ready?" he barked as they walked up.

"Almost," said SB, nodding at the growing crowd of Roughnecks, many of whom had come over with their breakfasts still in hand.

The sight made Tina smile. This was not how she'd envisioned getting married: in another world, with her armor as her wedding dress, surrounded by her guild, to SilentBlayde (not Haruto), by a paladin, in the Deadlands, et cetera. It was such an unlikely scene that she wouldn't have believed it if she wasn't standing in the middle. Her only regret was that James wasn't here to see it. She'd have to make sure he survived so she could tell him all the details later.

When everyone who was coming had gathered, Garrond cleared his throat pointedly, and the smacking and munching noises of breakfast died out as everyone paused to listen. SilentBlayde let Tina go reluctantly as Garrond grabbed him by the shoulder and physically turned him to face the east. He did the same to Tina, positioning them side by side in front of him with the light of the dawn rising over his head. Even in the gray of the Deadlands, it was an impressive sight, making Tina feel both giddy and nervous as she realized this wasn't just some display. This was a real ceremony—performed by an *actual* holy man—and it was happening *right now*.

"The Sun bears witness to all our deeds and words," Garrond announced, his big voice ringing across the steep gray mountains. "Today, we gather under its light to bless the union of *SilentBlayde*"—the commander almost choked on using SilentBlayde as an official name—"and Christina Anderson. Let their love be as pure as the dawn, as fruitful as the noon, and as comforting as the dusk, for as they care for each other, so does the Eternal Sun care for all its creation."

That sounded like the end, but then Garrond pulled a scrap of paper out of his belt pouch. He frowned at it for a few seconds, and then, with obvious annoyance and *great* disdain, he began to read.

"Do you, SilentBlayde, take Christina Anderson to be your wife? To have and to hold, in sickness and in health, for rich or for poor, forsaking all temptations, to remain true to her for the rest of your life?"

"I do," SilentBlayde said in a firm voice. Then he smiled at her.

Tina smiled back, head whirling in a dizzying combination of joy and nerves, because Garrond was looking at her now. "Do you, Tina Anderson, take SilentBlayde to be your husband with an understanding of all the requirements I just read?"

SilentBlayde shot the commander a furious look for skipping over the vows he'd so obviously given the man to read. Garrond glared right back, clearly at the end of his patience. Fortunately, Tina knew this part already.

"I do," she said confidently. "I take him to have and to hold, in sickness and in health, for rich or for poor, and forsaking all others for the rest of my life."

Garrond nodded like that was a good answer and tossed the paper away. "You may now exchange the symbols of your promise to one another."

His hands trembling, SB took her left hand in his, then they both stopped to laugh when they realized she was still wearing her armored gauntlet. She was shaking so badly that SB had to help her remove the plate glove so he could slide the ring onto her finger. Then their roles reversed, and she almost dropped his ring while waiting for SB to take off his gloves for her. They made it through in the end, though, their bare hands locked together with gold rings gleaming as they turned back to Garrond.

The paladin moved his hands over their heads, and Tina shivered as she felt warm magic fall over her like a blanket. "A promise made in daylight can never be broken," Garrond proclaimed in a ringing voice. "Let none deny what has been joined in the Sun's light! In the presence of those who

265

stand here as witness, I hereby acknowledge you as husband and wife. Blessings be upon your days and your children."

"May I kiss the bride?" Blayde asked hopefully.

Garrond huffed impatiently through his mustache. "If you must."

SB smiled and pulled Tina into a happy kiss. "I love you," he said, the words barely audible as the raid behind them erupted in applause.

"I love you, too!" Tina shouted back, hoping he could hear her over NekoBaby's incredibly loud *whoop whoops*.

He must have, because suddenly he was kissing her again, moving with that lightning speed she didn't know if she'd ever get used to. The roar from the Roughnecks grew louder and bawdier as she grabbed him back, kissing him with everything she had. Overhead, sparks flew across the gray sky as Sorcerers got carried away and ripped off magical fireworks. Garrond shouted at them to stop wasting mana and stomped back to his men, muttering under his breath about players making a mockery of the Sun's sacred ceremonies. He had a great deal to say on that subject, actually, but Tina didn't bother to listen. She was too busy trying to keep hold of her new husband as the whole raid surged in to congratulate them.

"I have to say, I'm a little jealous," Zen confessed, clapping Tina on the shoulder as she muttered something that sounded suspiciously like "never a bride."

"What?" Tina asked, struggling to hear the Ranger over NekoBaby's ongoing "I'm so right" dance.

"I said 'You look very happy,'" Zen said, flashing her a rare, wide smile. "Congratulations."

Several more people rushed in after that. Honestly, Tina found it all a bit overwhelming. Being a guild leader was one thing, but being the center of attention like this, especially when all her guildmates were so huge now, made her want to shrink away. Fortunately, SB had her back as always, though he was dealing with his own problems.

"What the hell, man?" Killbox said, socking SB hard in the arm. "No bachelor party? You're killing me!"

"This was just a battlefield wedding," SilentBlayde assured him. "When we're not at war and things are rebuilt, I want to have a real ceremony in Bastion."

Tina shot him an amused look. "Going for extra-married?"

"I've always dreamed of marrying you in the royal cathedral," he replied in all seriousness. "No reason I should give up on that vision yet."

"I can't say no when you say it that way," she said, squeezing his hand. Then she leaned in and hugged him, because she could do that now—just hug him or kiss him or hold his hand whenever she felt like it. She was seriously considering trying all three at once when a horn sounded from the Order of the Golden Sun's camp. The roar of men's voices filled the air a second later, and Tina sighed.

"Looks like the party's over," she said as she tugged her gauntlets back on. "Back to business, people!" she yelled to her guild. "We've got a world to save!" When they were all scrambling at acceptable speeds, she turned back to SB. "And a hell of a lot to live for."

Her husband smiled back and grabbed her armored hand again, pressing the articulated metal to his lips as they turned together to face the black spire of the Once King's Dead Mountain.

Chapter 12
James

A few hours earlier

Predawn in the Deadlands looked like midnight anywhere else.

Standing together in the pitch dark of the broken road, James and Fangs in Grass craned their necks back, staring straight up at the imposing, ghostfire-lit battlements of the Dead Mountain Fortress. The Once King's citadel rose so tall that its jagged peak was hidden by clouds. Even so, James could see a single point of bright blue-white light flickering through the haze at the very top. It was a light so intense that it could only be the Great Pyre, source of all ghostfire.

"So," Ar'Bati said, clearing his throat to hide the tremor in his voice. "What's your plan for getting in?"

James dropped his eyes to where the road they'd been following dead-ended at the fortress's massive doors, a three-story wall of black metal crisscrossed with flickers of blue-white magic from the raid-level ward that kept them sealed.

"I was thinking we'd knock."

He could hear the scowl in his brother's voice. "Sneaking would be more prudent."

"It would," James agreed. "But sneaking is for thieves and assassins. We're here to talk. Polite discourse requires polite introduction."

Fangs heaved a long sigh and motioned for James to lead the way.

Ears flat, James crossed the last dozen feet of the road and climbed the short steps to the massive door. This whole thing had been his idea, but that didn't make walking up to the towering undead fortress any easier. It didn't feel familiar, either, which was strange. James couldn't count how many times Tina had dragged him to the DMF to heal her raid, but while the large details were the same—the terraced battlements that divided the mountain's rise into tiers, the sheer black slopes without a single leaf of vegetation, the blue-white ghostfire sconces that danced and whispered on the endless wind—everything was so much…bigger, and not just in physical size. The fortress in front of him no longer felt like an art asset for bored gamers to play in. It felt like a castle, the seat of a king.

A dreadful, lonely, *terrible* king.

"Right," James said, swallowing against the sudden dryness in his throat. "Let's give this a try."

Trying not to cringe from the unnatural cold that oozed off the black metal like blood, James took a moment to brush the dirt off his armor and straighten his fur. When he was as presentable as he could manage—and, more importantly, out of viable stalling tactics—James lifted his staff and knocked, rapping the Eclipsed Steel politely against the ghostfire-lit metal doors.

Bang, bang, bang.

The metallic sound echoed through the silent valley. Lowering his staff, James squared his shoulders and waited.

And waited.

And waited.

"This is not working," Fangs said, stepping back to glare up the slope. "The peak is very far. Maybe he can't see us down here?"

James shook his head. "There's an army camped on his doorstep. He *has* to be watching."

"So knock again."

"But it's rude to knock repeatedly."

Fangs gave him a scathing look, and James raised his hands. "What? He's a king. An *old* king. That's two levels of stickler for decorum."

"Then knock again *respectfully*," his brother snapped, fur prickling. "We are not schtumple merchants hawking wares. We are princes of the Savannah! He's not the only one who's owed decorum."

That was a good point. They certainly weren't getting anywhere by waiting here. Glaring at the door, James steeled his courage and pulled himself to his full height, taking a deep breath to make sure he projected his words.

"Hear me, oh great king of old!" he cried in his best "herald" voice, using the old elven word for "king" that was the Once King's true name. "We are Fangs in the Grass, eldest son of Lord Rends Iron Hides of the Claw Born clan of the Savanna, and James of Claw Born, second son of Rends and adviser to the Holy King of Bastion! We have traveled many days and through great hardship to accept your offer of an audience!"

James ended with a bow, sweeping his head low to hide the nervous trickle of sweat that was making its way down his cheek. He didn't actually know if that was the proper way to make a courtly announcement, but it must have been good enough. The echoes of this voice were still bouncing across the valley when the flickering ward that guarded the door shifted, the ghostfire coalescing until the gathered flames formed the vague image of an elven face.

"I grant you the right to appear before me, sons of Claw Born," it said, speaking in a booming voice that made them both jump. Then they jumped again as the doors opened with a deafening *boom*. "Follow the torches to my court, but take care to stay in the light. Your safety is not guaranteed should you stray."

The way he said that made James's fur stand on end, but it was too late to back out now. The huge doors were trundling open with a grinding sound, revealing the cavernous entry hall James remembered from the game. When they were fully opened, the magical ward covering the doors snuffed out, taking the face with it.

Back when this had been a raid dungeon, the front hall had been a giant room full of skeleton patrols moving in a complicated pattern of interlocking circles that turned just fast enough to force raids to kill all of them if they didn't want to be surprised from behind. Now, though, the

270

airfield-sized, black-stone room was empty and silent. The only things that moved in the dark were the blue-white dots of the ghostfire sconces attached to the support columns that sprouted like stone trees from the paved floor at regular intervals. Several of the lights went out as James watched, leaving only the sconces in the center of the room, which stayed lit in a line to form a blue-white path through the dark, just as the Once King had promised.

"Well," James said, nodding at the remaining lights. "I guess we go that way."

Quiet as two cats, James and his brother crept through the door and into the first of several circles of light, if ghostfire could even properly be called light. The blue-white radiance was more like a different form of dark than a proper torch, but at least James could see well enough not to stub his toes.

"I don't like this," Ar'Bati growled under his breath.

James snorted. "Which part?"

"Take your pick," his brother said, glaring up at the dark above their heads. "We came here precisely because we knew the Once King had sent his army away, but I did not expect there to be no undead at all. No soldiers I can understand, but all kings have servants and attendants."

"Maybe he doesn't need servants," James said, ears swiveling. "It *sounds* empty."

"If he is truly alone here, then why is our safety in question if we leave the lights?"

James had no answer to that one. He could only follow the lit path through the room's center. Beyond the circle of the ghostfire's light, the shadows were so deep and black even his natural low-light vision couldn't pierce them. There could be an army hiding just a few feet away, and he wouldn't even know.

"Come on," he said, picking up the pace. "Let's get this over with."

Unlike other parts of the world, the Dead Mountain Fortress's layout still closely resembled how it had looked in the game. It had grown in scale,

271

of course, but not nearly as much as the Grasslands or Bastion had. The rooms were also still in the same order that James remembered. The huge entrance hallway ended at another pair of massive doors, thankfully open, that led into the wide, open-air courtyard that had been Grel'Darm the Colossal's boss room. Back in the game, raiders would have had to kill the giant skeleton *and* all of his undead boar patrols to gain access to the next part of the fortress. Now, though, the giant paved space was as empty as everything else. There weren't even ghouls in the ghoul-pits off to the side that Grel liked to bash players into.

At least the emptiness made for fast going. Running on all fours, James and Ar'Bati followed the ghostfire torches across the courtyard and up the stairs to the more reasonably sized castle complex built into the mountain itself. They passed through several more boss rooms, each as empty as Grel'Darm's had been. But while the general layout continued to be the same as it was in the game, James quickly learned that the devil was in the details. Big things like the encounter rooms and zombie storage warehouses were all still where he remembered, but there were countless smaller caves and passages that he *knew* hadn't been there before.

If it weren't for the ghostfire torches, they would have quickly gotten lost. But while James appreciated the Once King's thoughtfulness, he didn't like how they were being led deeper and deeper into a fortress that famously had no back door. He just hoped the king stuck to his self-imposed rules of hospitality, because they were in *way* too deep to turn around if the torches were leading them into a trap. Not that the Once King needed a trap to kill them, of course, but that knowledge didn't keep James from feeling like a very small mouse running headlong into a very big cage. He compensated for this by keeping his eyes on the floor in front of him, which was how he almost ran headfirst into a wall when the torchlight he'd been following suddenly ended.

"Whoa," James said, scrabbling back on all fours.

The "wall" he'd narrowly avoiding cracking his skull on wasn't actually a wall at all. It was another pair of giant doors. Stone ones this time, their surface carved into a blood motif so realistic James swore he could see them dripping. Artistry aside, though, they weren't that different from all the others doors they'd run through on their way up here, except that these doors were closed.

"This is Sanguilar's room," James said, running his fingers over the beautifully carved stone blood splatters.

"Are you sure?" Fangs asked.

James nodded. "I was in Tina's raid the first time they beat him. It took us seven attempts, and we had to do the stupid mini-game that opened the doors each time. No way I'd forget this place."

"Well, can you do it again?" his brother asked, jerking his head at the sealed doorway.

"I don't think that's an option anymore," James said. "Even if we still had the interface to start the event, Sanguilar was the one who sent out the zombies we needed to kill in order to get the quest items, and he's not even here."

"Then why is the door closed?"

James had no idea. There was no ward like there'd been on the fortress's front gate, but none was needed. The huge slabs weighed so much it would take a crane to get them open. He dug his claws into the tiny crack to try anyway, but he couldn't even get the door to wiggle.

"Is there a way around?" Ar'Bati asked, looking back at the line of ghostfire torches that had led them to this dead end.

"There wasn't during the game," James said, panting with effort as he let the door go. "Sanguilar was the last boss before the Once King. You had to go through his room to get to the stairs that lead up to the Once King's throne room and the Great Pyre on the peak. I don't know if that's true anymore, of course. It does seem really strange that the Once King would lead us all the way here just to stop before the end."

Fangs looked at him with new appreciation. "Have *you* fought the Once King?"

"Once or twice," James said, moving over to poke at the walls beside the giant doors. "I went on a few of Tina's raids against him as a healer. *Really* hope he doesn't hold that against me."

His brother looked impressed by this new information. For his part, James didn't want to think about it. The Once King fight had been everything he'd hated about raiding: stressful, hypertechnical, and super unforgiving. Even when you did everything exactly right, the Million Damage Blast killed you anyway the moment the Once King reached thirty percent. Talk about depressing. He'd never been to a Once King fight where everyone didn't leave pissed as hell. And Tina wondered why he never wanted to go with her.

"Look at this."

Startled out of his memories, James looked over to see his brother crouched a few feet away, staring at something metallic on the floor. Moving closer, James saw that it was a dagger. He didn't remember the item's name because Naturalists couldn't use daggers back in the game, but he remembered SilentBlayde carrying that exact weapon for months before he scored his silver swords.

"Lucky!" James said, picking up the darkly glittering dagger with his claws and offering it to his brother hilt first. "Here, you should use it. I've already got a top-tier weapon, and this dagger will hit way harder than your low-level sword."

Ar'Bati's expression turned sour. "No thank you. First, I like my sword. Second, I am level fifty. That dagger is for certain meant to be used by a level eighty. I'll not take the risk."

"Fair enough," James said, eagerly accepting the priceless dagger. "I could use a weapon that's actually made to stab things." Slinging his black staff onto his back, James cupped his new knife in both hands. When he reached out with his mana to bind the enchanted weapon to his magic, though, he stopped with a jerk, making his brother jump.

"What's wrong?" Fangs demanded.

"I can't bind it," James said, holding the weapon away from himself with two fingers. "It's still bound to someone else."

"Who?" his brother asked. "The Red Sands reported that all players raiding the Dead Mountain died during the transition. Not that I put much faith in that CincoDeMurder brigand, but we certainly haven't seen anyone."

"No, it's definitely empty," James said, looking back at the giant, silent, ghostfire-lit hall they'd come from. "Maybe someone made it out and dropped it while they were fleeing?"

That didn't seem likely, but there was no other explanation. Soul binding didn't break unless the owner died—or, in Tina's case, completely changed bodies. James didn't know who'd owned this dagger before, but their magic was still tied to it tightly, which meant he couldn't use it. Sighing at the waste, James tucked the dagger into his belt anyway and leaned on the wall below the last torch to try to come up with a plan. He was scowling up at the ghostfire flickering above his head when he realized the flame was bending in the wrong direction.

"Wait a moment," he said, stepping back.

The hallway they'd followed to get here had been just as still and quiet as everywhere else in the seemingly empty fortress. There were no windows this deep inside the mountain, which meant the airflow was nonexistent, but the last ghostfire torch next to Sanguilar's sealed doors was bending and fluttering sharply to the left. Bracing against the unnatural cold, James reached his hand up beside the flame, smiling when, sure enough, he felt a stiff breeze on his fur.

"Maybe this isn't a dead end after all," he said, walking down the wall with his hand raised to follow the breeze upwind. "The air is moving fast here, which means there's gotta be....*ah ha!*"

He stopped short as his fingers slid around a lip of stone. In the dark, it had just looked like another shadow, but now that he was touching it, James saw that it was actually a hidden doorway, the source of the fresh air. Inside, James found a spiral stairwell going up. It was barely big enough for them to climb single file, but James could see the faint blue flicker of another ghostfire torch just around the first bend, and his face broke into a smile.

"Looks like our invitation still stands."

Putting up their weapons, the two started warily up the spiral. Unlike the stairwells below, which had been broad and huge enough for an entire raid to climb, this stair was tight and incredibly steep, going up relentlessly toward the mountain's peak. After what had to have been several hundred revolutions, James was dizzy and out of breath. He wanted nothing more than to sit down and rest, but he didn't. He went faster instead, because the torches on the walls were getting brighter.

"We must be…getting near…the source," he huffed, nodding at the furiously burning ghostfire. "The Great Pyre is at the very…top of the mountain, and the Once King's throne is…directly beneath it. Can't be…much farther."

The panted words were barely out of his mouth when the tight spiral they'd been following suddenly ended, and they emerged from yet another hidden door into a richly decorated hallway. Its floor was carpeted in thick, rich black lined with silver trim, while the soaring walls were covered in richly colored tapestries depicting events and images James had never seen before. One showed a host of winged elves flying toward the sun with their hands raised in prayer. Another showed what was clearly the same group of elves, except now their backs bore only blackened stumps as they descended, weeping, into a cave.

"This is incredible," James said, moving in for a closer look. The embroidered images were so detailed they looked almost like paintings. Each tapestry was packed with long, interconnected sequences that told a story, and the hallway was packed with them.

276

"There have to be hundreds," James said, looking up and down the long corridor. "I wish we had more time to stay and look."

That was usually Ar'Bati's cue to remind him that they did not, in fact, have time, but when James looked over at his brother, the warrior was standing in front of a tapestry a few feet down the hall, his hand hovering over it as if he were dying to touch the gleaming threads but didn't dare.

Curious, James walked over. Unlike the others, this tapestry was a portrait, a larger-than-life image of a staggeringly handsome jubatus warrior. He wore armor made from Bird scales, and his fur had a distinct reddish hue to it that James had never seen before.

"Who's that?"

"The first lord of the Savanna," Ar'Bati said reverently. "Father of all our kind. He lived so long ago that no art of him remains, but this image matches his description in the ballads exactly." He looked back down the hall. "I wonder if there are more."

James wanted to know, too, but the ghostfire was flaring in the sconces on the walls, reminding James just whom they were keeping waiting.

"We have to go," he whispered, grabbing his brother's arm.

Fangs nodded, letting James drag him away from the picture of their shared ancestor.

They walked as quickly as they could without running, their footsteps silent on the thick carpet. Eventually, the tapestry hall ended at a much grander thoroughfare James recognized from the game. It was the Royal Hall, the path that led to the throne room where the first phase of the Once King's fight took place. If they managed to get the Once King down to two-thirds health, he'd blast through the ceiling and open a stairway to the top of the mountain for phases two and three. Not that anyone had ever *seen* phase three, since it started with the Million Damage Blast.

That memory did not make James feel more at ease. He led the way through the cavernous Royal Hall in silence, following the ghostfire breadcrumb trail to the end, where two tall doors made from richly polished wood were carved in relief to resemble a pair of glorious feathery wings, one on each door. At the bottom of the doors was a silver disk polished to a mirror gleam. There was clearly supposed to be a matching golden disk at the top, but it had been gouged out long ago, leaving only scraps of gold foil between huge, old claw marks.

"I don't understand," Fangs said, pointing at the destroyed disk. "That one is clearly the Sun, but what of the second? Casting the Sun in silver is sacrilege. It is only ever represented in gold. Even the Once King should know better than to disrespect a god."

James didn't know about that, but the silver disk had caught his eye as well. "I don't think it's supposed to be two suns," he said, running his finger over the mirror-bright metal. "I think it's the Moon." He looked over his shoulder at Ar'Bati. "On Earth, we frequently use silver or a silver crescent to represent the moon and its phases. Have you ever seen an image like this before?"

"Never," Fangs said, making a ward against evil with his fingers as he stared at the clawed sunburst. "But I wouldn't be surprised by anything in this place. It's clear that the Once King has forsaken all that is good and warm."

"I'm still not convinced it's that simple," James said, shaking his head. "The Moon was clearly just as important as the Sun in the theology at some point, but now no one seems to remember it ever existed, and I find that highly suspicious. Why are there still prayers to the Moon for crafting but nothing about it in any of the histories? And if it really was here once, where did it go?"

"I don't know," Fangs said, clearly uncomfortable with all this blasphemy. "Why does it matter? The Once King is firstborn of the Sun. What should he care of the Moon even if it did exist?"

James had no answer for that. He had no answers for anything, just hunches and theories that didn't add up. That was why they'd come here—to find out the truth—so he screwed up his courage and reached out to give the huge doors a push, jumping back in surprise when they swung open without a sound, revealing a three-story-tall room of black stone with a domed roof.

Though it was almost at the top of the mountain, the room had no windows or skylights. All the light came from a massive ghostfire chandelier that hung from the center of the dome like a crown. And seated below it on a massive throne made from twisting Eclipsed Steel was the Once King.

James stepped back again, his whole body trembling. The throne room was beautiful in a cold, dark, elegant way. It had been like that even back in the game, but seeing it now, James knew instinctively that he was looking at a shadow of what had once been glory on a scale no mortal could comprehend. Everything about it—the cursed steel, the blistered walls, the blackened metal of the chandelier—looked like what was left after a fire. There was no soot or ash, nothing dirty or out of place, but the feeling of ruin and loss hung in the air like smoke, making his eyes tear up as he looked upon the winged elf seated at its center, the most ruined of it all.

"Welcome," the Once King said, his deep voice scaled down from what it had been on the battlefield but still booming in the smaller space of his throne room.

Unsure what to say, James lowered his head, trying not to stare and failing miserably. Like everything here, the Once King looked almost exactly as he had in the game except for several small but critical details. He was still dressed from the neck down in his Eclipsed Steel armor, but his helmet was gone. In its place, he wore a simple crown of corrupted sun steel, leaving his white-blond hair free to tumble elegantly behind his long, pointed ears. His sheathed sword rested near his right hand, leaned up against the side of his throne next to a four-foot-tall stack of ancient books that James remembered from the game. Back then, the books had just been objects, uninteractable and unreadable. Now, though, they were open, their pages so well read they were falling apart. James was trying to figure out if they were written in Old Elven when the king spoke again.

"Enter and present yourselves," the Once King commanded, his smooth voice vibrating through James's very bones. "We run short on time to waste."

Exchanging a nervous look, James and Ar'Bati strode across the threshold into the home of FFO's only undefeated raid boss. When they reached the foot of the dais, James knelt and bowed his head low. Technically, as the older son, Fangs should have taken the lead, but his brother was staring at the world's oldest enemy like he didn't know if he should go for the throat or the eyes, so James decided to break decorum before the Once King broke them both.

"First of all kings," he said, as nobly as he could. "I am James of Claw Born, second son of Lord Rends Iron Hides. Beside me is Fangs in the Grass, heir of the Claw Born and Ar'Bati of the Four Clans. Thank you for allowing us into your presence."

"I acknowledge you," the Once King said, his cold, perfect face revealing no emotion good or ill. "Rise, sons of Claw Born. Your eyes and words are permitted to reach me."

James stood up, keeping his body tight to hide how badly his knees were shaking. This was it. The next words out of his mouth might save or doom everyone, starting with Fangs and himself. But while he had so many questions they were burning a hole in his brain, now that he was actually here, James realized he had no idea where to begin. How did you start a conversation with the first born of all creation? He was still scrambling for an opener that wouldn't make this sound like an interrogation when the Once King saved him the trouble.

"You have come to my court as the princes of the Savanna," the ancient elf said formally. "It is only fitting, then, that we speak first of matters of the state." With a wave of his hand, the Once King conjured a floating disk of ghostfire. As it moved and flickered, James realized he was looking at a top-down view of the military camp the Roughnecks and the Order had set up at the valley entrance. The image was so clear he could actually make out individuals moving between the tents, particularly the enormous form of Commander Garrond. He was still wincing at how good the Once King's scrying abilities were, and all the horrific implications of that, when the king closed his hand, and the image vanished.

"You have come to my lands with an army to siege my castle and two player raids intent on assassinating me," the Once King said scornfully. "What do you have to say for yourselves?"

The force of the king's displeasure hit him like a punch. James's instincts screamed in reply, demanding that he throw himself on the ground and beg forgiveness. At this point, though, James was very used to much bigger powers being angry at him, and he stuck to his guns.

"What else did you expect?" he demanded, proud that his voice only shook a little. "You have declared yourself the enemy of all life. Your armies sacked Bastion unprovoked and even now pursue our king into the Savanna. We are here in just defense of our land, our families, and our lives!"

The king looked disappointed. "I thought you'd be different," he said, his deep voice tinged with sadness. "You seemed ready to listen before, but now that you're here, you're just like the others. You don't understand." He sighed deeply, sinking back on his throne like a tired old man. But the illusion of weakness only lasted a heartbeat. When the elf looked up again, he was every inch the implacable, unreachable king. "Very well. What are your demands?"

James opened his mouth, but his brother beat him to it. "We demand that you extinguish the Great Pyre and cease all hostilities at once!" Ar'Bati cried, baring his teeth at the first king. "Only when you are no longer a threat to every living thing will we even consider peace!"

"No," the Once King replied without hesitation, his narrow brows furrowing in scorn. "Short-sighted kitten, I fight for the sake of all our eternities. Your current lives and complaints are insignificant by comparison."

281

"Then we will slay you and bring peace that way!" Ar'Bati cried, his brown fur standing on end as he reached for his sword.

The Once King stood up in reply, causing the two jubatus to scramble back, but something was off. James had expected anger or defiance in the face of Ar'Bati's open antagonism, but the Once King didn't look mad at all. Instead, the primal king's face looked relieved, almost eager, which turned out to be far, far more terrifying.

"I find your terms acceptable," the Once King said, reaching down to retrieve his own sword. "Your blade may be close to my throat, but mine is already piercing your heart. As we speak, Gregory, the man who uses my name as if it were a title, is fighting a losing battle at Red Canyon. When he inevitably succumbs, my victory will be all but guaranteed. The Nightmare has already done the rest of my work for me. All the zones of the world have already fallen or are in flames. Soon, the last of the Heraldsfords will be dead, and the Bastion he guards will be smashed. Without them, you have no more hope."

"We have ourselves!" Ar'Bati cried defiantly. "We are still here! We will fight you!"

"With what?" the Once King demanded. "Your forces' loyalties are already compromised. One breath of a promise from me and your raiders will perish on each other's blades. Your allies will do the last of my work for me, and the curtain will finally close on this wretched world. This land will return to what it was always meant to be: a shadow beloved only by the schtumples and the Birds. They will be glad to be rid of us, and we will be glad to be gone."

The way the Once King said that shook James to his core not because the king was angry or vengeful, but because he sounded so relieved. He'd said nothing James hadn't already guessed, but hearing it in his own words had finally made him understand the breadth of the Once King's nihilism. He wasn't waging a war against all life for some nefarious, unknown purpose.

The war *was* the purpose. Death was the end, not the means, but James still didn't understand.

"Why?" he asked, his voice cracking on the word.

"Because we were all doomed long ago," the king replied, his voice tired, as if he'd answered that question many, many times before. "Death is the only escape. I told you this before."

He had, many, many times. But now as then, James refused to believe it, because he'd seen this before. He'd heard that same resignation and hopelessness in SilentBlayde's voice, and in Grayson's. But before he'd selfishly ignored him, his friend had been asking for help, and now it was happening again. If the Once King was truly committed to his nihilism—if he *truly* didn't care—he wouldn't have invited James and Ar'Bati here. But he had. He *wanted* to talk, as Grayson had, which meant deep down, some small part of him wasn't ready to die. So long as that spark existed, James had hope. Now he just had to figure out a way to make the Once King feel it, too.

"I believe this concludes our negotiations," the Once King said, lifting his sword. "You have stated your demands, and I have refused them. You may now return to your army to face the inevitab—"

"Wait!" James cried, stepping forward. "I have one more demand."

The king arched a perfect eyebrow.

"It's more of a request, really," James hedged. "But we still have some time before my sister's raid arrives, and I still don't understand *why* we have to die. You keep saying we're doomed, but I've seen the people of this world, and they don't looked doomed to me." He looked at his brother, who nodded. "I don't doubt you're doing this for good reason," James went on, turning back to the king. "Even the Bedrock Kings said you were a dutiful ruler who always put his people first, so help us understand. Until we do, we'll never be able to reach a satisfactory agreement."

"That is fair," the Once King said, lowering his sword. "It would put my mind at ease to tell the tale one more time before the end. But such an intimacy would make our dealings personal, and you may not wish that."

"Why not?" James asked.

The Once King gave him a sad look. "Here, protected by the distance and formality of court, I am able to release you back to your people. But if I speak with you frankly, share my history and regrets, we shall become closer, and I will inevitably feel compelled to save you."

James swallowed. He knew what the Once King meant when he said "save." The ancient elf would tell them his secrets, and then he'd feed them both to the ghostfire. That was a pretty horrible fate, but as things stood, they were probably going to die anyway. Whether it happened now or in a few hours didn't really matter, and while they couldn't possibly face the Once King with just the two of them, James didn't want to kill the king anyway. He wanted to change his mind, and the chances of that were a *lot* better if he knew why the king felt this way to begin with.

Decision made, he glanced at Fangs in the Grass and flicked his ears toward the Once King. The warrior understood at once and nodded firmly. Fangs knew the odds, too, and he hadn't come here to back down. However this turned out, they were in it together.

"We understand," James said, turning back to the Once King. "And we accept. Even if it means our deaths, being in your confidence would be the highest honor."

"It is I who am honored," the Once King said, cracking a smile for the first time. "Follow me. A throne room is no place for casual speech."

Sliding his sword into the loop of his belt, the Once King descended from the dais. As the winged elf walked down the polished stone steps, James realized for the first time just how *big* he was. The Lord of the Undead was even taller than Gregory, at least ten feet from his armored boots to the arch of his ash-gray wings. That made sense seeing as he was a five-skull raid boss, but now that he was standing in front of them, the idea that James hadn't noticed the size difference before this moment felt ridiculous. Looking at the throne again, though, he could see why he'd made such a stupid mistake. The king hadn't looked huge when they'd first come in because everything in the room was scaled to match him.

Given the level of detail on his giant throne, James wondered if the Once King hadn't been this size even before the game. There was no polite way to ask, though, so James kept his mouth shut and followed the king around the throne, jogging to keep up with the elf's enormous steps as the king led them to the back of the room. Stopping in front of what appeared to be a solid stone wall, the king waved his hand, and a door emerged from the rock.

As it swung open, new light poured out, illuminating the king not in the blue-white cold of the ghostfire but with the warm, golden glow of *actual* fire from a hearth. After so much cold and dark, James could feel the welcoming heat all the way from here. It felt like paradise, but he was still in the presence of a king, so James forced himself not to run toward it. He compromised by stepping to the side instead, peeking around the enormous king to see a cozy stone room so stuffed with books, antiques, and curios there was almost no place to stand.

"This is my private study," the Once King said, removing the sword from his belt and leaning it against the wall beside the door. "Let us disarm so we may all be at ease."

Since the raid boss didn't need a sword to kill them, and James and Ar'Bati couldn't have killed him even if they'd been armed to the teeth, that seemed a bit ridiculous. But the Once King was clearly trying to be polite, and his insistence on formality gave James an idea. As he and Ar'Bati removed their weapons, James made a great show of fussing with his Eclipsed Steel Staff, knocking it over several times. During one of these bungles, he stealthily removed the dagger Ar'Bati had found earlier from his belt and shoved the narrow blade into the hinge of the hidden door. When it was in position, he set his staff on the ground as if he'd simply given up and turned back to the king.

"Sorry," he said, holding up his clawed hands. "Still not really used to having paws yet."

The Once King waved a hand in dismissal. "Your current condition was my doing. Think nothing of it."

"Thank you," James said as the door swung closed behind them. He didn't dare look, but his ears were listening closely, and he didn't hear the click of a latch. Satisfied he'd bought himself the best edge he could, James hurried to take a seat on the long sofa set off to the side of the large stone fireplace. The Once King was already seated in front of the blaze, his enormous body looking far more at ease here in the low-backed chair, which left plenty of room for his wings, than he had on his throne.

"James of Claw Born," he said, gesturing to his left. "Pour us wine so that we may speak as civilized beings."

"Yes, Your Majesty," James said, hopping up from the seat he'd just taken to hurry over to the place the Once King had just indicated, which turned out to be a giant sideboard cabinet filled with normal-sized bottles of wine that looked surprisingly not ancient and were stamped with the mark of Bastion.

That made sense, James supposed. Where else was the Once King supposed to get his booze? It wasn't as if you could raise grapes in the Deadlands. But strange as it was to pour a drink for the enemy of all life, seeing the wine gave James more hope than ever. For all his talk of suffering and death, the elf still clearly enjoyed at least *some* of the fruits of living.

Likewise, this room was a treasure trove. In addition to a lost library's worth of ancient texts, the Once King's shelves were lined with all manner of interesting objects. There were petrified corals from the deep ocean and uncut gems as big as James's head. Carved bones and wooden figures had been arranged in neat rows, and large decorative clay bowls held heaps of coins and glass beads. The ancient king even had player toys and vanity items from the game, tons of them. Clearly, the Once King was an elf of intellect and curiosity.

James could work with that.

"Here you are, Your Majesty," he said, trying not to sound too happy as he handed the Once King his glass.

The elf took it with a nod, watching as James poured for himself and his brother. When they were all served, James returned to his seat, hopping a little to get up onto the couch that was clearly built for much bigger people. The size made him wonder if the Once King sat in here with Sanguilar and his other raid bosses. Or maybe the Once King just liked to take naps? He didn't see a bed or a wardrobe, but the room still felt intimate and secret, reminding James of when he used to sneak into his parents' bedroom.

"So…" James said when he was settled at last. "Now that we're less formal, how would you prefer we address you? Should we just call you *king*?"

He used the old elven word Assets had taught him. But while the Once King had already acknowledge that as his true name, saying it in this context felt wrong, like wearing a tux to the pool. Without it, though, James was at a loss. He wanted to take full advantage of the Once King's offered intimacy, but there was simply no casual way to address a man whose name *was* "King." His discomfort earned him an amused smirk from the Once King, who'd clearly guessed his dilemma.

"*King* is what I am," the timeless elf said with an elegant shrug. "But long ago, when I still had friends and confidants, they called me 'Ar'Kan.'"

Ar'Bati jerked at that. "You speak the old tongue of the Savanna?" At James's quizzical look, he explained, "Ar'Kan means 'The Head of all Clans.'"

"The Head Warrior speaks correctly," Ar'Kan replied, his voice pleased. "The old tongue of the Savanna is a dialect of the Unbounded Language, albeit a very distant one."

Fangs in the Grass puffed out his chest, his tail swishing with jubatus pride. For his part, James didn't see how "Head of All Clans" was any less formal than "King," but that was what the Once King wanted, so that was what he used.

"All right, Ar'Kan," James said, working his tongue around the new word. "Why did you declare war on life?"

"I didn't," Ar'Kan replied calmly, taking a sip of his wine. "You are quoting my detractors' propaganda. I declared that I would bring all the souls in my charge to the peace of oblivion."

"Okay…" James said slowly. "I'm afraid I don't really understand the difference."

"I'd think it should be obvious," the elf said, giving James a frustrated look. "I have no quarrel with *life*. The trees and plants and animals, even the schtumples and the Birds, they are none of my concern, for I am not their king. My responsibility is to my people. I alone have the knowledge and power to save them from their horrible fate. Death is but the tool I use to do so."

"How can you say that when your 'salvation' is the greatest single source of suffering?" James demanded, barely avoiding shaking a finger at the primordial king. "You call it a horrible fate, but people's lives would be enormously better if they didn't have to contend with your undead armies! If you really want to save people, why don't you run around slaying evil and empowering good instead? Aren't you firstborn of the Sun itself? Why not follow its—"

"*Do not speak of the Sun to me!*" the Once King snarled, making James's ears go flat. "You know nothing of it!"

"Then *tell* me," James pleaded. "Help me understand. Everything I've ever heard about the Sun says it's a good and merciful god. Now you say that's wrong. Do you see my dilemma?"

"I do," Ar'Kan sighed, reaching up to pinch the bridge of his elegant nose. "But perpetual ignorance is part of mortality's curse. Allow me to illuminate you."

Setting down his wine, James leaned forward eagerly. It felt foolish to listen to the enemy of life's opinion on the god of life, but Gray Fang's trick with the lore rugs had taught him just how little he knew of this world's

288

actual history. Now he had a primary source in the form of an immortal king with a long memory. James was sure any of his history professors would have given up a kidney for a chance like this, and while he was certain there was bound to be a lot of bias to the Once King's version of events, it was still priceless information he could get nowhere else.

"You have heard of the Age of Skies," the Once King began, waiting for James to nod even though it wasn't a question. When he did, the king continued.

"Until recently, the four gods moved freely through the Boundless Sky," Ar'Kan said, his voice taking on a wistful, nostalgic tone. "Water formed the clouds, Wind made the weather, the Sun's heat made life, and the Moon's pull made planets. Working together, the four of them filled the vast emptiness with sustenance, giving birth to countless new universes. Your home is one such, though it was created a very long time ago. You see, the four gods never stopped moving, and the worlds they left behind quickly became cold and dark, losing their magic. Some eventually ceased to exist entirely when the power of the gods left them completely.

"But where the gods were, there was creation. Wind and Water were free flowing, fickle and unbiddable, but the Sun and the Moon were different. They were locked together in an endless dance, circling but never touching, and together, they made wonders. I was the first, created by the Sun the same time as Zthr was made by the Moon. Happy with their creations, the gods made more. From the Sun came the Celestial Elves and from the Moon the Birds. When the Moon's position eclipsed the Sun, the Birds would rise up from its dark surface to hunt us, and we hunted them in return. During the day, we would fly outward to explore the never-ending marvels created by the four gods. It was beautiful."

He stopped there, his voice too choked with emotion to go on. James waited silently until, at last, the king continued.

"I tell you this because to understand our problem, you must first understand our essence," he said, staring with such intensity that James flinched back. "The Sun created us to fly and discover, to be its joy and wonder as we explored everything it had made. This was our purpose, our reason for living, and live we did. We were immortal—the unaging, undying children of the Sky. Staying in one place for too long is very painful for Celestial Elves, which is why we never settled down on any of the planets the gods made. No matter how beautiful they were, we who were born to fly and move could never live placid on the ground. So we followed the wandering gods endlessly through the Boundless Sky. We hunted and were hunted by the Birds, and we were happy."

Pain flitted across the king's gray-tinged face as he looked up at the walls that surrounded them now, and James winced. After the loving way he'd spoken of exploring the Sky, James couldn't imagine how he stood being stuck inside this fortress. It was a wonder he hadn't gone mad. Then again, considering that he was out to destroy every person on the planet, maybe he had.

"This glory was our existence for a long, long time," Ar'Kan went on, his voice strained, as if he were forcing himself to continue. "How long, even I can't say. There was no need for time in the Boundless, Infinite Sky. But then, one day, it ended."

"How?" James asked.

The Once King's face grew furious. "The Sun," he hissed, hands clutched so hard around his glass James was amazed it didn't shatter. "Suddenly, without warning or provocation, the Sun attacked and burned the Moon. I can still remember it so clearly, as if it happened yesterday. I was leading my people back from the hunt at dusk when half of the silver god erupted in sunfire. Consumed, burning, the Moon cried out in pain. The Water and the Wind rushed to save it, as did my people and the Birds. Save for the Sun itself, the entirety of the heavens came together to fight what would later be called the Conflagration. For time untold, we fought and pushed and died until, at last, the fire was put out." His eyes flicked to the ghostfire torch that hung on the study's wall. "Mostly."

"But you won," James said, leaning forward. "You saved the Moon."

"We did," Ar'Kan said bitterly. "But the cost was great. Even burned to a cinder, the Moon's nature is that of form, cycles, and returning. When the battle was finally over, the Water and the Wind tried to return to the Sky only to discover they could not. They had stayed too long on the Moon's surface and been trapped by its nature. We *all* had. Even with our wings, we could no longer fly above the high atmosphere, for without the Wind and the Water, the Boundless Sky had no air or sustenance. The Sun still flew, but either in shame or continued cruelty, it had retreated so far from the Moon that the air above it was icy and dark."

The king paused to take a shaky gulp of his wine. "Any one of these factors we might have been able to overcome, but we could not survive them all. In our desperation to save the Moon, we had become trapped by it, unable to leave its orbit lest we perish in the cold, dead emptiness the Boundless Sky had become."

It took all of James's composure not to jump up and yell "ah ha!" at that, because he'd suddenly realized that he *had* heard this story before. What the Once King was telling him now in plain language were the same events described obliquely in the Origins Poem. Lines he'd once dismissed as some developer's overwrought dramatics like "the Celestial Elves were born to wander" and "All were trapped" now made actual sense. He also finally understood why the Once King seemed so hopeless.

"I think I get it," he said with new empathy. "The Celestial Elves were an entire race born to fly and discover, and now you couldn't."

"You can never understand," the Once King said, though not cruelly. He was merely stating a fact, and James supposed it was a true one. He wasn't immortal or celestial. He wasn't even an elf. He was human—well, jubatus—which meant he had no instinct to roam like the Once King's people. If they couldn't even stand to set foot on a planet, how had they dealt with this?

"Many of my people went mad from being confined," Ar'Kan said, answering the question he hadn't asked. "Others destroyed themselves attempting to cross the void. They knew it would happen, but they could not bring themselves to stand on the prison of the ground for one more second. I tried my best to hold us together, to lead as I always had, but I had nothing to give them. My people *needed* a new frontier to explore like your kind needs air or food, but all that remained accessible to us was the Moon itself."

"Surely the Moon was welcoming?" James asked tentatively. "You saved it, after all."

"We did," the king said. "And it tried, in its way. But the Moon was the domain of the Birds, and it was not our god. In all the ages we'd flown with it through the Sky, we'd never once touched its shadowed surface. As well we shouldn't, seeing what had happened to the Water and Wind, never mind the wrath of the Birds. Now, though, we were trapped in its pull. Forever."

James looked down at his glass. The king's grief had filled the room like smoke, making it hard to breathe. But while that sounded like the end of the story, James knew it wasn't. "What did you do?"

"The only thing I could," Ar'Kan said. "I was their ruler. I had to save them, but I was facing an unwinnable situation. So I turned to the only one left with the power to help us. I got on my knees and beseeched the Sun for salvation." He bared his teeth. "I wish it had never answered my prayers."

"Why?" Curiosity made the word slip from James's mouth before he could stop it. If the Once King minded the interruption, though, his flawless face didn't show it.

"Because it betrayed me," the ancient elf whispered, clenching his fist so tight he *did* break the glass this time, sending dark wine flowing like blood down the plates of his cursed armor. "I begged it for mercy, and the Sun replied, 'Come to me.' I'd seen what it had done to the Moon with my own eyes, but like a *fool*, I trusted it still. I gathered up my people and sang the Sun's praises to them once more. I made promise after promise, trusting the Sun to keep them. I told everyone that salvation was waiting for us and sent my people flying toward our creator in the Sky, but then…"

He trailed off, leaving James and Ar'Bati sitting tensely. "But then?" James prompted when the silence had stretched too long.

The king's voice came back in a broken hitch. "It burned off their wings," he said, his own ash-gray wings pulling in tight around his body. "They fell from the Sky like broken toys, their backs bearing only blackened stumps. I alone was spared, for I alone had stayed behind. I wanted to go last, to be sure that all my people would be saved."

The final word was spoken with such bitterness James winced, but this still didn't make any sense. "Why did the Sun do that?"

"I don't know," the Once King whispered, clutching the arms of his chair as his sadness turned into rage. "But I should have. After what it did to the Moon, to its own divine partner, I should have *known* it would betray us, but I was a fool! I sent my people into the embrace of a monster who mauled and deformed and destroyed what they held most dear! A quiet death in the cold void would have been kinder, but I took that from them. In my blindness and stupid trust, I doomed my people to a fate worse than death!"

The room fell silent. The Once King sat still as a statue, petrified by his loss and guilt. James was struck just as dumb. The Once King's story flew in the face of everything he'd ever seen, read, or heard about the Sun. Aside from what was happening right now, James had never heard a bad word spoken about the Sun god. *All* the lore from the game painted it as the ultimate benevolent force, and with the notable exception of the Once King, every actual denizen of this world sang its praises earnestly. Even the player Clerics he'd met liked the Sun, and it wasn't even their religion. All that made the Once King's story very hard to believe, but it was obvious to James that the king absolutely believed he was telling the truth. The only thing James could think was that there'd been some horrific miscommunication, but how did that end up with wings getting burned off? What had the Sun been trying to do?

"So what happened to them?" Fangs in the Grass asked.

The Once King and James both looked up in surprise. "What do you mean?" Ar'Kan demanded.

"Your people," Fangs clarified, lifting his chin stubbornly. "You said the Sun burned their wings to stumps, but all the elves I know have backs that look just fine. So where did the Celestial Elves go after this supposed betrayal? Did they all die?"

James's first instinct was to apologize for his rude brother, but Fangs had actually asked a very good question. Where *had* the Celestial Elves gone?

"They did not *die*," the Once King said, curling his lip in disgust. "They wished they had died at first, and I tried my best to help them, but after a very brief period of time, they forgot."

James boggled at him. "What do you mean they forgot? Like forgot their wings?"

"They forgot everything," the king sneered. "As their burns healed, they became enraptured by the Moon and its ever-changing surface. Without their wings, they forgot the Sky and their destiny and became obsessed with making this world their home. They became like *schtumples*."

He said that like a curse, but several things James hadn't understood before were now coming together, including the Grand Schtump's claim that the elves had come down from the sky and taken everything. He didn't know if that was exactly what had happened, but he was pretty sure the Celestial Elves hadn't been peaceful refugees trying to find a new place to live. The fallen elves had probably been more like Jack from *Nightmare Before Christmas*—grabbing everything shiny and making a mess of it all. No wonder the local inhabitants had been pissed.

"Still, everything might have been all right if not for mortality," Ar'Kan went on, making him jump. "Even without their wings, my people were creatures of the Infinite Sky. Unlike the Birds, we were not built to handle all of this finiteness and gravity. Being trapped in the Moon's ever-grinding grasp wore down my people's souls. Since my wings were still intact, I was able to cling to my true nature and resist, but I could not save

294

them. I was forced to watch, helpless, as my beautiful, immortal people were twisted into mockeries of themselves, eventually breaking down into the various lesser bodies you now call jubatus and humans and ichthyians and all the other descended races. And as their souls eroded, my timeless subjects began to age and die."

"Did you not die before?" James asked, confused.

"We did," the king admitted. "But not like this. In the Sky, an elf killed by a Bird could be mourned for all eternity, but their soul was free to fly back to the Sun. Here, though, even that was stolen from us. Elves who died bound to the Moon did not return to the Sun or even to the Sky. Instead, their souls were trapped in an endless cycle of rebirth. There was no more heaven for us, no more flight. Only a ceaseless hell of being born an ignorant child, growing up painfully, gaining the tiniest measure of our former power and glory only to almost immediately lose it again to old age, sickness, and infirmity. Even in death there was no escape, because the moment my people died, the Moon's pull forced their souls right back to the start. Another weak mortal body. Another brief, painful life. Another death. Over and over, *forever*."

James blinked in surprise. It was common knowledge, at least on the wiki, that all of FFO's humanoid races except schtumples were descended from Celestial Elves, but he'd never read anything about reincarnation in the lore or heard about it from Gray Fang. "Wait, wait, wait," he said, holding up a hand. When the Once King scowled, he added, "Please?"

Glowering, the monarch motioned for him to go ahead, and James jumped on it. "The clans of the Savanna teach that our souls join the Wind when they die," he said in a rush. "The Church of the Sun, on the other hand, says that good souls go to the Sunlight Heaven while the wicked sink into the Lightless Realm. Real Naturalists like Gray Fang and Thunder Paw—not me—are also priests of the Water and Wind, and the church has the High Priest who can talk directly to the Sun itself. What you're saying about reincarnation contradicts all of these religious authorities, so how do you know it's true?"

"Because I was there," Ar'Kan growled. "I've watched it happen! It's true the Wind catches some souls, but they live with it only temporarily. It does this as a tiny mercy for those who praise it, but holding on is not the Wind's nature, and it's as trapped as the rest of us. In the end, *nothing* escapes the Moon, and *all* souls must pass through the Lightless Realm. As for the Church of the Sun..." The king sneered. "Their top clerics know perfectly well that there is no heaven, sunlit or otherwise. I know this for a fact, because the current high priest came to me."

"Whoa," James said, eyes wide. "High Priest Raffestain came *here*?"

The king nodded. "Decades before the Nightmare, right after he ascended to his current exalted position, Raffestain came and sat right there in the space you now occupy, and he was not the first high priest of the Sun to do so. Almost all of them come to me eventually in a desperate attempt to resolve their inevitable crisis of faith."

His voice changed as he spoke, the sneering tone changing into something that sounded suspiciously like jealousy.

"You see, whenever they prayed to the Sun, it would answer. The god showered its blessing upon them, granting miracle after miracle. It even permitted the casting of the Resplendent Aegis, a spell that requires direct divine intervention. And yet despite their god's clear and constant presence, whenever the priests asked about what happened after death, their beloved Sun became silent and cold."

"So they came to you instead?"

The king's lips curled into a superior smirk. "Who else could they ask? I am the oldest being in creation. They came to me for answers, and I told them the truth just as I have told it to you, but every single one of those wise men rejected my knowledge and left. Since new priests kept arriving at my door every few decades, I can only presume they all decided to keep perpetuating the myth of a sunny land where good souls go." He shook his head. "I suppose one of the benefits of being mortal is that your life is short enough to choose the bliss of ignorance over the discomfort of reality. By the time you're forced to confront the truth, you're already dead."

He said that like it was a personal failing, but it didn't take any of James's imagination to guess why a High Priest of the Sun would never in a million years share this secret. The risk of irrevocably damaging their religion—or pissing off the Sun itself—was simply too high. It was also easy to dismiss such unpleasantness when it came from the lips of the enemy. Easy and not entirely wrong. James had to remind himself that, while the Once King was very authoritative, he was still just a person recounting his highly personal interpretation of events. His story was not a whole or even an unbiased picture but the recollections of an angry man with an ax to grind.

Lacking any grains of salt nearby, James took a sip of wine instead. "So this world, the ground we stand on, *is* the Moon, then?"

"It is," Ar'Kan said. Then he frowned. "Though your word, 'Moon,' is not entirely correct. The magic that allows you to understand our languages chose that name because your planet's satellite resembles how this world used to look to us when we flew in the sky. A more accurate translation from the Unbounded Language would be 'that which circles,' and it used to refer to both the god and time, since the first instance of time was calculated by the Moon god's turning. But that was long ago. Now, 'Moon' is just the name of a long-lost god. This thing, this *corpse* we live on is all that remains of a once beautiful divinity."

"But the Moon can't be *totally* dead," James argued. "It still has magic."

"Would that it had died," the king sighed. "Then we would not be trapped, and none of this would have happened. Alas, in our efforts to save the god, we forced it into this lessened, crippled state, dooming it and ourselves. Truly, no good deed goes unpunished."

He heaved a long, bitter sigh, and Ar'Bati shot to his feet. "Enough!" the head warrior cried, baring his teeth. "We did not come here to listen to you talk in circles! You promised to tell us the truth!"

"I have," the king said, his regal voice dripping with displeasure that Ar'Bati—in classic Angry Cat style—completely ignored.

"You have told us complaints and old wrongs!" Fangs snarled. "But aside from the gods themselves, everyone you've ever known is long dead, so why are you still here? You go on and on about saving your people, but by what you have just said, *we* are your people! If you have indeed spoken the truth, then we—all peoples of this world save the schtumples and the Birds—are what the Celestial Elves became, but we are the very ones *you* are killing!" He stabbed his finger at the Once King. "How can you call yourself a king when all your works and powers are bent toward slaughtering the very people you should be protecting?"

That wasn't how James would have phrased it, and it certainly wasn't the right tone, but his brother's questions were good ones. They had indeed learned much, more even than James had hoped, but nothing had actually changed. The Once King was still their enemy, and James *still* didn't understand why.

"My brother's right," he said, standing up to take Fangs's side against the increasingly furious king. "I believe everything you've told us, but that just makes what you've done—what you're *still* doing—even more wrong! What kind of king kills his own people and then enslaves their corpses to form an army so he can keep killing? What good monarch tends a fire of hate? What do you think salvation is that *this*"—he stabbed his finger at the ghostfire torch flickering on the wall—"is your answer?"

"Ignorant children," the Once King sneered, his handsome face pulling into a furious mask as he shot to his feet. "I have told you everything, and yet you refuse to learn! You speak of enslavement, but there is no freedom in this world except for what *I* bring!"

"All you bring is *death*!" James cried. "Worse than death! I've seen what your ghostfire does. I watched it ravage a child! An innocent little gnoll pup who did nothing to deserve so much suffering! How can you call that freedom?"

The king stared at them in shock. "You still don't understand," he whispered, sinking back into his chair. "You still don't know what the ghostfire does, how it works."

"I know," James spat. "It burns souls and turns beautiful living things into undead monstrosities!"

Ar'Kan scowled. "I'll overlook your rudeness because I see now that it comes from an even deeper ignorance than I realized. I should have known, but it is so difficult to keep in mind just how much you have forgotten." He shook his head in despair and then straightened up. "Sit," he said, gently now.

Looking warily at each other, James and Ar'Bati sat back down on the sofa. When they were still, the Once King removed his black armored gauntlet and lifted his hand, summoning a candle flame–sized wisp of ghostfire into his bare palm.

"This is death," he said, holding the blue-white flame up for them to see. "*True* death, not the tragedy of ever-cycling mortality. After the Sun's second betrayal, some of my people retained their sanity. They were not seduced by the Moon's call, but without their wings, they could not escape the grasp of age. Grieving, I rallied everyone who would listen and led them deep underground, away from the cruel Sun. At first we thought only of finding shelter, but down there, deep, deep in the dark, I found something greater. The solution to our problems."

He pushed the ghostfire at James, who flinched away. "You found the ghostfire?"

"No," the king said, stroking the flame like he would a cat. "This was a complicated creation of my own hand. What we found was an ember left over from the Conflagration. After the Sun burned the Moon, we learned

299

just how hard it was to extinguish sunfire. It is the oldest magic, so primal and eternal that even the Wind and the Water could not fully destroy it all. I mourned that fact while we were fighting, but that wretched tenacity proved to be our salvation."

He cupped the flame in both hands. "I took that ember just like this, and I turned to my people—my poor, dying, wingless people ravaged by mortality—and I told them my plan. When they heard it, they rejoiced and sang my praises once again as I fed each one of them into the fire. As they were consumed, I used the magic of the Sky—magic that still lives in all of us—to merge their deaths with the flames, creating *this*." He smiled lovingly at the tongue of blue-white fire. "A pyre, death made flame. I took my enemy's power and made it my own. With the ghostfire, I could burn the souls of my followers to create magic more powerful than anything ever seen in the whole of the Boundless Sky, but even that was only a byproduct. A highly useful but ultimately unnecessary side effect. The *true* purpose of ghostfire is the destruction of souls."

"But...but *why*?" James demanded.

"Because a soul consumed by ghostfire cannot be reborn," the Once King said simply. "Those my ghostfire turns undead are freed from the Moon's eternal cycle. No longer are they forced to endure the pain of birth, life, and death, making the same mistakes over and over and *over* again. Instead, their souls are simply *gone*. At peace. No more." He smiled. "That is how I will save my people. That is how I will save *you*. By sending your soul to oblivion, I will finally free you—all of you—from the Moon's grasp. Even you players. If you stay here for more than one year, your souls will be trapped as well, but you don't have to be afraid. You are not my people, but I will save you all the same. With my ghostfire, I will save *everyone*, all the souls in this world. Then, when you are all free, I will feed myself to the flames, and I, too, will have peace at last."

James shrank back into the couch. The beatific smile on the Once King's face was a thousand times more terrifying than his rage had been.

Anger, sadness, righteous fury, those were things James could fight, but he didn't know how to respond to this eagerness. He'd thought the Once King was hopeless, but the man in front of him was doing all of this *because* he had hope: hope for his people, hope for himself, hope for a future in which no one suffered. If it hadn't meant the death of the entire world, James could have gotten behind it. But no matter how good the Once King's intentions, his plan was madness. He *had* to be stopped, but how?

"Your first followers," James said cautiously. "The ones you killed to create the ghostfire. What happened to them? Are they gone?"

"I didn't *kill* them," the king said, insulted. "They threw themselves on the fire of their own accord. There were six who said I was tainted by the Sun's fire and refused. Those fools I cast aside, flinging them even deeper under the ground, but the others saw what must be done as I did, and they serve me still. They are my generals and advisers, my commanders in the field. While I am trapped here tending the ghostfire, they are already one with the flames. So long as I keep the fire burning bright, they can go wherever they are needed to do my work in the world."

James nodded. Of course. Those first dead Celestial Elves had become the powerful sentient undead bosses like Sanguilar or the Lich of Red Canyon. He'd suspected as much, but knowing for certain that the Once King's original followers were still alive confirmed an important fact: souls fed to the ghostfire *weren't* consumed immediately. Maybe Celestial Elves just burned very slowly, or maybe the Once King controlled which souls got consumed and which simply smoldered. Either way, the fact that beings like the Lich existed at all proved that souls fed to the ghostfire weren't necessarily gone, and that gave him hope. If they could destroy the Great Pyre, maybe the souls of those who'd already been turned could still go back into the cycle and be reborn.

It was definitely worth a try, but James still had to figure out how they were going to *get* to the Pyre. It was now clear that convincing the Once King to stop fighting was not going to happen, at least not through him. He

301

didn't know if there *was* someone the Once King would listen to, but so long as the ancient elf saw him and Fangs as foolish children, he wasn't going to take anything they said seriously, which meant their usefulness here was done. He'd learned a ton, not that he knew how any of it could be useful yet, but he still needed to get the information back to Tina. His sister was smart, and so were her people. Together, James was sure they could find something in the Once King's history to use against him. Before he could escape, though, there was one last thing James had to try.

"Thank you, Ar'Kan, for telling us so much," he said, bowing respectfully. "My heart breaks for your history of tragedy, disaster, and betrayals."

The Once King smiled, banishing the flicker of ghostfire with a wave of his hand. "It is I who should thank you. I am glad I let you live, James of Claw Born. It is good to be understood at least once before the end."

"I understand you very well now," James said, bracing himself. "I just don't agree."

The ancient king froze, his huge body going perfectly still. For a terrifying moment, James thought that was that, but the elf didn't lash out. He simply slumped in his chair, shaking his head in despair.

"I am disappointed," he said at last. "I'd thought here, at last, I'd found someone wise and open-minded enough not to reject the truth."

"I'm not rejecting the truth," James argued. "I believe everything you said, I just don't agree with your conclusions."

The Once King's head shot up. "Explain yourself," he ordered.

James scooted forward on the couch. "You say you want to burn all the souls of this world in the ghostfire to free them from the Moon's eternal cycle of rebirth. I understand how you reached that conclusion, but all of your plans are based on the premise that your people are suffering because of their mortality, and I don't think that's correct."

"How can you say they do not suffer?" the king demanded. "Have you *seen* how they live?"

302

"Have you?" James asked, looking the king straight in the eyes. "I'm not saying there isn't pain, but just because suffering exists doesn't mean that's all there is to life. Even in the worst conditions, people still find happiness. They raise families and fall in love and make beautiful things. The existence you condemn isn't nearly as horrible as you think. If it was, why would we fight so ardently to defend it?"

"You say that because you are still young," Ar'Kan said bitterly. "You haven't yet had to watch, helpless, as old age steals away your vitality and power. You haven't yet crossed the threshold where there are no new horizons, only the dark void of death. You will see."

"Yeah, a long time from now," James snapped. "But focusing only on the end ignores all the good things that come before it. Even when life *is* brutish, painful, and short, the people of this world get another shot when they're reborn. That's way better than my world. We *still* don't know what happens when we die, but the races here get to go on forever. To experience all life has to offer again and again. That's not suffering, that's not hell. That's *amazing!*"

"Spoken like a spoiled child," the Once King said dismissively. "I've seen your world through Leylia's eyes. I know how soft you live. This world is different."

"Because of you!" James cried. "Your armies have caused most of the destruction in this world! And as for soft, you're the one acting as if any hardship at all is intolerable! I don't know where you got that idea. I mean, the Celestial Elves knew suffering, right? You fought and struggled and died in battle. Did that mean the Age of Skies was hell?"

"You are deliberately missing the point," the king said angrily. "Of course we suffered, but we were free, children of an infinite future and explorers of untold worlds! Now all of that glory has been exchanged for squealing in the mud. No sane creature would want this."

"How do you know?" James challenged. "You haven't left this castle in a thousand years, *and* you're still immortal. Of course you think life is

303

terrible! You've been living on and on and on alone in the dark with nothing but grudges, guilt, and ghostfire to sustain you. You claim your people are suffering, but how can you possibly know? You haven't even tried being alive."

"I am aware of my hypocrisy," the Once King acknowledged. "But this is for their own good."

"I don't think you are aware," James said, ignoring the instinct screaming at him to stop before the very large man lost his patience. "All you talk about is how everyone betrayed you and how we're all too ignorant to know better, but we're the ones who are actually out there living. Have you ever stopped to consider that maybe you're wrong, and all those people fighting so hard to stop you aren't unaware of their suffering but actually want to *stay alive?*"

"*I do know better!*" Ar'Kan roared, shooting to his feet. "I am older than any other being save the gods themselves! I was made by the Sun itself to rule and guide, while you are all children who know nothing but petulance! My way has been the way of the Celestial Elves since before your Earth existed, and it will be their way to oblivion's end!"

James shrank back into the couch. The Once King hadn't made any overtly aggressive motions, but being shouted at by someone who could kill him in a blink was still terrifying. Beneath the fear, though, he was rejoicing, because anger meant he was getting through. Locked up in his fortress, the only people the Once King had to talk to were his ardently devoted undead servants and the occasional high priest. James bet he hadn't been actually challenged in thousands of years, which was why he was getting so flustered and making so many mistakes now. Mistakes James was just crazy enough to jump on.

"You can't claim the Sun's authority in one breath and reject it with the next," he argued, going back on the attack. "Admit it: this whole crusade is personal. If you truly cared about your people, you'd ask them what *they* wanted. But you never have, because this isn't about them at all. You're not burning the world because your people are suffering. You just can't stand how *you* feel when you look down on us mortals."

"Of course I can't," the king said, defiant. "It kills me to see how my people live now because I remember what they were. I am the only one who knows how far they have fallen, but just because they are ignorant of the crime doesn't mean it didn't happen. The Sun wronged us all! It turned its back on its own creations and then tried to cover up its sin by burning our wings so that we would forget what it stole. But I cannot, I *will not* forget! I will free my people from this pit if I have to drag them kicking and screaming, but I will *never* stand idly and watch as they roll in filth and think it is fine because filth is all they've ever known!"

James sank back in his seat with a frustrated sigh. This was going nowhere, and they were running short on time. He didn't know how long it had taken him and Fangs to get up here, but it had to be after dawn by now. Tina's army would be attacking any moment now, and he didn't want to be here when they arrived. The last thing his sister needed was for him to be used as a hostage against her. But as he turned his thoughts toward escape, his brother's voice broke the silence.

"Have you ever asked the Sun why it burned your people?"

The Once King's mouth pressed into a tight line. "Of course not."

"Why?" Fangs asked stubbornly.

"Because it made its intentions obvious," the ancient elf hissed. "It burned us *twice*! Once immediately after I beseeched it for help! Only an idiot would go back for more after that."

"Perhaps," Fangs said, crossing his arms over his chest. "But I know a thing or two about grudges. They seem obvious and necessary while you're holding them, but just because you're the one making it doesn't mean the poison isn't deadly." His eyes flicked to James. "A wise Naturalist once told me that sometimes the only way to win a battle is to let it go. You have sat in here cursing the Sun for a thousand years now, but it has continued to shine and give light to all the world. It would shine on you, too, if you'd part the clouds of the Deadlands and let it. I'm not saying it deserves forgiveness. For all I know, it truly did betray you. But even if that is true, nothing you do now can change what happened. This anger, this hate, it's only hurting you. You are the last immortal Celestial Elf, and you're wasting your endless life hiding in a fortress feeding a fire with your hate. *Literally*. That seems a shameful way for the Head of All Clans to behave."

"I have no care for your seeming," the Once King said, but his voice was more sad than angry. "Pride and shame are for mayflies whose only immortality is to live on in tales. A true king does not have such luxuries. No matter what you say or how you try to twist my words to make me a villain, I know my duty. I *will* save my people, and there's nothing you can do to stop me."

James sighed again, this time in defeat. "Then it seems we're at an impasse."

"Indeed," the Once King agreed, rising to his feet. "This conversation is over. You'll have to forgive me. I'd intended to offer you the choice of becoming sentient undead, but I think your souls would be best fed straight to the ghostfire. As powerful servants as you would make, I don't think I could tolerate this insolence on a regular basis."

A drop of sweat rolled down James's neck. That was right. The Once King had said he was going to kill them when this was over.

"One last question!"

The king looked annoyed. "Do not attempt to stall. You knew this was coming."

"I did, and I'm not," James said quickly, putting up his hands. "But this is super important. Before we die, I have to ask: can you actually send us home?"

"What does it matter if I tell you or not?" the Once King said flippantly. "You're about to die."

"Yeah, but knowing for certain would make me feel better."

The Once King frowned, thinking that over. "I'm not sure it would."

"Please, I need to know," James begged. "Think of it as my last request."

"Very well," the king said. "The connection to your world still remains in my memories. I know how to find Earth and send my magics to it, but it took me ten years' worth of channeling my mana from the Nightmare to create the spell that cut your threads and brought your souls to this side. It would take a similar amount of power to send them back."

Ten years...

James sagged in his seat. He supposed he should be happy to know it was possible, but ten years was practically a death sentence. Even with the ten-to-one time difference, only the luckiest of players would have a living body to return to.

"I, too, would prefer you to be gone sooner rather than later," the Once King said at James's crestfallen expression. "It would be far simpler to just return you all than to defeat you. Alas, I would have to use all of the Great Pyre's energies to get the power I needed, and that magic is already spoken for. But look at it this way: in ten years, your souls would be trapped by the Moon just as my people's are. You are all destined to suffer just as they do, and again, I apologize for that. I did not intend for your people to become trapped here when I freed us from the Nightmare, but I will not abandon you." He smiled at James. "You are not elves, but I still think of you as my own, and I promise I will set you free."

"Yeah, well, you'll forgive us if we don't say thank you," James grumbled.

"Being king is a thankless job," the Once King said with a shrug. Then he reached out his arm toward them. "Farewell, sons of Claw Born. Be at peace, and know the rest of your kind will join you soon."

Eyes flying wide, James rolled off the couch. Ar'Bati did the same in the opposite direction. There was no way they could beat the raid boss—even without a weapon, the Celestial Elf was strong enough to crush their bones barehanded—but if they could just get to the door he'd propped open with the dagger, they could make a run for it.

At least, that had been James's plan. Now that it was actually happening, though, he was starting to realize just how badly he'd underestimated the Once King's speed. The ancient elf moved with a grace and precision that made even SilentBlayde look bumbling. James couldn't even dive off the couch before the Once King grabbed his tail.

Panicked, James jerked away, leaving the Once King with a handful of fur. Too terrified to feel the pain, James lunged for the closest bookshelf, sending books and art objects flying as he scrambled up the shelves. He was planning to wedge himself into the tiny gap between the top of the heavy bookcase and the stone ceiling when his frantic hand closed around something familiar.

When they'd first entered the room, James had noted the Once King's impressive collection of curios included several player toys. The box his hand had just found was one of these: an ornate silver cube with a slim crank handle poking out one side that he recognized immediately. It was the Music Box of Sim Salrin, and the moment James saw it, he broke into a grin.

On paper, the Music Box of Sim Salrin was a totally useless vanity toy. In practice, it was FFO's favorite trolling item. Turning its crank summoned an illusionary chorus to perform the "Ballad of the Sea's Sadness," a seven-minute dirge that told the story of a doomed ichthyian princess, *loudly*. In addition to being super long and annoying, the illusionary chorus who appeared to sing the dirge counted as intractable objects, meaning you couldn't walk through them.

Because of this, activating the music box basically created a seven-minute blockade anywhere it was played, so of *course* people loved cranking it up in front of the mailbox or the auction house or the entrance to a dungeon. It eventually got so bad that raiding guilds started advertising their "Zero-Tolerance Music Box Policy" when recruiting. Tina in particular hated that box with a passion, but James had never been happier to see anything in his life. He was still tightening his fingers around it when the Once King's fist slammed into his side.

That should have been the end. If he'd been in his old scavenged armor, it would have been. But thanks to his brother, James was now wearing a full set of level-eighty gear. That still shouldn't have saved him, but the sword the Once King had left outside must have been more important to his damage than James had realized, because when the raid boss slammed him to the ground, he wasn't dead. The side of his chest was caved in and all of his ribs were broken, but he was still very much alive and kicking, which was exactly what he did.

Kicking off his back, James rolled sideways a split second before the Once King's boot landed where his head had been with enough force to crack the stone floor. He was technically still close enough for a kick, but James didn't wait to see if the king was angry enough to kick him while he was down. He was already cranking the music box's handle as fast as it would go, yelling to his brother as he wound the magical mechanism tight.

"Fangs! Hit the ground!"

He heard a soft thump across the room, which he could only hope meant Ar'Bati had obeyed. Either way, it was too late. The Music Box of Sim Salrin was already glowing in his hands, its lid cracking open with a watery light and the mournful wail of a hundred crying fish-women. Then, with a swell of music, the silver box split open, and the cozy study was filled with green-scaled, wall-eyed ichthyian maidens, their diaphanous dresses floating in the currents of an illusionary sea as they opened their gaping fish mouths to begin their ancient lament.

The Once King cried out in surprise as the surging illusion shoved him out of the way. James had no idea how the music box worked now that everything was real, but it seemed the singing fish ladies were just as solid here as they'd been back in the game, their bodies crowding out the raid boss just as they'd once crowded players out of countless trade-profession huts. Fuming with rage, the ancient elf grabbed the figures to fling them aside, but while they were real enough to stop movement, the illusionary chorus wasn't actually alive. They were made from magic. Every time the Once King grabbed one to throw it, the illusion flowed away like water only to reform itself a split second later, forming the loudest, most annoying impenetrable wall imaginable.

James gave himself precisely one second to gloat over his cleverness, and then he was on his hands and knees, crawling through the forest of ichthyian legs toward the door as fast as his wounded body could go. Fangs met him halfway, eyes flying wide when he saw his brother.

"You're bleeding!"

That was news to James. He'd thought he just had a chest full of broken ribs, but the Once King's punch must have broken more than he'd realized, because his armor was indeed soaked with red when he looked down.

"How badly are you hurt?" Fangs demanded.

"Not bad enough to stop me," James said, hoping more than believing that was true. "*Door!*"

He resumed shoving himself through the chaos, but he must not have been going fast enough, because Fangs grabbed him with a growl. Slinging James onto his back, the head warrior dropped to all fours and bolted, zigzagging through the narrow gaps between the singers' legs like a true cat. By this point, the Once King's angry growling had turned into a roar. Every now and then, James caught a glimpse of the king as he punched and grabbed at the fish maidens, but there were just too many, and he was too big. He couldn't even use his wings in here because the ceiling was too low. For the next few minutes at least, the Once King was well and truly trapped. Glancing at the door, which looked pretty closed, James desperately hoped they weren't, too.

"Well?" he gasped when they reached it.

Fangs lowered him to the ground and dug his claws into the crack where the hidden door met the wall. It had been flush against the stone when the Once King had first opened it, so the fact that his brother could get any purchase at all meant James's ploy with the dagger had worked at least a little. Sure enough, after much pushing and huffing, Ar'Bati got the door to move just enough for them to slip through.

"Go!" he ordered, his eyes bulging with the effort as he braced his shoulder against the magical door to hold it open.

James nodded and did as he was told, eyes watering with pain as he squeezed his broken chest through the narrow gap. The moment he was clear, Fangs dove after him, but as he was wiggling his armored body between the stones, James caught a flash out of the corner of his eye.

By the time he looked up, it was too late. Across the room, the Once King had spotted them. He still couldn't get to them through the warbling singers, but now that his eyes were on them, that didn't matter. He simply grabbed something shiny off the shelf beside him and flicked his hand, sending the object hurtling through the illusionary-water heads of the fish maidens and straight into Ar'Bati's chest.

It happened so fast his brother didn't even seem to notice he'd been hit at first. Only when the object—an engraved silver pen sized for the Once King's hand, which made it nearly a foot long—clattered off the back of the Eclipsed Steel throne did the warrior finally stop and look down. Then he slumped sideways, blood pouring from his mouth as he landed at James's feet with a wet, broken *slap*.

"*Fangs!*"

Clutching his own wounds, James fell on his knees at his brother's side. Without Ar'Bati's strength to hold it open, the stone door had mostly closed again, but not enough to hide them from the Once King's deadly gaze. Baring his teeth in heartbroken fury, James lashed out with his foot, kicking the dagger out of the hinge to close it fully. He grabbed his staff next, snatching the Eclipsed Steel off the floor where the Once King had ordered them to disarm and waving it over Ar'Bati's body as he began the healing spell.

"Hold on, Fangs!" he cried, frantically gathering the green, glowing life magics that floated through the air even in this dead place. "I've got you!"

He was still building the spell when his brother reached up with a bloody hand to grab his staff.

"Don't."

"Don't be stupid!" James hissed, tugging at his staff, which Fangs had a surprisingly tight grip on for someone who was dying. "I have to heal you before you bleed out!"

The warrior shook his head. "Don't waste your mana," he wheezed, letting go of James's staff at last to push himself over onto his back. "I've got too much health, remember?" He gave James a bloody smile. "Two-skull boss of Windy Lake."

As if James could ever forget. Fangs's huge health pool had saved their bacon countless times, but all that HP didn't mean squat if all his blood was on the floor instead of inside him. When he tried to cast again, though, his brother knocked his staff away with a furious look.

"I said *no*," Fangs rasped. "If we both die, this was all for nothing. You have to get what we learned to the others. Heal yourself and get out of here."

"I'm not leaving you!"

"You're not leaving me. I'm bravely staying behind so you can complete the mission."

"But—"

Fangs shook his head. "This is something only you can do. To be honest, I didn't understand half of what the Once King was saying. You're the one who has the knowledge to search what he told us and find a way to defeat him."

"But I don't know how!" James wailed, tears flowing down his face. "I don't have a plan!"

"You'll think of one," his brother said confidently, closing his eyes. "You always do. But you can't think of anything while you're bawling here, so go. Get to your sister, tell her what we've learned. I'll hold him off."

That was ridiculous and they both knew it, but there was nothing else James could say. Ar'Bati was right. By the time James finished healing him, he'd be out of mana, the music box diversion would be over, and the Once King would be on them both. If he was going to run, it had to be now, but he couldn't carry his brother with his own chest hanging open. He was already feeling lightheaded, a sure sign that he needed to take his own advice and heal up before he bled out and wasted both their lives. He could already hear the ballad wrapping up through the closed door, so with a sob and a final squeeze of his brother's hand, James gathered his magic again and cast it on himself.

For once, he barely noticed the bliss of the magical healing washing over him. The fist-shaped dent in his broken side was still pulling itself back together when he turned and fled, limping, then jogging, then sprinting down the cavernous ghostfire-lit hallway back toward the front of the fortress, where, he desperately hoped, his sister would be waiting.

Chapter 13

Tina

Tina stood on the road to the Dead Mountain Fortress. It was well after dawn, not that they could see the sun through the Deadlands' eternal ceiling of gloomy, ash-gray clouds. Admittedly, part of that lateness was her fault. Another, oddly, was Richard's. The usually punctual Sorcerer had suddenly found a million things he had to do in camp, pushing back their march by almost an hour. But the majority of the blame for their late arrival fell squarely on the huge, skull-armored shoulders of the sulky-looking Berserker in front of her.

"Took your sweet time," she growled, glaring at Cinco as the Red Sands *finally* shuffled out of camp to join the rest of them. "Finally done licking your wounds?"

"Fuck you," he replied, glaring at the ground.

"Uh uh," Tina said, shaking her head. "The loser doesn't get to say that shit to the winner. From here out it's 'Yes, Roxxy' and 'How high, Roxxy?' Anything else and I'm taking your guild and giving it to Killbox, get me?"

"Whatever," he said, still not meeting her eyes.

"Wrong," she snarled. "Do it again."

CincoDeMurder raised his head at last. "Yes, Roxxy," he said through gritted teeth.

Oh, those words were sweet in her ears. Grinning like the bad winner she was, Tina waved for him to get back in line. Muttering under his breath, Cinco went, stepping out of the way of Commander Garrond, who was marching in Tina's direction.

"Will he be a problem?" the commander asked, eying Cinco's back as the Berserker rejoined his subdued raid.

"Nah," Tina said. "We're his only way home. He made his play and lost. Now his choices are follow orders or pitch a fit and risk being stuck

314

here forever. And while I'm sure CincoDeMurder can throw a mantrum with the best, I don't think he's going to risk his ticket back to Earth just to screw me over."

The commander looked confused. "Mantrum?"

Tina shrugged and turned back to the dread mountain citadel towering in the sky. "Ready to move out?"

"My men have been ready since before dawn," Garrond said sourly, but he left it at that, turning to study the fortress of their enemy with her. "The Order will take point. We have enough men to surround your raids completely. We'll escort and protect you until it's time to face the Once King."

"That wasn't the plan," Tina said angrily. "Your guys are here as backup, remember? The DMF is our turf. We go first."

"You players are the only ones who stand a chance against the Once King," Garrond argued. "That's why you're here. If the fortress is not actually as empty as it appears, we're all in for a fight. We can't risk your raiders taking casualties before you even get to the top."

"If there are monsters in there, they're going to clean your clocks!" Tina argued back, annoyed that she had to crane her neck to yell at him now. "The Order are all level-eight one-skulls. Even the trash mobs in the Dead Mountain are two-skull at least. If you take point, a ton of your guys are going to die. And *don't* say you're going to use your mass rez, because that ace is spoken for. If you spend all your mana using your big resurrection spell on the way in, it won't be ready again in time for the Once King fight."

"I am aware of the tactical situation," Garrond snapped. "But my men know what they are facing, and we remain committed to our oaths. If you players are truly the only ones who can free this world from the Once King, then it is the Order of the Golden Sun's duty to deliver you to him unscathed. On my honor, we will get you to the top of the mountain fresh and ready for the fight no matter what."

Tina gritted her teeth, pissed as hell at Garrond for putting this on her. The men behind them were actually people now, not just NPCs. He could talk about duty all he wanted, but those deaths would be on her hands if she let the Order slaughter themselves. That said, Tina knew a losing battle when she saw one, and butting heads with Garrond was *definitely* losing. She'd just have to cross her fingers and hope the fortress really was as empty as it looked.

"Fine," she growled. "You can escort us, but *no* resurrections before we reach the top! I don't think the Once King has recovered enough mana for a Million Damage Blast yet, but if he does get one off, you're our only insurance."

"Again, I am aware," the commander said, looking down at her. "I will not fail you."

Satisfied as she was likely to get, Tina nodded and gave the order to move out.

It wasn't a long march. They'd camped so close to the mountain, practically in its shadow, that even with their giant army, it took less than half an hour to reach the citadel's enormous front gates, which were mysteriously open.

Tina frowned. The last time she'd been here—before her ignominious transformation from stone to flesh—the enormous metal slabs had been sealed tight. Now, though, they were flung wide, almost like the Once King was inviting them in. She didn't like that at all, but there was no turning back. Garrond was already leading his troops inside, forcing Tina's raid off the road to make room. When she looked back to see if her Roughnecks were ready, though, what she saw made her beam with pride. Every player was in position, arranged by class and armed to the teeth, their enchanted weapons and armor glowing blindingly bright in the dim Deadlands morning. She'd never seen anything more beautiful in her life. It was almost enough to make her cry as she hopped up onto the ancient skeleton of a broken catapult.

"Roughnecks!" she cried, raising her small voice as loud as she could over the din of the Order's marching. "It's time! I'm so damn proud of how far we've come. We're gonna kick all the asses today!"

The raid answered with a roar she felt all the way through her chest. SilentBlayde appeared beside her a second later, flashing her a smile he no longer needed his mask to hide.

"Everyone's ready to rock and roll," he reported. "We could kill the Once King right now if he was here."

It was technically Zen's job now to tell Tina that sort of thing, but the Ranger looked happy to let SB take over reporting duty. Tina was happy, too. It was occurring to her yet again that this amazing man was her husband. She didn't need to hide her feelings when he got close anymore. She could just reach out and touch him or hug him or kiss him. In the end, she did all three, pulling him down to her mouth right then and there.

"Ugh!" Neko cried, making a noise like she was horking up a hairball. "If I'd known there'd be so many PDAs, I wouldn't've helped you guys hook up!"

Fortunately, the rest of the raid didn't seem to mind. Everyone was too busy watching the Order march into the fortress, gripping their weapons nervously as Garrond's soldiers vanished into the dungeon's cavernous front hall.

"So why do you think the door was open?" SB asked when she finally let him go.

Down on the ground in front of them, Killbox snorted. "Duh. Obvious trap is obvious."

"Actually, I bet this is James's doing," Tina said, but even as the words left her mouth, she wasn't sure she believed them. The fortress being empty was the whole reason they'd decided to come here, but as the mountain swallowed Garrond's army like it was nothing, she couldn't help feeling that this was wrong. No matter how cocky, bosses who were home alone didn't

317

just leave their front doors open. For the millionth time, she wished she hadn't let James go.

"Everyone, keep your eyes open for stray jubatus!" she called to her raid. "We might have a side quest to rescue my brother today."

As her people nodded, SB reached out to squeeze her hand. "He'll be fine. James always lands on his feet."

A week ago, Tina would have scoffed at that. Now she could only nod. Even so. "Would you mind taking point?" she asked, squeezing his hand back. "I'm not sure Garrond knows where he's going, and I need someone who can get back here fast if there's trouble. And if you see James…"

She couldn't finish. The idea of James being undead was a very real possibility that she couldn't handle right now. It was selfish to ask Blayde to do it, but her husband nodded. "I'll be your eyes," he promised, lifting their joined hands to press a kiss to her armored fingers before vanishing into the Lightless Realm, his presence a comforting weight in her shadow before he flitted away.

Satisfied she could trust him to do the right thing—or at least come back and tell her if the right thing had to be done—Tina settled in to wait. When Garrond's forces were finally through the doors, Tina ordered her players to move in as well, keeping her eyes on the gray sky in case the Once King decided to cut to the chase and drop down on them again. But no terrifying winged shadows appeared. She didn't even see one of his undead vultures. Just the low clouds hanging over their heads like cinderblocks as the Roughnecks marched at long last into the Dead Mountain.

It felt slightly surreal walking back into the familiar raid dungeon after everything that had happened. This stupid place had been Tina's home for most of the last year, and it still looked exactly like she remembered. The scale was a little bigger, but the rest of it—the undecorated black stone walls, the eerie blue light of the ghostfire torches, the grisly stains on the floor—was the same. The biggest difference was the emptiness. This room should have been packed full of skeleton patrols. Just walking through the doors, part of Tina was already braced for their horrifying, bandsaw–like alarm scream, but there was nothing. Just the echo of metal boots bouncing off cavernous stone and the nervous whispers of her raiders as they followed Garrond's troops through the forest of stone columns to the doors that marked the entrance to Grel'Darm's courtyard.

This, too, was empty. Like, super empty. Not only were there no patrols, but the dungeon's static dangers like the ghoul pits and giant corpse-spewing machines were quiet and still. What really got Tina, though, was that *all* the gates were open, even ones that had been permanently shut during the game. The iron portcullis that forced players to detour through the poisoned lab? Gone. They just walked right up the gently sloping ramp to the third terrace. Didn't even have to take the stairs.

"I don't like this," Tina muttered, clutching her shield closer.

"What are you talking about?" Neko asked beside her. "This is awesome! I hate the poison level."

"*Everyone* hates the poison level. That's what makes this so strange. Even without any undead to knock us in, crossing the bridge over the poison pools would probably still have killed a bunch of us. Why didn't the Once King make us go through that? Why let us just stroll in?"

The Naturalist shrugged. "I dunno. Maybe James hit the 'Hold Door' buttons on his way up. He's thoughtful like that."

Tina hoped rather than believed she was right.

The next two tiers of the mountain were more of the same: empty rooms, open doors, terrifying silence. The constant waiting for the ax to fall was making Tina jumpy as shit, so when something *actually* came out of her shadow, she nearly punched it in the face before she realized who it was.

"Whoa!" SB said, dodging her left hook.

"Sorrysorrysorry!" Tina cried, clutching her fist to her chest. "What's wrong? Did you find James?"

"Not yet," he said. "I'm here because we hit a dead end. Sanguilar's boss room is locked up tight. Garrond tried to bash the doors open, but they're too heavy. There doesn't seem to be any magic holding them together, though. It's just weight, so I came back for some extra muscle."

That sounded straightforward enough, but Tina still didn't like it. "Of all the doors, why would Sanguilar's be sealed?" she asked, motioning for the rest of the players to follow as she and SB started up the stone corridor, which was built for an undead army to march down and was thus plenty wide to accommodate both the Roughnecks and Garrond's anxious-looking Order troops. "He's the last boss before the Once King himself. We're only one terrace away from the throne room level. I mean, if you were going to block an invading army, surely you'd want to do it *before* they were in your face?"

"Maybe he got scared," NekoBaby said, brandishing her claws as she bounced up between them. "We're pretty pwn-tastic!"

"It could be left over from the game," SilentBlayde said, flitting through the shadows to Tina's other side, where Neko wasn't blocking him. "Sanguilar was the only encounter that required a mini-game to open the door. Maybe all that programming that didn't translate well when things got real."

Considering every other door had been open before this point, Tina didn't think that was it. There was no way to know until they got through, though, and from the look of things, that was going to take some work.

"Wow," she said, gazing up at the pair of huge stone doors. Like everything else in this world, Sanguilar's doors were a lot bigger than they'd been in the game. That was really saying something, because Sanguilar was the Once King's general. Everything in his part of the Dead Mountain Fortress was sized for armies that included multiple corpse giants and siege weapons. His doors were no exception: a matched pair of fifty-foot-tall stone slabs whose black surface had been carved to resemble dripping blood. They looked just like Tina remembered, except now all that intricate carving was broken up by a series of huge, smoking slashes, almost as if the doors had been attacked by a giant, angry cat.

320

Tina's lips quirked. "Holy sword not cutting it?" she asked Garrond, who was glaring at the gates as though he found their existence offensive.

"No," came the terse reply.

"Okay then," she said, cracking her knuckles. "Everyone with knowledge of modern physics to the front!"

Richard came forward first, inspecting the doors with obvious fascination. Surprisingly, NekoBaby joined him, bouncing over to help him tap and push at the stone. She even climbed up the outer wall like a cat climbing a tree, peering into the hair-thin crack at the top of the doors before dropping back down to converse rapidly with Richard. After several minutes of this, they returned to Tina.

"What's the word?" she asked.

"The doors operate on a simple hinge mechanism," Richard reported. "But the hinges are recessed into the walls." He turned and pointed at the smooth stone where the giant doors met the rest of the fortress. "This positioning prevents us from attacking the hinges directly, but there has to be a gap somewhere else, or the doors would not be able to swing open. They must also be lifted off the ground, else the friction of so much weight would prevent them from opening at all."

"And it would rip up the floor hella bad, too," NekoBaby added.

Richard nodded. "Since the floor is *not* scraped up, we know the doors can't actually be sitting on the ground. That means their full weight *must* be resting on the hinges, so if we destroy those—"

"The doors should fall over on their own," Tina finished. "Gotcha. But you just said the hinges are hidden inside the wall. How are you going to get at them? Go through the stone?"

"No way, I've got a super-sweet and way better idea," NekoBaby said, bouncing with excitement. "I'm going to need a caster convention up here. Also, everyone else is gonna want to stand waaaaaay back. Like, a hundred feet."

Nodding, Tina called for all the Roughnecks' casters to come forward. Everyone else she ordered to the minimum safe distance. Then she had them move back an extra fifty feet, because Neko. While the rest of the players were shuffling, Neko and Richard divided the Roughneck casters into five teams. Four pairs of Naturalists and Sorcerers—one for the top and bottom hinge of each door—and a fifth team of Clerics that Neko designated as "emergency blast shield." When everyone was in position, Richard walked back to his group and look expectantly at Tina.

"Ready," he called.

"Great!" she yelled back, reaching up to cover her ears with her hands. "Knock 'em down!"

The roasty smell of fire magic filled the corridor as Richard and the other Sorcerers began collecting smoldering red magic in their hands. As they worked, the Naturalists waved their staffs around in circles, creating huge whirlpools of glowing water that they fed in streams through the tiny cracks where the doors met the walls. When the gaps for the hinges were absolutely full of water, Neko gave Richard a thumbs up. He nodded back and raised his staff, signaling the Sorcerers to unleash the magic they'd been building.

All at once, four huge gouts of white-hot flame hit the four corners of the doors. The intense magical fire superheated the stone instantly, turning the black rock red, then orange. It was getting even brighter when Tina felt a rumble under her feet.

"Oh, crap!" Neko said, launching herself toward the Clerics. "Blast shield up! *Dive! Dive!*"

Golden light filled the tunnel as the Clerics erected their magical shields over the casters. As for Tina and the others, they were forced to hit the decks as the giant stone doors exploded, blown outward in a shower of stone shrapnel and superheated water.

Tina kept her head down, using her armor to protect SilentBlayde as thousands of needle-sharp rock shards peppered the hallway. When she raised her head again, the giant stone doors were gaping away from the wall at perilous angles, their faces so spiderwebbed with cracks they looked ready to crumble.

"Wow, guys," Tina said, awestruck by the destruction. "That was big even for us."

Richard's flat expression showed a glimmer of pride. "Flash-heating water in an enclosed space results in a cavitation collapse due to the rapid expansion of gasses."

"He means we caused a steam explosion," Neko translated. "Rock couldn't handle that shit!"

"Good job," Tina said, impressed.

"It was Neko's idea," Richard said quickly, clearly far more concerned with accuracy than any sense of humility.

Shocked, everyone turned to stare at the cat girl.

"What?" Neko cried defensively. "I know things! I've gotten past way harder puzzles than this in D&D. My regular DM is a fucking sadist. The Once King needs to up his game to at least an adamantium door collar and dwarven time-skipping locks before I'm gonna have trouble."

"Word," was all Tina could say. She offered Neko a fist bump. "So now we just push them down and walk in?"

They all stared at the crumbling hundred-ton doors.

"Not it," Killbox said.

"Ladies, *please*," Neko said, swinging her staff like a golf club. "Gust!"

Magical wind exploded from NekoBaby's weapon as she sent the Naturalist's PvP knockback spell sailing down the hallway. The winds crashed into the unbalanced, unsupported, thoroughly cracked slabs of rock at hurricane force, sending them tipping over into Sanguilar's room. As they toppled like redwoods, Tina realized far too late that she had no idea what was beneath Sanguilar's room or if the floor could take the impact.

For once, though, the impenetrable nature of the Once King's fortress worked in their favor. The crash shook the whole damn mountain, but the floor didn't break as the doors collapsed into two huge piles of rubble. Waving the rock dust away from her face, Tina let out a huge sigh of relief. She was lifting her hand to order everyone forward again when she spotted something in the dark ahead of them. A *lot* of something.

"Hold!" she yelled, squinting through the billowing dust.

The inside of Sanguilar's boss chamber was uncharacteristically dark. The huge room—one of the biggest in the entire fortress—was normally lit by red fonts of enchanted blood and the ever-present ghostfire torches. Now, though, the giant doorway they'd just cleared looked like a hole into deep space, complete with hundreds of glittering stars. Stars in pairs, all standing at roughly head level.

"Tina," SB whispered, grabbing her arm.

He didn't have to tell her. Tina was already drawing her sword, moving her shield in front of her as she stared at the hundreds of blue-white spots flickering in the dark ahead of them. Flickers of ghostfire, burning in what had once been *eyes*.

"Roxxy," Garrond demanded, coming to stand beside her. "What monsters lie before us?"

Tina squinted, letting her eyes adjust to the dark. Back in the game, the Sanguilar fight had included legions of zombies that poured out of holes in the walls. Every time a zombie died, Sanguilar got health back. To beat him, the Roughnecks had had an off-tank team sit in the back of the room and keep all the zombies contained while Tina lured Sanguilar to the opposite corner, where the rest of the raid could kill him safely away from his reinforcements.

With that in mind—and Sanguilar on another continent—the obvious answer was that the ghostfire eyes belonged to the zombies the Blood General had left behind. But they hadn't seen any undead the whole way up here, and these figures were bigger than the little trash zombies had been. They were also armed and armored, their shapes bulky in the dark. Now that her eyes were adjusting, Tina could make out the faint glow of enchanted gear. Really, really *nice* enchanted gear, which wasn't normally something you saw on zombies.

It was, however, a feature of players.

"Oh shit," she said, taking a step back. "Shit, shit, shit."

"Those are raiders," SilentBlayde whispered, his voice shaking in horror. "Undead *raiders.*"

Tina cursed herself for an idiot. How had she not seen this coming? She'd seen other raids going into the dungeon the whole time she'd been trying to get her own group together. She'd heard the screams coming down the mountain the day of the transition. Hell, Richard had been here and escaped. He'd flat-out told her that all the other players raiding the Dead Mountain had died, but death was just the beginning in this place. The Once King hadn't left his castle unguarded when he'd sent his army to Bastion. He'd saved the best for himself.

"*Shit!*" she swore again, lifting her shield against the sea of ghostfire eyes staring back at her.

"You're saying those are players?" Garrond asked, his voice afraid for the first time she'd ever heard.

Tina didn't have the heart to tell him it was so much worse than that. Those weren't just any players. They were the guilds who'd been raiding the DMF at the time the transition hit. Every single one of those players was level eighty and wearing gear that was at least as good as her current Roughnecks possessed, probably better. These were the groups Tina had been competing with for world firsts. They'd been at the top of the game, and they were all soaked in ghostfire.

"Order of the Golden Sun, to the doors!" Garrond cried, raising his gleaming sword. "Keep them bottled! If we let them get into the hall, they'll surround us!"

"Wait!" Tina yelled, but her voice was drowned out by the roar of the soldiers as they thundered after their commander. The Roughnecks had to hug the wall to keep from getting trampled as the Order filled the broken doorway. On the other side, ghostfire eyes flared in the dark, and then the air was choked with the smell of blood and the screams of dying men.

"*Fuck!*" Tina stomped her armored foot. "This is a disaster! Those poor Order bastards don't stand a chance against geared raiders. He's feeding them into a meat grinder!"

"How many are in there?" Frank asked, his face pale.

Tina had no idea. Fortunately, SilentBlayde was more observant.

"I saw at least twelve shield-bearing Knights at the front," he said quickly. "It was a bit chaotic, but they looked like they were in groups of two."

Tina nodded as she saw where he was going. "Main-tank and off-tank pairings. Good thinking." Then she gritted her teeth. "Shit, that's six raids at least."

By this point, the entire Order army was pressed into the door to Sanguilar's room, blocking the way with their bodies. Literally, in some places. The golden troops were tough NPCs, but their gear was only as good as the Deadlands entry quest items. They were better than Bastion's knights, but they were nothing compared to players in DMF gear.

"Ugh," NekoBaby said, ears back. "I've never seen the concept of a 'meat shield' used quite that literally."

"Maybe Garrond can handle it," SilentBlayde said hopefully. "He's a raid boss himself and has two thousand guys with him. Six full raids is still only about three hundred people. If he pushes into the room, he can surround the players and crush them with superior numbers."

From the orders he was shouting over the din, it seemed like that was exactly what Commander Garrond was trying to do, and despite the bloodshed, the Order was making headway. They'd already made it over the crushed doors and into the dark room, which was now lit up by the paladin's gleaming holy sword. Watching from the back line felt wrong, but Tina had promised Garrond she'd hold the Roughnecks in reserve for the Once King. She was determined to make good on that, but then flashes lit up the dark as the undead players' abilities started going off. Soon, the doorway was full of Sorcerers' Fire Tornadoes and volleys of Acid Arrows from the Rangers. The attacks ravaged the Order's lines, filling the air with the stench of charred flesh.

"That's it," Tina said, hefting her shield. "He's being slaughtered. We need to get in there."

"What makes you think you can take it any better?" asked a smug voice behind her.

Tina closed her eyes with a curse. "You don't want to start this shit with me right now, Cinco," she said, turning around to see that Red Sands had finally made it up here from their spot at the rear. But while he could never look not-arrogant, CincoDeMurder at least didn't look deliberately antagonistic as he walked up to join her.

"I'm not starting anything," he said, rising on his toes to get a better look at the slaughter in front of them. "I'm just stating facts. You guys are all DMF geared, but so are they. That means anything you do in there is gonna be an even fight at best. Even if you do win, you'll be too shredded by the time it's over to go on to the Once King."

Tina bit her lip. "Yeah, but—"

A blast of golden light interrupted her, and her head whipped back around in time to see Sanguilar's room lit up by hundreds of pillars of sunlight.

"There goes Garrond's mass rez," SB said.

"You mean 'there goes our ace in the hole,'" Tina growled furiously. "*Now* we're screwed!"

"Not yet, but we will be if we keep wasting time," Cinco said. "If the NPCs want to soak up the damage, let 'em. We need to get through to the Once King before Garrond's army breaks and we get overwhelmed." He pointed at the door with his spear. "There. Go in the side and hug the wall, and we'll see if we can't get around."

After yesterday, Tina wasn't inclined to do a damn thing Cinco said. But while he was definitely an asshole, he was still one of the best PvPers in the game, and strategically speaking, that wasn't a half-bad idea. It was certainly better than standing here talking while all their backup died.

"Let's go!" Tina said, trusting the others to follow as she ran forward, clutching her shield tight. When she reached the rubble in the doorway, Tina leaped up the pile in one jump, landing on top of a six-foot-tall chunk of broken stone to see what they were in for.

As she'd noted before, Sanguilar's room was *big*. In this immense underground stone box, waves of golden troops repeatedly crashed and broke on not six but *eight* knots of undead players. Garrond's mass resurrection spell had just gone off, but the ground was already littered again with the Order's burned and broken bodies. She was trying to get a feel for just how many of their side were dead versus the enemy when Cinco grabbed her shoulder.

"Change of plans!" he yelled over the carnage. "This fight's already fucked!"

"How do you know that?" she demanded. "We just got here!"

"It's fucking obvious!" he shouted, pointing at the growing piles of bodies. "The momentum's lost! Garrond already tried to save it and failed. The whole plan's FUBAR. We have to fall back!"

"There's no falling back from a Hail Mary play!" Tina roared, but it was hard to argue with what was happening right in front of her face.

No matter how many of Garrond's soldiers crashed into them, the undead players' lines were rocks. Any damage the Order soldiers did was immediately erased by floods of healing ghostfire from the undead Naturalists and Clerics. Garrond's troops had had a lower ratio of healers to begin with, and those they had already looked to be out of mana. Meanwhile, the undead raiders' DPS was pouring abuse onto the Order's back lines, taking out their reinforcements before they could even get to the front.

Tina's shoulders slumped as the reality of their situation finally hit her. It didn't seem possible that everything had gone to hell so quickly. But even with Cinco tugging pointedly on her arm, she knew to her core that retreat wasn't an option. Even if they *could* find somewhere safe to fall back, what was the point? As everyone had been saying for days now, they were this world's last hope. King Gregory and his forces were desperately defending the Savanna right now, waiting for Tina and her raiders to keep their word. If the Roughnecks couldn't kill the Once King right here, right now, everything was over.

"Fuck it!" Tina yelled, pointing her sword at the door on the other side of the room, multiple raids away. "We're going through!"

"Are you crazy?" Cinco screamed.

Tina left that for him to decide as she leaped off her vantage point and charged into the room. She didn't look back to see if Cinco had followed, but from the shouting of her officers, she knew her Roughnecks had, and that was what mattered.

Gritting her teeth, Tina pushed through the back lines of the Order's troops. She had to hot-foot it over the bodies like an obstacle course just to get to the central section of the room. Behind her, her guildmates cursed and stumbled as the less agile classes tried to keep up. Tina knew she was going too fast, but she could already see the battle lines softening as the raiders' superior damage started to win out over the Order's numbers. If she didn't make it before the Order folded, those raids would turn on her, and then it really would be Game Over.

Scanning the battlefield for the safest route, Tina caught sight of Garrond. The four-skull commander towered over everyone else. He had two Assassins stabbing him in the back and a spear sticking through his right leg, but there were two dead player Knights on the ground in front of him, and he killed a Berserker as Tina watched, tearing the ax out of the player's hands and slicing him in half with it. He spotted her as he finished, his face desperate and despairing before he hid his weakness behind a stony scowl.

Sprinting through the chaos, it was all Tina could do to give him a running salute as she shot by.

I'm sorry, Garrond.

There was no chance to say it aloud, but from the look on his face as her raid thundered past, she knew he understood. The paladin had said over and over that he would gladly lay down his life to beat the Once King. Now he was getting a chance to prove it, not that knowing that made Tina feel any better about leaving him behind.

Tearing her watering eyes away from the desperate commander, Tina forced herself to focus on her own fight. She was halfway across the room now, close enough to see the staircase at the back that led up to the Once King's throne room. Or rather, the giant royal complex that ended at his throne room. For once, though, Tina was happy the fortress was so massive. All those fancy empty halls and giant doors would be good distance to put between her and the undead player army when they finished off the Order, especially if the Roughnecks could find something to collapse and block the way. First, though, they had to actually get out of here. But in a rare stroke of good fortune, the undead players seemed about as observant as normal undead, which was not very much. The dead raiders were so intent on wiping out Garrond and his troops that they didn't even look at Tina's army as they ran around the room behind them, pouring through the door at the back and up the ghostfire-lit stairs to the next tier.

Refusing to celebrate such a bitter victory, Tina grimly led her strike force up and away from the battle as fast as she could. Thankfully, this was the part of the Dead Mountain she'd spent the most time in recently. She'd come up to these damn halls five nights a week while her raid had been working on killing the Once King, and despite all the new passages, she knew the way by heart.

Careening down a black-carpeted hallway, Tina blasted past tapestries and ghostfire torches until she spotted her goal at last: the beautifully decorated wooden doors of the throne room. That was where the

Once King fight started, and since he'd said they would fight "in the manner of the game," she'd assumed it was where he'd be waiting for them now. The giant wooden doors with the wings carved into them were already opening on their own, but as she lifted her sword to signal her people to get ready, she saw what was inside.

Tina slid to a halt, her sharp metal boots tearing up the rich black carpet. The throne room doors were open, but the throne itself—a twisted spire of Eclipsed Steel as big as a minivan—was empty. Instead, the room was full with yet *another* group of undead players. This was the worst one yet, because while every player in here was a DMF raider by definition, these ghostfire eyes shone out of a glittering array of top-tier gear. There was stuff in there that even she'd never gotten, but the real tell was the Knight standing in the front: a towering male stonekin wearing an exact copy of Tina's gear right down to her almost-unique-in-the-world sword.

"Goddammit!" Tina yelled, stomping her feet at the unfairness of it all. "That's fucking Protato!"

"Who?" Cinco said, skidding to a stop next to her.

"Asshole main tank for Six Ways From Raiding," Tina explained quickly, pointing at the glittering wall of undead players standing where the Once King should have been. "They're the group who was ahead of us on the Once King fight, the number-one raiding guild in the world. They must have been in here working on him when the transition hit."

"Ah, crapballs!" Neko swore, ears going flat as she looked at Tina. "What do we do? Six Ways outgeared us back when we were actual Roughnecks! We don't have a prayer now!"

"Sure you do," Cinco said, planting his spear on the ground. "'Cause this time, you've got us." He flashed Tina a bloodthirsty grin and lifted his voice. "*Red Sands!* It's time to show these Care Bears that raid gear don't mean shit for PvP!"

"Are you serious?" Tina demanded, too shocked to be insulted. "They're the best-geared players in the *world.*"

331

Cinco winked at her, a bit of the old charm coming back. "Can't loot skill, baby. Once King's gotta be around here somewhere. Go find him and kick his ass. We got this."

Tina stared at him for a moment. Then she turned on her heel and started running back the way they'd come. "Red Sands has this!" she shouted at her people. "Roughnecks, follow me!"

Behind them, arrows screamed through the air as what was left of Six Ways From Raiding launched a volley at the Red Sands. With a bellowing roar, Cinco cut the arrows out of the air while Shankfest and his two Assassin buddies appeared in the middle of the raider's back lines, their blades sinking into the backs of the enemy healers while spells and arrows flew in all directions. It was an effective start, but Tina couldn't stick around to see if Cinco's raid-on-raid PvP skills were really as badass as he claimed. She was already sprinting around the corner, tearing off the main hallway into one of the Royal Quarter's less-used side wings.

"Where are we going?" Neko cried, running beside her on all fours, jubatus style. "This is the top of the dungeon! The only place left is the Terrace of the Great Pyre at the peak, but you can't even get up there until the Once King breaks the ceiling when he moves to phase two!"

"Maybe back in the game," Tina said, turning down a hall that led out to one of the dungeon's many huge, scenic balconies that overlooked the Deadlands. "But as I keep telling you, *this isn't a game.* We make our own way now!"

"Is that why we're headed to Mthr's balcony?" SilentBlayde asked, keeping up with her nimbly.

Tina nodded. "If we can't go through the throne room, we'll go straight up the outside of the mountain itself. Bet old Mr. Pigeon Wings hasn't thought of *that.*"

She smirked at her own cleverness as they pelted through the arched doorway onto the football field–sized balcony that the undead Bird Mthr used to come and go from the fortress. The balcony that, since she'd watched Mthr go down fighting Xthr back in Bastion, was *supposed* to be empty.

"*Goddammit!*" Tina cried, skidding to a halt.

"Huh," SB said, stopping much more gracefully beside her. "Looks like he thought of that."

Yet *another* raid of undead players stood in front of them, taking up the whole outer half of the semicircular balcony in perfect formation. It was hard to recognize the characters without their nameplates, but even with its golden sun steel turned to black Eclipsed Steel by undeath, there was no mistaking her own damn shield. That was the Sun's Resplendent Bulwark, albeit a far less dented version than the one in Tina's hands, and holding it was a tall human Knight with black hair that Tina would know anywhere.

"Goddammit," Tina swore again, sadly this time. "They got Isabella."

"Wait, you know her, too?" Frank said, huffing up beside her. "Dang, did you know everybody in this game?"

This high up in the raiding ranks, everyone knew everyone, but Isabella was special. She was the only other girl besides Tina who played a DMF-level tank. She and her husband ran El Major, the guild who'd been ahead of the Roughnecks before Tina's group beat Sanguilar and took their spot. There'd been a lot of drama over the upset, but she and Isabella had always been tight. Tina used to get drunk in real life just so she could log in and meet Izzy at Bastion's Royal Mile Pub for drunken shit talk and gossip. Her friend had been so funny, so full of life, and now she was here, staring at Tina with eyes full of ghostfire.

"SB," Tina whispered, blinking the tears out of her eyes, "is there any way to—"

She hadn't even finished before the elf shook his head. "The ghostfire has spread completely through her. The best we can do for her now is to end this before she suffers more."

She'd known he was going to say that, but that didn't make hearing it any easier. These weren't random players like the ones in Sanguilar's room.

These were her former rivals and friends. She'd done co-raids with El Major when times were tough and attendance was low. Fighting them now, even when they were like this...It was too cruel. She refused.

"Roughnecks!" Tina yelled, pointing her sword at the undead players. "External on the Enemy!"

She'd never given an order like that before, but to her raid's credit, they rolled with it.

"Got it!" Anders yelled, and then the balcony was filled with golden light as he cried, "*Sanctuary of the Four!*"

The golden shield-dome slammed down over the undead raid in the nick of time. The enemy players' terrifying volley of spells and arrows rattled off the inside of the barrier, bouncing back to strike them instead of the Roughnecks' HP.

"Eight seconds, Roxxy!" Anders called.

She nodded and turned, pointing her sword at the far end of the balcony, where the intricately carved railing met the sheer stone of the mountain itself. "Roughnecks, that way! We're going up!"

The raid sprinted forward. Halfway there, the golden bubble holding in the enemy raid popped. "External on the Enemy!" Tina yelled again, and the undead players were suddenly trapped inside a Circle of Thorns instead.

"Good work! Keep them canned!" Tina yelled, ditching her backpack and slinging her shield onto her back instead. "Neko, hop on!"

The jubatus leaped onto Tina's shield, clinging to her like a monkey. When she was secure, Tina hopped the banister and hurled herself at the cliff, digging her armored fingers into the slick, icy stone.

Looking up, Tina saw nothing but rock, which was exactly what she'd hoped for. The second and third phases of the Once King's fight were held at the very top of the Dead Mountain on the Terrace of the Great Pyre, a huge, flat, circular stone courtyard that was cut like a bite into the very top of the mountain's sword-like peak. Back in the game, the only way up was a secret stair that broke open when the Once King crashed through his ceiling at the end of phase one.

But Tina had been up that spiral staircase many, *many* times. She knew it had huge panorama windows to show the passing players just how high up they were so they'd be properly terrified when they reached the top and entered the part of the fight in which the Once King could knock them off the mountain. If she remembered correctly—and assuming the vistas had been actual features of the fortress and not just art assets—one of those windows should have been right above them. Sure enough, Tina could just see the neatly laid stone bottom of the enclosed stairwell that spiraled up the mountain's peak jutting out from the icy cliff almost a hundred feet above their heads.

"There!" she cried, pointing up at their goal. "That's our in. Let's go!"

Order given, Tina gritted her teeth and started to climb.

It was one of the hardest things she'd ever had to do. Fear in battle was nothing compared to the terror of hanging from what was basically a sheer frozen wall by her fingers and toes. The wind tore across the cliff-face like a tornado, spattering her with ice and grit. The biggest gusts were strong enough to physically lift her off the rock, making Tina miss her stonekin body something fierce as she hauled herself and Neko up the mountain on nothing but pure adrenaline. Whenever she couldn't find a handhold, she used her magically augmented strength to punch one into the rock, leaving a ladder of holes for the others to follow.

"How're we doing?" she yelled to Neko.

"Fuckfuckfuck!" was the Naturalist's reply. An arrow screamed past Tina's head a second later, making the rock next to her explode. "*Fuck!*" Neko yelled, whacking Tina in the head with her staff as she cast the next Circle of Thorns. "STAY PUT, YOU ASSHOLES!"

"Good job," Tina said, kicking her metal boot against the cliff to make a foothold.

"Only if you don't look down," Neko groaned, burying her cat face in Tina's hair.

Tina looked down. She must have been making better progress than she'd realized, because the balcony was now far below them. Her guild was spread out over the cliff face below as everyone looked for the way up that was best suited to their body. The Agility and Strength characters were helping the casters just as she was helping Neko, but no one was having an easy time. A Sorcerer slipped as she watched, falling a good ten feet into the gray abyss below before a Ranger snagged him back onto the wall. Far below, Neko's latest external on Isabella's raid was already fading. A Cleric picked them up again the moment Circle of Thorns ran out, but Tina could feel their hold on the situation fraying.

"We're almost there!" she yelled over the wind. "Faster, people, faster!"

Leading by example, Tina launched with her legs, jumping up the cliff to grab hold of a tiny stone crack no wider than her pinky finger. It held, thankfully, but the worst was yet to come. They were nearing the enclosed stairwell to the Terrace of the Great Pyre. This close to the peak, there wasn't actually room to put the raid-sized spiral staircase inside the mountain, so it ran around the outside of the mountain instead, circling up the sheer peak like a stone snake. Unfortunately for them, this arrangement meant that to reach the windows, they were going to have to climb *upside down* across the bottom of the stairwell and then up the other side, which meant their climb was about to go from straight up a sheer cliff to dangling off an inverted ledge above a thousand-foot drop.

"Uh, Roxxy," NekoBaby said, her voice even higher pitched than usual as she realized what they were about to do. "Are you by any chance a skilled mountaineer?"

"Nope," Tina said, digging her fingers into the underside of the thick stone ledge that supported the stairs. "Just gonna beast-mode it."

"*I hate this plan!*" Neko cried, wrapping her arms around Tina's neck.

Fighting not to choke, Tina braced her legs and pushed them both onto the underside of the ledge. As the angle got sharper, she let go with one hand to draw her sword, stabbing the magical blade into the rock. This gave her something to hold on to, but the scariest part was coming next. Somehow, they had to go from dangling under the overhang to climbing over it.

There was no easy way to do this, so Tina took a deep breath and winged it, holding onto her sword with one hand while she swung her body like a pendulum. After three swings, she got enough momentum to hook a metal-booted foot onto the outside wall of the enclosed stairwell. Another swing got her spare hand up there. Digging her fingers into the cracks between the huge stone slabs that protected the stairwell from the drop she was now dangling over, Tina used her new hold as leverage to wrench her sword free and stab it above her head instead.

The first try ended with broken stone falling on her head, but the second stab went in deep, giving her a solid anchor on the stairwell's outer wall. From there, it was just a matter of hauling herself up one handed to the window ledge. She grabbed it so hard that her metal glove left a handprint in the granite, but she didn't slip. Neko was already clambering up her extended arm like a terrified cat, jumping through the window onto the stairs inside before turning around to help haul Tina the rest of the way.

"*That was the worst part of my life!*" the Naturalist yelled as Tina flopped through the window to sprawl on the stone stairs inside. "You just gave me PTSD!"

Tina was pretty sure that wasn't how PTSD worked, but now wasn't the time for definitions. They'd finally made it to the stairwell that led up the mountain to the Once King's terrace. Now they just had to figure out how to get the rest of the raid in here, too.

Still huffing from the effort of the climb, Tina hauled herself off her back and stuck her head back out the window, using her sword—which was *still* stabbed into the wall outside—as an anchor to lean her whole body out the window so she could see what was happening on the cliff below. As she'd feared, her guild had made it to the bottom of the stairs but was stalling at the ledge. The Agility classes could handle dangling upside down from sheer rock, but everyone else seemed too terrified to try, which she supposed was fair. If she wanted to get everyone up here safe and sound and ready to fight, she was going to have to think of something better than beast mode.

"We need some rope," she said, turning to Neko. "Don't you do vines and shit?"

"Way ahead of you, chica," Neko said smugly, digging into her pack to pull out a hundred-foot coil of giant metal chains glowing with amber enchantments.

Tina gaped at her. "You mean you were carrying those the *whole time*?!"

"What?" Neko cried. "It's not like you handed me a customs form before kidnapping me up a mountain! These are the chains Zen brought for our totally boss Once King beat-down plan. Someone had to carry them, since it's not like the mailman was going to deliver them up here for us! And before you bitch about the added weight, I watched you lift a fully armored CincoDeFatty over your new tiny head just yesterday. You could totally handle me plus hardware."

Since she'd just done exactly that, Tina couldn't say a damn thing except "Thanks" as she took the chain from Neko and started wrapping one end around the metal banister. While she secured the anchor, Neko tossed the other end of the chain out the window.

"Heads up!"

There was a surprised shout and a grunt of pain. Then the chain stopped swinging, and Killbox's flushed face appeared over the ledge, his black hair soaked in nervous sweat. "This place fucking sucks!" he announced in a terrified voice, hauling himself—and the two casters clinging to his shoulders—across the final sheer few feet to dump himself through the window. "I don't feel so bad anymore about never actually going on a DMF raid. This is some *bull*shit!"

"We didn't go this way in the game," Tina said, bracing against the chain for extra support. "How are we doing?"

"Everyone's on their way up," SilentBlayde reported, stepping out of her shadow with the perfectly unmussed appearance of someone who hadn't just had to scale a mountain upside down. "But *El Major* is still coming. The moment we got too far up to keep them bottled with externals, they started coming up the cliff after us."

"Freaking zombies, man!" Neko cried as she helped the next batch of raiders through the window. "They never quit!"

"Neither do we," Tina said, handing the end of the chain to Killbox so she'd be free to go back to the window, leaning her body way out again to see—*ah ha.*

"Anders!" she cried, reaching down to grab the fish man off Frank's back. "We got zombies incoming! I need you and Neko to do that Holy Water combo thing from Bastion again."

"I can try," Anders said, the gills in his neck still flaring from the terror of the climb. "But it's really hard to do holy magic in this place. I didn't realize just how much the cloud cover interfered until I cast Sanctuary of the Four."

"Just do your best," Tina said, pushing him back toward the window. "And try not to wash any of our people off."

"You say that like we have fine-tuned control," Neko grumped, giving Anders some deadly side-eye as she stepped up next to him. "But whatever. I'm awesome. We got this so long as Fish Face doesn't fuck it up."

Anders slumped, but he didn't fight back, and Tina sighed. "Just do it," she ordered, peering down the mountain at the ghostfire-filled raiders she could now clearly see scaling the cliff just a few hundred feet away.

With a final glare at Anders, Neko held out her hands to summon a ball of glowing water. The Cleric waved his staff next, whispering what sounded like a deeply sincere prayer. It took a few seconds, but eventually golden light blossomed from his weapon to fill the swirling ball. Neko was hauling back to hurl the thing down the cliff like a beach ball when Tina said, "*Gently.*"

Rolling her eyes, Neko nudged the golden-blue ball of magical water out the window instead, using her staff to arc the ball in midair so that it flew around the overhang where the Roughnecks were still climbing before landing like a water balloon on the cliff face just below Zen, who was bringing up the rear.

"Any reason in particular you wanted me to go easy?" Neko asked. "Cause I could have fire-hosed them."

"But that would have blasted them off the cliff into a thousand-foot drop," Tina said, holding the chain steady as the last of her raid climbed up. "El Major deserves better from us, and this was just as effective. Look."

Neko, Anders, and everyone else crowded to the window.

"Damn," Killbox said. "They're all sliding back down!"

Tina grinned in victory. "Holy water becomes holy ice when you blast it with freezing wind," she said smugly, nodding at the zombie raiders as they slid all the way back down to the balcony below. "That should keep them busy long enough for us to finish this."

And speaking of, everyone was inside now. Zen was the last. She climbed through the window as Tina watched, hopping into the enclosed stairwell with her usual flawless grace, which meant it was time.

"All right, folks," Tina said, hauling the chain back in and handing it to Neko, who returned it to her pack. "Showtime."

The others nodded, gripping their weapons tightly as Tina turned to lead them up the ghostfire-lit stair.

"What do we do if the Once King isn't there?" SilentBlayde whispered, climbing silently beside her.

"Celebrate," Tina whispered back. "If he's not waiting for us on the terrace, then we get to destroy the Great Pyre for free."

"You think we'll get that lucky?"

Tina didn't bother to answer. He already knew. They all did. There was only one place left in the mountain that the boss could be, and it was the one that gave him the greatest advantage. Up on the open mountaintop with no walls to box him in, the Once King could use his wings freely, *and* he was right next to the source of all ghostfire. Tina didn't know if proximity to the Great Pyre actually made him stronger, but she wouldn't be surprised. If nothing else, the king could physically toss them into the undead flames—or off the mountain entirely. Just as it had back in the game, the Terrace of the Great Pyre gave the Once King ultimate home-field advantage. Of *course* he'd be there.

Everyone else must have come to the same conclusion, because the normally rowdy Roughnecks were silent behind her. Even the clang of their armored boots on the stone steps sounded muffled as they closed the final distance, emerging from the dark of the artificial tunnel into the open air of the mountain peak.

Tina's feet missed a step as she strode onto the terrace. She'd made this trek so many times during the game—usually at a dead run, since she had to be the first one up here so she'd be ready to taunt the Once King when he landed and entered phase two—but the transition from mountain tunnel to sky had never hit her as hard as it did now. All at once, the protective layer of stone vanished, leaving her puffing in the thin air beneath the eternal gray clouds. She could see the whole of the Deadlands from up here, as well as the surrounding snow-capped mountains and even the faint green speck of the Verdancy far to the west. It felt as if the whole world was spread out like a blanket beneath them, and perched high above it like the monarch he was stood the Once King.

Tina had to hand it to him: dude knew how to make an entrance. The enormous winged elf was standing at the center of the enormous circular stone terrace, his white hair crowned with the brilliant blue glow of the wall of ghostfire rising from the huge black bowl on the dais behind him, the Great Pyre.

Honestly, Tina had never bothered to look much at the pyre itself. She'd always been too focused on the boss and her upcoming world-first kill to waste attention on yet another batch of ghostfire. Now that things were real and not just rendered images, though, it was impossible to miss just how aptly named the Great Pyre was. Not only was it absolutely enormous—a great black cauldron of Eclipsed Steel the size of a swimming pool, spouting blue-white flames as tall as trees—but the bowl itself was packed to the brim with the enormous, beautiful, twisted bodies of Celestial Elves. There were hundreds of them, their backs still bearing the burned-off stumps of wings that must have been as big as the Once King's.

Given where they were, Tina's first thought was that their wings must have been consumed by the ghostfire. But despite being the foundation of an eternal undead fire, no other parts of the Celestial Elves' bodies were burned. Quite the opposite. The corpses looked perfectly preserved, so much so that Tina could still clearly see the terrible anger and sorrow on their faces. That expression was mirrored in the face of the last living winged elf standing in front of them now.

"Welcome, players," the Once King said in a terrible, final voice, "to the end of the world."

"Oh yeah?" Tina growled, snapping back to herself as she raised her shield. "Because I've got a fresh raid here that says otherwise."

The king shook his head like a disappointed parent. "Always so rash," he chided. "There is no need to be in such a rush, Roxxy of the Roughnecks. You have always been my most tenacious opponent. Ineffective, admittedly, but I can't help but respect your undaunted spirit. Even now, in that diminished form, you have made it all the way to my feet yet again. Such spirit demands special recognition, and so I wish to make you an offer, a final boon before we cross blades one last time."

Tina held her breath, mindful of the raid doing the same behind her. *Fuck.* She could guess where this was going. Frantically, she debated attacking the Once King right now just to shut him up, but it was already too late. He was already speaking, lobbing his best attack at her raiders without even raising his sword.

"This world is destined to end," he pronounced in a ringing voice. "But *you* do not have to end with it. I am willing to send the Roughnecks home. All of you, right now. I can make the portal right here. All you have to do is step through it, and your Nightmare shall finally end."

He hadn't even finished his offer before the players erupted. Shouted questions and accusations rang out over the howling wind, making Tina wince. Fuck, fuck, *fuck.* Forget knocking them off the mountain. This was so much worse. That bastard had just thrown a wedge into the crack she'd been frantically papering over since Bastion. Now she had to find a way to fix it before her whole raid flew apart.

"*Shut up!*" she yelled, turning her body sideways so that she could address her raid and the king at the same time. "You're asking us to abandon an entire world! Do you know how many of our friends have died to get us this far? What kind of people do you think we are to step over their bodies just to save ourselves?"

By the end, she was talking straight to her people, but it was the Once King who answered. "I don't know who you are," he said slyly. "But you do. You all remember who you were back in your own world. If you kill me, that home will be lost to you forever. I'm giving you a chance—your *last* chance—to leave this place forever. You can return to your families and your comforts. All you have to do is put your weapons down and accept."

"Screw you!" someone shouted from the back.

"Screw *you!*" someone else shouted. "I want to go home!"

"How selfish can you be?" Anders cried, stepping out from the crowd to point a webbed finger at the Once King. "He wants to destroy this entire world!"

"So what?" a voice yelled. "This place sucks!"

"And it's not like we actually had a chance," another pointed out. "No one's ever beaten this fucker!"

"Guys," Tina said, trying not to sound as panicked as she felt. "Stop and think a moment. The Once King wants to kill everyone. He's only saying this to drive a wedge between us. We don't even know if he *can* send us back to Earth."

"Then why are we here?" an ichthyian Sorcerer yelled. "I only voted for this plan because *you* said the Once King was our way home! I don't want to be a fish anymore!"

"That doesn't mean you can burn this world to the ground!" Anders yelled at him. "What about those of us who can't go home anymore?"

"Yeah!" Frank said, stepping up beside the Cleric. "My body was falling apart on the other side. I reckon I'm already dead over there, which means I got no place for my soul to go home to. You gonna kill me as well just 'cause you don't like having fish eyes?"

"Don't be such goddamn wimps," Killbox said, flexing. "Stay here and be awesome with us! Elf titties be rocking over here, and we're gonna be heroes! We're gonna get so much action when this is over."

"Fuck you, dude!" Neko said furiously, thrusting her leather-bound but still enormous bosom at the Berserker. "You try saying that after getting stuck carting this crap around! You'd be crying on the ground to get your dick back if you had to go through half the shit that I have! I'm sick of being a hero for everyone else! I. Want. *Home!*"

"You'll regret selling out," SB warned. "If you do this, it'll haunt you to the end of your days. Trust me, nothing is worth that."

"Easy for you to say," ZeroDarkness spat, jabbing a finger at the elven Assassin. "You just got married to your teenage sweetheart, *and* Roxxy has her original body! Of course you want to stay. This place is a total win for you! But I've got kids waiting for me to come home. What about them?"

Tina clenched her sword tightly. Behind her, the Once King was smirking, but she wasn't keeping more than a cursory eye on him anymore. Her attention was on her raid, which was splitting apart in front of her. Forget the Million Damage Blast. This was *so* much worse. At this rate, the Once King wouldn't have to lift a finger to beat them, but she had no idea how to stop it. This wasn't an attack she could tank for them, but she had to do something. This was her raid, her Roughnecks, dammit. But how could she fix this? She'd promised SB she'd stay here, but she'd also promised to get Neko home. How did she keep both of those pledges? There seemed to be no way. Whatever they decided, someone was going to get fucked today, and it really looked to Tina like it was going to be *everyone.*

Then, just as her panic was reaching the breaking point, Tina caught a flash of movement. Someone was coming up the stairs behind them.

For a crazy moment, she hoped it was Red Sands. No, scratch that. Cinco would only make this situation a million times worse. Garrond was *way* better, but it wasn't the paladin. It was a player, the one she'd been hoping to see more than any other. He was alone and exhausted, dragging himself up the stairs without even an Angry Cat to help, but Tina didn't care. She'd never been happier to see anyone in her life than she was to see James emerge, blinking, into the gray daylight.

"Everyone be quiet!"

Her yell echoed across the mountains, shocking her raid into silence. Nodding, Tina turned and pointed at James. She had no idea what he'd found or why he was here or if he'd been successful, but if there was one thing Tina had learned about her brother since coming here, it was that he always knew what to say to make people stop fighting. Everything was falling apart anyway, so she decided to take a chance, gambling it all on her brother as she turned to glower at her Roughnecks with the best poker face of her life.

"Shut up and listen," she told them calmly. "James has something we need to hear."

Chapter 14

James and Tina

James stared at his sister in horror. Ahead of him, the Roughnecks were divided into two opposing groups, proof that the Once King's plan had worked perfectly. And from the smug look on his face, Ar'Kan knew it.

The wave of defeat that followed that realization was almost enough to send James to his knees. After leaving Fangs on the floor of the Once King's throne room, James had tried to find his sister, but all he'd found were other raiders, their undead eyes filled with ghostfire. Cornered at every turn, he'd eventually fled back to the hall of tapestries where he and Ar'Bati had emerged from the secret stair after Sanguilar's room.

At the time, James had considered this a stroke of good fortune. Unlike Gray Fang's rugs or the FFO wiki, the tapestries told the whole of this world's history, or at least the Once King's version of it. Since he was stuck there anyway, James had invested his time poring over the pictures, looking for anything he could use, anything to gain leverage, but all he'd found was more bitterness. So far as he could tell, the Once King's life was divided into two halves: the paradise before the Sun's betrayal and the hell that came after. But nowhere in the pictures did he see anything about *why*, and the more he thought about that, the less sense it made.

The tapestries at the beginning of the hall, the ones that showed the awe and majesty of the Age of Skies, depicted the Sun as a kind and benevolent force spinning in an eternal dance with its beloved partner, the Moon. The gods were always depicted as two halves in balance, even as their children—the Celestial Elves and the Birds—hunted each other across the Sky. From everything James could tell, the Age of Skies seemed to be a paradise for the Sun as well, so why had it attacked? Why would a seemingly warm and loving god destroy its own happiness?

Clearly there was something going on that the pictures didn't show. James refused to believe that the benevolent Sun had up and turned evil one day for no reason. There must have been something—an event, a miscommunication, a mistake, *something*—that explained why the Sun had suddenly burned those most precious to it.

Sadly, unlike the rest of the bad history, James couldn't go to a primary source on this one. The only being in the universe who knew this truth was the Sun itself, and it wasn't talking. Even the priests didn't know the truth.

And thus he'd found himself right back at the beginning. He was still going round and round when he'd finally heard the familiar shouts of the Roughnecks. By the time he'd found them, though, Tina and the rest were already halfway up the mountain with an undead raid hot on their heels. Unable to follow them up the sheer, icy cliff, James had backtracked to the throne room, where yet another fight had been going down between CincoDeMurder's Red Sands and an incredibly geared group of undead players. He didn't raid enough to know which guild they were on sight, but that kind of loot didn't grow on trees. Still, raid gear had always been a disadvantage in PvP, and Cinco's team was holding its own, which turned out to be James's salvation. With the undead players so focused on Red Sands, he'd been able to slip right past. He'd tried to slip all the way to the back where he'd left Ar'Bati, but that would have meant going through the enemy healer camp. Even zombies would have noticed that, so he'd forced himself to stay on target, slipping in just as far as he needed to get to the wall that concealed the hidden spiral stairway.

One blast of lightning had been all he'd needed to punch through the false wall and open the way. He'd hoped to catch Tina on the stairs so he could tell her everything and they could come up with a plan together, but like everything else today, things hadn't gone his way. Now he was up here with everyone looking at him, waiting for him to tell them what to do, but James didn't know. He didn't know if there *was* a way out of this, and once again, he could see that the Once King knew it.

Desperate to avoid his sister's trusting stare, James looked up instead. It was nearly midday, not that you could tell in this place. Day or night, the sky in the Deadlands was always gloomy and dark thanks to the eternal blanket of thick gray clouds. Back in the game, he'd assumed that was for the spooky ambiance, but there was no programming holding the clouds in place now.

Suddenly curious, James squinted at the sky. He hadn't spent much time in the Deadlands since the Nightmare had ended, and that which he had had been constantly busy. Now that he was thinking about it, though, James could think of no climatological reason for the constant clouds to remain here on their own. Something had to be keeping them in place, and now that he was looking for it, James realized he could see the lines of magic floating over his head.

He stepped back, awestruck. There was a huge spell in the sky, a net of air and water magic held together by blue-white tendrils of ghostfire. Not that that was a surprise—everything here was touched by the ghostfire—but that much of it in the sky *had* to be deliberate. The heavy clouds weren't part of the Deadlands art design. The Once King was keeping them there on *purpose*, holding them in place so the Sun would never shine on his lands.

And just like that, James knew what to do.

"Listen, everyone!" he cried, snapping his head back down to look at the raid. "The Once King is lying to you! He already told me he doesn't have the mana to send us home without draining the Great Pyre, which he'll never do. He's trying to trick you into fighting each other so you won't be strong enough to fight him, but he wouldn't have to stoop to such tactics if he wasn't afraid. He *knows* you can beat him! And if you ever want to go home, that's exactly what you have to do." He pointed at the sky. "I think I know how to save this world *and* get everyone home who wants to go, but the only way to get there is to bring the Once King to his knees, and that's only possible if you fight him together."

"You heard him!" Tina yelled as the raid began to murmur. "Did you all forget the plan? Since when do we negotiate with the undead? Of course he's lying to us! We've got him running scared!" She turned and pointed her sword at the Once King, who was no longer looking smug. "Screw his cheap tricks! Roughnecks don't compromise, and we *don't* sell out! We're going to kick his winged ass *and* go home. Now get back in formation, and *let's do this!*"

The raid roared in agreement, their cries shaking the stone as the two opposed groups rushed back together into one formidable whole. Breathing hard, James rushed forward as well, pushing through the crowd toward his sister. He was trying to get past a group of huge Berserkers chanting *"Roughnecks! Roughnecks!"* when something stepped out of his shadow.

"Nice timing, James," SilentBlayde said with a grin. "We knew you'd make it."

"You don't know how happy I am to see you guys," James said, grinning back at his friend. "Can you get me to Tina?"

Rather than answer, SB took the lead, parting the raid easily to where Tina was waiting at the front.

"Glad you're alive, bro," his sister said, never taking her eyes off the Once King. "What's the plan?"

"It's a long story," James said. "You see, back in the Age of Skies—"

"Yeah, we don't have time for that," Tina interrupted. "I'll listen to the whole thing later, after we've won. For now, just tell me what I have to do."

Fair enough. "Run him out of mana," James said, gripping his staff. "And I don't mean too low for the Million Damage Blast, I mean *all* the way. When he's too drained to cast so much as a counterspell, I'll take over."

Even knowing what he planned to do, that felt like a stupidly ballsy thing to say. To his amazement, though, his sister just nodded. "Will do,"

349

Tina said, lifting her sword. "All right, Roughnecks, let's do this like we planned. Ready?"

The raid roared in answer, and a hungry smile spread over his sister's face. "Let's give him hell!"

The players roared again. James felt like roaring himself. He didn't know how his little sister did it. She wasn't even a stonekin anymore, but that had never really mattered. Whatever was in her that made people want to grab their weapons and follow her into battle, it had *always* been Tina, not Roxxy. All the game had done was give her a way to let it out, and she did so now, setting her shield fearlessly as she charged the enemy.

"*Go!*"

James had already taken a step forward before he remembered that the order didn't include him. It felt wrong to sit out of the fight when so much was on the line, but he needed the mana he'd recovered while he'd been studying tapestries. Even if he'd had extra to spare, though, he knew the Roughnecks had this. Tina had more experience fighting the Once King than anyone left alive. If anyone could do this, it was her, so James decided to trust his sister, leaving the fight to her as he slipped back into the tunnel to wait for his chance.

***

Tina had never been so pumped in her life.

She'd thought it was over, and then James—blessed, *wonderful* James—had appeared from nowhere and done what he did best. Now her raid was united. They were fresh, they were ready, and the Once King was going down. She was going to get her world-first kill at last, and she was going to save the goddamn world while she was at it.

Didn't get much better than that.

"Melee, move in!" she cried as she closed the final distance. "Rangers, Casters, healers, spread out! Zen's in charge of the back line; everyone else on me!"

The orders weren't technically necessary—since she'd spent their last day of practice mastering One For All, Tina actually had the least experience with the plan of anyone here—but she'd learned long ago that players forgot their own names in the excitement of a charge. If you wanted people to actually do their jobs, it never hurt to remind them what those were, so she did, yelling out assignments at the top of her lungs as she rushed the Once King, who looked nonplussed.

"You're really going to do this?" he asked, drawing his sword with great resignation. "Waste everyone's time?"

Tina's answer to that was a thrust at his groin, the easiest part of him to reach now that she was short. The king parried easily, his face disgusted. "*Mortals,*" he sneered. "I will never understand how you can choose the shortsighted arrogance of hope over reality. Truly, you are blind."

"Save it for someone who cares," Tina growled, swinging her shield next. The Once King dodged that, too, flapping his wings to jump back to the rim of the Great Pyre's basin.

"It is clear you are beyond reason," he announced, lifting his sword high. "But I will do my sacred duty whether you understand it or not."

Tina responded by lifting a finger over her shield. The middle one. "*Do it, Frank!*"

From both sides of the terrace, the melee who'd moved in at her command began to charge, sweeping in toward the Once King from both sides. The winged elf's sneer deepened as the Knights, Berserkers, and Assassins rushed in, and then he flapped his wings, lifting high out of their reach into the sky before turning to charge the healers.

Which was exactly what they'd hoped he'd do.

"He's up!" Zen yelled from the back. "Flak defense!"

The Once King had already swept past her position, which was a real shame. Tina would have given a nonvital organ to see his sneer fall off when, instead of panicking, all the Roughnecks assigned to the back line turned and unloaded into his face. Agility-stacked Rangers fired glowing arrows like machine guns while the raid's Sorcerers unleashed a stream of fast-cast Fireballs. There was no way to tell without damage numbers, but the fusillade had to be worth several million damage at least. Whatever it was, it was enough to force the king to abandon his charge, peeling off into a barrel roll instead as he tried in vain to dodge the hundreds of arrows, fireballs, and lightning bolts cascading into him. When he turned to fly out of range of the damage, though, Tina raised her hand.

"Uh uh!" she shouted up at him. "No being a chicken! Zen, show him what happens if he runs!"

At her command, the Ranger officer turned and fired a glowing arrow over Tina's head. The deadly green bolt whistled across the terrace to land inside the bowl of the Great Pyre. The explosion of acid that followed was quickly burned off by the ghostfire, but not before the magical attack left pits on the bodies of the dead elves.

"Your choice, asshole!" Tina yelled up at the flying Once King, who'd gone still. "We're gonna DPS something! You or your fire, what's it gonna be?"

For a delicious second, the Once King stared at her with real fear. Then he inverted his climb and spun around, plummeting toward the raid like a meteor. As he dove, he waved his free hand in a spell, using his mana to call an enormous tendril of ghostfire. At their master's command, the blue-white flames erupted, rising from the Great Pyre's basin to surround the king's sword in a wall of unholy flames as big as he was.

"Shit," Tina said, eyes going wide at the sheer size of the attack before she ducked behind her bulwark. "Ready the windshield!"

It was undignified, but this was one of the hardest lessons they'd learned from fighting Gregory. Smart bosses could guess a lot from their shouted orders and the context of battle, enough sometimes to counter tactics they'd never seen before. The Roughnecks had quickly discovered the best way to avoid this was to use terms that were easy to understand and remember for gamers and/or people from Earth but that sounded like nonsense to the people of this world. Even this strategy was limited, though. A smart boss might not be able to guess what they meant the first time, but he'd remember it the second. All the more reason to make every attack count.

And every defense, Tina thought to herself, staring nervously from behind her shield at the tractor trailer–sized blade of ghostfire coming straight at her. For a moment, it looked like their whole raid was about to get whacked all the way back down through the mountain. Then, without any callouts of ability to give it away, golden light blossomed beneath their feet as multiple overlapping Sanctuary of the Four bubbles, the Cleric's invincible golden shields, popped open like umbrellas to cover them.

The timing was even better than in practice. A split second after the golden wall appeared, the unstoppable force of the Once King slammed into it at full speed.

Like a bug on a windshield.

A grin spread over Tina's face as the wall of ghostfire exploded over them, creating a ring-shaped shock wave that flew off into the distance. The golden dome rang like a temple bell from the collision, and Tina swore she heard the crunch of the ancient elf's bones.

"Cancel!" she yelled, unwilling to wait the full duration. The Clerics dissolved their spells immediately, and Tina got her prize. The Once King fell toward them in a stunned tangle of his own wings, scattering the melee as he crashed to the ground. Knowing the weakness wouldn't last, Tina ran forward. The rest of the Berserkers and Knights followed suit, surrounding the downed king in a ring of enchanted steel. She was giving the order to start a good old-fashioned dog-pile hackfest when the Once King shot back to his feet.

And paused.

The grin on Tina's face got even wider. "See it now, don't you?" she taunted. "You go up, we shoot you down. You run out of range, we take a swing at your precious ghostfire. Looks like you've got no choice but to stay down here in the mud with us. But hey, if you want to run back to the sky, we'll be happy to keep up the focus fire."

The Once King's burning eyes narrowed at her. "Only fools crow their victory at sunrise," he growled, sweeping his sword at the encircling ring to make them jump back. "I will show you the fate of the sparrow who challenges the hawk."

"Ooooh, I'm scared," Tina taunted. "Whatcha gonna do, bird brain? Tickle m—"

The towering elf used his wings and his legs to launch himself along the ground like a bullet—straight at her.

Tina scrambled frantically get into her protective crouch. Of all the potential targets, she hadn't *actually* expected him to pick the tank. But apparently taunting sometimes worked in real life, too, because the Once King's giant armored knee was already slamming into her shield, sending force exploding through the bulwark and into her.

And it was here, in the first real hit of the fight, that Tina learned just how big a difference there was between a normal five-skull like Gregory and the Once King. The hit didn't just take her off her feet, it launched her into the air. She would have flown right off the mountain if Killbox hadn't caught her boot at the last second, sending the whole world spinning as he checked her momentum and sent her slamming back into the ground.

She landed hard enough to crack the stone. The impact knocked the breath clean out of her. She was still trying to get it back as Killbox dragged her to her feet again. But then, before she could get back into position or even resume breathing, someone started to scream.

Tina's head snapped up, looking frantically for the raid boss. She found him on top of Frank. Her fellow Tank was on the ground with the king's sword sticking out of his thigh like he was a bug on a board. The Once King yanked his blade free as she watched, whipping the point hard enough to send Frank spinning before he turned and swept his sword up to meet the two Berserkers who'd been going for his back.

Everything went to shit after that.

The Berserkers landed their attacks, but their colossal axes drew mere flecks of blood before the Once King cut them both down in an arc of crimson. Meanwhile, heals were landing on Frank, but just as he was getting back up, the Once King turned and kicked him into an oncoming Knight, sending them both tumbling across the paving stones. Keeping the move going, the Once King used the momentum to land a haymaker on the next Berserker coming in from his left. The hulking player blocked the hit on his canned-ham arms, but it didn't help at all. Tina could hear bones snapping from across the terrace, followed by his cries of agony as he hit the ground like a hammer.

Never one to miss a chance, Zen yelled an order, and a volley of arrows screamed in through the gap left by the falling Berserker. The Rangers couldn't use their acid or explosive shots with so many friendlies in the area, but the geared players' normal arrows were still deadly. Or, at least, that's what Tina had thought. But the screaming shots that should have perforated him barely scratched the Once King's armor instead, not even distracting his attention as the king threw his sword left. The dark, gleaming blade moved so fast that Tina had trouble following its movement, but she saw all too well where it stopped in the chest of a Roughneck Knight named Jonsey.

The Knight looked down in surprise, staring at the huge sword sticking out of his ribcage like he didn't understand what had happened. Then Jonsey's body went slack, his giant two-handed sword clattering to the stone like a cymbal as he fell over with a brilliant red *splat*. Tina was still staring at the copious red blood in horror when she realized the Once King was now looking at *her*.

"Steady Ground!"

It wasn't even a conscious thought. She'd activated the defense reflexively, which turned out to be a very good thing when the Once King charged her like a rocket. Her feet sealed to the floor just in time as the boss's Eclipsed Steel boot slammed into her shield with the force of a runaway train carrying fifty miles' worth of bricks. For a moment, she was driven down into the ground as the floor cracked and crumbled beneath her, then hot sparks singed her face as her shield's slightly curved surface deflected the king's kick over Tina's head.

The world went dark as the Once King's body passed over her. Vaguely, in the distance, Tina was aware of flashing light as the healers poured magic into Jonsey, but all she could see was the shadow of the Celestial Elf's wings as he leaped over her, his lightning-fast sword already flitting down to stab into her unguarded back.

Dropping Steady Ground to unlock her feet, Tina whirled to face him, but not fast enough. She didn't know if there was a "fast enough" as the burning-cold steel punched through the side of her enchanted armor to enter her guts. But as bad as it hurt to be run through by a sword as thick as her arm, that pain was nothing compared to the searing heat of the ghostfire as it caught inside her.

Tina wasn't entirely sure what happened after that. She remembered screaming and thrashing as she tried to get herself off the Once King's blade. Then ZeroDarkness leaped from the king's shadow, his twin daggers stabbing the elf's back between the wings at high speed. SilentBlayde emerged from Tina's own shadow at the same time, his arms clamping around her waist like a vise as he yanked her off the Once King's sword. A hail of blessed, pain-removing healing magic landed on her a second later, and she collapsed into SB as they both landed on the ground.

"Tina!"

Too shaken from the blistering pain to move, Tina lay slack on top of him. She wouldn't even have opened her eyes if his hands hadn't caught her face.

"Tina," he said again, forcing her to look at him. "This is bad. We're supposed to be running him out of mana, but he hasn't even cast anything yet, and he's *still* mauling us. We need a new plan!"

Tina's head was ringing too hard to remember the old plan. Now that her eyes were open again, though, there was no denying that Blayde was right. The Once King had already abandoned her to launch himself into their back lines. More screams rang out, more blood splattered on the ground, then the terrace lit up as the Roughnecks returned fire, taking advantage of every gap the Once King left. There were many—even he couldn't defend from every angle—but Tina already knew it wasn't going to be enough. They were getting damage in, but it was hardly dinging his two billion HP. At this rate, they'd all be stains on the pavement before they hurt him enough for the king to notice.

"We're not gonna last five minutes like this," she gasped, pushing off her elf at last. "Healing's keeping pace so far, but if he keeps getting those big hits in, it's only a matter of time before someone loses a head." Couldn't heal that.

"What are we going to do?" SB asked, looking nervously at her side, where her freshly healed skin was visible through the gaping hole in her armor.

"We need more mud," Tina growled, hauling herself back to her feet. "Tell Zen it's chain time. I'll make the opening, and then you do it just like you did at practice."

"Right," he said, sinking into the shadows. Then he popped back out to press a desperate kiss to her cheek. "Love you."

There was no time to say she loved him back. No time for anything. It was all happening so much faster than she'd planned. The chains were supposed to be their big finisher. Using them now meant they'd have no cards left, but Tina didn't see any other choice. The flashes of gold and green from the healing camp were going off constantly now, and the terrace was slick with so much of their blood. As things stood, the healers' mana pools were the only reasons they weren't all dead already. Once those ran dry, it would *really* be over.

Another scream rang out as the Once King crushed a Sorcerer's ribcage before Frank managed to get in between them, catching a blow to his own head in the process. Wincing at her fellow tank's gasp of pain, Tina scanned around for Zen to see if SB had delivered her order yet. Thankfully, the Ranger's height and bright-green hair made her easy to spot. She met Tina's eyes and raised her bow in reply. Satisfied that part of the plan was ready at least, Tina lifted her sword, trusting SB to do his part as she raised her voice over the chaos.

"*Hey, chicken wings!*" she bellowed, banging her shield with her armored fist. Fifty feet away, the Once King looked up from the Ranger he was disemboweling to give her a sneer.

Tina sneered back. "That last hit didn't do jack!" she cried, lowering her shield to show him her healed side through the hole in her armor. "You gotta try harder than that to hurt me! Put your legs into it next time!"

The eternal elf arched a perfect gray eyebrow as arrows rattled off his back. Then he turned back to his victim with a condescending shake of his head, ignoring her.

Tina cursed under her breath. Clearly, words weren't going to be enough this time. If this was going to happen, she needed to go all in, so Tina forced herself to unclench her hand, putting her life in SilentBlayde's hands as she released her shield, dropping the giant bulwark on the ground with a deafening *clang*.

That got his attention.

"Come on, fucker!" Tina cried as the Once King's head snapped back to her. "You want to kill me? You'll never get a better shot than this!"

She threw her arms wide, showing him her now completely unguarded torso. Sure enough, the Once King's eyes flashed eagerly when he saw an open shot, and Tina shifted her weight in preparation for the charge. But he didn't charge. He just flicked his arm, his sword hand suddenly empty as he launched his sword through the air like a missile straight at her.

Tina's eyes flew wide. *Oh shit,* she thought as her death approached at supersonic speeds. *SB, you'd better be fast. You'd better be fast as—*

A shape launched out of her shadow. It moved so fast she couldn't see more than a blur, faster than even the Once King's sword as it flashed between her and the incoming weapon. Then the flash solidified into the body of SilentBlayde, his swords crossed in a guard in front of him. Silver blades met black in a shower of sparks, and then it was Tina's turn to catch as the force of the Once King's thrown weapon crashed into them both. She staggered backward, getting a foot behind her as she caught her husband. Then she heard the immensely satisfying clatter of the Once King's Eclipsed Steel blade landing on the stone floor.

Wasting no time, Tina leaped out from behind SB to grab the Once King's sword. Seizing it in the hand that normally held her shield, she waved the huge blade like a flag at the boss, making damn sure he saw it before sliding the black sword into the sheath her tanking blade normally occupied.

It was a horrible fit. The Once King's blade was thinner and much longer since it was sized for him, but she didn't think it was going to fall out. Even if it did, Tina didn't care. The real victory was the look of naked rage on the elf king's face as he stopped ripping into their back lines and whirled to face her again.

"Well, well," Tina said in her most obnoxious, way-too-loud voice. "Would you look at this? I just scored some loot without even killing the boss!"

"Too bad it's old and ugly," SilentBlayde said, getting in on the act as he rolled deftly off the ground to stand at her side. "The Sephiroth look is *so* outdated." He pointed at the circle of Eclipsed Steel on the Once King's brow. "Crown doesn't look half bad, though. We should go for that next."

"Maybe we'll get his shirt, too!"

SB made a face. "Pass. I bet it has sweat-stained pits. That's probably why he wears so much black."

"Totally," Tina agreed, wrinkling her nose. "But what else can you expect from a dude who lives alone in an attic with nothing but a bunch of zomb—"

Her vision suddenly filled with dark wings and the Once King's enraged face. Tina only had a second of warning before he struck, and she used it to grab her shield back, hunkering down so low behind it she was practically horizontal. But there was no bracing against this impact. The loss of his sword meant that he could no longer slice through her, but the Once King was still ten feet of immortal fury as he hauled back and slammed his fist down on top of her.

The first punch rang her whole body like a bell. The second made her arms go numb. The third hit so hard that her knees buckled, causing Tina to lose her stance as she crumpled to the ground.

The Once King's foot came in as she fell, kicking the loose edge of her shield wide. Tina's grip held, so at least he didn't kick it away, but the attack sent pain exploding through her shoulder as something in her arm popped loose. She didn't even get a chance to cry out in agony before the king's foot landed on her chest.

"Foolish child," the Once King snarled, crushing her with his full weight. "I don't need my sword to end this indignity for you."

Tina gritted her teeth, saying nothing. This was partially because she couldn't breathe but mostly because she didn't want to give anything away. Shouting things like "Do it now!" was how surprise attacks got ruined, and Tina wanted this one to be the shock of his life. Of course, given the way her ribs were popping, it might end up being the shock of *her* life if this went on much longer.

Any time now, guys.

Finally, just as the Once King was bending down from his enormous height to retrieve his stolen sword, Tina heard the faint whistle of metal flying through the air. This was followed by a flash of light as an amber-glowing chain—the same one NekoBaby had pulled from her pack to get them up the wall—flew in from the side to wrap around the Once King's neck. Two more chains followed from the left and right to wrap around the king's arms, their spiked ends hooking into the king's armor to lock them in place. Bowstrings twanged as the Rangers fired their Grapple Shots into his wings, pinning them temporarily to the ground to make way for even more chains.

They flew in like fishing lines after that, tangling the raid boss from every angle until he was buried under a pile of enchanted metal. Roaring in fury, the Once King released his hold on Tina to rip them off, and she seized her chance to scoot away, using her good arm to drag her body across the cracked stone floor as fast as she could manage.

The Once King roared again when he realized what she was doing, dragging at least six Roughnecks forward as he lunged to try to catch her. Tried and failed. As players fell over, more rushed in to help, the Knights and Berserkers piling onto the chains' ends like players in a tug-of-war game. When half the raid had dug in their heels, the king ground to a stop at last, his furious cries echoing off the mountains below.

"Shoot him!" Tina yelled, switching her shield to her undislocated arm to cover her head as she scrambled away. "*Shoot him!*"

The order was hardly necessary. The moment she was clear, the area around the Once King was engulfed in a whirlwind of elemental destruction. Fireballs, arrows, and lightning bolts poured down until his trapped, hunched figure was no longer visible behind the glare. There was so much fire that the stone under the king's feet was starting to turn red, but Tina wasn't taking anything for granted.

"*Full DPS!*" she yelled as SB rushed over to help her back to her feet. "Don't worry about killing him, he can take it! *Push push push!*"

Shouts rang out in answer to her command as the Roughnecks activated their big, damage-boosting cooldowns, and the storm of fire and lightning around the Once King grew even more intense. It was getting so hot that she was starting to worry about the chains, but they'd been enchanted with toughness and strength by the Naturalists of Windy Lake for exactly this purpose. Even if they had been popping, though, it was too late to change tactics. The king was in the trap. The only thing they could do now was make it count.

Since the boss was busy getting owned, Tina waved for a heal. Both NekoBaby and Anders jumped to obey, bathing her in a glowing shower of pain-relieving magic. The doubling was wasteful, but Tina didn't complain as her health refilled.

When it was over, NekoBaby rolled her eyes and flashed the ichthyian a rude gesture before stalking away. The look of regret on Anders's face as she left was almost enough to make Tina feel sorry for him. She definitely regretted the promise she'd made to the high priest back at Windy Lake. She didn't think Neko was ever going to forgive him, but Anders still deserved to know the stakes he was up against. Especially since that was the only way they were ever getting access to the Resplendent Aegis spell, which would be *really useful* right about now.

She was trying to think of something leadery and encouraging she could say that might nudge the obviously repentant Cleric in the right direction while not actually going back on her word when a shout went up from the raid. It wasn't until she realized she couldn't see why, though, that Tina realized she'd put her back to the Once King.

Swearing at her own stupidity, Tina spun on her heel, shield coming up just in time as a hundred-foot-tall blade of blazing ghostfire sliced its way through the tornado of flame and lightning from top to bottom. The fire cut through the chains as well, leaving the melee flailing as the lines they'd been pulling on with all their might went slack and the Once King shot back into the sky.

He threw out his arm as he flew, sending another wave of blue-white fire down at Tina. Since she already had her shield up, she wasn't too worried, but then she saw that she'd got it wrong. The ghostfire wasn't aimed at her. The boss had sent it over her head, throwing the wall of fire straight at NekoBaby, who was still stalking away from Anders behind her.

"*Neko!*"

Tina leaped from her crouch, but she was miles too late. All she could do was watch in horror as Neko looked over her shoulder, ears going flat on her fluffy head as the enormous blue-white wave of death filled the sky above her. Her mouth was still moving in a screamed *"FUCK!"* that was lost in the roar of the flames when Anders appeared from nowhere, tackling her to the ground. That was the last Tina saw before the ghostfire slammed down on top of them, punching a ten-foot hole straight through the terrace floor and dropping the healers, burning, into the dark below.

***

Anders woke up in blackness.

No, he realized groggily, not blackness. Black rock. He was lying in a pile of rubble on the floor of the Once King's throne room. Directly above him, high, high overhead, he could see the hole the ghostfire had punched through the Terrace of the Great Pyre. Down here, though, all was quiet, which struck him as strange. Last he'd seen, this room had been a PvP battlefield between Cinco's killers and the undead players of *Six Ways From Raiding*. He didn't know if the stillness was because the fight had moved on or if someone had won. Or maybe they'd all died just now in the rockfall. Either way, he needed to get up. He'd never atone if he just lay around here.

Pressing his fish lips together, he tried to push himself up only to find he had nothing to push with. Both of his legs were broken. So was his

363

collarbone, though that was nothing compared to the shattered stump that was all that remained of his right arm. He must have been deeply in shock, he realized belatedly, because none of the horrific wounds actually hurt yet, though the sight of his sharp, blindingly white fish bones sticking out through the skin of his shoulder where his arm should have been was almost enough to make him pass out. Looking quickly away, Anders decided to focus on summoning up the holy energies with his left hand, the only appendage he had that was still working.

It shouldn't have been hard. He knew the healing spell's motions so well that even one-handed casting should have been a breeze, but the Sun was so distant here in the Deadlands. The unnatural clouds muffled the warm god's voice and dimmed its power. After fumbling the spell twice, Anders groaned and gave up, collapsing on his back to stare up at the battle he was no longer part of.

High above him, Anders could hear Roxxy's brother yelling his name as he ran down the stairs, which was a surprise. He'd forgotten James was here. But even a jubatus could only run so fast, and there were ten spirals of the hidden stair between them. Given how cold he was already feeling, Anders was certain he'd bleed out before James arrived. He wanted to yell back at the Naturalist not to bother. That he was done for, and honestly, glad of it. All his life had been one of shame. He'd shown signs of insanity well before FFO had earned him the label of Leylia's disease. And then, when he'd gotten a second chance at life, he'd destroyed it within seconds with his perversion and misery.

Truly, he was a waste of the Sun's benevolence. His one solace was that at least he'd managed to die well. The ghostfire had been blinding, but he was pretty sure he'd managed to knock Neko clear of the blast before the floor gave out. He didn't think one good act was enough to counter a lifetime of selfishness, but at least he hadn't been a bastard at the end. That had to count for some—

"*Anders!*"

His eyes shot open in surprise. He knew that high-pitched voice, but it couldn't be. He'd knocked her out of—

"Anders!" the shrill voice cried again. "Don't die, idiot! If you see a light, stay away from it!"

Heart pounding, Anders rolled in his soon-to-be grave, looking up through the billowing dust at the green light that was rapidly filling the broken throne room. As his eyes adjusted to the glare, he saw a bloody but very much alive NekoBaby weaving a big healing spell over him. Desperate, he reached out to grab her slender arm but stopped just short of her sleeve. Even now, he couldn't bring himself to touch her, especially from this angle. Looking up from the ground, he had a perfect view of the boxy shoulder pads and chest bindings the jubatus used in an attempt to make herself look more masculine. Those things weren't his doing, but Anders felt guilty for them all the same. Truly, he'd made everything worse for her from start to finish, a monster outside and in. He didn't deserve to keep living.

"Stop, Neko," he begged, closing his eyes against the building green light. "I don't want to keep living."

"Too bad," NekoBaby growled. "The raid can't afford to be down a healer right now, so buck up, buttercup."

"It'll take too much mana," he argued, gesturing at his broken body with his only working hand. "Just leave me. It's better this way. You're owed your revenge, and I'm glad to give it to you. You don't even have to do it yourself. I'll die all on my own. Just let me—"

"*Fuck you!*" she yelled, baring her little fangs as she started shoving gobs of green nature magic into his chest. "You don't know me like you think you do!"

Euphoria washed over Anders as the magical healing kicked in, washing away the cold and the shock and numbness. It wasn't a full heal, but the stump of his right arm was no longer leaking, saving him from death by blood loss. Nodding in satisfaction, NekoBaby started working on the next spell immediately, leaving him staring at her in bewilderment.

"Why won't you kill me?" he asked, his warbling voice cracking. "I know we need a healer, but James is here. He can take my spot at any time and my death is the only way you'll have peace. I know you've been stalking me and looking for your chance. I've been bending over backward to give it to you: being alone, letting you follow me, standing near dangerous stuff. Why won't you put us both out of our misery?"

"Because, *Ryan*," NekoBaby said, slapping a watery mass of healing magic into his face, "that's not my fucking bag to carry anymore. Yeah, you gave me some mental scars, and yeah, I love thinking about the best way to fillet you, but the battle for Camp Comeback was a goddamn educational slideshow about what revenge does to people. I'm a smart cookie. Smart enough to know that if I kill you, it's going to haunt me for the rest of my life, and you're not fucking worth it! I am motherfucking *NekoBaby*! My greatness is way more important than some sad little fishstick like you, so get over yourself."

Anders couldn't believe his earholes. "Are you—Are you forgiving me?" he asked, breathless with hope.

NekoBaby rolled her eyes. "What part of that sounded like forgiveness? I've just decided to move on. I'm sick of carrying this load of bricks, so I'm making the boss move and setting it down. You can keep dragging your end for the rest of eternity if you want. Ain't none of my business. But I'm over this crap, so 'be healed' and shit."

Another spell burst over him as she finished, bathing him the final burst of radiance needed to heal him to full. But while his body felt whole and hale again, his right arm remained a smoldering stump. He knew he should probably be freaking out about that, but honestly, he was too confused right now to care properly. Lying where he'd fallen, Anders realized he had no idea what to do next. He'd meant what he'd said, but now that he was no longer at death's door, he wasn't actually keen on the idea of dying. If he wasn't going to die for Neko's revenge, though, where did that leave him? What did he do with himself if she didn't want his guts or his atonement? He was still wrestling with that when Neko stood up and offered him her hand.

Anders stared at that small, clawed paw for a long, long time. Long enough that the cat girl's tail started lashing with irritation. Not wanting to add yet another sin to his pile, he reached up his lone remaining arm and slid his shaking webbed fingers into hers.

"*Finally,*" NekoBaby huffed as she yanked him to his feet. "Roxxy's going to skin us both if we don't get back up there."

Anders nodded dumbly, still too jumbled up inside to speak.

"Thanks for saving my tail up there, by the way," she continued casually, hopping over the rubble with catlike grace. "I thought my number was up, but your push got me clear of the worst of it. I even landed on my feet!" She glanced over her shoulder with a pitying look. "I'm sorry about your arm. I tried to force the life threads back in so it would regenerate, but it was too damaged and the ghostfire was too deep. I had to let it burn."

"It's all right," Anders said, reaching down to pick up his golden staff with his remaining hand. "Thank you for saving my life."

"That's what I do," Neko said, lifting her nose into the air. "Now if you'll excuse me, the Roughnecks' best healer has to get back to the battle so we can become legends." She chuckled evilly. "I'm gonna leave this world with the best troll *ever*. For centuries, school kids here are gonna have to stare at my statue and learn about how the Great *NekoBaby* saved them all! It's gonna be da bomb."

There was absolutely nothing Anders could say to that. Neko was already darting up the hidden stairwell anyway, running on all fours with her staff in her mouth. Anders couldn't move nearly as fast, but that was fine with him. As much as he wanted to get back to the battle, he needed time to absorb what had just happened. He'd lost an arm today, but somehow he felt like he'd become more whole. He wasn't a good man yet, but the knot of guilt inside him was unraveling, and something good was growing in its place. Something warm and calm, like sunlight shining on his face on a peaceful summer afternoon. It was a truly blessed feeling in this cold place, and Anders held it as tight as he dared, leaning on his golden staff as he hobbled up the Once King's broken staircase after Neko.

Chapter 15

Tina and James

The fight was not going well.

Tina slid across the terrace on her back, skidding to a halt by the stairs in a shower of sparks. Even after she stopped, her head kept spinning from the blow that had sent her flying, or maybe the one before that. They were all running together at this point, but at least she was still getting back up.

"*Tina!*" Her brother rushed over as she drunkenly staggered to her feet. "Are you all right?"

"Of course I'm not fucking all right," she said, wincing at how badly her voice was slurring. "We're fucking losing. Those chains were our best shot, but he broke out in thirty seconds and killed my two best healers."

God, that hurt worse than anything. The only reason she wasn't bawling her eyes out was because she had no time. She *had* to kill this winged bastard and get revenge, or Neko would troll-haunt her for the rest of eternity. But as she was scrubbing the tears out of her eyes, she realized belatedly that James was still talking.

"What?"

"I said 'they're not dead.' The blast sent them crashing down into the throne room, but I saw Neko healing Anders. They're both on their way back up as we speak."

Now Tina really was going to cry. "Well, at least one good thing happened," she said, swallowing her sob. "But we're still fucked."

James said something then about not giving up hope, but Tina was not in the mood to listen. She knew a losing battle when she was in it, and this one was going down in flames, but the worst part was that she had no idea how to fix it. Her raid was doing everything she could ask of them, performing even better than they had in practice, and it wasn't making a damn bit of difference. Their damage was simply too low, and the Once

369

King's HP was too high. Fucker knew it, too. He hadn't even tried to get back the sword Tina still had in her sheath. He wasn't casting spells anymore, either. He was just flitting around, cleaning their clocks the old-fashioned way, pummeling them with his boots and fists until they broke.

"It's not what it looks like," James said, reading the despair on her face. "I've talked with him. I know Ar'Kan has a really good poker face. He's capable of playing the evil raid boss, but I know he doesn't actually enjoy making others suffer. Never forget: he thinks he's doing this to *save* you. He must be having more trouble than he's letting on, or he would have killed all of you already to put you out of your misery."

Tina supposed it was nice to know the Once King wasn't drawing their suffering out just for laughs, but that didn't change the fact that they were going down. "Then what do we do?" she asked her brother, grabbing her shield off the ground to get back into the fight before Frank nearly died for a third time.

"Call his bluff," James said. "Stop letting him control the fight and force him to do something big. If he's faking as bad as I think he is, he won't be able to take it."

She almost asked, "And if he's not?" but there was no point. She already knew the answer, so Tina gave James a thumbs up and hurled herself back into the fight.

"*Richard!*" she yelled, running back toward the center of the battle-scarred terrace. "What's our mana status?"

"At the current rate of burn, DPS should have fifty percent remaining on average," the Sorcerer officer replied calmly, pausing to sling a fireball through a gap in the melee line. "Healing is most likely down to twenty-five, give or take a few percent."

That was better than she'd feared. "Okay, new plan," she said, grabbing the beanpole Sorcerer by his shoulder to stop his next attack. "I want you to take all the casters and get them over there." She pointed at the far side of the mountaintop, the farthest point of the circle from the Great

Pyre. "*All* the casters, including healers. Get everyone together and start team casting like Neko and Anders do."

Richard looked intrigued. "What's the spell?"

Tina forced a confident grin onto her face even though she had none. "I want you to make me a magical storm. I don't care if it takes all our mana, I want every last watt of lightning, fire, and holy power we can scrape together, and I want it to be a big area-of-effect attack. Think 'orbital nuclear strike.'"

This description earned her a frown. "We can probably manage something like that," Richard said. "But it'll take sixty seconds at least to gather so much power, which means the Once King will almost certainly interrupt us. Also, targeting will be impossible with so many casters. It's a matter of when, not if, we'll lose control of the attack. Even if we did somehow keep it together, the sum total of our remaining mana isn't close to what's needed to kill him. Even if we do everything perfectly, we'll be left with an only half-dead boss and no mana for heals."

"That's fine," Tina said. "I've already got it covered. You just focus on getting everyone together to blast him with as much AOE bullshit as possible. I'll take care of the rest."

The Sorcerer looked doubtful, but he followed her order, yelling and waving his hands as he ran over to the remaining healers. Satisfied he'd do his part, Tina turned to look for her next target, who turned out to be only a few feet away.

"Zen!" she cried, running over.

The Ranger officer didn't stop firing to answer, "What?"

"Do you have any super-speed left?"

"I've got all of it," she said as she calmly fired an arrow through the six-inch-wide gap between two Knights to graze the Once King's shoulder plate. "Why do you ask?"

"Because you're about to need it," Tina said, pointing at the basin of burning elves sending tongues of ghostfire high into the overcast sky. "I want you to go stand by the Great Pyre and hurt it as hard as you can. Make yourself unignorable."

Zen almost dropped her bow. "Are you crazy?" she cried. "The Once King will swat me like a bug!"

"Then don't let him," Tina said. "I know you can see as well as I do that this shit ain't working. If we don't shake things up, he's just going to keep knocking us down until we can't get up anymore."

Looking at the tiny scratch left by her own arrow, Zen's face grew grim. "So you want me to get his attention by shooting the ghostfire and…what? Dodge and hope for the best?"

"You *are* a goddess of Agility," Tina reminded her. "Unlike Assassins, Rangers don't need to pack on Strength for stabbing. You've got more jump than even SB. If *anyone* can pull this off, it's you."

Zen sighed. "This is crazy," she muttered. "But I guess last stands always are." She took another deep breath, reaching up to push the sooty green hair out of her face. "When do you want me to go?"

"Right now," Tina said, looking nervously at the battle raging behind them. "Before he kills Killbox."

That was going to be a tall order. The Once King had already grabbed the Berserker by his chestplate, trying to hold the wiggling human steady long enough for a decapitation. "Crap," Tina said, gripping her shield as she started to charge. "*Do it, Zen!*"

The Ranger was at the pyre before the order was out of Tina's mouth. The moment her first arrow hit the ancient elves whose bodies fed the flames, they all had to duck as the Once King whirled around. He dropped Killbox a heartbeat later, launching himself at the dark-skinned elf with his lightning speed. Zen moved just as quickly, jumping out of the way and spinning in midair to launch yet another arrow into the pyre. This one burned up before it could land, but the shot still struck true. With a roar of fury and maybe a flicker of fear, the king charged after her, beating his wings as he ran to pick up speed until the two of them were just a blur. The other

Roughnecks—including Killbox, who was still lying where the Once King had dropped him—watched the chase in awe. They would have sat there forever if Tina hadn't started banging her shield.

A sea of panicked, bloody faces whirled on her, their eyes too full of battle adrenaline to properly follow an explanation even if she'd had time to give one. Fortunately, they didn't have the time, so Tina didn't even have to try.

"Assassins here!" she ordered, pointing at the stone under her feet. "Knights form a line twenty feet behind them. Berserkers, I want you twenty feet behind the Knights. Frank! You're twenty behind the Berserkers. Rangers, you're back with the casters. Keep the flak in the skies. If he tries to fly, shoot him down!"

The raid stared at her dumbly, and Tina banged her shield again. "*Move,* people! This is not a drill!"

Everyone leaped after that, scrambling into the positions she'd just laid out. As the lines formed, Richard finished gathering all the casters at the far edge of the terrace. *Very* close to the edge. It was a dangerous position, but it was the only place far enough back to work. If she was going to pull this off, Tina needed as much HP between the Once King and the casters as possible.

"Listen up!" she bellowed as her raiders fell into line. "This is our final play, so use it if you got it! Cooldowns, potions, buffs, everything is cleared! Our only goal is to keep him off the casters until they finish their spell. Any way we can accomplish that is a good one, so go for broke!"

With that, Tina moved into her own position twenty more feet behind Frank, which put her practically in the caster camp. This close, she could feel the first rumbles of the magical storm building behind her. Setting down her shield, Tina picked up a ten-foot length of the enchanted chain the Once King had broken earlier and wound the end around her right arm. When everything was exactly as she wanted, she looked up to see how Zen was doing.

She tried, anyway. Her eyes weren't actually good enough to keep up with the deadly game of cat and mouse going down on the other side of the terrace. The Ranger was moving so fast that she seemed to flicker between footsteps, only touching ground once every few seconds. But the Once King was just as quick, slashing his empty hands through the air only a hair more slowly than she vanished. The only reason he wasn't able to slash her was because he had to keep pausing to snatch the arrows she continuously loosed at the Great Pyre out of the air. Other than the painfully close shaves, though, Zen's gambit was actually going spectacularly well. Tina was starting to think they might not even need the rest of the plan because the Ranger could distract the king the entire time on her own.

Then, suddenly, Zen's speed gave out all at once.

The Ranger must have hit her limit face first. One second she was flickering through the air, the next she was gasping on her knees, her dark-brown face turning a terrifying shade of purple. Her bow hit the ground next as Zen clutched her throat, gasping for oxygen. Then the Once King appeared in front of her, his fist already pulled back for the finishing blow.

Tina was sucking in her own breath to bellow at the Assassins to get Zen out of there when lightning cracked overhead, bathing the entire mountain in blinding light. Even the king stopped at the flash, buying SilentBlayde enough time to flit in and drag Zen to safety before slipping back through the shadows to resume his position. He certainly had plenty to work with. The always-dim Deadlands sky was now black as pitch over their heads, the clouds low and angry and full of unnatural flashes, only some of which were lightning. There was also fire and water and golden holy light, plus whatever the weird purple stuff Sorcerers cast was. All of it was swirling together over their heads in a black, cloudy vortex. There was so much magic in there that even Tina—who'd never had mana as a stonekin and not much now—could feel the weight of it building like a hammer in the sky.

The Once King *definitely* felt it. All at once, he forgot about Zen and turned, his gaze fixated on the circle of casters at the opposite side of the terrace. Then his wings beat down once, shooting him up into the air straight at them.

"Here he comes!" Tina yelled as the gigantic elf rocketed skyward. "Rangers, get him down here!"

She didn't even need to say it. Her archer gallery was already firing, shouting out their damage-boosting cooldowns as they launched their biggest shots straight at the Once King. Even for the world's best raid boss, it was a staggering amount of damage. More than he could take, clearly, because the king swooped back down almost immediately, putting himself back in range of the rest of the Roughnecks.

Being the closest and the fastest, ZeroDarkness and SilentBlayde got to him first. "Shadow Dance!" "Flying Blades!" Her two Assassins called out their abilities as they turned everything on, leaping onto the falling Once King with blades that moved so fast Tina couldn't even see them. After being left out of the chain attack earlier since they couldn't stand in the conflagration of spells without being consumed themselves, both Assassins were fresh, and they laid all of that saved energy into the Once King.

The winged elf fell to the ground with a crash, his blood flying everywhere as he defended. But even with his hands flickering at max speed and sparks flying from his gauntlets from the hundreds of parries, even he couldn't stop it all. Plenty of hits got through before the Assassins ran out of speed just as Zen had.

"Fifty seconds, Roxxy!" Richard yelled.

Part of her knew that was important, but the rest of Tina's attention was focused on the Assassins, both of whom she could now see again as their speed and defenses ran out. As they wound down, the momentum flipped back to the Once King's side. Moving as fast as ever, he flitted around Zero's parry to plunge his fist into the jubatus's chest, dropping the Assassin in a single, near-fatal hit. His foot moved at the same time, crashing into SB's crossed blades and sending him flying. Blayde almost saved it, flipping in midair with supernatural grace, but the Once King wasn't done. As he flew through the air, the winged elf's hand flicked down to the ground, grabbing a piece of the shattered floor and winging it at him like a knife. The stone, which had looked so small in the king's oversized hand, crashed into SilentBlayde like a cannonball, smashing him to the ground with a force that shook the mountain and nearly broke the floor again.

Crying out her husband's name, Tina rushed forward, only to stop a second later. She couldn't go. SilentBlayde was writhing in the crater a good thirty feet away, but he was still alive. So was Zen, panting on the stairs where SB had dropped her. They'd need serious healing, and soon, but as of right now, no one was dead, and she meant to keep it that way.

Forty seconds.

"Knights forward!" she yelled as the Once King started toward the casters again. "Don't let him through!"

"Blades of Glory!" the Knights bellowed in reply. "Steady Ground!"

Just like the Assassins, the Roughnecks' Knights gave it everything they had. They'd always been a melee-heavy group, but that normally bad comp finally worked to their advantage as the whole pack of armored players crashed into the Once King like linebackers, swinging their swords with all their overgeared strength. For a moment, the impact was enough to check even the five-skull boss's strength, forcing him back several feet. Then the king filled his hands with pure concentrated ghostfire, swinging the flaming mass like a bat into the knot of armored muscle pinning him in.

To their credit, Tina's Knights didn't give up. They threw themselves at the Once King, weighing him down with their bodies even as he bashed their armor and broke their swords. In the end, though, even their strength wasn't enough. A few heartbeats later, the king bashed himself free, leaving them bleeding and wreathed in ghostfire as he staggered forward.

Thirty seconds.

"Roxxy!" NekoBaby cried, making her jump. She hadn't realized the healer was back in action yet, but when she looked, the Naturalist was standing in the casting circle with everyone else, weaving her magics frantically. "They need heals! Do you want us to—"

"*No!*" Tina cried, forcing the word out. It went against every instinct she had not to call for healing for her downed raid members, but this was the plan. It was all or nothing. If she chickened out and broke the casting early, she'd gotten everyone hurt in vain.

"Stick to the plan!" she bellowed. "Berserkers in! *Don't let him through!*"

The building magical storm crackled over head as the last group of her melee rushed in. "Reckless Strikes! Dogs of War!" came the callouts as the Roughnecks' Berserkers crashed into the increasingly desperate Once King. Metal screeched on metal, men roared in pain, weapons shattered, but no one backed down. They weren't as armored as the Knights had been, but that didn't matter. Killbox and the others stalled the king with their sheer fury, swinging their weapons like whirlwinds so fiercely that even the Once King stepped back. But no player ability lasts forever. When their cooldowns were up, the king overpowered them as he had all the others, breaking through their line with a savage arc of blood and broken bones.

Twenty seconds.

Sweat poured down Tina's neck as the Once King reached Frank.

"Iron Wall! Last Stand!" Frank yelled, slamming his shield into the ground as he set himself like a boulder in the king's way. Sneering at the off tank, the Once King drove his shoulder into Frank's shield. The resulting impact should have hurled him off the mountain, but for once Frank had set his shield at the exact right angle, tilting the metal wall so that the force of the blow traveled down into the ground instead of into him. A gunshot-like *crack* rang out as the stone under his feet broke, forcing both Frank and the Once King to jump away as yet another hole opened in the floor.

Whooping with victory, Frank reestablished his position, banging his shield to taunt the boss back to him once more. Any other time, Tina would have been beside herself with pride. Now, though, she could only watch in terror as the Once King roared with impatience, gathering the ghostfire once more into his hands to slam it down on Frank's head. Again, though, Frank got his shield into the right position, using what was left of Iron Wall to fend off the blows. But, like all of their techniques, Iron Wall's perfection was short lived. Tina knew to the heartbeat when it would run out, and as it did, so did Frank.

The moment the Knight's ability was no longer holding his shield in place, the Once King knocked it wide open. But in a move that shocked even Tina, Frank was ready. The moment the Once King knocked his shield out of the way, Frank charged in, using his own broken guard for a surprise tackle that took the Once King off his feet.

"Go, Frank!" Tina yelled, heart soaring. "Get on top of him! Punch his face!"

Frank was trying to do all that and more, but while the tackle had caught the Once King off guard, he was still a raid boss, and Frank was just one man. A single hand was all it took for the king to pluck the shieldless Knight off his chest, crushing his body in an iron grip before throwing him away. Frank landed in a fresh crater right next to SB's, wrapping his arms in pain around what had to be a whole chestful of broken bones. Nodding in satisfaction, the Once King rolled back to his feet and turned on Tina, the last obstacle left between him and his goal.

Ten seconds.

Tina met his sneer with her own and raised her shield, ignoring the blood that was still trickling down her face from the many, many hits. This was it. Her raiders had given every inch of themselves to reach this moment. She would not be the weak link here at the end. She would not fail them.

With that, Tina roared her battle cry and charged straight at the king. The massive elf met her head on, forming the ghostfire in his hands into a blade as big as she was as he swung for her chest. But not being a stonekin anymore had its advantages. Using the Once King's own blinding attack as cover, Tina ducked and rolled, slipping between the raid boss's legs to come up behind him instead. When she reached the other side, she spun and threw the enchanted chain she'd picked up earlier, slinging the barbed end around the enormous elf's waist. The moment the other end came back to her hand, Tina grabbed the chain and wrapped it around herself, locking them together.

"Idiot child!" the Once King bellowed when he realized what she had done. "Did you forget that you are no longer a stonekin?" He took a step forward, dragging her effortlessly with him. "You cannot stop me alone!"

"I'm not alone," Tina said, clutching the chains tight. "And even you can't counterspell twenty-five people at once."

"I don't have to," the Once King spat. "I will break them instead. They cannot channel mana if they are dead!"

"We'll see about that," Tina snarled, checking her internal count. Five seconds left. Good enough.

"Sorry, pal," she said, slamming her feet into the stone floor. "Buck stops here. *Steady Ground!*"

The words were still leaving her lips as the terrace's paving stones turned to bedrock around her feet, transforming Tina into an unmovable anchor. Realizing he was trapped with her, the Once King began to strain against the chains tying them together, denting her armor in the process. But sun steel was not broken so easily. Neither were the stone-enchanted chains, especially at this angle. She might not be as good at grappling as James was, but while she hated it with a passion, Tina hadn't entirely escaped PvP as a stonekin. She knew how hard it was to get someone off your back when you were huge and they were small. Even when the Once King did manage to grab hold of her shoulder, he lacked the leverage to rip her free, breaking her collarbone instead as he roared in impotent fury.

Zero seconds left.

"Roxxy!" Richard screamed, his panicked voice coming right on time. "We've lost control!"

"That's fine!" she shouted. And then, because this was how one ruined surprise attacks, she yelled out, "*Do it now!*"

The words worked like a charm. All at once, the Once King stopped thrashing and looked up. Tina looked up as well, peering between the king's ashy wings.

The multielemental storm filled the sky. Flame-lightning crashed wildly from cloud to cloud, striking not in single strikes but entire sheets. Black-gold clouds roiled with enough power to sink entire battle fleets, and the winds howled like the eye-wall of a category five hurricane. Below it, her casters had collapsed, their faces terrified as they screamed about losing control, but Tina didn't see how such a giant storm could ever be *in* control. Already, the wind wall was spinning even faster, whipping up fire tornadoes whose points were already extending toward the lightning-lit mountain below. It was easily the most terrifying thing Tina had ever seen, and she'd seen some doozies over the last week and a half. She was still staring in wonder when the ancient king she was tied to began to laugh.

"A marvel of casting," he said appreciatively. "Truly, you players are masters of destruction. But while that storm is more than enough to kill all of you, it will not kill me."

"Maybe not like this," Tina said, summoning up all her courage as she stared at the wonder her guild had made. "But that much storm concentrated down to a single point? That's another story."

The Once King looked down in confusion, but Tina just clenched him harder, reminding herself that she was the glorious guild leader of the Roughnecks. Even when she'd gone from being Roxxy to Tina, they'd acknowledged her, listened to her. Several of them were probably *dying* for her right now. She would never let down that trust, and she would *never* allow them to lose. At this final moment, when it counted most, she would lead them all to the victory their bravery so richly deserved.

With that, Tina turned her face to the sky and hurled all of that determination—*her* determination—at the storm, challenging the heavens themselves as she yelled out.

"One For All!"

380

The entire storm froze. For one terrifying moment, the enormous spinning clouds were as still as stones. Then, like she'd just kicked the whole thing into overdrive, they started to spin much, *much* faster. Already-hurricane-force winds began howling like band saws as the eye of the storm shrank in toward Tina, concentrating the flames, lightning, and holy power into a frantically spinning blender of blindingly violent power aimed straight at her...and the king she'd chained herself to.

"Eat it, fucker!" she yelled as all hell and fury descended upon them.

"*No!*" the Once King cried, his normally booming voice filled with panic for the first time. "I cannot perish here! Not yet!" Tina felt the universe itself heaving as the ancient elf reached for his mana, the last of the Eternal Sky that lived within him. "Great Pyre, *your master commands you!*"

Ghostly screams exploded into Tina's ears as the Once King's entire body erupted in a bonfire of blue-white flame. Then Tina was screaming too, writhing against the chains in agony as the ghostfire ate her alive. It hurt like nothing had ever hurt before, but somehow she held on. Even when her flesh scorched and her armor superheated around her, turning the world white with pain, she did not let go.

She would *never* let go.

Roaring in fury, the king thrust his hands aloft, hurling a torrent of ghostfire at the eye of the still-concentrating storm Tina had called down on them both. The elemental hurricane tilted as the ghostfire slammed into it, but it didn't stop spinning. Chest heaving, the Once King reached into himself again, pouring more and more of his mana into the ghostfire that was searing the sky. As it burned, Tina felt her One For All ability straining, pulling against his pushing as they fought over the storm. For several long seconds, the two of them hung in balance, and then the raging storm snapped as the ghostfire won out, blowing the spinning clouds apart in a flash of power that ate all sound and whited out the world.

For a moment, Tina could feel nothing. She couldn't hear, couldn't see. The world was just white and stillness. If she wasn't already so experienced with the feeling, she would have thought she was dead. But she knew death in this place, and this pale quiet was nothing like it. It was just shock, which meant there was nothing to do but wait it out until, in bits and pieces, the world began to come back.

The first thing she felt was the chain. The enchanted links, once strong enough to bind the Once King himself, were now brittle as ash in her hands. They crumbled when she moved her fingers, leaving her slumped against the smoking armor of the Once King. Her armor wasn't much better. The whole front of her suit was half melted and steaming, the inside hot enough to singe her flesh and turn her padding to charcoal. But for all the pain, she was still alive. And so was her enemy.

"You have failed," the Once King whispered, breathing hard as he broke away from her at last. Then he pointed up at the sky, which was once again covered in the Deadlands' flat gray clouds. "Your ultimate attack is done, and still I breathe." He sneered at her. "I've won."

"Not hardly," Tina gasped back, sucking a breath into her ragged lungs for one last cry. "*Hit it, James!*"

The Once King jerked and whirled around, his eyes landing on James a second too late. Her brother was already standing at the center of the circular terrace, his tall body lit up with the glare of all his mana as he threw his hands skyward, launching a spell. What spell, Tina didn't know, and she didn't care. The panicked look on the Once King's face was all she needed. Desperately, he tossed her aside and extended his hand for a counterspell, but nothing happened, because they'd done it. They'd drained his mana dry, leaving him with nothing to stop James as his magic leaped up toward the heavens, splitting the Deadlands' heavy clouds like a knife to let the golden sunlight through.

***

James stood on the broken battlefield, his heart pounding. It had taken everything he had to get out here, to walk past dying friends without dropping even a tiny heal. Seeing Tina had been the hardest. His little sister looked like a burn victim, tiny as a sparrow in the Once King's looming shadow. That had almost broken him, but then he'd seen the grin on her face. Heard the trust in her voice as she yelled for him to do it.

How could he let her down?

With that, James had grabbed his mana, all of it, and honed it to a point. The counterspell was an ability every caster class learned. It was so simple in concept, just a spike of mana you used to pry apart your enemy's magic, but even the easiest things became hard when you upped the scale, and James had never gone bigger. Even the ritual to summon the Bedrock Kings seemed trivial compared to the blade of magic he stabbed into the sky. The blade made from himself, for it was *all* his mana. There was no wind, no water, just the pure memory of the Unbounded Sky that lived inside him, inside every descendant of the Celestial Elves. How fitting, he thought, that that power should be what saved them all now, shooting into the sky like a spear to pierce the ghostfire-fueled magic binding the clouds together.

And it was *just* enough.

Once again, he whispered a silent thanks to his brother for his new armor. The level-eighty gear had increased his mana pool even more than he'd initially thought, giving him the capacity to hold all the power he was now using to rip open the sky. As his magic tore the clouds apart, all James could think was that the jubatus of Windy Lake had been justified in their fear. Players *were* terrifying. They were unspeakably powerful and unspeakably ignorant, but they could learn. He just hoped he'd learned enough to guess this right as his counterspell ripped the clouds apart, exposing the Deadlands to the light of the Sun for the first time in a thousand years. And as the golden light burst forth, the Once King cried out as he never had before, not even when Tina had slammed a zone-sized magical storm into him.

"*NO!*"

The king lunged forward, tossing Tina aside like so much trash to charge at James. "*Never!*" he roared, his ageless face a mask of fury. "I will tear you apart with my own hands before I allow you to—"

"*Resplendent Aegis!*"

The warbling voice was Anders's, but the power inside it was something James had felt before only once, when the Bastion had activated. All at once, golden light surrounded him, stopping the Once King's charge cold. The ancient elf cried out in pain and jumped away, abandoning his attack to flee back toward the stairs instead, but James was having none of it.

"No!" he yelled as the sunlight poured down. "No more hiding in the shadows! It's time for you to face this!" He whirled back to the remains of the caster camp, where Anders was the only one standing, his small fishy-form bathed in radiant light that did not belong to him. "Do it again!"

The Cleric—a true Cleric now, James realized—raised his staff in triumph, his fish face bathed in the wonder and understanding of someone who'd finally found the answer he'd searched for all his life.

"*Resplendent Aegis!*"

Again, the golden light poured down from the sky, blocking the Once King's escape back into his mountain. Stuck in the blinding light, the king roared with a fury greater than anything James had ever experienced. Great and *deep*, the sort of whole-self emotion that changes lives forever. As if it could hear the Once King's anger, the sunlight streaming down grew even brighter, bathing the mountain in light so intense that the dark stone glittered like desert sand.

But though it was easily the strongest sunlight James had ever felt, it did not burn. Quite the opposite. Wherever the golden light touched him, his body felt renewed. His mana was still empty, but the accompanying exhaustion vanished completely in the warmth of the Sun's light, and he wasn't the only one.

Across the terrace, Tina stood up, her burns fading away before his eyes. The healing touched her golden armor as well. James didn't know if that was because her suit was made from sun steel or if the god was simply that powerful, but the dented, melted plates turned to molten gold as he watched, flowing back into their usual perfect shape while Tina stared in awe. Others were getting up too now. Frank, SilentBlayde, Zen, all the Roughnecks who'd used their lives to block the Once King's way rose back to their feet whole and unharmed.

But as the light lifted all of them up, it sent the Once King to his knees. Crying, the king cursed the dazzling brilliance, using his huge wings to shade his face from the Sun riding at the zenith of the sky. This time, though, there was no hiding. Anders hadn't cast the spell a third time, but James felt the power of the Resplendent Aegis slam down yet again, trapping the Once King in a sphere of golden light. As the barrier solidified, James felt something else condensing in the air.

Something unfathomably immense was turning its attention to the mountaintop. From the horror on the Once King's face, James had a good guess as to what, but he didn't dare speak. He didn't dare do anything but fall to his knees as the light grew stronger and stronger, brighter and brighter, until...

"*No!*" the king cried, lifting his head at last to bare his bloody teeth at the blinding sky. "You can force me to kneel, but I will *never* acknowledge you again! You were our light, our hope, and our love, and you betrayed us! You burned the Moon! You cast your children into damnation! Your radiance may be enough to dazzle these short-lived idiots, but I *know* you! I know your evil, and I will *never rest* until I have freed this world from what you have done to us!"

He was screaming by the end, his furious words echoing across the mountain, but the light did not answer. It simply bore down on them all even harder, filling the air with an emotion so huge, James thought it would break him apart.

SORROW.

The world went blurry as his eyes filled with tears. It wasn't even his sorrow, but the god's feeling was greater than any sadness he'd ever experienced, breaking his heart even as he struggled to understand why. There was no context, no reason, just a secondhand sadness so strong it threatened to drown him. Struggling to hold himself together, James pitied the Sun in that moment. He knew instinctively that it had no words with which to explain itself, no way to translate such divine emotions into something lesser beings could understand. It could only show them, beaming its great sorrow down from the heavens in the hope that its target would understand. Since the Once King had the same tears in his eyes as the rest of them, James hoped he did.

Then the king spoke, and all his high hopes fell.

"It is too late for petty regrets," the first born of creation growled, glaring up at the sky with a hate so old and deep even the sorrow of a god couldn't move it. "And not even you can stop me now! Your chosen king has lost! The armies of Bastion are being defeated even as we speak, and these players are all but dead. Your light may have healed their wounds, but mana belongs to the Sky! Theirs is gone, and you cannot restore it! Without it, I will kill them easily. I will kill *everything,* and you will be forced to watch, as helpless as I was when you burned my people and threw them to the ground!"

He started crying then. A great king on his knees, sobbing in fury like a child. It would have been pathetic if it hadn't been so sad.

"I will free them," he whispered, fisting his hands on the sun-warmed stone. "I will take back my people, the souls you stole from me! I will free us all, and then I will never have to see you again."

The king was still crying when a beam of sunlight struck the ground in front of him. It grew brighter as James watched, its golden hue turning yellow then white. It shivered as it changed, glittering like sunlight on water.

Then, in a move James's mind couldn't wrap itself around, the light grew solid, taking on the form of a person.

Not an actual person. This shape was vague and featureless and even taller than the Once King. But there was something unmistakably human about the way it dropped to one knee, reaching out a brilliant golden hand to touch the ancient elf's soiled wing.

The Once King froze. Then his ashen face lifted, his teary eyes wide as a child's as his wings folded flat against his back in awe. "How?" he whispered, his voice so breathy and quiet that James had to strain to hear. "I've never heard of... Never seen...How are you here?"

"For...you..."

James clapped his hands over his ears. The golden figure had no mouth that he could see, but its whisper was as huge as the mountain. The figure's edges blurred as it spoke, obviously holding itself together with great difficulty. Given what he'd learned of the gods, James supposed it would be very difficult for something so huge to make itself this small, but the Sun was trying, crouching closer to its kneeling creation as it struggled to form the words.

"I...am...sorry," it said in that world-sized whisper. *"For...what...I did."*

The words came out halting and slow, each one clearly the product of great work. It was trying so hard, but the Once King was having none of it.

"Why?" he demanded, his vaunted royal composure shattering as he stabbed an accusing finger at the avatar. "Why did you burn us? What did we do?!"

"Nothing," the Sun said. *"You...did...nothing wrong. It was...accident."*

The Once King's face went from furious to horrified. "Impossible," he spat. "It *can't* be that simple."

"But...it was," the god whispered, the strained golden voice so sad. *"I...loved the...Moon...too much, I loved. My partner. My balance. So much, I loved.....that I flew too close. I only wanted to be nearer...but I....I burned."* The

387

golden avatar dropped its huge head, bending down almost to the ground. "...
I am so sorry."

"How can you be sorry?" the Once King asked, but not in accusation.
He seemed truly baffled, as if his world had just been turned upside down
and violently shaken. "You are perfect. You are the *Sun!*"

"*I am finite,*" the Sun replied. "*And therefore...fallible.*"

"But I trusted you to save us!" the Once King cried, clenching his
fists. "You told us to fly up to you, and then you burned off my people's
wings! Was *that* an accident?"

"*No,*" the Sun said. "*That was trying to...fix. I could not return you to the
Endless Sky...Without the Sky, your wings were a curse. I did not want you
to...suffer...So I took...them away.*"

"Took them away?" the king repeated, furious. "You mutilated my
people!"

The avatar shook its head. "*They do not suffer. You have seen them
happy and thriving...granted eternal rebirth by...the Moon's mercy...*" The figure
reached out again. "*My first and precious child, I wish I could take your wings
too...You are owed peace more than any other...You have tried so hard for so long to
do what is right. You deserve...rest.*"

The Once King recoiled from the golden hand. "I cannot accept this,"
he spat. "There is no rest in an endless cycle! We must end. It is the only way
to escape!"

The avatar of the Sun moved closer, leaning in until the Once King's
long hair began to singe and crinkle.

"*You are not doomed...*" it whispered. "*And you were never alone...I loved
my children always...watched you, always...I hear and answer your prayers. I put
my light inside each of you, to protect your souls when they pass through the
Lightless Realm. We are still together...always...Come home.*"

The Once King lowered his head with a sob. Even without seeing his
face, James could feel the king's longing, his desperation to run back into his
creator's light, but he did not move.

"If you are right," he said at last in a dark, quivering voice, "then I am wrong. Terribly, horribly, unforgivably wrong for so many years." He took a shuddering breath. Then, to James's almost mortal shock, the Once King's arm flew up to point at him. "Even *he* knew it, and he hasn't been here two weeks!" The king buried his face in his hands. "How was I so wrong?"

The Sun said nothing. Instead, it turned its formless face to James, who was almost knocked over by the force of such direct, divine attention. Despite the burning terror, though, James knew why. This wasn't something the god could say. There was too much anger, too much resentment. For these words to be heard, they had to come from another. The Sun, in its wisdom, understood that. James thought he did, too. He just hoped he was up to the task.

"Even the Sun makes mistakes," he said gently, breathing deeply to hide how badly he was shaking. "But you can move on. If a god can admit it is wrong and seek forgiveness, surely you can, too."

"How?" the Once King asked bitterly. "I am the enemy of all life. All this world sees me as such—you said so yourself. How can I come back from that? How can I be forgiven?"

James shot a nervous look at the Sun, but the god remained silent, giving him no help. "That's the mercy of rebirth," James said at last, hoping he was right. "Everyone makes mistakes, everyone does wrong, but there's always another day. We always get to try again."

"But the hatred lives on," the king said, staring down at the ground. "I may die, but I will be hated forever."

"You can't make people forgive you," James admitted. "But you can forgive yourself, and you can *stop* doing the things that hurt everyone so much. You can't change the past, but you don't have to let it rule your future, either. You can always choose to be better. There is *always* a way forward. Time takes us all to new places eventually. You just have to let yourself go there."

The Once King said nothing, just lowered his head to the ground. Then, in a tiny voice, he whispered, "I am sorry."

James jumped in surprise and looked at the Sun, but the god shook its head. *"That is not for me,"* it whispered in its booming voice. *"I am owed no...apology. It is for you."*

James nodded, understanding the Sun didn't mean him in particular. The Once King's apology was for everyone, all the souls he'd trapped in the name of freeing them. But as the Once King had just told the Sun, words were not enough.

"If you're sorry, then fix it," James said, crouching down beside the king. "Put out the ghostfire and let your followers rest. Stop the undead before they really do kill off the last of Bastion. Free the souls you've trapped so that they may be born again. Send home the players you trapped here. You may not be able to force people to forgive you, but you can give them a reason to try. If you are truly sorry, then mend your wrongs. Show it in deeds, not just words, and I think you'll be surprised."

The Sun nodded in agreement. *"He speaks...wisely."*

The Once King's head shot up at that. "You're not going to punish me?" he asked, shocked. "But what of the monstrous things I've done?"

"I could ask the same...of you," the Sun whispered, its avatar wobbling. *"I burned the Moon...I ended the Endless Sky...I did not mean it, but the fault was...mine. Can you still love me?"*

"I never stopped," the Once King said, his body sagging. "How else could I have been so mad?"

"You forgive me?"

The king nodded, and James felt the golden avatar smile. *"If you can forgive me...after so...long. Then there is nothing that...cannot be forgiven."*

The Once King took a deep breath. James did too, impressed. Truly, the Sun was a wise god. Even Tina looked like she was eating it up, and she normally hated this stuff. But while the god was beaming with a job well done, the Once King looked more lost than ever.

"But what do I do now?" he asked the Sun, looking down at his hands. "I don't...I don't want to die. I was willing to do so for my people, but now..." He took a deep breath, his face conflicted. "I must die, though. How else am I to be reborn?"

"*You are already...born anew,*" the Sun said, reaching out to touch his face, but careful—oh so careful—not to burn it. "*My dearest child...every day is a new life. You do not have...to die. The only thing you have to do...is live.*"

With that, the blinding figure vanished, leaving them all blinking sunspots out of their eyes. The intense light faded next, leaving them standing on the broken mountaintop in the perfectly normal light of a bright summer afternoon. Even the chill of the Deadlands was gone, replaced by the refreshing cool of the high mountains. The Once King breathed it in deep, raising his face to the bright sky overhead.

"It is gone," he whispered.

"I don't think the Sun is ever really gone," James said, approaching the huge king nervously. When the elf didn't move, he glanced at Tina. This turned out to be a bad idea, because his sister started frantically motioning for him to do something, but James had no idea what. How did you follow up for a god? Fortunately for him, though, the Once King was still a king. Monarchs did not remain indecisive for long, or on their knees. It took a few moments, but eventually he got back to his feet, looking around at the players he'd been frantically trying to kill not five minutes earlier with an expression that—on a lesser face—James would have called sheepish.

"It appears matters have changed," he announced regally, brushing the burned blood off his armor self-consciously as he turned to Tina. "We have much to discuss."

"You bet your winged ass we do," Tina said, folding her arms over her chest. "But let's start with your army that's attacking—"

"Already stopped," the king assured her. When Tina arched a skeptical eyebrow, he explained, "I control all undead, sentient or otherwise. My army stopped in its tracks the moment the Sun asked my forgiveness."

From anyone else, that would have sounded cocky, but from the Once King, it just sounded sad. Sad and heavy with the regret of a man who had just realized how much of his life he had wasted. James could absolutely relate, and he walked forward to put his hand on the king's arm with a warm smile. "Well," he said cheerily. "Since no one's dying right this very second, we have time to talk. Let's start with my brother. Is he...?"

"Undead?" the Once King finished. "No. He was faking being dead when I passed, or perhaps passed out. Either way, I was in a hurry and didn't consider him worth the effort, so I shoved his body into one of the zombie spawners."

James recoiled in horror. "You put Fangs in a *zombie spawner?*"

"I figured it would save time later when he inevitably died and turned," the Once King said with a practical shrug. "I didn't feel his soul join the Pyre, though, so he's probably still in there."

"Right," James said, turning to his sister. "Why don't you two find somewhere to negotiate. I'm going to rescue my brother."

"Don't take too long," Tina said, eying the Once King warily as James turned and started running toward the stairs.

"Be careful with Angry Cat!" Neko yelled after him. "He's going to die legit when he hears us players saved the world!"

That was both more and less true than she knew, but James didn't have time to explain. He was already loping down the stairs toward the throne room, scrambling to remember where all the zombie spawners in the Royal Quarter were so he could narrow down which one the Once King had unceremoniously crammed his brother into.

Chapter 16
James and Tina

As the Once King had said, James did indeed find his brother in a zombie spawner. Thankfully, it was an empty one, and the warrior was unconscious. James made sure to drag him well away before he started the heals, though, because the hidden chute in the wall that dropped undead behind player raids was disgusting. Not as gross as it could have been—the Once King's undead weren't as drippy as movies would have one believe— but dead bodies were still dead bodies, and they got *rank*.

Trying not to gag, James dragged his brother to the center of the hallway that led to the Once King's throne room and sat down to mana up. There wasn't much dried meat left in his pack since he'd already done this once today, but he got enough in to cast a healing spell big enough to at least wake the warrior up.

"Ugh," Fangs said, his cat eyes blinking open. Then they spotted James, and the warrior sat up so fast he nearly passed out again.

"Easy!" James said, helping him back down. "I only had enough mana to get you out of danger. If you crack your head open on the granite, we're in trouble."

"My head is not afraid of floors," Ar'Bati replied in such a deadpan voice that James had no idea if he was joking or not. "More importantly, you are here and alive. Does that mean we won?"

"Yeah," James said, smiling widely. "We did. We did win!"

He got more excited with every word. There'd been so much going on that he hadn't had time to fully realize what they'd just accomplished. The undead had stopped. The war was over. No one had died! They were all going to *live*!

Whooping with victory, James grabbed his brother in a huge bear hug. "We won, Fangs!!" he cried, jumping up and down. "*We did it!*"

"Ow," was his brother's only reply.

393

"Sorry," James said, releasing his hold on his brother's chest, which still had a hole that was only minimally healed.

"Never be sorry for celebrating a victory," Ar'Bati said, clearly striving to be tough despite the pain on his face. "So the Once King is dead?"

James frowned. "Not exactly…"

"Defeated, then?" the cat warrior pressed. "Bound in chains to pay for his crimes?"

"It's kind of hard to explain," James said slowly. "But I'll try."

***

"Let me be sure I've got this straight," Ar'Bati said, tail lashing. "Your sister cornered the Once King into a trap that forced his surrender, and then you summoned the Sun to talk some sense into him?"

That wasn't how it had gone down at all, but they'd been here so long already that James had recovered enough mana to drop another heal on his brother, and he wasn't telling this story again. "Sure," James said, exhausted. "Whatever. The important thing is that the Once King's agreed to stop attacking, and now we're negotiating. We need to be polite and keep an open mind."

"I'm not forgetting what he's done," Fangs growled. "His lich tortured me for hours untold! My sister had to suffer undeath thousands of times because of him!"

"I'm not asking you to forgive anything," James assured him. "But I do need you to listen. This is important. What we do here and now will shape the future of this entire world. We just ended a thousand-year war. Let's not start another one just yet, okay?"

"If the Sun itself could forgive the undead, then I suppose I can be civil," the warrior grumbled, lashing his tail. "But no more than civil."

"Good enough," James said, rising to his feet. "Let's go. Everyone's waiting on us."

Ar'Bati lifted his hands for James to pull him up, and then, leaning on each other, the two brothers started down the long, far-too-large-to-be-practical hall toward the throne room, which was open and full of people. All of the Roughnecks were there, and surprisingly, so were the Red Sands. The PvPers were all injured, and several had the shaky, thousand-yard stare of the recently resurrected, but they were alive, which seemed like a miracle given how much blood was splattered across the hallway leading in.

The throne room itself was clean, though. Someone had cleared all the rubble from the ceiling collapse *and* scoured the blood off the stone floor. They'd even righted the toppled throne, which made James suspect this was the Once King's work. Strange as it was to imagine the giant king cleaning up, imagining him holding court in a filthy, wrecked throne room was even more implausible. His pride would never allow it. He was actually up on his dais right now, though he was not sitting on his throne, probably because it would be too awkward sitting on the cursed Eclipsed Steel after making up with the Sun. Or maybe he just felt like standing. Either way, the king was clearly tired of waiting, gesturing impatiently at James the moment he walked in to come and join him and Tina on the dais steps.

"Now that we are *all* here," he said, his voice back to its usual imperiousness as James leaned his still-wobbly adopted brother against a pillar and took his place on the stairs. "Let us begin negotiations."

There was a long pause, and Tina leaned over to James. "That's you," she whispered.

"But you're the great general," he whispered back.

"Exactly," she said. "I'm the stick, not the carrot. You're the one who always wanted to be a diplomat, so diplomat him!"

James didn't think she could use "diplomat" as a verb like that, but he cleared his throat anyway. "Your Majesty," he began, trying not to think about how terrifying it still was to be the object of the Once King's direct attention. "You have already ended the war in the Savanna, and for that we are very grateful. However, much damage has been done. The city of Bastion lies in ruins, and hundreds of thousands of lives have been lost. Many of those souls are trapped in your ghostfire. I would ask that you release them."

"And send us home!" a raider from the back yelled out.

The Once King scowled at the outburst, and then he sighed. "What you ask is complicated," he said, his ash-gray wings twitching like drumming fingers. "The ghostfire was created to keep souls out of the Moon's cycle of reincarnation, which I now understand to be folly, but it is also the source of my power. I used it to bring you all here in the first place. Without it, I do not have the magic necessary to send you home."

"That's fine," Tina said. "You're quitting the Evil Undead Overlord gig, right? If you're not running zombie armies and doom fortresses anymore, what do you need ghostfire for? Let's burn it up and get us home!"

"What do you think it burns?" the Once King asked coldly. "It is *ghost*fire. Its necromantic flames are fed by the very souls I now know I must free. If I 'burn it up,' as you so crudely suggest, I'll be continuing the wrong actions that led me to this point in the first place."

Tina's face fell in despair. James didn't blame her. That was a pretty big catch, but he wasn't giving up. "How do we free the souls from the ghostfire?"

"That is...tricky," the Once King admitted, his expression grim. "When I created the ghostfire, I did not plan on ever reversing it. I do not honestly know if it *can* be reversed. It is a combination of the Sun's fire and death, neither of which is simple to undo. Just as a log fed into a blazing hearth cannot be pulled back out again whole and uncharred, a soul fed into the ghostfire is forever changed. I don't know if I can retrieve them."

"Well, that's just great," Tina said, throwing up her hands. "We're screwed."

"Don't give up hope yet," James said, thinking the problem through. "'Changed' is different from 'gone.' The pile of Celestial Elves in the Great Pyre proves that souls can burn for a *really* long time without being destroyed. Those are the bodies of Ar'Kan's very first followers, the ones whose deaths created the ghostfire in the first place. If they're still in there, then everyone else must be, too."

"But how do we get them out?" Tina asked. "And if we do, how does anyone get home?"

"I don't know," James said, turning back to the king. "We saw you in Bastion, but you only appeared briefly. According to the wiki, you're trapped in this mountain because you can't go far from the Great Pyre. Is that correct?"

The Once King nodded. "The flames require constant tending. If I leave it for too long, the Pyre will burn down, and my powers will fade." He turned to glare at Tina's Ranger leader, Zen. "You clearly know this."

The green-haired elf smirked, unrepentant, and James hurried to get things back on track. "But that's good!" he said quickly. "If the Great Pyre is full of souls *and* the flames are constantly in danger of burning out, that means there must be some part of those souls that the ghostfire can't burn. I mean, you've got people who've been in there for a thousand years! If they haven't been consumed yet, they're not gonna be. They're just trapped in there. But if you stop stoking the fire and let it burn out, there will be nothing holding them down anymore, and they'll be free to go back into the Moon's cycle."

The Once King looked down, clearly deeply disturbed by this idea. "I....I see no technical reason this would not be true," he said at last. "But you must understand, those are my people's souls. I've tended the fire for so long, I don't know what will happen if I stop. The souls trapped inside could be consumed entirely and be gone. That was always my intention, the reason the ghostfire exists. I don't know if it can be thwarted."

"That doesn't make sense, though," Tina said stubbornly. "I don't know diddly about magic, but if all those souls haven't burned up yet, I don't see how they're going to suddenly poof the moment you stop feeding new fuel into the flames. That's not how fires work. Stuff either burns or it doesn't."

"She's right," James said, grinning. "There's clearly something enduring about the soul, or it wouldn't be able to survive passing through the Lightless Realm over and over again. The Sun said it put its essence in all of you so that you could pass through death without fear, but I wouldn't be surprised if that gift had other benefits as well. I mean, it would make sense that sunfire wouldn't burn."

The Once King covered his face with his hands. "It is true," he whispered in a small voice. "It seems even in my greatest heresy, the Sun never abandoned us. But if I haven't been actually burning the souls, what *have* I been burning?"

"You already answered that yourself," James said, his eyes going wide as it all came together. "It's hate. Your drive for revenge, the fury of the original Celestial Elves, all the sorrow and rage of the people whose lives were cut short by your undead, *those* emotions are what fan the flames. That's why the ghostfire always felt so angry and out of control even though you were calm. *And* that's why it needs constant feeding to stay going. It's a *literal* fire of hate."

"Then we should put it out," Tina said.

"It'll do that all on its own," James assured her, turning back to Ar'Kan. "You built the ghostfire out of death and anger, but it's still a fire, and that belongs to the Sun. You told me the original spark for the ghostfire came from one of the Sun's own embers after the Conflagration, but you fought that fire alongside the Wind and the Water. You *know* how hard it is to put out! The fact that the ghostfire requires constant tending *proves* that it's not as strong as the spark of the Sun that helped create it. The only reason it's still here is because you've been feeding it with your resentment and hatred all these years. But if you just *stop*, the ghostfire will burn out all on its own, and all the souls trapped inside will be free."

His eyes flicked to Ar'Bati as he spoke. The circumstances were entirely different, but those were almost the exact same words James had said to his brother in the gnolls' wagon back in the Savanna. He was worried

Fangs would take offense at the implicit comparison, but the warrior was nodding in agreement. The Once King was nodding, too, though he did not look nearly as confident.

"I believe you," he said. "But I am still afraid. I have been the master of this fire for so long that my name has become synonymous with it. It is the center of everything I've built. If I let it die, what will I have left?"

"You have an entire world," James said. "You're the king of a race of born explorers, but you haven't even been outside of this fortress in a thousand years! Don't you want to see what your people have built over their many lives? Aren't you curious?"

The king looked down, so James stepped forward, putting himself directly in the towering monarch's vision. "Remember what the Sun said," he whispered. "The ghostfire was your prison, too. If you let it go, you won't just be freeing the souls trapped inside. You'll be free as well. You're the only Celestial Elf left who still has his wings. Don't you want to fly?"

"More than you can ever know," the elf replied. Then he took a deep breath. "I have come to a decision," he announced. "I have many sins to atone for. Wrongs done to my people and to you." He nodded down at the players. "This isn't even your world, but I still found a way to hurt you, and for that I am deeply sorry. As an act of repentance, I will use the last of the ghostfire's power to send back to Earth any who wish to go. When it is done, the fire's power will be consumed. It will burn out, and those trapped inside will be free to be reborn, as will I."

The finality in his voice as he said that made James panic. "What do you mean?" he demanded. "You're not going to—"

"Take my own life?" The Once King shook his head. "No. My god bade me live, and it is long past time I listened. But my immortality came from the Eternal Sky, and that is forever lost to me. Though I still have my wings and my nature, I am trapped by the Moon's pull same as everything else. The only reason I have lived on as long as I have is because I, too, burned in the ghostfire. Without it, my eternal life will end. Not instantly, but time will wear me down the same as any other, and that is fine. I am no longer afraid of death, nor do I long for it. I have been obsessed with endings for far, far too long. I am eager to try actually being alive."

He chuckled, smiling down at James. "You see?" he said quietly. "I am not too old to learn."

James nodded, too choked with emotion to answer. All this time, all his pushing for the Once King to let go of the ghostfire, he hadn't realized he was asking the elf to give up his own life. Knowing that now made him feel horrible, but the king actually looked more relaxed than James had ever seen him. He was even smiling. The expression made his timeless face look young and even more perfect, which scarcely seemed possible.

"Well, this is great and all," Tina said, breaking the moment. "But I believe you just said you'd send us home, and I'd like to get on with that. I've got a lot of promises to keep and a lot of people who want to get back while they still have bodies to go home *to*."

"Of course," the Once King said, stepping down off the dais. "Follow me."

He led the players back up the spiral stair to the top of the mountain. The peak was warm and sunny when they arrived, the broken terrace looking almost picturesque with its epic three hundred sixty–degree view of the surrounding snowcapped mountains and the Deadlands, which now looked white rather than gray in the full light of the sun.

"Whoa," Tina said, looking around in wonder. "I am *never* gonna get used to that."

"It does look very different than it did when we were raiding," SilentBlayde agreed, leaning in to kiss her.

James did a double take. "Wait," he said, rushing over to them. "Wait, wait, *wait*. Are you guys actually together now?!"

SB and Tina shared a smirk. "Oh, we're together all right," his sister said, trying and failing to hold in her laughter. "We kind of got married."

James stared at them, his eyes going wider and wider. "You got *married?*" he squeaked at last. "H-how? *When?!*"

"Garrond did it this morning," Tina said happily, leaning into SB, who looked like he was going to float away. "It was a bit of a battlefield wedding, but hell if I was dying without..." She trailed off, her brown eyes going wide in horror. "Oh *shit,* where's Garrond?! We totally forgot him! He'd better not be dead."

"He is not dead," the Once King said, his booming voice making all three of them jump. When they whirled around, the king looked slightly embarrassed.

"Even now that I am no longer catching their souls, I can still feel whenever someone dies in my mountain," he explained. "Commander Garrond survived everything I threw at him. He was still fighting when I bid my armies cease."

"That's fantastic!" Tina cried, grinning widely. "Though I'm not surprised. Dude is the Energizer paladin. He takes a licking and just keeps on ticking. But if he's alive, why isn't he here?"

The Once King's look of embarrassment deepened. "Garrond is a paladin of the Order of the Golden Sun. He's devoted his entire life to destroying me. I...did not wish to deal with him just yet, so I locked him in Sanguilar's chamber."

"Holy crap, he's still in there?" Tina said, blanching. "He's going to be pissed as shit."

"He and his remaining soldiers are currently building a battering ram to bash down the doors I closed," the Once King confirmed. "He's a long way from breaking through, but I have no doubt he will make it eventually, which is why we should make haste. I'd like to have all complications with your world settled before I begin the long process of atonement in this one."

James could see how making peace with Garrond was going to be tricky, or impossible, but that was Ar'Kan's bear to wrestle. He'd done his part. Now it was time to go home.

So he, Tina, and SB walked up to join the rest of the raiders who were gathered around the Great Pyre. The crowd parted wide to let the Once King through as he walked up to the giant metal brazier. When he reached the fire, he thrust his hands into it. As always, the flames came to him eagerly, but it was clear he no longer delighted in their power. Instead, the king looked sad—horribly, shatteringly sad as he clutched the blue-white fire to his chest.

"Not much longer, old friends," he whispered. "One last miracle, and then you shall rest at last. I promise."

James looked down at his feet. The magical interaction was fascinating—he could actually see the dark shadows of the death magic wrapping around the ancient king like encircling arms—but watching felt wrong, like he was intruding on something personal and intimate. He stared down at the broken paving instead, distracting himself by wondering how much of the blood that still stained it was Tina's until, at last, the Once King stepped back.

"*Rise!*" the elf ordered, throwing up his hands. The ghostfire obeyed at once, shooting up to the sky in a screaming pillar. When it was so high James could no longer see the top, the Once King clapped his palms together and brought his arms back down.

"*Return!*"

The word echoed over the mountains like thunder. The tower of ghostfire roared in response, collapsing back down into itself to form a swirling vortex in front of the Great Pyre's brazier. Everyone except the Once King jumped back when it landed, covering their faces against the necromantic fire's burning cold. When James finally managed to look up again, what he saw was not what he'd expected.

The Great Pyre was still there, still burning merrily, but it was *much* smaller, and in front of it was a portal. It actually looked just like the portals from back in the game, except this one was ringed with ghostfire rather than myriad magical colors, and the place he could see shimmering on the other side wasn't anywhere in FFO. It was a highway. A four-lane American highway complete with green road signs and panicking traffic. Probably somewhere in the southwest given the arid landscape, but James couldn't actually read the signs through the shimmering magic, so it was impossible to be more specific than that.

"There," the king said, his chest heaving with effort as he turned back to the players. "You are free to go."

"Holy Toledo!" NekoBaby cried, bounding up to the portal's edge. "So we just go through this and what? We're back in our old bodies again?"

"Those of you who still have bodies will be instantly transported back to them the moment you step through," the Once King said. "Those of you whose bodies have died will retain the forms you inhabit now."

"Wait, really?" ZeroDarkness said, his cat jaw hanging open. "So if I'm dead over there, and I walk through, I stay a jubatus? Like, walking down the highway?"

The Once King nodded proudly. "It took a great deal of magic and finesse to make that possible, but I wanted no one to be harmed by my actions any more than you already have been." He smiled. "Think of this as my apology gift."

"Fuckin-A!" NekoBaby cried, running back to hug Tina. "Girl, I'm gonna miss you! Those other guilds are shit."

"Hold on," Tina said, clutching Neko to her partially out of friendship but mostly to keep her from running off. "Wait, wait, wait, this is too fast. We're here, but what about all the other players? This world is full of people who want to go home, but they're scattered all over. Hell, we left thousands in the Savanna. That's on another continent! How long does this portal last?"

"It is tied to the ghostfire," the Once King said. "It will remain open for as long as the Great Pyre burns."

"How long is that?" Tina demanded.

The elf glanced over his shoulder at the flames. "It is difficult to say. A year, perhaps? Maybe slightly less."

Tina sagged in relief. "Thank god. I thought you were going to say fifteen minutes or something. A year we can work with."

"Is it one way?" James asked, staring through the portal at the people he could see getting out of their cars on the other side.

The Once King scoffed. "Of course. I am not a fool."

"Well, I guess that's that," Neko said, slipping out of Tina's hold to throw her arms around SB. "Take care of it, guys! I'd love to help, but I've got a totes rip, noncat body to get back to. Also, my mom is probably freaking out."

Tina snorted. "You still live with your mom?"

"Damn straight. My mom's awesome," Neko said. Then she hugged Tina and SB again. "Take care of yourselves, all right?" she whispered.

"We will," Tina said, hugging her hard. "Be good, Neko."

"It's Rashid," Neko said, whapping Tina with her tail one last time. "And I'm the *best*."

Having had the last word, the cat girl turned and bounded off, running full speed at the portal. It flickered when she reached it, and then NekoBaby's jubatus body vanished, turning into a spark of fire that shot off toward the horizon, and presumably his real body.

"I'm gonna miss her," Frank said, wiping away a tear.

"Yeah," Killbox muttered, kicking the ground. Then his head shot up. "Wait, she didn't leave us any of her stuff! That selfish cat! Her gear was priceless!"

This kicked off a riot as those who wanted to stay swarmed those who didn't, filling the mountain with tearful goodbyes and unabashed loot trading. James watched the chaos with a heavy heart, and then he turned to his brother.

"Here," he said, removing his rings and necklace and handing them to Ar'Bati. "Give those to Gray Fang and tell her thank you. I'd give her my staff, too, but even with the undead gone, I don't think she's going to want anything made of Eclipsed Steel. Also, please tell our father that—"

"You can tell him yourself," Fangs growled, shoving James's stuff back at him. "Because you are *not* leaving!"

"But I have to," James argued. "I have hundreds of thousands of dollars in student debt waiting for me. My parents were co-signers on the loans. I can't leave them with that kind of burden. They just got to retire!"

"You have family here," Fangs argued back. "We need you, too! You're a hero and a prince of the Savanna! You cannot actually want to go back to your old life of debt and labor."

"Of course I don't want to go back," James snapped. "But I have obligations." He looked at Tina. "Are you going back?"

"Nope," Tina said, smiling at SB. "I've got promises to keep here, and a library to start. It's gonna be awesome."

Hearing that filled James with jealousy. He wanted to see Tina's library. He wanted to stay and see everything, all this world could be when it wasn't tied down by games or being destroyed by undead. He wanted to keep his magic; he was just starting to get good! But he couldn't.

"It's my fault," he told Ar'Bati. "I can't leave them to carry my burdens. It's not right."

Fangs snorted. "If money is your only problem, we have that in plenty."

"But I don't," James said. "I spent all my gold to get us out of Bastion, remember?"

His brother gave him a scornful look. "What family do you think you joined? The Claw Born are rich! We will gladly pay your debts if it means you stay with us."

James couldn't believe his ears. "Really?"

"Of course," Fangs said, insulted. "We might not have the 'dollaz' you players used to brag of, but we have gold in plenty. Surely that has value in your world?"

"It does, but…" James trailed off, shaking his head. He'd been so sure he was going back—back to his dead-end job, back to being a failure—he didn't know what to do now that he might have a chance to stay. "Gold would probably work," he managed at last. "But how would I get it to them? The Once King just said the portal's one way."

"You're making this way too complicated," Tina said. "All we have to do is find someone who *is* going back *and* who knows they'll be keeping their body and send the gold home with them. And probably letters. If we don't tell Mom and Dad we're not dead, they'll freak."

"*Is* there someone who knows they're going back in an FFO body, though?" James asked, terrified to hope.

His sister shrugged. "I don't know about our group, but there's tens of thousands of people trapped here. There's gotta be *someone* who—"

"I'll do it."

Tina and James both whirled around to see ZeroDarkness standing behind them. "I'm going back," he said. "And I know for a fact that I'll be keeping this body. I'm actually lining up a bunch of FFO-to-IRL courier jobs right now."

"Really?" Tina said, impressed. "Dude, way to hustle. But how do you know your real body's dead on the other side?"

The jubatus Assassin flashed them a cat smile. "Because that's what I told them to do. I got in a car accident last winter. I still have brain function, obviously, but the rest of my body's been paralyzed from the nose down for the last five months. It fucking sucks, which is why I've been playing so much FFO. At least here I could still walk and talk. Anyway, I told my wife to pull the plug if I ever became unresponsive for more than a week. I was holding on for my family, but I know caring for me was bankrupting us. I was still going to go back for my kids, but this is so much better! All I gotta do is hang out in this world for a while until I'm sure the old me is dead, and then I'll go through the portal and come out the other side in a brand-new body!"

"A cat body," Tina said, biting her lip. "Are you sure that's what you want?"

406

"I'll take cat over vegetable any day," Zero said with absolute certainty. "Also, have you *seen* me?" He flexed his arm to show off his lean muscle. "I'm super cut, and I've got ninja moves!" He turned to grin at SB. "Even without the Lightless Realm, can you imagine doing the jumps and flips we do here in the real world? Add in the fact that I'm a cat, and I'll be famous in no time. The internet *loves* cats."

"He has a point," SilentBlayde said.

"I would be excessively grateful if you'd take gold to my parents to pay my debts," James said, not believing his luck. "Thank you, Zero. What do I owe you?"

"It's on the house for you guys," the Assassin said, grinning at Tina and James. "I owe you two at least four of my nine lives. I think that's worth a little free travel. Just give me contact info and a letter so they know I'm not a weirdo and we're good."

"Done," Tina said. "Thanks, dude."

"Don't mention it," Zero said, waving the words away. "Consider it a wedding present, though it'll have to be a late one since I'm planning to stay here for at least six more months. Can't take the chance of going back before they off me."

"That's fine," James said. "I'll need time to get the gold together, anyway."

"And I'll need time to drum up all my new business," Zero said, rubbing his paws together greedily. "You guys get a freebie, but everyone else pays ten percent commission. I'm gonna be *rich!*"

"That's the spirit," Tina said, laughing.

The Assassin smiled back and bounced away, leaving them staring at the train of players going through the portal. CincoDeMurder had already left, as had most of the rest of Red Sands. Roughnecks were leaving, too, and soon Tina was pulled away into a line of tearful goodbyes.

"Man," James said to SB. "I'm almost sad I'm not going home now. Things are going to be crazy over there. I wonder if magic works on the other side?"

"Leylia was born a Portal Keeper in our world, so there has to be something," SilentBlayde said, then his eyebrows shot up. "Speaking of, I just realized I need to go talk to Anders. I know we promised to keep her secret, but he's had Leylia's Disease for a long time. He deserves to know the truth."

"Go for it," James said. "I don't think she'll mind."

"Thanks," SB said, then his smile got wider. "Brother."

"It's brother-in-law," James called after him as the elf darted off.

"I can't believe you're fine with your sister marrying the Assassin who tried to kill us," Ar'Bati grumbled.

"Considering that was Tina's idea, I can't hold it against him," James said with a shrug. "I'm just happy he finally told her the truth. I knew they'd work it out eventually. They weren't nearly as good at hiding being in love as they thought they were."

He really was happy, he realized. There was so much still to do, so much to rebuild and fix, but for the first time ever, James was looking forward to the future. They'd won so much more than a battle today. They'd won a chance to start over, a chance at a new life, and not just for the players. The Once King had moved away from the portal once the rush began. He was now standing at the edge of the terrace, staring out over the now glaringly white desert of the Deadlands, his face pensive.

"I wonder if the trees will return now that there is sunlight again," he said as James approached. "This land was verdant once. Perhaps it will be so again in time."

"I'm sure it will," James said. "It'll certainly be busy. Every player in the world who wants to go home will have to come here to do it. Back when the portal system worked, that wouldn't have been a problem. Now, though, I have no idea how we're going to manage it."

"The Bedrock Kings will help," the Once King said with certainty. "They always said I was wrong, but they never gave up on me even when I banished them. I'm sure they'll be so happy to be proved right at last that they won't mind keeping the Timeless Tunnels open for a while. I'll need those tunnels myself in any case. There are many I must apologize to."

James nodded, unsure what else to say.

"I do not expect the world to welcome me," the king said quietly. "But if I am to make amends, I must start soon. Once the Great Pyre burns out, I don't know how long I'll be able to support my life. But I suppose that is what it means to be mortal. You never know how much time you have."

"That's why smart mortals don't waste it," James said, smiling. "I'll be happy to help you if you need it."

"I won't," Ar'Kan said, starting toward the stairs. "But thank you."

James waved after him, watching the winged elf's back as he descended the stairs back to...James had no idea, actually. The fortress was the king's home, and it had been a very long night and day. Maybe he was going to bed. He could go anywhere now that he wasn't tied to the Great Pyre or forced by the game to sit in his throne room waiting for people to come by and kill him. He was honestly surprised the Once King hadn't already flown away. Maybe he was saving that for later, when the world knew he wasn't trying to kill everyone and people wouldn't try to shoot him out of the sky.

Either way, it was a beautiful day. Sitting up on top of the mountain, James watched the sun set over the Deadlands for the first time in who knew how many years. Ar'Bati sat next to him, telling his brother of all the honor they would reap once the world knew of their deeds. It honestly sounded like a lot of work, but James liked it anyway. He liked everything that involved his new future here in this world he'd always loved so much. They were discussing how best to get back to the Savanna now that things were over when a huge *bang* sounded from below. A few minutes later, a very bloody

409

Garrond rushed up onto the terrace, loudly demanding to know what was going on.

"Hoo boy," Tina said, walking up to clap the furious paladin on the shoulder. "Have we got a story for you."

***

In the end, fewer people went through the portal than Tina expected. Tons wanted to, but now that the Once King had given them such an unexpectedly long timeline, a surprising number were no longer in a hurry. They were far more interested in getting their money out of the bank and living it up like kings for a bit before returning to their lives, and honestly, Tina couldn't blame them. She wanted her bling back, too.

They couldn't stay on top of the mountain forever, though. It was cold up there, and structurally unsound thanks to all the holes and cracks in the floor. Everyone who was going through the portal today had already gone anyway, so when the sun started to sink below the mountains, Tina ordered everyone to pack it in and head back down to camp.

Garrond had already gone ahead. The Order commander had flat-out refused to believe what had happened at first, even when Tina told him about the Sun's direct intervention. It had taken both James and Anders working on him before he finally stopped trying to go down and tear the castle apart so he could kill the Once King once and for all. Which, in hindsight, was probably why the winged elf had made himself scarce, the sneaky old bastard.

"You staying too, Roxxy?" Frank asked as they all started down the spire. "I'm glad. I ain't ready to be main tank."

"I thought you did great," Tina said, grinning at him. "You finally learned to use your shield! It was beautiful. I legit cried."

"Well, I'm staying," Killbox said over Frank's shuffling and "aw, shucks." "No way I'm abandoning all this"—he slapped his rock-hard eight-pack—"and I *still* haven't gotten my elf hottie."

"Probably because you call them 'elf hotties,'" Tina said flatly.

"Try treating women like people," Zen suggested, cutting in gracefully to join them. "I think you'll have more luck."

"Whoa, Zen?" Tina said, cutting off Killbox's explanation of how "elf hottie" was a *compliment*. "You're still here? Weren't you hell-bent on going back?"

"I was," Zen said. "And I'm still thinking about it, but I realized while everyone was saying goodbye that I haven't actually made up my mind."

"Fair enough," Tina said. "But what about your body? Aren't you worried about it?"

"I was, I *am*," the Ranger said. "But I forgot I'd promised my mom I'd meet her for lunch on my day off. She knows I'm never late, and she has a key to my place. She's probably already found me."

"That's a relief," Tina said with a smile. "But don't you still want to go back? I thought you loved your job."

"I do, but the hospital won't fall apart if I'm out for a week, and I can't go back in good conscience without at least finding out if Gregory and the others survived."

Tina homed in at once. "*Gregory*," she said in a suggestive voice. "Not *King* Gregory?"

Zen rolled her eyes. "Tina, we left them to *die*. I don't think it's weird to be worried."

"No, no, I think it's sweet," Tina said, batting her eyelashes.

"I also want to get back to the Savanna, because I don't think they have another modern medical professional," Zen went on, ignoring her. "Healing spells are fine and dandy, but there's a lot they don't handle. Someone has to teach the Bastion medics about germ theory at the very least. They don't even wash their hands! It's barbaric."

"Well, I'm glad you're staying," Tina said with a smile, glancing over her shoulder to locate her husband, who was safely tied up in conversation with Anders. "I want you to remain on as my second in command. I need someone who can yell at me when I'm being stupid. SB was no good at that even before we got together. Now that we're married, he's utterly hopeless."

"I don't like yelling at you, either," Zen said gruffly. Then she smirked. "Maybe you should try being less pigheaded."

"Yeah, I don't ever see that happening," Tina said proudly. "My head is stone to the end!"

"Amen to that," Zen said, shaking her head in defeat as they all walked together down the stairs, out of the empty fortress, and into the surprisingly beautiful calm of the Deadlands' blue twilight.

***

After a good night's sleep and much partying, it was decided that a player force would stay and guard the portal and the Dead Mountain Fortress. Commander Garrond wanted to tear the place apart brick by brick, but James and Tina managed to talk him down. He still refused to leave until every spark of the ghostfire was gone, which James felt was fair, but there was no way they could leave the zealous holy warrior alone near the Great Pyre that fueled the portal until every single player was out.

In the end, they compromised on building a temporary Order base located in what had been Grel'Darm's courtyard. James wasn't sure how the Once King would feel about that, but the elf wasn't there to complain. No one had seen him since yesterday, actually, which was both convenient and scary. Even with his new epiphany, having the world's most dangerous raid boss MIA felt like a Very Bad Thing. But for once the undead were not at the top of James's concerns. He was much more concerned with getting back to the Savanna.

Thankfully, the Once King appeared to have been right about the Bedrock Kings. They showed up bright and early the next morning all on their own, no summoning circle required, and offered the extended use of the Timeless Tunnels until all players were where they wanted to be.

"Dude," Tina said as they hurried under the ground on their way back to the Savanna. "My stone parents are *so* awesome! Almost makes me sad I'm not a stonekin anymore."

"I'm just glad someone's happy to hear the Once King's still alive," James replied. "I was starting to get worried."

Tina rolled her eyes. "Only *you* could be worried about a raid boss." Then she smiled. "And that's a good thing."

"Glad you think so."

"I *know* so," she said, punching him in the arm. Lightly, thank the Sun. "Now that I'm not spending every second being down on you, you're actually a pretty cool dude. I'm super glad you're staying. I'm fine with the fighting and stuff, but all this political crap is *way* over my pay grade. I need you here to tank the nobles for me."

As nervous as James was, that mental image made him laugh. "I'm happy I'm staying, too," he told her as they ran into the dark, sprinting through the distance-warping tunnels toward what, James hoped, would be a victory celebration.

When they finally reached the circle of daylight at the other end, though, he realized that his joy was premature.

"Whoa," Tina said, skidding to a stop.

James stopped too, eyes wide in horror. At his request, the tunnels had brought them straight to Red Canyon, the gnolls' fortress where all of Bastion was supposed to be making their last stand. But while they were definitely in the right place, the fortress—and all the grassland for a mile around it—was a smoking ruin. Undead were everywhere, their bodies lying in pieces as if they'd simply fallen apart where they stood. Given what the Once King had told them, that was probably exactly what had happened, but

413

that still didn't explain the emptiness. James didn't see so much as a bird in the morning sky, and it was terrifying.

"Where is everyone?" Ar'Bati demanded, voicing what everyone else was thinking as he bounded up from the tunnel.

"They can't be dead," James replied quickly, looking around at the destruction. "There are only zombies and undead out here. No fresh corpses."

"Then why is no one on the walls?" the warrior demanded, pointing at the smoking fortress. "And why do no flags fly from the towers?"

"Oh, crap," Tina said in a small voice. "Did the Once King stop things too late?"

Everyone lapsed into horrified silence, and then James slapped his fist into his hand. "I bet they're underground!"

"You mean in the Red Canyon dungeon?" Tina said skeptically. "Wouldn't that place be crawling with monsters?"

"Not since we cleaned it out," James said, grinning at his brother. "Thunder Paw is no fool. I bet he saw that army coming and led everyone straight down the canyon."

"Then what are we standing here for?" Ar'Bati said, dropping to all fours. "Let's go!"

The two of them raced into the Red Canyon fortress, followed quickly by Tina and the rest of the players. The destruction was even worse in here. Gnoll and jubatus bodies littered the streets beside humans wearing the red of Bastion. James even spotted a few player bodies, which meant the lowbies they'd left behind must have decided to fight after all. It was a gruesome spectacle, but James remained hopeful, because while the dead were many, there were still not nearly enough corpses to account for everyone. Wherever the main force was, it hadn't fallen here. He just prayed they were still alive as he and Ar'Bati sprinted down the canyon toward the dungeon at the bottom.

Just like the fortress above, the base of the canyon was littered with broken undead. There weren't nearly as many of Bastion's corpses here, though, and that gave him hope. That hope rose even higher when they reached the entrance to the lich's former stronghold and discovered that the hall where the dungeon portal had been was choked with the remains of countless undead boars, their bodies hacked to pieces by gnoll axes.

"There was an incredible battle here," Ar'Bati said, leaning down to examine the wounds. "But where are they?"

"Keep going," James said, hopping over the boars to continue the search.

It was a brutal one. Every inch of the Red Canyon dungeon appeared to have been a battleground. There were bodies everywhere, mostly undead, but too many not. James and Ar'Bati called out to their allies as they searched but got no answer. By the time they reached the bridge where the Naturalists had made their last stand during their last visit to Red Canyon, James was starting to lose faith.

"There's only one room left," he whispered nervously to Tina. "What if they—"

"Here!" Ar'Bati called.

James sprinted over to see what his brother had found. The warrior was standing on the steps next to the portcullis they'd used to lock themselves in with the lich what felt like forever ago. When James arrived, Ar'Bati pointed up the stairs, where the massive enchanted steel doors of the lab were closed tight.

"You think they're in there?" James asked breathlessly.

"Only one way to find out," his brother said, running up the steps two at a time.

James followed eagerly then slowed, his eyes going wide. Now that they were closer, he could see that the lab's doors were nearly destroyed, their heavy surface riddled with slashes and dents. At their foot, the body of a giant elf lay crumpled. When Ar'Bati turned him over, James realized he was looking at the remains of Sanguilar.

"He must have collapsed when the Once King stopped the army," James said quietly.

"Couldn't have happened to a nicer asshole," Tina said behind him, kicking the former raid boss in the gut with her boot. "Let's get these doors open."

James nodded, stepping over the boss's body to pound his fist against the damaged doors. "Hello!" he called out. "If you're in there, it's James of Claw Born. We won! It's safe to come out now!"

For a minute there was no answer. Then the huge doors jerked against his hands, causing James to leap back in surprise. As he retreated, the doors began to rattle and bulge, as if some immense power was pounding on them from the inside. James was still trying to make sense of that when Tina tapped him on the shoulder.

"Hinges are warped," she said, pointing up at the huge, boss fist–sized dents at all four of the door's corners.

"Can we break them free?" James asked.

His sister grinned. "We can break anything." She looked over her shoulder. "Team Hulk to the front! It's clobbering time!"

James stepped out of the way as the Knights and Berserkers came forward, wedging their hands or blades into any crack in the doors they could reach.

"Ready?" Tina asked, getting in there as well. "*Heave!*"

The players pulled with all their might, and the doors of the lab ripped free with an ear-splitting screech. Everyone scattered as the huge sheets of metal crashed to the ground, rattling back and forth on their bent, uneven surfaces. When the dust cleared, James broke into a huge grin.

"*They're alive!*"

King Gregory stood in the open entranceway with his two captains beside him, the source of the pounding they'd heard earlier. Behind them, a ragtag army of knights, gnolls, jubatus, and a large number of players huddled in the huge room that had once been the lich's workshop. Gregory's golden armor bore dozens of deep slashes and was still covered in his dried blood, but the giant red-headed king looked overjoyed, his face bursting into a huge smile when he saw them.

"By the Sun!" he cried, rushing forward to clap James's shoulders. "It is you!"

He said more, but even the king's booming voice was drowned out then by a flood of cheers from the army behind him. Weapons were dropped as all their terrified discipline dissolved into hugs, tossing each other around, and crying in joy. A few of the soldiers ran deeper into the lab, bringing out the women, children, and wounded to join in the joy. James spotted Gray Fang in the back next to a bandaged Rends. His adopted father spotted him at the same time, bursting into a grin even his injured face couldn't hide.

"*We are saved!*"

The cry grew into a roar as the others joined in, thousands of jubilant voices blending together as the survivors of the Savanna burst forth from the dark room they'd been holed up in for what must have been days now.

"Did you destroy the Once King?" Gregory yelled over the chaos. "The pounding on the doors stopped a day ago, but we didn't dare hope." He looked around at the still corpses of the undead, his eyes going especially wide when he spotted the body of Sanguilar. "You *must* have done it!"

Tina and James shared a look. "We did it," James said. "But it's sort of...complicated."

"Then you shall tell me over dinner," Gregory said happily, pulling them both toward the exit.

Several days later...

In the end, everyone agreed that the battle of the Savanna was one of the bloodiest ever fought. It took days to burn all the corpses and still more to mourn the fallen. When all the ceremonies were done, King Gregory announced that he and his people would be returning to Bastion.

"Are you sure that's a good idea?" James asked. "The city's a smoking ruin."

"And it will be that way forever if we don't go home," the king said grimly. "But there's more to Bastion than just one city. We have many principalities and territories, all of whom will be looking for guidance. I am their king, too, which means I must go back. The world must know that the Bastion still stands. But I do have one question for you."

"Shoot," James said.

The king looked nervous. "Will you stay with us?" he asked, looking at James and Tina. "I know you have a way home now, but many players are staying, and frankly, we don't know how to handle them. There are also many dangers left over from the Nightmare that have yet to be addressed. Even with the undead defeated, whole zones are still overrun, and I no longer have an army to help them."

"That's fine," Tina said, smiling her best mercenary smile. "The Roughnecks are always available for the right price. We'd be happy to stomp some lowbie quest zones in your name in exchange for, say, tracts of land and good pay?"

"Quite fair," the king said. "It shall be done."

Then he looked at James.

"I'm staying," James assured him.

The king's instant smile was the best compliment anyone had ever paid him.

"We have much to do," Gregory told them both happily. "But there's no one I'd rather do it with! With your help, I am sure we can rebuild this world to be what it was once again."

"We'll do it better," Tina said proudly. "There's so much knowledge from our world that we can share. Now that this is our home too, I'm hoping people will actually listen."

"Cheers to that," James said, lifting his tin cup of water. "It's not every day you get a chance to rebuild a world. I'm looking forward to it."

"I'm looking forward to peace," Gregory said, his shoulders slumping. "But even with the Once King gone, I fear it will not be easy."

"Nothing worth doing ever is," Tina said. "But we've got this."

"We've got this," James agreed, wrapping an arm around his little sister's armored shoulders. "Together."

Epilogue

There were many things that happened in the world once called *Forever Fantasy Online* after the Once King's defeat. But while there are more victories and defeats in the long life of a living world than can be recorded in any history, here are the stories of the figures who stood tallest.

After much cajoling, **Tina Anderson** finally accepts a noble title from King Gregory to make the accounting easier in her new role as Bastion's field general. Due to the many, many conflicts left behind by the Nightmare, Baroness Anderson and her husband SilentBlayde spend their first several years together in their wedding present from James, a yurt, leading the Roughnecks on a worldwide campaign of pacification. When every last raid dungeon and quest hub has been dealt with, SilentBlayde puts his foot down and insists they move back to Bastion and raise a family.

Living in peace with his wife at last, **SilentBlayde** commissions an "elven Ikea"–style apartment in Bastion right next to his second passion project, Bastion's only ramen noodle shop. He and Tina retire from their lives as generals and use the funds from the publication of the world's first collectible card game to found the Public Library of Bastion. Somewhere in the midst of all this, they have their first daughter, an elf named Hanabi. She is the light of SilentBlayde's life, and Tina is forced to intervene on a regular basis to ensure that her feet occasionally touch the floor.

James Anderson stays in the Savanna to help rebuild. When Rends's marriage plots grow too dire to ignore, he allows himself to be "kidnapped" by his mother Acacia when she returns to her diplomatic post in Bastion. Desperate for competent help, King Gregory snatches him up at once and makes him the kingdom's foreign affairs adviser. James eventually goes on to actually use his political science classes, founding and leading the first Diplomatic Corps of Bastion.

Fangs in the Grass eventually succeeds his father as the head of the Claw Born clan. Despite his protests, James insists on giving him full credit for the jubatus' treaty with the gnolls, a deed that earns him the title Ar'Bati, He Whose Fangs Brought Peace Instead of War. It takes Fangs a full year to forgive his brother for this indignity.

After six months of drumming up work, **ZeroDarkness** goes home loaded down with a giant bag full of letters, James's payoff gold, and a very hefty commission. After much media attention and an uncomfortable stint in a government facility, he is reunited with his family at long last. He goes on to be quite internet famous, as intended, but the real winners are his kids, who think it's the coolest thing ever that their dad is now a "super cat ninja."

Killbox stays with the Roughnecks for a few years until he gets bored doing "lowbie quests" and returns to Bastion to open an Ax Gym, which promises to give wealthy patrons the "player body." It's modestly successful, though most of his clients are actually other players looking to keep their game-given physiques. Not one to be modest in anything, Killbox gives up on the gym and opens a brewery instead, eventually winning a Royal Warrant for his amazingly smooth lagers.

Leylia seduces her Red Sands bodyguards during their escape from the Battle for the Savanna and runs off with them, never to be heard from again.

Anders joins the priesthood, going on to earn even Raffestain's grudging respect through his humility and hard work. His career as a priest is marked by always taking assignments in the most run-down and disadvantaged areas, particularly those inhabited by players. When the statue honoring the Roughnecks is finally built in Bastion's new Founder's Square, he makes sure that NekoBaby's figure is right up front with her name in huge letters so that not even the smallest schoolchild can miss it.

Rashid "NekoBaby" Patel is the first player to wake up from the "Forever Fantasy Online Incident." He goes on to be mega-famous, starting with talk shows and eventually building an entire lifestyle brand around himself. He later writes a best-selling fantasy series retelling the events that happened to the players trapped in FFO—moderately embellished, of course. When not on tour, Rashid spends a great deal of his time and money championing LGBTQ+ rights and causes around the world. He also captains the FFO survivors' reunion once every two years. He is still the best healer in the game.

Frank successfully guilts the Grand Schtump into giving him all of DarkKnight's gold so that he can found an orphanage for children who lost their parents in the post-Nightmare chaos. He later teams up with Baroness Anderson to found the world's first free public school. 'Cause kids need to go to school, dang it.

Zen stays in the world of FFO and has a very different life than she expected. All of her cats back home are fine.

The Once King uses his newfound freedom to actually explore the world he once considered his prison. He is occasionally sighted flying in the blue sky by excitable peasants, but for the most part, no one knows what he does or where he goes. He dies peacefully a year after the last of the ghostfire is extinguished. James only discovers this when he is invited to attend Ar'Kan's sun-drenched royal funeral by the Bedrock Kings, along with King

Gregory and Commander Garrond. The Great Birds Zthr and Xthr also show up to pay their respects, causing a great deal of panic.

After the death of the Once King, **Commander Garrond** devotes the Order of the Golden Sun to the task of restoring the Deadlands to life. He dies of old age shortly after reopening the Grand Sun Temple at the top of the (formerly) Dead Mountain.

The End

Book 3 of 3

Thank you for reading *The Once King*! If you enjoyed the book, or even if you didn't, we hope you'll consider leaving a review. Reviews, good or bad, are vital to every author's career, and Travis and I would be extremely grateful if you'd consider writing one for us.

What a ride it's been, huh? Thank you so much for reading all the way through our FFO trilogy! Endings are sad, but we've got tons of new projects in the pipe. If you want to be the first to know when new stuff is available, sign up for our New Release Mailing List! List members are the first to hear about any new projects plus you get bonus content such as the list-exclusive Heartstrikers short story, *Mother of the Year*! The list is free, and we promise never to spam you or give your information to anyone else, so sign up and join the fun! You can also follow us on Twitter @Rachel_Aaron and @TravBach.

Need something new to read *right now*? Check out one of Rachel's other completed series! Just flip over to the "**Want More Books?**" page or visit www.rachelaaron.net for the full list of Rachel's novels complete with their beautiful covers, links to reviews, and free sample chapters!

Thank you again for reading, and we hope you'll be back soon!

Yours sincerely,
Rachel Aaron and Travis Bach

Enjoyed FFO?
Need a new book *right now*?!

Try one of Rachel's other completed series! Just keep going to see
the list, or visit
www.rachelaaron.net
for full sample chapters, links to reviews, and lovely covers in
high resolution!

Minimum Wage Magic

The DFZ, the metropolis formerly known as Detroit, is the world's most magical city with a population of nine million and zero public safety laws. That's a lot of mages, cybernetically enhanced chrome heads, and mythical beasties who die, get into debt, and otherwise fail to pay their rent. When they can't pay their bills, their stuff gets sold to the highest bidder to cover the tab.

That's when they call me. My name is Opal Yong-ae, and I'm a Cleaner: a freelance mage with an art history degree who's employed by the DFZ to sort through the mountains of magical junk people leave behind. It's not a pretty job, or a safe one-- there's a reason I wear bite-proof gloves-- but when you're deep in debt in a lawless city where gods are real, dragons are traffic hazards, and buildings move around on their own, you don't get to be picky about where your money comes from. You just have to make it work, even when the only thing of value in your latest repossessed apartment is the dead body of the mage who used to live there.

"A catchy title, a plucky protagonist and a maximum effort by the author, honestly readers can't ask for more in the urban fantasy genre."- **Fantasy Book Critic**

"I love what Rachel Aaron has done with this novel to expand her stories within this unique world of her creation. I have developed a trust in her ability to write engaging stories of great characters which I feel most comfortable and eager to spend time with, and this book is no exception." - **TS Chan**

The Heartstrikers Series

As the smallest dragon in the Heartstriker clan, Julius survives by a simple code: stay quiet, don't cause trouble, and keep out of the way of bigger dragons. But this meek behavior doesn't cut it in a family of ambitious predators, and his mother, Bethesda the Heartstriker, has finally reached the end of her patience.

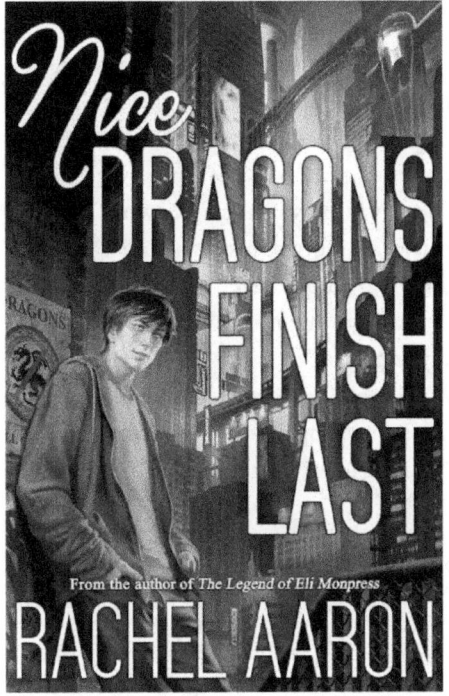

Now, sealed in human form and banished to the DFZ--a vertical metropolis built on the ruins of Old Detroit--Julius has one month to prove to his mother that he can be a ruthless dragon or lose his true shape forever. But in a city of modern mages and vengeful spirits where dragons are seen as monsters to be exterminated, he's going to need some serious help to survive this test.

He just hopes humans are more trustworthy than dragons.

"Super fun, fast paced, urban fantasy full of heart, and plenty of magic, charm and humor to spare, this self published gem was one of my favorite discoveries this year!" - **The Midnight Garden**

"A deliriously smart and funny beginning to a new urban fantasy series about dragons in the ruins of Detroit...inventive, uproariously clever, and completely un-put-down-able!" - **SF Signal**

The Legend of Eli Monpress

Eli Monpress is talented. He's charming. And he's the greatest thief in the world. He's also a wizard, and with the help of his partners in crime--a swordsman with the world's most powerful magic sword (but no magical ability of his own) and a demonseed who can step through shadows and punch through walls--he's getting ready to pull off the heist of his career. To start, though, he'll just steal something small. Something no one will miss. Something like... a king.

"I cannot be less than 110% in love with this book. I loved it. I love it still. Already I sort of want to read it again. Considering my fairly epic Godzilla-sized To Read list, that's just about the highest compliment I can give a book" - **CSI: Librarian**

"Fast and fun, The Spirit Thief *introduces a fascinating new world and a complex magical system based on cooperation with the spirits who reside in all living objects. Aaron's characters are fully fleshed and possess complex personalities, motivations, and backstories that are only gradually revealed. Fans of Scott Lynch's* Lies of Locke Lamora *(2006) will be thrilled with Eli Monpress. Highly recommended for all fantasy readers."* - **Booklist, Starred Review**

The Paradox Trilogy
(written as Rachel Bach)

Devi Morris isn't your average mercenary. She has plans. Big ones. And a ton of ambition. It's a combination that's going to get her killed one day - but not just yet.

That is, until she just gets a job on a tiny trade ship with a nasty reputation for surprises. The Glorious Fool isn't misnamed: it likes to get into trouble, so much so that one year of security work under its captain is equal to five years everywhere else. With odds like that, Devi knows she's found the perfect way to get the jump on the next part of her Plan. But the Fool doesn't give up its secrets without a fight, and one year on this ship might be more than even Devi can handle.

"Firefly-*esque in its concept of a rogue-ish spaceship family... The narrative never quite goes where you expect it to, in a good way... Devi is a badass with a heart."* - **Locus Magazine**

"*If you liked* Star Wars, *if you like our books, and if you are waiting for* Guardians of the Galaxy *to hit the theaters, this is your book."* - **Ilona Andrews**

"*I JUST LOVED IT! Perfect light sci-fi. If you like space stuff that isn't that complicated but highly entertaining, I give two thumbs up!"* - **Felicia Day**

About the Authors

Rachel Aaron and **Travis Bach** are two giant nerds who love gaming, reading, writing, and hiking through the great outdoors while talking about gaming, reading, and writing! When they're not terrifying the wildlife, Rachel and Travis enjoy anime, manga, MMOs, table top gaming, cooking, pampering their old lady dog, and helping their son build secret bases in Minecraft.

Rachel and Travis live in Athens, GA, but dream of moving out west where the humidity isn't 90% all year long. If you love gaming and manga as much as we do, hit us up on twitter at

@Rachel_Aaron
@TravBach

Or send us a note at www.rachelaaron.net!

Cover Illustration by Daniel Schmelling
Cover Design by Rachel Aaron
Editing provided by Red Adept Editing

As always, this book would not have been nearly as good without my amazing beta readers! Thank you so, so much to Christina Vlinder, Paul Carroll, and Kevin Swearingen.
Y'all are the BEST!